WYNNER

Also by Mel Tormé

The Other Side of the Rainbow

Mel Tormé

WYNNER

STEIN AND DAY/*Publishers*/New York

Library of Congress Cataloging in Publication Data

Tormé, Mel, 1925–
Wynner.

I. Title.

PZ4.T6857Wy   [PS3570.0687]   813'.5'4   77-92714
ISBN 0-8128-2462-8

For my children: Steven, Melissa, Tracy, Daisy and James

And with deep gratitude
to
Sterling, Sol, Michaela and Marilee
for their encouragement, creative assistance
and belief in this book

WYNNER

Chapter

1

Wynner stood on the stage of the Scheherezade Room, which was full—but only because of a convention. He'd been pulling in half a house all week, not like in the old days.

He glanced back at the orchestra as the five strings played the final bar that would lead him into the song.

Day after day I must face a world of strangers,
Where I don't belong.
I'm not that strong.

When he opened the damn place almost ten years ago, he'd had a slew of violins and cellos and violas and a harp and two extra percussionists and a trio of French horn players. Now look. The drunks in the audience weren't even listening to the song they'd requested.

It's nice to know there's someone I can turn to
Who will always care.
You're always there.

Forty minutes to go. He could hear the lead trumpet player out of tune behind him.

1

I can take all the madness the world has to give
But I won't last a day without you.

Wynner closed his eyes on that note and thought of Mary Frances. He had lasted for years without her. She had never rocked him in her arms. She'd envied his fame, his success, his independence. She hadn't really loved him. At least, not in the way he had loved her.

Anyway, that was a very long time ago.

Chapter

2

Commerceville sat nestled in the hills of northern Pennsylvania's coal-mining region, unchanged in all of its fifty-one years of incorporated existence in the Pennsylvania Commonwealth: an unremarkable town of ten thousand three hundred and twenty-two souls, mainly of Slavic or Irish extraction, the former mostly working the mines, the latter involved in the everyday commercial business of supply and demand. Of this latter group, no one had been more successful in the plying of his trade than Thomas Edward Maguire.

In a town the size of Commerceville, there was room for only one large supplier of meats, vegetables, and general comestibles and that privilege fell to Mr. Maguire, devoted churchgoer, hard-working businessman, dedicated civic leader, husband of Emily Ann Maguire nee Kennealy and father to Mary Frances Maguire.

Maguire's Meats dwarfed its neighbors in size and volume of business. Its owner was generally well liked by his fellow businessmen and his customers, although one had to concede that warmth was not his long suit. He conducted his affairs with a minimum of affability since he was capable of no more. His dealings on all levels were scrupulously honest. No one had ever accused him (or for that matter even suspected him) of placing a stealthy finger on his meat scales to heighten the price of a rib roast, and his piousness with regard to his dedication to St. Anthony's plus his generous donations to that worthy Catholic edifice of worship sufficiently offset his personal shortcomings. In the minds of his customers, Slavs and Irish alike, Thomas Edward Maguire was a good man, and so his business flourished.

At home he was the complete patriarch, a large, beetle-browed husband and father, dominating a delicate, birdlike wife and a pretty little girl just-turned-teenager. After Mary Frances was conceived, whatever ardor Thomas possessed fled his body, and Emily's short, unrewarding sex life came to a sudden, final halt. Sex, remarked Thomas one evening shortly after the child's birth, was a waste of time and energy, and he needed both of the aforementioned in the pursuit of his business. Of course, he had been careful to impart these words of celibate wisdom to his wife within the carefully sequestered confines of their bedroom. The subject was private. You didn't just go around talking about these things in the parlor or the kitchen. The fact that the only other human being privy to these comments in the Maguire household was a newly born infant was not a consideration. All things in their proper place, that was Maguire's Law.

Mary Frances was no longer a baby. At thirteen she was uncommonly pretty, showing every indication of becoming tall and graceful. She was already well endowed. Her breasts, her father noticed, were precociously large for a child who had recently been confirmed, and as they grew larger (almost daily it seemed), they became a source of embarrassment to him. One night, after dinner, he ordered the girl to go to her room. She left the dining table, bewildered, not knowing what she had done to be punished. Emily Ann sat erect in her chair, quiet and expectant. Maguire tried to speak twice but could not bring himself to discuss "it" at the dinner table. All things in their proper place. Maguire's Law.

He rose, threw his napkin upon the table, shoved his chair back, and headed up the staircase for his bedroom. (Long

4

ago, the Maguires had agreed to the privacy and comfort of separate bedrooms.) Emily Ann followed him dutifully. She entered his bedroom and automatically closed the door behind her. She walked over to a chair near his writing desk and sat down, waiting for him to begin. He paced back and forth in front of the window for a few moments for dramatic effect, then stopped and turned to her.

"Well, then, missus woman," he began in a brogue as thick as Christmas gravy, "have you taken a good look at your daughter lately?"

"Why of course, Thomas," she replied in her high-pitched, quaver-toned manner. "She's getting prettier every day, don't you think?"

"Prettier, huh? Prettier! Brazen is what I call her. Have you no eyes, woman? Are you blind as well as foolish?"

"Now, now, Thomas, there's no need to shout. Tell me what's wrong?"

"What's wrong, she asks," he said, looking at the ceiling expecting to find God there commiserating with him. "The Saints preserve us! Her—her—*chest*, that's what's wrong!"

"Her—*chest?*"

"Well, good. You're not deaf, at least. That's right. Her chest."

Baffled, Emily asked, "Why, what's wrong with her chest?"

"I'll tell you what's wrong with it. It—it's—" The subject was painful for him, difficult to discuss. "—It—sticks out too far! She's—my God—she's near as big as you are!"

"Don't swear, Thomas, please. You know I cannot abide swearing!"

He walked over to her, bent down, and placed his nose within inches of hers. "I'll swear all I want! I'll swear till the cows come home if I've a mind to!"

She shook her head, placing her fine-boned fingers to her mouth.

"What would Father Aloysius say if he could hear you now?!"

"Never mind *me*, Emily Ann." In all the time he had known her, courted her, and lived with her, he had never

5

called her, simply, Emily. It was always the more formal Emily Ann, just as his daughter would forever be addressed as Mary Frances.

"Never mind me," he repeated. "What would the good Father think if he could see our daughter lookin' like a common—a common—" He could not bring himself to say it.

"Now, Thomas . . ."

"Don't 'Now Thomas' me! You've been too lenient with that girl. She goes to the pictures too much, she spends too much idle time. Why does she never seem to do any homework? I never see her bring her books home from school."

"Why, of course she does homework. The minute she's in from school. It's all finished by the time you get home."

He went on as though he had not heard her. "It was the same when she was learnin' her catechism. No responsibility to her church or her family. I work my fingers to the bone to provide for this family, and how does she repay me? By walking around this town with everything she's got on display."

"Thomas!"

"Well, it's true! Now I want something done about her!"

"All right, Thomas, all right. But what?"

"I don't know. But I'll not be seen with that child in church this Sunday unless her appearance is suitable for the occasion."

"Thomas," Emily said rather sadly, "your little girl is no longer a little girl. She's next to being a young woman. She'll be fourteen in a few months. Fourteen!" she said, half to herself, suddenly surprised. "Where did the time go?"

"This is no time for reminiscin', woman. You'll do as I say, and that's the last of it!"

Emily Ann opened her mouth to speak and closed it again. When her husband's mind was made up, it was useless to argue or to try to reason with him. His Victorian prudery was fashioned of Irish old-country bedrock.

She sighed. "All right, Thomas. I'll talk to her. But . . ."

"But me no buts, Mrs. Maguire. Just do as I tell you."

Mary Frances was by turns furious, frustrated, tearful, and

6

rebellious when her mother delivered her father's ultimatum.

"*Bind* myself? *Mother*! This is 1920! None of the girls at school *bind* themselves!" She said "bind" as though it were a dirty word.

"Now then, darling," her mother cooed soothingly. "You must do as your father says. You know he means it for your own good. You're . . . developing real fast, dear. Faster than I did." She blushed modestly. "You don't want people staring at you, do you?"

"What's wrong with people looking at me? I'm pretty. Everyone says so. I like being looked at. Georgie, the boy who delivers groceries for Daddy, says I look like Mary Pickford."

Emily Ann took no notice of this. "I didn't say 'looking' at you," she corrected her daughter. "I said 'staring.'"

"Oh, Mama!"

"Now, you do as your father wants, and I'm sure he'll buy you something real nice for your birthday. There! Let's not talk about it any more."

That was the way most problems were resolved in the Maguire household. The edict came down from the summit and was usually obeyed without further discussion by the subordinates.

On Sunday, Mary Frances appeared in church with her parents, decked out in a dark blue skirt and middy blouse that offered no evidence of her ripening condition.

On the following Thursday, her father nearly had an apoplectic fit followed closely by a coronary.

At precisely 5:12 P.M., he opened the door to his storeroom, a small frame building directly behind Maguire's Meats, and found his daughter, naked as the day she was born, atop a pile of Idaho potatoes. On top of his daughter, equally unclad, was Georgie Westerman, his delivery boy. Mary Frances' mouth formed a surprised "O," and Georgie raised himself, lost his balance and slid down to the floor to the accompaniment of several dozen loosened potatoes, landing on his bare rump, and depriving Mary Frances of the protective covering his body had provided. She lay there, her legs splayed southeast southwest, her breasts astonishingly full, her sparse brown pubic hairs blatantly displayed.

7

Thomas Maguire ran forward and kicked Georgie so hard in the left kidney that the boy carried the effects of the blow with him for the rest of his life. Gathering his clothes as best he could in an on-all-fours position, he began to crawl toward the door.

"Oh, no ya don't!" thundered Maguire. "You'll not crawl through that door naked as a jaybird for the world to see. No one's goin' to know about this. No one, you understand? Now, get into your clothes and get outta my sight! If I ever see you near me or my daughter again I'll shoot you, so help me!"

The boy scrambled frantically into his pants and shirt, fumbled with the laces of his shoes, and painfully straightening up, ran for the door.

"Slowly, you blatherskite! Slowly! You'll walk out the door slowly, get on your bicycle, and ride away. Slowly. Now git!"

George Westerman looked as though he would cry. He glanced once at Mary Frances in mute apology, then slowly opened the door and vanished.

Mary Frances had, by now, covered her nudity with her discarded clothing, her skirt draped over her breasts, her blouse clutched tightly in her left hand, covering her lower extremities. Her father moved toward her. She shrank from him, clutching her clothes tighter to her body.

He slapped her face resoundingly.

She did not cry.

Angrily he asked, "Did he? . . . Did you two? . . ."

"No," she answered in a small voice.

He trembled angrily as he said, "You may still be a virgin, but you're about as pure as sewage. I know you now for what you are, Mary Frances Maguire. It galls me to even give you the benefit of my good name in addressin' you. A thirteen-year-old girl . . ."

"Almost fourteen . . ."

". . . Dammit! A *twenty*-year-old girl, attemptin' to commit fornication out of wedlock is guilty of a cardinal sin!"

She pleaded with him through tears of frustration. "Daddy, this—is—nine—teen—twenty! Things are different

8

from when you were a kid. The whole world has changed. But you're blind to it all. You're still stuck back in . . . in the *old* days, when people were afraid to kiss, and to love. . . ."

"I don't need a lecture from the likes of you regardin' kissin' and lovin'. Goodness is goodness, and rottenness and evil are still the same and always have been and always will be." She could sense a sudden resolution in him now.

"You're my daughter whether I like it or not, and under my supervision. You're goin' to do exactly as I say, or you'll rue the day you were born. I mean it, believe me!"

She did.

Father and daughter went home together in silence. Mary Frances repaired to her room without a word. Maguire told Emily Ann his plans for Mary Frances with the added admonition to not question them.

She did not.

Mary Frances was taken out of Commerceville Elementary School and enrolled in St. Theresa's Convent for Young Girls. She would become a novice, study, reflect on the path she had nearly taken with Georgie Westerman and perhaps, one day, be properly repentant, with the help and guidance of the sisters, Mother Superior, and Father Aloysius. Like it or not, she would forsake the secular life and eventually take the vows.

Strangely enough, Mary Frances found the convent to her liking at first. She had some degree of privacy, a certain amount of independence, a chance to be away from her domineering father. After a few months at St. Theresa's, however, boredom attacked her like a severe case of scarlet fever. She could feel the heat of it, the sting of the long, eventless hours, cloistered as she was within the dull brown walls of St. Theresa's. Yet she had become stronger, more hardened in the convent.

She decided to bide her time, to wait. She would endure the endless lessons, the monastic existence, the daily multiple prayer sessions, the itchy clothing, the relentless quest on the part of the nuns for true humility, the dull, stupid girls who made up the contingent of fellow novices. One day, some-

9

time in the near future, she would escape. How, she did not know, but somehow the opportunity would present itself and she would grasp it eagerly. More than in God, she believed in this.

That opportunity was two long years in arriving.

Chapter

3

She first laid eyes on Joe Wynocki during the Thanksgiving bazaar, held by St. Theresa's and St. Anthony's jointly for the benefit of underprivileged families. The year 1922 was not an especially good one in the mines, precipitating many layoffs among the miners. These distressed people had applied for relief to both the state and Federal governments with little or no success. The combined forces of the convent and the church meant to see to it that those families had turkey and trimmings on the third Thursday in November as well as Christmas dinner, toys, and clothes for the children come December 25th.

In addition to various raffles and drawings, games and prizes, foodstuffs (much of which was donated by Thomas Maguire), and personal effects auctioned off in the good cause, boxing matches were held in a makeshift ring set up within the convent grounds: amateur matches to be sure, but enthusiastically entered into by many of the young men of the community on both sides of the ethnic fence. One of the participants was a young coal miner named Jozef Wynocki.

Since all the entertainments of the bazaar were church-sanctioned, the nuns and novices were allowed to enjoy them on this special day. The moment Jozef Wynocki stepped into the ring, he caught Mary Frances' attention. He was strongly built and far better looking than any coal miner she had ever seen; far handsomer, in fact, then *anyone* she had seen in Commerceville. Ever.

Sitting next to her parents in the jerry-built bleacher stands, she was careful not to let them see the interest in her eyes as Jozef moved around the ring, cautiously sizing up his opponent.

He had no real skill as a boxer. He moved, flat-footed, first to the left, then to the right, avoiding the jabs of the auburn-headed young Irishman he'd been paired off with, not trying very aggressively to counterpunch. His long, well-muscled arms were effectively holding the other fighter at bay, out of reach, and the first round produced little action. Neither did the second. During the third and final round, the spectators began booing good-naturedly, and the Irishman, piqued, slipped under Jozef's guard and planted a solid right hand to the ribs that hurt the Pole. There was a cheer from the crowd, Mary Frances excepted, and heartened by their encouragement, the redheaded man delivered two swift left jabs to the pectorals and completed the combination with a stunning right cross to the jaw.

Jozef, hurt and shaken, involuntarily raised his left arm in a gesture of self-protection and lashed out with his right.

The single lucky blow, a clumsy roundhouse attempt, caught the Irishman on the left side of the head at the hairline near the temple. His legs buckled under him and he sagged to his knees, eyes glazing slightly, then found it necessary to fall forward, on all fours, palms flat on the canvas, shaking his head from side to side. Instantly Joe Wynocki forgot his own pain, dropping on his hands and knees to face the young man.

"Are you all right?"

The Irishman expelled his breath and kept shaking his head.

"Please," Joe implored. "I not mean to. . . . Please. Are you all right?"

The crowd was silent. Then the thatch of red hair bobbed up and down. The fighter rose shakily to his feet and the crowd cheered. Joe stood up, greatly relieved. The Irishman reached out with his glove-encased hands and clasped the Pole's right glove in them. He raised Jozef's hand to indicate the Pole's victory.

The crowd roared.

Jozef smiled shyly and climbed out of the ring. It had been the last of three bouts, and now the crowd began dispersing, milling around inside the enclosure, moving toward the exits. It was late in the afternoon and most people would be heading home for Sunday dinner. For the nuns and novices, Vespers would be observed followed by their evening meal.

Mary Frances bid her parents goodbye offhandedly, distracted as she was by the prospect of not being able to find and detain Jozef Wynocki, should they linger awhile. They did not. It had been a long day, and Thomas Maguire was tired. Exchanging peremptory kisses on the cheek, the parents left their daughter to the nuns and God's beneficent care.

Mary Frances prayed that, if all went well, she would never have to see her father again.

Making sure she was unnoticed, she made her way toward the small cloakroom near the chapel where she was certain the young Pole would be changing back into his clothes. After a half hour of standing well camouflaged near a large oak, the chill November wind numbing her right through, her patience was rewarded. Several of the afternoon's amateur pugilists had come and gone from the cloakroom. The last to leave was Jozef Wynocki.

As he closed the door behind him, Mary Frances stepped out of the deepening shadows.

"Excuse me, sir."

"Yes, miss? . . . Sister?"

"Oh, I'm not a sister. I'm just a novice. Do you know what that is?"

"Uh . . . no. I not . . . My English . . . is . . . uh . . . not good . . . I . . ."

"That's all right. I understand. I am not a nun. Do you understand that?"

He looked at her: the white, full dress, the head covered by the nunlike hood, a band of black material peeking through the white cloth covering the brow. He did not understand. She *looked* like a nun. He gazed intently at her face. She was very young. And beautiful. The most beautiful girl he had ever seen.

He shook his head slowly. "I ... I am sorry. Not understand. I ..." He held his hands up in a gesture of his lack of comprehension.

She smiled. "I would like to talk to you," she said.

"Talk? To me? For what?"

She looked around. The grounds were deserted, the light leaving the sky. She would be missed at Vespers. She had to move quickly. She shivered.

"Is anyone left in there?" she asked, indicating the cloakroom.

"No. Is empty. All gone."

She stepped past him, opened the door, and beckoned. "Come on."

He stood there for a moment, unable to understand this strange and beautiful young girl's actions.

"Come on," she insisted. "It's cold out here."

He sighed and followed her inside.

As he closed the door behind him and stepped into the gloom of the unlit cloakroom, she suddenly closed the gap between them and slipped her arms around his neck. "I like you," she whispered throatily. "You're very good-looking."

Jozef recoiled in horror, breaking her hold. "What are you doing? This is wrong! You are nun!" His voice trembled as he whispered the words.

He could see her quite clearly in the light that came in through the transom over the door he had just closed behind him; fading daylight, to be sure, but sufficiently strong enough to define her shapelessness in the novice's gown, her wide-set eyes, her smile, patently seductive.

"Stand there," she commanded. "Don't move."

Her hands moved to the knot on the rope halter that hung down over her hips, ending in a "V" below her abdomen. Slowly she undid the knot, letting both strands of the halter

14

fall away to the sides. Next, she removed her headpiece, and the effect was jarring to Jozef. Her rich, dark hair tumbled out and down over her shoulders. She kicked her slippers off. Jozef's heart was pounding. Mary Frances crossed her arms over her chest, her fists grasping the material of her dress under both armpits.

Jozef looked away.

"No," she almost shouted. "No," she repeated more quietly, insistently. "Please look. Watch me."

In one practiced move, she drew the dress over her head and tossed it casually to the floor. Her only garment now was a cotton slip.

"Do I look like a nun now?" she inquired softly.

Jozef stood mute, spellbound. No longer swimming in the tentlike novice's uniform, her body screamed at him, no curve or swell left to the imagination.

Her lips parted in a wide smile, white teeth shining in the semidark. With unexpected swiftness, she repeated her cross-armed dexterity with her slip. Now she stood completely naked, save for the long, black woolen convent stockings she still wore. She let her weight rest on one leg, bending the other at the knee, arching the calf, pointing the toes, the heel elevated, the sole barely resting on the floor.

"Now?" she asked even more softly through slightly parted lips. "Now do I still look like a nun to you?"

Jozef Wynocki was mesmerized. He knew it was wrong to keep staring at this goddess of a girl, yet he could not help himself. He was twenty-three years old and still a virgin. Most of the men his age who worked in the mines were already married with families. He had taken a few girls to the movies and one to a dance in the neighboring town of Wilkinsburg, this last having rewarded him with a kiss at the end of the evening. Mainly, he had kept to himself.

He looked at Mary Frances standing there posing for him; looking, in her woolen stockings, for all the world like one of those French whores depicted on the postcards Zivik had once shown him. He had blushed and looked away then.

He was not blushing now.

15

He felt a stiffening between his legs. She saw the change taking place. She extended her arms toward him. "Come here," she entreated him.

He did not move.

"Come here," she repeated, pouting.

As if in a trance, he moved toward her. She placed her hand on his shirt, unbuttoned the first three buttons, and fingered the curly wire hair on his chest. Then she traced her fingers down, down past his belt, lingering tantalizingly on the flap that covered his pants buttons, and slowly, slowly she closed her hand over his aroused penis.

In the course of the next ten minutes, she seduced him, succeeded in deflowering herself, and came to the conclusion that the culminated sexual act was not what she had imagined (and hoped) it would be. Jozef's total lack of expertise and her own inexperience robbed this first attempt of any real gratification on her part. Yet she had entered into the act with a will born of desperate necessity.

She had to get away: away from the convent, away from Commerceville. Jozef was her ticket to freedom.

That very night, having completely hypnotized him into using his savings to get them out of town, Mary Frances slipped out of the convent at eleven o'clock and met the young immigrant at the railroad station. She wore the middy blouse and skirt and knee-length woolen coat she had worn upon entering St. Theresa's two years before. They were tight and uncomfortable on her, but no matter. She would buy new clothes—all she wanted. Her imaginative mind had already formulated plans for the future.

She would become Mrs. Jozef Wynocki (Ugh! What a name!).

Jozef would become a professional fighter. He had done well that very afternoon against a tough young Irishman, hadn't he? She did not know a great deal about fighting, but she had once read that Jack Dempsey had made a fortune. True, Jozef had looked awkward in the ring, but he was strong and young and he could learn to fight. It was certainly a better future for him than slaving away in the Pennsylvania coal mines. He would become rich and famous, and one day, he would fight in California. In Hollywood, to be precise. That's where I'm going to wind up. In Hollywood.

As far as Mary Frances was concerned, her mental diagram for Jozef (*God! I can't call him Jo-ZEF. Make it just plain Joe.*) was practical and sound. That he would accept her plan was a foregone conclusion. I'm only sixteen, she thought. Well, nearly seventeen, but I'm a lot smarter than he is. Maybe it's just that he speaks English so badly, I don't know. He is good-looking, though, she added to herself. Even their first crude attempt at lovemaking offered promise. She had never really gone all the way before (she thought wistfully of Georgie Westerman), but her instincts were good. She would practice making love a lot. She would teach him—Joe—how to be a good lover. It would all work out.

A light rain was falling when she reached the station. Joe was waiting for her, sitting on a bench outside, looking forlorn and dazed. In the course of a few hours his life had suddenly changed, the comfortable safe pattern shredded by this incredible young girl. He sat with his legs stretched straight out in front of him, his wool cap pulled over his eyes, his hands jammed in his pants pockets. He wore no overcoat.

"You'll catch cold," she said by way of greeting.

"I am all right," he mumbled, punctuating the lie by sneezing.

She reached into the small carpetbag she was carrying and brought out a black woolen shawl. She draped it around his shoulders.

"Haven't you got a coat?"

"I am wear my coat."

"I mean an overcoat."

"No."

"My shawl ought to keep you a bit warmer. Have you bought the tickets?"

He looked up at her, brows knitted quizzically. "Where we go anyway?"

Exasperated, she replied, "Who cares? Anywhere. Away from here, that's all. To a big city. When's the next train out?"

He shrugged unhappily. "I not know."

She sat down next to him. Was he going to change his mind about leaving? Ruin her plans?

"Is anything wrong?" she asked him quietly.

Without looking at her, he replied moodily. "Yes. Is very wrong. Everything. I leave my friends here. I have no work now. No job. Everything . . ." He struggled for the words. ". . . Everything happen . . . so . . . *fast.*"

She placed her hand on his arm. Mustering as much huskiness as her near-seventeen-year-old larynx would permit, she said softly, "You will have work. And new friends. And me. You have me."

She squeezed his arm for attention and he turned to look at her adorable face. Impulsively, she leaned forward and kissed him. Her mouth was wonderfully fresh and sweet-tasting.

"Aren't I worth it? Leaving your job and friends?"

Lamely, he attempted, "But why so quick? In morning we could talk to . . . tell . . . your mama and papa. I could work in mine for . . . few more months. Have more money to go away . . ."

Angrily, she retorted in a cold tone of voice he would become accustomed to over the years, "Don't be silly! My parents would never let me out of the convent. Certainly not to marry some hunky coal miner."

She saw that hurt him, so she added, coquettishly, "But they don't know you. How handsome you are. How well you make love." She kissed him again. "Trust me, Joe. It'll all work out. You'll see."

She removed her hand from his sleeve and opened her palm. "Now," she said, all businesslike efficiency, "give me some money for the tickets."

Less reluctantly, he removed from his right pants pocket two ten-dollar bills, three fives, and eight ones. She took them and placed them in her carpetbag. She opened her hand again.

"Any more?"

"Yes, but . . ."

"Give it all to me. I'll take care of the money from now on."

Joe hesitated.

"Come on, come on," she insisted. "I was first in my class in arithmetic. It'll be better if I handle the finances from here on in."

Resignedly, Joe gave her the rest of his hard-earned savings.

She dropped the rubber-banded wad into her bag with a triumphant flourish. "There. That's better. Wait here," she commanded.

Joe watched her rise and go inside the station. He jammed his hands back in his pockets and slouched in his seat again.

The next train out, Mary Frances learned from the lone, sleepy ticket-seller was the 12:17, the local for Columbus, Indianapolis, and Chicago, with many intermittent stops along the way.

Chicago! Absolutely perfect!

Was the train on time?

Yes. Be pullin' in in about twenty-five minutes.

Mary Frances bought two coach tickets.

Joe was tired and wanted to sleep once the train lugged out of the station, but Mary Frances had never been on a train, had never taken a trip anywhere, had never been free before. She wanted to talk. They sat up all night in the straight-backed, dark-green, plush-covered double seat, unmindful of the snores and grunts of the other passengers. This was high adventure for Mary Frances Maguire.

o

Joe said: "Excuse me."

She turned to him. He looked tired. "Yes?" she replied.

"What is your name?"

"Pardon?"

"Your name? What is your name? How do I call you?"

She laughed merrily. It was truly funny. It *had* all happened very swiftly. In the excitement of her prospective escape, she had forgotten to introduce herself.

In mock seriousness, she replied, "Well, now that you have taken my cherry, I suppose you *are* entitled to know my name." She laughed again.

"Excuse ... I not ... understand. What means cherry?"

"It means," she said happily, "that, thanks to you, I am no

19

longer a virgin. I'm a woman. And," she added, "I have a feeling I returned the compliment."

Joe was completely lost.

"I mean I get the feeling you were never with a girl . . . like *that* . . . until today. Am I right?"

He grinned shyly and nodded.

"Good," she cried. "We're starting out even. We'll both get better at it as we go along."

Joe blushed and changed the subject.

"Your name. You were going . . ."

"Oh. Yes. My name is Mary Frances. Mary Frances Maguire. I am an only child. I am an Irish Catholic and I'm neither proud nor ashamed of it. For the last two years I have been imprisoned in St. Theresa's Convent for Young Girls, and I never thought I'd get out of the tower till you, my Polish prince, showed up today—" She looked at her watch. It was one-forty-five in the morning. ". . . Yesterday," she corrected herself ". . . and saved me from a fate worse than death. Aren't you proud of yourself?" She was prattling away now, talking compulsively out of relief, excitement, a blissful sense of freedom. "Wynocki, is that right? You are Polish, aren't you?"

"Yes. Polish."

"I have nothing against the Poles," she said. "People are people. Some of my father's Irish friends say the Poles are a bunch of dummies, that all they're fit for is working the mines."

Without warning, she put her hand on his crotch and squeezed. Joe swallowed and turned beet red. "But I know one Pole," she grinned, "who's good for something else."

Just as suddenly, she released her grip on the slight bulge that had quickly formed beneath her hand and said, "You know all about me now. Tell me about yourself. If I'm to marry you . . ." She paused. "You do intend to make an honest woman out of me, don't you?"

He did not understand.

"I'm sorry. That's a saying some people have when a girl who's made love to a man gets him to marry her. You will marry me, won't you?"

20

"Of course. Of course. I want . . . I wish to . . ."

She settled back in her seat, content, her dark hair pressed against the plush covering. She raised both legs, tucking them under her thighs, clasped her hands together over her kneecaps, and said: "All right. Begin. Tell me everything about yourself. Everything."

Haltingly, he told her. She listened, fascinated, wide-eyed, unbelieving. Good God! She had chosen to run away with a man who she had assumed was just another dumb Polack coal miner. Good-looking, yes, but ignorant and boring, like all the rest of them. Now, as he spoke, she realized she was heading for Chicago with a man whose life, prior to his arriving in America, sounded as exciting as one of her favorite Pearl White serials!

Chapter

4

To her dismay, Mary Frances Maguire discovered she was too young to be married in Illinois without the consent of her parents. The runaways took a room in a boardinghouse on Clark Street, north of the Chicago River. It was run by a blowsy harridan named Thelma Malloy, a worldly-wise, well-used ex-hooker who had saved her money, bought the building she had worked in (after a police raid put an end to the carnal activities it had previously housed), and had gone "straight."

She liked Mary Frances immediately. The pretty kid was Irish, wasn't she? And tough. She wound that big Polack around her little finger. Just a baby she was, with the body of a woman and the instinctive sense to put what she had to good use. She'd do.

Mary Frances spent a great deal of time with Thelma that first week, getting acquainted, telling her about her life in Commerceville, the convent, her meeting with Joe, the seduction in the cloakroom, the decision to run away. Thelma, between sips of gin from a water tumbler, wept copious tears. It was beautiful, it was sad, it was so damn sweet, these two good-looking young kids, hand in hand, running away to the big city, with nothing but each other to hold onto. Jesus, what courage!

By the end of her first week of residency at Malloy's Boarding Home, Mary Frances was being pampered, petted, flattered, adored. The assorted types living in the house came to resent the fact that she never failed to receive extra portions at the dining-room table. A long-time boarder was unceremoniously moved out of his room, the choicest in the house, so that Mary Frances and her Polack could occupy it. When Mary Frances coyly protested to Thelma that the new, large room would be too expensive for Joe and her, Thelma patted her arm, kissed her cheek, and told her not to worry about it.

Determined as she was to have her own way with life, Mary Frances had not lost her sense of propriety. She and Joe were living in sin. She was a fallen woman in the eyes of the Catholic Church. Yet she convinced herself that if she could find a way to marry Jozef, she would be magically restored to grace.

She confided in Thelma, who solved the problem by driving the young lovers to Crown Point, Indiana, where an old reprobate of a justice of the peace, who years before had been one of Thelma's most ardent customers, performed the ceremony.

Now Mary Frances Wynocki began Phase Two of her plan. She told Thelma about Joe and his "victory" in the prizefight at the convent. Girl to girl, she admitted that Joe was hardly a genius. He had been talking about finding a job in the steel mills out in South Chicago, "but honestly, Thelma," (eyes cast down, hands twittering), "I'd just die if I had to go live somewhere else. I love it here, and I love you, you know that, and I want Joe to be something better than a common workman."

Thelma Malloy was sentimental, but she wasn't stupid.

"All right, Mary Frances, that's enough blarney. What's on your mind?"

Mary Frances smiled brightly. "Well, Thelma, we don't know a soul in Chicago. You know everyone, I'll bet. If I could just get someone important to see Joe fight, I honestly think there's a big future for him as a boxer."

Thelma smiled. This Little Miss Wide-Eyed Innocence

had a way of getting 'round you. It was that damn pretty face.

"Okay, okay. I'll make a call or two and we'll see."

True to her word, the erstwhile soiled-dove set up a meeting with Barney Riordan, owner of a well-attended professional gym and sometime promoter of club fights in and around the Chicago area; not the biggest nor the best-connected of the entrepreneurs, but by the same token, a rank amateur didn't deserve any better.

At first Joe objected to keeping the appointment Thelma had made for him with Riordan. The thought of fighting again made him physically ill. Only after Mary Frances pouted, raged, and threatened to leave him, did he capitulate and go to Riordan's establishment.

The gym operator called Thelma late that afternoon.

"I never knew you to kid me, kid," he scolded. "This Polack lad you sent over's a joke."

"You're foolin', Barney."

"Thelma, he stinks! He's got no timing, no footwork, he ain't aggressive. In fact, looks to me like he don't wanna be a fighter. Mind you, I'll say this for him. He's got a good built. Plenty of muscle, but what the hell! He sure ain't ready for no fight."

"But you're goin' to teach him, aren't you, Barney darlin'?" Thelma pressed him.

Barney withheld his reply for a moment. "Yeah, yeah, I guess so. For you, Thelma."

Chapter

5

For the next seven weeks, Joe Wynocki arrived at Riordan's gym promptly at ten o'clock every morning except Sundays and went through the ritual of learning how to box. At first, he hated the stifling atmosphere of the gym, the sour smell of sweat that hung over the large room like a cloud, the deadly routine of rope-skipping, bag-punching, foot-shuffling, the nonstop barking of the trainers ("Keep your left up, dumbbell," "The gut, the gut. Hit 'im in the gut!" "Jab, for Chrissakes, jab!"). In a few weeks, however, he became inured to the rough talk and the cold eyes of managers and trainers, and the seemingly pitiful patience with which the various practitioners of the art went about their business.

At the dinner table one evening barely two months after Joe had begun to train, Mary Frances asked, "When are you going to have your first fight?"

"I not ... don't know. I maybe need learn more, before ..."

"But I saw you beat your sparring partner today!" she persisted. "And you told me he's good, with lots of experience."

"Mary Frances," Joe explained slowly, "is different making sparring contest at gym from fighting in ring for money. You tell her, Thelma."

Thelma was in the process of helping herself to a third portion of mashed potatoes. The large tablespoon poised in midair.

"He's right, honey. Be patient. Barney'll get him goin' when the time's right. You don't want to see your handsome hubby hurt, do you?"

"Of course not," Mary Frances answered defensively. "It's just that I think he's ready now." The truth was she had grown tired of Thelma's gin-soaked reminiscences and longed to be out of the boardinghouse. Once Joe got going in the fight game, they would travel, see the country and eventually . . . California!

The next day, Mary Frances left the boardinghouse, walked to Division Street, and used a telephone at a corner Walgreen's Drugstore.

"Hello, Mr. Riordan?"

"Yeah, who's this?"

"It's Mary Frances Wynocki, Joe's wife."

"Oh, yeah. How are ya, girlie? What can I do for ya?"

"Could I meet you somewhere? Oh, but I wouldn't want Joe to know."

"I getcha. How's about the Loop Bar and Grill over on Wells and Randolph? It's good and private!"

"Oh, thank you. I sure appreciate it. I know how busy you are."

"Aw, hell, babyface, I ain't ever too busy for a pretty girl. See you in . . . say, twenty minutes, okay?"

"I'll be there."

Mary Frances was purposely ten minutes late. She wanted to make an entrance. She had dressed very carefully in the most demure of the three dresses she had bought since she came to Chicago: a Kelly green wool ensemble, with a multicolored imitation silk scarf tying back her long, dark hair. It was an unseasonably warm February day and she had risked going out without wearing her coat. The moment she walked through the door, every male eye, and a few female ones as well, followed her from the front entrance all the way back to Barney's table.

Uncharacteristically, for him, Barney rose from his seat and pulled out her chair, shoving it gently under her as she sat down.

"You get prettier every time I see you, kid," Barney smiled.

Mary Frances managed a maidenly blush. Barney cleared his throat and offered her a menu.

"I'm not very hungry, Mr. Riordan. You order for me, would you?"

"Sure, kid, sure. And the name's 'Barney!'" He snapped his fingers and one of the waitresses shuffled over. He ordered two open-faced hot roast beef sandwiches with mashed potatoes and gravy and coffee for two.

"May I have milk instead?" asked Mary Frances. Barney amended the order.

"Awright, now. What did ya wanna talk about?"

Mary Frances looked down into her lap. "Gee, now that I'm here, I . . . I don't know whether I should . . ."

He reached out and put his fist beneath her chin, raising it.

"Come on now, little soldier. Nothin' can be that bad. Tell Barney all about it."

"Well," she smiled wanly, "the thing is—I'm pregnant."

Barney whistled softly. "Are ya now? Well, that's wonderful news. Bet Joe's proud as punch. And Thelma, boy I'll bet . . ."

"No, no, Barney. I only just found out myself. You're the first one I've told."

"You haven't called your husband?"

"Don't you see? Joe would start worrying about money. Thelma would insist on paying for everything 'cause she knows we're broke, and I couldn't stand that. No one's going to pay for this baby except me. And Joe, of course. That's the way it's got to be."

"Well, what about your family, then? I mean your father. Why don't ya call him? I'm sure he'd send you some money if he knew about your condition."

"But Barney, I can't. My daddy taught me self-respect since I was a little girl. Stand on your own two feet all through life, he said, time and time again. You know how Irish fathers can be."

Barney's eyebrows arched in surprise. "Hey! You Irish, kid?"

"My family name is Maguire."

"I'll be damned! Thought you looked like a mick, but I wasn't sure."

"Well, I am," she stated, "and all the Polish married names in the world will never change that."

He looked at her, sitting there, her head held high and proud.

"You're one hell of a young woman," the gym owner declared.

"Barney," she lowered her voice confidentially, "my father was opposed to this marriage from the start. Kept telling me Joe wasn't good enough for me. Finally, I couldn't stand it any more. I decided to break up with Joe, much as I loved him, rather than defy my father."

"Yeah? Well then, how come . . .?"

"Joe talked me into running away. He actually threatened to kill himself if I didn't."

The waitress interrupted with their food and Mary Frances stopped talking until she went away.

Barney shifted uncomfortably in his chair. He was slightly ashamed to admit that he had had some prurient thoughts about Wynocki's wife right up until a few minutes ago. But of course, that was before she had imparted the news of her impending motherhood. And her Irish origins. No, she was a good Catholic girl and he would be "Uncle Barney" to her if she'd let him.

"I never even knew about the facts of life, until Joe got hold of me. He's taught me everything . . ." She blushed, an embarrassed young girl, unable to continue this delicate discussion.

He changed the subject. "Ahem. Well, let's get down to it, then. How can old Barn be of service?"

"Please, Barney, if Joe could start fighting. For money. I know he isn't going to make a great deal right away. But if he could at least start earning *something,* that would help."

"Hmm, I suppose so. But I'm not so sure he's up to it yet. You know, it's not good to push a man into the ring before he's ready . . ."

"*Please,* Barney!"

28

"On the other hand," he laughed, "me old Irish father once threw me in a pond with the good advice that if I was ever goin' to learn to swim, then was the opportune time!"

She laughed with him delightedly.

"Eat your sandwich, little missy, and relax. Uncle Barney'll work things out, you'll see. We Irish have to stick together, right?"

She smiled, sighed contentedly, and picked daintily at her food. He forsook dessert, sweetening his mouth instead by taking Mary Frances' hand in his and kissing it, once again committing an act uncommon to the likes of Barney Riordan. He looked at his pocket watch. "Gotta be gettin' back to the gym. Now don't you worry." He squeezed her hand reassuringly, rose, and left.

Mary Frances sat there, slowly drinking her milk. Never before had she been so pleased with herself. *I'll do well in Hollywood someday,* she thought. *I can act. I just proved it.*

Suddenly she experienced a cramping abdominal pain. She grimaced, put down her milk, arose, and headed for the ladies' room. It was always the same dreary discomfort, the first day of her period.

Chapter

6

Mary Frances' excitement was uncontainable. For Joe's first fight, he was to "go" four rounds with a man called Spider Ferris. She tried to instill some confidence in her husband as he dressed to leave for the arena, but he insisted (the big booby!) on worrying.

Joe threw his robe, shoes, trunks, and supporter into a green duffel, mumbled goodbye to Thelma, kissed Mary Frances absently on the cheek, and barely acknowledged the cries of "good luck" from the other boarders in the dining room as he passed out of the house into the cold evening air. He trudged his way toward the streetcar line and boarded a red-and-yellow for the Loop. Mary Frances and Thelma would be along later, in time for the bout.

"He didn't eat anything," commented Thelma.

"Don't worry," chirped Mary Frances. "We'll celebrate after the fight. A victory dinner!"

o

"And in this corner, making his first professional appearance in any ring, weighing one hunnerd and sevveny-nine pounds, from the coal mines of Pennsylvania to the bright lights of the Windy City, in the purple trunks ... Joe Wynocki!"

Joe stood up in his corner, letting the robe fall away from his shoulders. He walked to the center of the ring and stood face to face with his opponent.

Spider Ferris' nose had been broken and reset several times. Scar tissue had built up around his eyes to such a degree that they were mere slits in his face. His lips were still swollen from his last fight. He would have no trouble keeping his mouthpiece in; he had no teeth.

He was slightly shorter than Joe, but he had seven pounds on the Polish neophyte, and as long as Joe's reach was, Ferris' was longer, the length of his arms in radical disproportion to the rest of his body. His midsection was ridged with hardened muscle. The only legs Joe had ever seen that appeared as strong and solid as Ferris' were those of a weight lifter who worked out at Riordan's.

When the referee finished his charge to the fighters, Ferris smiled at Joe. Or was it a smirk? Joe returned to his corner, sat down on the stool, and allowed Cokey, his coffee-colored trainer, to place the mouthpiece between his teeth. He was trembling. This was much worse than he had imagined it would be. He felt naked, on display, surrounded by posts and ropes and smoke and noise and hundreds of hostile faces all hungry for his blood.

Iisus Khristos, what am I doing here?

The bell.

He rose to his feet and moved reluctantly toward center-ring. Ferris came dancing at him and delivered an uppercut that caught Joe at the breastbone, then came in again with surprising speed and planted twin thunderbolts to the stomach.

Joe rocked on his heels and backed away into a corner. Ferris stalked him to the ringpost, wedged him in, and served up a flurry of lefts and rights, his arms working like perfectly timed pistons. The blows caught Joe everywhere his ineffectual guard was not: on the arms, the head, in the gut, the ribs, the kidneys, the nose, eyes, mouth. The blood pounded in his head and mingled with the roar of the crowd. They were screaming for the kill.

The arena was spinning now, the ring lights a hot white-blue, as his legs threatened to give way. Had they forgotten to ring the bell? Surely the three minutes were up!

The first round was only forty-five seconds old.

Joe's superb condition saved him. To everyone's surprise, he was still on his feet when the bell ended round one. He staggered back to his corner and sagged onto the stool. Cokey applied a cotton-tipped stick dipped in astringent to a cut which had opened under Joe's left eye. Joe recoiled from its sting. His head swiveled around as he squinted through sweat and blood flecks, searching for Mary Frances wherever she might be in the noisy maelstrom beyond the ring.

Too soon, the bell sounded and Joe rose, determined to make a good showing so that his wife would not be ashamed of him.

As the two fighters met in the center of the ring a huge roar went up from the spectators. As far as they were concerned, the fight was cut and dried. Hell, this was only a prelim anyway. Get it over with.

The moment Joe Wynocki was in range, Spider hammered him with three good left jabs. Joe realized he had to stay out of reach of those apelike arms. The fight took on a comic aspect: Ferris crouched, advancing; Wynocki, guard up, retreating. The crowd began to boo.

"How about it, girls?" roared one wag through his rolled-up program. "Save a dance for me?"

"Come on, Spider. Put the bum outta his misery!"

"Yeah, Ferris, quit playin' with 'im, will ya?"

"Hey, Spider, my old lady's expectin' me home sometime tonight!"

Mary Frances sank into her seat. Did this crowd know she was the wife of that clown up there? She hoped not.

Spurred by the catcalls from the crowd, Spider bored in. There was no escape for Joe. Fists (there had to be more than a mere pair of them!) exploded from everywhere and a massive tattoo of pain traveled the complete length of Joe's upper torso. The cut under his eye was bleeding profusely now and he prayed the referee would stop the fight. He held his arms up over his face, trying to protect his eyes, and Spider took advantage of his raised guard to pummel his midsection. Why the hell didn't the dope go down?

32

Frantically, Cokey yelled, "Clinch, Joe! Get him in a clinch!"

What a good idea! Joe stepped into a straight right that grazed his cheek, and wrapped his arms around Ferris. That was fine with the superior fighter. He had been punching hard; he welcomed the breather.

In the flush of confidence, he said into Joe's ear, "Get ready, dumbbell. I'm goin' to wipe up this ring with your ass!"

Ferris now remembered having seen Joe's wife on one occasion when he had stopped by Riordan's. He hugged Joe tighter and rasped: "Talk about ass, your wife's a real choice piece."

Ferris pushed Joe away with both hands, breaking the clinch. Wynocki's features were contorted with rage. His lips were compressed so tightly around his mouthpiece the shape of it protruded under his nose. He sprang forward, oblivious to the blows being rained on him. Forgotten now were the rudiments of boxing, drummed into him daily for the past few months. Clumsily, he smothered Ferris with roundhouse lefts and rights, most of them missing their marks.

"Keep your head, Joe," yelled Cokey. "Box him, boy. Combinations!"

Spider was not grinning any more. He had to put this idiot away before the fight got out of hand. He stuck his left arm out, the glove in Joe's face, while he cocked his right for the clincher. He saw an opening as Joe's tired arms lowered slightly. He swung his right, putting his whole body into it. His fist slammed into Joe's jaw, dead center. He gawked at the young Pole, and lowered his own guard in surprise.

The powerful right cross seemed to have no effect!

In that off-guard instant, Spider Ferris was caught by a Wynocki sledgehammer of a right, just above the left eye. Ferris fell heavily to the mat. Joe stood there, looking at his fallen foe, with the fans yelling their approval at the odd turn of events.

The referee guided Joe into the neutral corner and began his count.

"Eight ... Nine ... *Ten,*" the crowd shouted with him as his hand dropped for the last time. A great cheer went up as

33

the white-shirted man walked over to Joe and raised his gloved right hand in victory, even while the arena doctor was climbing through the ropes to attend Ferris.

The doctor knelt beside Spider and waved an ammonia capsule under his nose. He took Ferris' wrists between his hands and rubbed them. He slapped the downed boxer's face, gently at first, then with open-palmed blows. He turned toward someone outside the ring and asked for his bag, as the clamor in the arena subsided.

Spider's trainer and manager climbed into the ring and stood over the prone figure of their meal ticket. The doctor took his thumb and raised Spider's eyelid. The eye rolled back into the head, filmy and unseeing. The crowd grew quieter. The doctor reached into his bag and removed a stethoscope, placing the curved earpieces in his ears and the chromed metal cone at the other end over Spider's heart. He shook his head unbelievingly, and once again listened for a heartbeat.

The doctor rose to his feet and murmured something to the other men in the ring. As he signaled for a stretcher, the referee walked into the glare of the center lights and announced through a megaphone:

"The winner, by a knockout, in two minutes, twenny-two seconds of the second round . . . Joe Wynocki."

There was a smattering of applause.

"The management regrets to announce," continued the referee, "that Spider Ferris was seriously injured in the knockdown . . . and has succumbed to his injury. There will be a fifteen-minute intermission."

Two ambulance attendants carried the body up the aisle toward the exit. Joe watched them disappear into the archway. Tears glistened on his battered cheeks as he climbed through the ropes and headed up the center aisle toward the dressing rooms. As he ran the gauntlet of the crowd he felt a few sympathetic pats on the back.

"Don't blame yourself, fellah. It wasn't your fault."

"Tough luck, kid."

"Yeah, too bad about Ferris. But it was a hell of a fight!"

And from a fat, grinning slug of a man with a bottle of beer

34

gripped in his paw: "Hey, Joe boy! You really stepped on that Spider. Get it? I mean you squashed him like a bug!"

Joe stopped and glared so fiercely that the moron blanched and shrank away.

For weeks after the fight, Joe kept mostly to his room, silent and grieving, despite all the pleas and preaching of Mary Frances. He had been cleared of any blame by the Illinois State Boxing Commision. A well-known promoter called to say he thought Joe had "color," that there was a real future for him in the ring.

Joe, staring out the bedroom window for hours on end, ate little, lost weight, and was uninterested in all that went on around him. Mary Frances tried to cheer him up by offering herself to him one night, all bathed and smelling good from the lilac water she had borrowed from Thelma. Joe did not participate in the lovemaking, he submitted to it. She might as well have been making love to a stone.

One day, Joe surprised his wife by rising from his place at the bedroom window and saying: "I go look for job today."

"Joe, oh, Joey, you . . . you talked to me! I began to think you'd stopped speaking for the rest of your life. Really, Jozef! You *have* been difficult. I mean, it's impossible to communicate with someone who won't talk. Now let's go downstairs, have a nice lunch with Thelma, and then we'll come back up here, just the two of us and uh . . . I'll be nice to you, all right?"

Joe walked past her and put on his coat and hat.

"I go look for job today."

"But you've got a job. You're a fighter."

Joe looked at her. "No more. I never hurt anybody again."

He turned and left the room, walking downstairs and out the front door.

Joe Wynocki headed for the steel mills like a homing pigeon; to his way of thinking, they were the Chicago equivalent of the Pennsylvania coal mines. After four days of looking for work, he was hired by the Belanger Mill. When he told Mary Frances the news, she threw a tantrum. Through the locked door of their bedroom, her curses and threats were heard by every guest in the boardinghouse until

35

they subsided into rasping sobs and, finally, no sound at all.

In the morning, Joe's few belonging were packed. Mary Frances sullenly watched him from bed, the coverlet drawn up over her nightgown as if to shield her body from the eyes of this stranger walking out the door. As for going with him, not a chance. Mary Frances Maguire (in her mind she had already reverted back to her maiden name and single status) had no intention of wasting her life as the wife of a common laborer. He had implored her to accompany him to Steeltown, that area of South Chicago where the workers lived with their families. He had arranged to rent one of the small frame houses near the mill, and he was sure Mary Frances and he could be comfortable there. She would have none of it.

Two weeks passed, during which Mary Frances pondered her future. She had made a mistake, marrying that Polack. She did not love him, and the only chance he'd had to make something of himself was lost because of his selfish stubbornness. She was almost out of money and Thelma had cooled toward her. She could not stay at the boardinghouse indefinitely without paying. Envelopes had been arriving in the mail containing half of Joe's wages, but his weekly take-home seemed so meager, she didn't have enough spending money to go to the movies.

Then, just when she was wrestling with what seemed an insoluble problem, nature stepped in and made the decision for her. She was really pregnant, this time.

Now she had no choice. Bitter in defeat, she packed her belongings, walked to the streetcar line, and rode the long rattling ride out to the South Chicago address erratically printed on the backs of the envelopes she'd gotten from Joe.

Chapter

7

Joe Wynocki stood in the center of the saucer-shaped open hearth, took off his smoked goggles and, turning away from the furnace, wiped his forehead with his shirt-sleeved arm. The temperature in the huge blast furnace was nearing the 3000 degree mark. At first, Joe had been physically repelled by the intense heat. For several months after he came to work at the Belanger Steel Mills he could not rid his body of what his fellow workers called "the burn." No matter how many icy showers he took in the company lavatory, his skin felt as though a stove was cooking it from within. And then, one day he found he had become inured to the heat of the furnace. It became a natural element of his daily life, and he actually came to look forward to it during the cold months when the cruel winter wind howled and whistled off Lake Michigan and knifed through his coat on his way to work in the mornings.

No, he admitted to himself, the furnace heat wasn't at all bad in the winter. But this was an especially hot summer even for Chicago, the summer of 1933, and ten hours of hard work on a scorching July day made a man bone-weary. Oh well, he thought, this is Friday. I will have weekend. . . . I will have *the* weekend . . . (Mary Frances kept reminding him to

37

speak better English. "Talk more American," she would scold, but he found it extremely difficult to overcome the accents and syntax of his native Poland.) . . . *I will have the weekend to rest. Unless Mary Frances wants to get on the streetcar and go downtown to the World's Fair* . . . He sighed.

Early that morning he and the rest of the crew had begun preparing for the day's steel output. The larger mills were using big, automatic pieces of equipment that picked up the preweighed boxes of limestone and scrap and fed them into the furnace. But at Belanger, this work was still done by men. For the first half hour of the morning, Joe and the rest of the crew, Warnacek, Markhovic, O'Ryan, and Soszinko, repaired the hearth. Then Kosciusko, the melter, lit the furnace as the charging began. The crew lifted box after box of raw materials from the cradle cars that ran on a track in front of the hearth. First the limestone was flung into the brick-lined enclosure, each man lifting a box at a time. Then, two men to each box of scrap steel, muscles bulging and straining as perspiration dripped from arms and legs and the backs of necks, and brows knitted with concentrated strength, the second phase of charging was completed as box after box found its way into the rising heat of the large kiln.

Two hours later, hands holstered in thick, heat-resistant work gloves, the men guided the huge ladle again and again as it traveled on its single-cable overhead trolley to and from the furnace, spewing molten pig iron into the hot stew. Now, as the elements began to fuse into steel, the crew stepped back for a breather. The iron, they knew, upon rising to the surface of the bubbling mass, would give off carbon-dioxide gas which, in the large quantities produced by the furnaces, could be fatal. While the gas rose and quickly dissipated itself through the thin slots in the corrugated-steel roof of the furnace shed, the Belanger family insisted that as a safety precaution the men move away from the hearth. With material readily obtainable and operations reasonably trouble-free, the Belanger Mill was a thriving little business. Keep the men busy and reasonably content (work crew: $24.00 a week per man; melters: $40.00 per week), and progress would be made with a minimum of adversity.

"I look forward to the time," barked J.W. "Old Man" Belanger on the occasion of the Fourth of July company picnic not three weeks earlier, "when the Belanger Mill will be as big and as famous as any mill in this great country of ours." (Cheers from ths captive audience.) "Hell, this Depression isn't going to last forever, not that we're not doing okay in spite of it, right, men?" (He winked broadly as the men cheered once more.) "Now you watch! Next year this picnic will be bigger and better, more beer, more prizes, more everything! And you know why? Because we're going to do even better in 1934 than we did this year! And," he added, his plump face flushed with the afternoon heat and the best part of a bottle of bourbon, "I think *this* was one hell of a year! Your pardon, ladies." (More cheers, but less vociferous this time.)

Now, as Joe walked away from the furnace, removing his gloves, he thought about Old Man Belanger and smiled. He liked the boss. He liked his job. Working at the mill made him feel as though he were part of the Belanger family. He felt warm and protected in that knowledge, misplaced though his values might have been. One bad year, any tightening of the already anemic national economy, and the "family" would unceremoniously lay him off. Yet Joe Wynocki was an inveterate believer and, in his heart, he could simply not conceive of any other way of life anywhere except working at the mill.

He sat down on the wooden bench at the back of the hearth, a good seventy-five feet from the roaring furnace. The handkerchief he had tied around his forehead was clammy with sweat.

"Hot bastard today, ain't it," said Markhovic as he sat beside him.

"Hot every day," Joe managed to grin, as he rubbed the bandanna under his armpits. He had developed into a handsome man in his strong-jawed, high-cheekboned Slavic way, with dark-blond curly hair, eyebrows set close to pale blue eyes, teeth that were very white and attractively

39

irregular, protruding slightly from a mouth that grinned easily. He was popular with the men on Furnace III except for Kosciusko, who was forever teasing him, calling him "Lover Boy" and "the pretty Polack." Joe accepted these taunts good-naturedly, although he flinched when anybody, even another Pole like Kosciusko, called him "Polack."

Some of the work crew were gathering around the rest bench, opening lunch pails, gulping huge draughts of water from a large tin cup connected by a thin metal chain to a solitary water faucet near by. Joe reached under the bench, his hand groping for the lunch pail he placed there first thing each morning. When his hand failed to locate it, he swung his body forward between his legs and looked under the bench. Puzzled, he sat up slowly.

The lunch pail dangled before his eyes, suspended from the thumb and forefinger of Anton Kosciusko's right hand.

Joe grinned sheepishly. "Ah, Anton. You always make fun."

Kosciusko was a powerful man, barrel-chested with a cruel mouth and a shock of straight black hair. He looked at Joe and snorted, as Joe reached for his pail. Withholding it, the melter's brittle voice demanded, "All right, what's my name?"

"What? What you mean?"

" 'What? What you mean?' " mimicked Kosciusko. "How long you been in this country, Wynocki?"

Joe counted on his fingers. "I am here now eighteen years."

Kosciusko shook his head disdainfully. "And you still talk like a greenhorn."

"I know," Joe shook his head sadly. "I not talk good. Mary Frances keep telling me, 'Joe, you got to speak more American.' "

"She's absolutely right. This ain't the old country. It's the U.S.A." He leaned down and placed his face close to Joe's. As if he were speaking to a two-year-old child, he made his lips into a pout and said, "You want people to think you're a dumbhead, Lover Boy?"

Joe flushed, conscious of the grins of his fellow laborers.

"No. 'Course not. What you t'ink I am, anyway?" He

40

reached for the lunch pail once more, and again it was denied him.

"No," laughed Kosciusko, "no lunch until you tell me my name."

"Aw, Anton . . ." Joe pleaded.

"Not *Anton*, you dimwit. *Tony. Toe*-knee."

"Oh, yeah, I'm sorry. I forget. Tony Kosciusko."

"Wrong again. Tony Kosko. See? Short. Easy to remember. More American. Kosko. I told you a dozen times. Kosko. You don't like your job, I guess, you can't even remember your boss's name."

Markhovic looked up at the melter. "Cut the crap, Tony. You're not the boss. You're just the melter."

"Oh yeah? I earn nearly twice what you dumb oxes get. That makes me the boss."

"Some boss," muttered O'Ryan, as he placed his head beneath the faucet and turned on the water full strength.

"Wha'd you say, Irisher?" growled Tony, taking a step toward him.

"I said," replied O'Ryan, shaking the water from his head like a dog drying himself, "why in hell don't you leave Joe alone and give him his pail?"

"And who asked you to poke your big mick nose in this? Unless you're lookin' to get it broken."

O'Ryan grinned. He was a beefy Irishman with a perpetually red nose, a physical anomaly since he was a teetotaler. This kind of talk was the standard fare every day when the lunch break came around. He pulled himself up to his full height, which was considerable, and said, "I'd like to see the day when any hunky can break the nose of any Irishman." He bowed slightly toward his co-workers. "No offense intended, lads."

Kosciusko was taking it more seriously than usual today. "You fat loudmouth! If you really think you can—"

"Oh, for God's sake, Tony. It's too damn hot for this sort of thing. Now be a good fellow and give Joe his—"

"I can take care myself," Joe said suddenly, as he snatched at the lunch pail, but Tony was too quick for him. He retreated a few steps and opened the pail. "Let's see what the beautiful Mary Frances packed for Lover Boy today." He rummaged through the wax-paper-wrapped lunch. He nodded and pulled the corners of his mouth down in appraisal. "Not bad. Now, if that pretty little mick wife of yours is as good in bed as she is in the kitchen . . ."

Joe sprang to his feet, took two short quick steps and grabbed the lunch pail from the melter's hand.

"Enough, Anton! I don't like when you make such talk."

Kosciusko smirked at him for a moment and walked away. Joe took a deep breath, looked around at the other men self-consciously, and slowly sat down again. The crew lapsed into silence. It was too hot to talk. Sandwiches, pint bottles of milk, coffee thermoses appeared.

Joe unwrapped his lunch, a bologna and cheese sandwich, and started chewing on it thoughtfully. He had tried hard to like Kosciusko. After all, did the man not bear the name of a great Polish hero? Still, it was difficult to be friendly toward him. For some reason the melter seemed to relish hazing him; he wondered whether the real trouble between Anton and himself did not stem from that evening not long ago when he had refused to accompany Kosciusko into the South Shore district.

While Joe Wynocki was well liked by his comrades at the steel mill, he did not extend that camaraderie into his evening hours. He enjoyed being at home with his family (even though Mary Frances seemed to be more and more dissatisfied with him and her life in general in recent weeks). One hot Friday Kosciusko had braced him at the end of the work day with an invitation.

"Hey, Wynocki," he said. "Bunch of us are goin' into South Shore tonight."

"South Shore?" asked Joe, uncomprehending.

"Yeah. You know. Sheenyland. Where the Jews live."

"I still don't . . ."

Kosciusko rolled his eyes toward heaven. "Mother of God, I don't believe it! Look," he began again patiently. "Bunch of us are goin' over around 71st and Jeffery, find us some kikes, and beat the shit out of them. We want you to come along."

"Why?"

"To help beat the shit out of them."

"I not go."

From that day until this one Kosciusko had chided, taunted, ragged, and embarrassed Joe with monotonous regularity. On several occasions Joe had had to exercise extreme self-control to keep from hitting him. Afterward, he had broken out in cold sweats, his body trembling with the realization of how very dangerous that would have been. In view of Joe Wynocki's past history, he could not afford the luxury of physical anger toward *anyone.* He was happy to be in America, happy to have the chance to work every day, proud to be married to a beautiful girl like Mary Frances, father to a fine boy like Martin, who would grow up to be "more American" than Anton Kosciusko could ever hope to be.

Chapter

8

Joe Wynocki had not thought about the horrible events of his early life in Poland for some time. The knowledge of what had happened to him and what he had done was so painful that he had forcibly shuttered the memories from his conscious mind.

When his son Martin, a boy closely cast in his father's image, pressed him to tell about his former homeland, Joe, in halting English, would recall stories his parents had once told him. Fairy tales in some instances, accounts of valorous Poles of bygone days, anecdotes about Joe's ancestors—these were all Joe Wynocki cared to remember where his native land was concerned.

They were invariably recounted as bedtime stories and, for Joe and Martin, those moments spent together became the best time of the day. Martin respected and loved Joe who, in turn, worshipped the boy. The younger Wynocki liked the sound of his father's voice, the imperfect use of the difficult foreign tongue, English, spoken softly and gently in the dark.

These nightly sessions were exclusively father's and son's. Mary Frances had long since been bored by Joe's rambling reminiscenses. She either sat in the parlor, leafing through screen magazines, or went to a movie.

One evening, Joe's powers of recollection ran dry and Martin, under the covers, said, "Papa, you already told me that one. Last week. Remember?"

Joe struggled to dredge up some heretofore unrelated tale. He could not. Mary Frances, sitting in the parlor, toying with a jigsaw puzzle, rose from her chair and walked over to her son's bed.

"There's one story your daddy remembers, I'll bet. He told it to me once, on a train, when we first came here." She looked at Joe, seated on a chair by the boy's bed in the darkness. "Why don't you tell him that one?"

Joe shook his head. "I not know which one you—"

"Don't be modest, Joe," she mocked. "Your son has a right to know about his bold, brave papa."

"Mary Frances," Joe said.

"Please, Papa," begged Martin. "Tell me. What kind of a story is it? Is it really about you?"

"Martin," Joe said lamely. "Is not—I don't want you—"

"Oh, for God's sake," Mary Frances interrupted. "Tell him. It's just another fairy tale anyway." She shrugged and walked back into the parlor.

"Papa," Martin quietly urged him. "Please."

Joe sighed. He supposed the boy would have to know sometime.

He began to talk.

o

It was snowing, a thick, dry, huge-flaked snowfall, as if someone had cut open a giant goose-down pillow in the sky and was shaking it gently over the earth. Young Jozef Wynocki held his mother's hand as they left Janicki the baker's sweet-smelling shop. In the fading light of what remained of the day, the dim electric bulb in the window of the bakery threw a pale yellow shaft on the fallen snow in the street. It was one of the few incandescent luxuries in the rustic village of Podlasz.

Now mother and son would trudge three and one-half

45

miles back home through the snow, to the near-blackness of the farmhouse, lit only by candles, and there would be chores to do before dinner. The hens would have to be fed, as would the goat and Koniek, their sway-backed excuse for a horse, beloved and respected by Jozef and his mother for his tirelessness in dragging the plow during the week and pulling the little troika on Sundays to church, waiting outside patiently in the cold and the rain and the heat of summer while Father Mikolaczyk extolled the virtues of Christ the Redeemer and counseled his parishioners to count their blessings in this essentially cruel world.

This evening, like every other evening in the last year and a half, Jozef would pass the cemetery on his way home and automatically peer in the gloom toward his father's grave. Stepan Wynocki had died eighteen months earlier of bronchial pneumonia. His mother could not bring herself to look toward the cemetery, her eyes never wavering from the road ahead, her hand gripping Jozef's even tighter, her wedding band cutting into her son's trapped fingers.

As they left the protecting frame structures of Podlasz behind them, a cold wind drove the snowflakes into their eyes and noses and mouths. Jozef recalled his father once telling him that it only snowed when the temperature of the air was warm enough, but surely the elder Wynocki had been wrong. The cold sliced through his jacket, and he bent his head against the frigid air, releasing his mother's hand momentarily to adjust his scarf over the lower half of his face.

He did not, therefore, see the horsemen as much as hear them at first. He sensed a muffled drumming in the ground like far-off applause. As it became louder he looked up and saw a group of mounted figures approaching, vague and diffused in the swirling snow. Jozef peered at them, his eyes straining to make out details and identify the contingent, although he knew that so many horses could only be found at the Russian cavalry outpost on the outskirts of Brest-Litovsk, seventeen miles away.

Now they were much closer, about twenty of them, coming

toward Jozef and his mother at a brisk trot, the horses breathing and blowing loudly, their breaths making puffs of steam in the cold air. The cavalrymen, dressed in their heavy greatcoats with collars of lamb's wool and the familiar peaked caps, were singing as they rode, a lusty air in a minor key.

The officer who led them caught Jozef's eye, and the young boy stared at him in unabashed admiration. He was a young, handsome man, with a lean face, the best feature of which was an aquiline nose that complemented a dark, slightly drooping mustache. He wore a coat and *papacha* made of the finest sable, and his boots gleamed dully through the veil of falling snow. He sat erect in his saddle, his gloved left hand loosely holding the reins, his right hand closed around a bottle of vodka which he now brought to his lips, throwing his head back and draining the last drop.

He threw the empty bottle into the snow with a gesture of disgust. How dare it be empty! Now Jozef could see the man sway slightly in his saddle. His superb animal made a slight correction, an almost imperceptible shifting of weight that allowed the young officer to maintain his balance. The horses and men were only yards from Jozef and his mother now, and the young officer became aware of their presence. He shouted two words to his men, and they stopped singing. A few of them hooted in drunken glee and Jozef saw something bright and shining appear in the right hand of the officer. The trotting horses converted to a canter and almost immediately shifted to full gallop.

As the mounted group bore down on Jozef and his mother, she recognized with fear the curved steel cavalry saber in the officer's hand. She grabbed Jozef and moved in front of him protectively. Frightened and confused, he cried questioningly, "Mother?" He strained his neck and shoulders, first to the left, then to the right of his mother's obscuring body, trying to see what was happening. Through the crook of his mother's left arm he saw, almost as if in cameo, the Russian officer lean over the neck of his horse, and gracefully swing his saber in a perfectly described arc. He was right on top of the Wynockis now, and his suddenly gentle smile was almost benign, as if he were offering his sword as a benediction. Jozef pressed his head against the rough wool of his mother's shawl, his eyes tightly jammed shut in an effort to suspend what he knew was coming.

He heard the swoosh of the sword and the slight jar of contact it made as it cleanly decapitated Jania Wynocki. Jozef did not see the blow struck, but he felt a huge tremor course through his mother's body, and her blood, warm and sticky, running down his face. His mother's legs bent at the knees and the whole torso sagged. Jozef tried to hold her up, but it was futile. She fell heavily in the snow and he swayed between screaming and gagging as he watched her severed head roll slowly into the ditch at the side of the road, an oversized red and white snowball, functionless and irrelevant. The troop of cavalry galloped by, with no more than a few backward glances. There was more fun to be had in the village.

For more than an hour Jozef lay on the road next to his mother's stiffening, headless body, his right arm encircling her gently. He felt the warmth leave her by degrees until her skin became tight and cold. He did not cry. From the village he could hear screams and shouts, the occasional firing of a gun. Finally, because he was chilled to the bone, he left his mother's side and went to the ditch to retrieve her head. It lay there like a forgotten globe, completely covered with snow.

Twice he tried to bring himself to pick up the severed head of his mother but his mind rejected the act. Then, because he knew the Russians would have to come back this way, he overcame his horror and reached for the head. Snow fell away to reveal Jania Wynocki's nose, and Jozef cradled her head in his left arm while he gently brushed the glistening crystals from her mouth, her cheeks, her hair, her eyes.

Her eyes.

Open and staring, frozen at the moment of her death in surprised shock. He looked into them for an instant, as if to find some message for him. There was nothing.

After pulling her torso off the road and into the ditch, he

took her shawl, still incongruously draped over her shoulders, and covered her head. He ran all the way to the farm, got Koniek out of the barn, hitched him to the troika, and went back for her body. At first he wondered whether to take her directly home. To bury her properly, though, he knew he would have to see Karpuszko, the village undertaker. He somehow got the separated parts of his mother's body into the little sleigh, and drove into the village.

The Russians had departed. Corpses were strewn in the street like neglected mounds of garbage, buildings were burning, a few dogs howled at the sides of their dead masters. Jozef drove slowly, looking from side to side in revulsion at the carnage visited upon Podlasz. He passed the baker's shop where only two hours ago his mother had bought their daily loaf of bread. The long cord and socket in the window now held only the shattered remnants of the wonderful electric light. The window was smashed, and Janicki lay over his counter, his legs on the floor, his body bent at the waist, his arms dangling loosely over the table edge, the left side of his face resting flat on the counter. Blackish-red blood from the bullet hole in his right temple had coagulated and caked upon his cheek in the cold night air.

The village lay in darkness except for the light of the fires still licking at several of the frame structures. As Jozef headed for the undertaker's, he passed a child crying alongside a body. He recognized Anna Warszawski. She too had lost her mother. For a moment he considered stopping to comfort the little girl, but he was possessed with a strange sense of purpose.

He drove on to Karpuszko's. The undertaker's establishment had been spared. He had hidden in one of his own coffins as the Russians kicked his door down and entered the place. When they realized where they were, they had crossed themselves hurriedly and departed.

Jozef offered him all the livestock on the farm and the troika in exchange for a Christian burial for his mother.

"What about your horse?" the undertaker asked. He was of the living and he had, after all, to live.

"Not the horse," Jozef answered shortly. "I will need Koniek."

Karpuszko considered haggling, but the look on the boy's face changed his mind and the bargain was made.

Jania Wynocki would have one of Karpuszko's finer coffins, and her grave would be dug alongside her husband's. Jozef left without looking at his mother again. He had said goodbye in the ditch when he had been alone with her for the last time.

Chapter

9

Jania Wynocki was buried the next day under leaden skies. Father Mikolaczyk spoke over her remains as the coffin was lowered into the ground. The previous day's events were of such staggering enormity that even the usually comforting words of the priest seemed empty and useless. The village lay in smoldering ruins, a full third of its population annihilated during the course of one evening of Russian diversion.

Jozef stood, cap in hand, a cold wind blowing his hair and chilling him as Gromycz, the gravedigger, shoveled large clods of earth into the hole where Jozef's mother lay. The boy's eyes were fixed upon the disappearing coffin, and when its shape and form could no longer be seen, he turned and walked slowly away.

o

Piolek Martwicz was the closest thing Podlasz had to landed gentry. Most of the surrounding farms were occupied by near poverty-stricken families who paid the owner, Martwicz, a semiannual sum of money far in excess of what six months of tenant farming was worth for the privilege of having a roof over their heads and a little food in the cupboard. Jozef's father had been one of the few men to own his meager cluster of acres free and clear. They now belonged to Jozef, and he knew the only man in Podlasz who could afford to buy was Piolek Martwicz.

Jozef reined Koniek to a halt in front of Martwicz's neat, white house on the eastern edge of the village. The boy thought, Why, God, do You allow good people like my mother to be killed, kind men like Janicki with his wonderful electric light and Kovak with his jovial smile, and little Anna Warszawski's mother, who never, not one day of her entire life, hurt so much as an ant in the road; why do these people die and suffer, and have their houses and shops burned to the ground, while here in front of me stands the home of Martwicz, untouched? I do not understand You, God.

He dismounted and walked up the path to Martwicz's front door, upon which he knocked softly four times. He waited for a reply and when there was none, he knocked again, louder, less respectfully. He knew Martwicz was inside and had heard the knocking. He also knew that out of shrewdness and a touch of perverse satisfaction at holding the upper hand, the landowner would answer the door in his own good time. Jozef sighed and waited. He would skin his knuckles no more.

Presently, the door opened. Piolek Martwicz stood there feigning surprise.

"Jozef, isn't it? Jozef Wynocki?"

Games, thought Jozef.

"Yes, Komisarat," he replied, purposely using Martwicz's official title, his cap in his hands, his head bowed, his eyes downcast. Now he threw a quick glance at the man and was pleased to notice the look of self-satisfaction on the land-owner's face.

"What do you want? What are you doing here?"

As if you did not know. Where else can I go to sell the farm?

"Komisarat Martwicz, may I come inside for a minute?"

Martwicz hesitated for the briefest of moments, enjoying the cat-and-mouse aspect of this little charade. Then, expansively, he waved the boy inside.

Martwicz's house, Jozef noticed, was just as handsome inside. There was a whole room just for dining, with a table and four chairs, as well as a sitting room with a desk made of dark wood, a *double* electric lamp on top, and two large overstuffed chairs, covered with a nubby, russet-colored material. They looked very comfortable and Jozef was tired but, although Martwicz seated himself, he neglected to invite Jozef to do the same. The boy remained standing, as Martwicz, sitting behind the desk, leaned back in his chair, pressed his fingertips together and said, "Your mother. I heard. Too bad. I'm sorry."

"There were many who lost mothers yesterday."

"Yes, of course. The Russian scum. Some day they will pay."

He waited for Jozef to acknowledge his last remark and when he did not, Martwicz cleared his throat.

"I am a very busy man, Jozef Wynocki. What is it you wish to say to me?"

"If you please, Komisarat, I want to sell my mother's—I mean, my farm."

Martwicz laughed. "*Matka Boska!* Mother of God! *Your* farm? What makes you think it is your farm?"

"Of course it is mine, sir. Now that my mother is—gone, there is no one left of my family. The farm is mine."

"Would you be surprised, boy, to learn I hold a mortgage on your farm? That at this very minute it is right here in this drawer?"

"You said you were a busy man, Martwicz. How, then, have you the time to make foolish talk today? You are playing with me. You have no papers, no mortgage. My father owned the farm, and then my mother, and now me. I want to sell it. Do you want to buy it or don't you?"

Martwicz slammed the drawer shut. "Don't you get sharp with me, boy."

Wearily, Jozef said, "I have not the strength to be sharp. I did not sleep last night. I buried my mother today."

Martwicz leaned back in his chair and eyed Jozef speculatively. "How much do you want for the farm?"

"Whatever you think it is worth, Komisarat Martwicz. I know you will be fair with me."

"You are clever with words, boy. But if you think

53

compliments will influence the price I will pay, you are badly mistaken. I know exactly what that measly patch is worth. I will mention a figure. You will not like it, but you will either take it or you can keep the place and work it alone." He chuckled. "You are a little young to marry, so you cannot count on the help of a wife for a few years. What are you, sixteen?"

"Fifteen, sir."

Jozef stood, cap in hand, waiting, as Martwicz pondered. After what seemed an interminable pause, Martwicz said, "Here is what I will give you for your farm." He named a figure which surprised Jozef for its fairness.

"Well, well? Come, come," said the Komisarat. "What do you say?"

Jozef swallowed and said, "Why ... why I say yes. And thank you, Komisarat."

Martwicz smiled. "You thought I would cheat you, didn't you, boy? You thought I would take advantage because of what happened here yesterday."

"No, no, I did not," Jozef protested weakly.

"If you were anyone else, I would probably try to buy your property as cheaply as I could. But you are Jania Wynocki's son. And I will tell you a secret. I wanted her. There was something about your mother. ..." The landowner permitted himself a moment's reverie.

"Everything," said Martwicz abruptly. "You must leave everything at the farm. The furniture. The livestock."

Jozef explained his dealings with the undertaker involving the livestock and the buggy. Martwicz nodded his understanding.

"Yes, yes, all right."

"One more thing."

"Yes?"

"My horse. I will need him."

But Martwicz would not agree to this last stipulation. Horses were scarce in the village, and renting or selling the Wynocki farm would be far less difficult if a workhorse were included. With the livestock gone, Jozef would have to leave the horse.

54

With great reluctance, Jozef agreed.

"Would you allow me to ride him back to the farm to pick up my own things? I will leave him in the barn."

Martwicz hesitated for a moment. Would the boy ride off on the horse and never give a thought to having bilked him? He thought not. This was the son of Jania Wynocki, and she had raised him to be a good boy.

"All right, Jozef. I will get you the money. Wait here. We will have to go to your house anyway to get the papers of ownership so you can sign them over to me. It must all be legal and proper."

Jozef reached into his jacket and brought forth an envelope, dog-eared and slightly crumpled.

"Komisarat, I brought them with me."

Within ten minutes they had concluded their business, and Jozef's coat pocket bulged slightly with the bulk of gold coins. He thanked Martwicz once again, and paused in the doorway as the landowner said, "I will visit your mother's grave, Jozef."

The boy looked at him, nodded, and left.

o

When Jozef reached the farm it was late in the afternoon. He led Koniek into the barn, slipped his halter, and guided him into his stall. Then he filled a bucket with oats from a large sack and placed it at the far end of the stall. His body ached as much from emotion as fatigue. It had been a grueling day and an eventful one. He had buried his mother and sold the farm. In a village where momentous events were as rare as eclipses, it seemed as if some unseen force had speeded up all the clocks and managed to condense enough shattering experiences into one day to last a lifetime.

Snowflakes were falling as he left the barn. It had grown chilly again, and as Jozef approached the house, it seemed, for the first time in his life, forbidding.

He could not bring himself to sleep in his room. Instead, he got a blanket and curled up on the kitchen table, sleeping restlessly and crying out twice in the night, a victim of terrible dreams.

In the morning, he carefully wrapped his mother's dark

blue glass string of beads in an old black shawl she had worn to church on Sundays. There was nothing else of real value to take away with him. He picked up a half loaf of three-day-old bread. As he took a bite of the stale dough, he remembered the last loaf of bread his mother had ever purchased. Was that only the day before yesterday? It was hard to believe. Chewing the crust thoughtfully, he felt a single tear on his cheek. It trickled across his jaw and fell onto his worn jacket, and in that instant, aware of emotion that could only be a burden to him, he shook his head violently from side to side and wiped away the tear streak with his coat sleeve. If he were to succeed in carrying out the plan he had formulated, he had to put a tight rein on his feelings.

He slung the bundled shawl over his shoulder and pushed open the door into the yard. He looked up into the overcast, squinting his eyes against the falling snow, and with his free hand gathered his coat collar around his throat.

He had a long walk ahead of him.

Chapter

10

Fyodor, Count Pavlovich yawned and stretched before the mirror. In the predawn light of his comfortable quarters, with only a gas lamp for illumination, he leaned close to the mirror and inspected his teeth. Even and white, they gleamed in the near-darkness like so many pearls framed by the well-shaped droop of his stylish mustache.

At thirty-one, he was in the very peak of physical condition. His chest was matted with ringlets of fine, dark hair, with perfectly developed pectorals giving way to a rock-hard abdomen and flat stomach. He flexed his right arm and his biceps obediently bulged into a satisfying mound. Considering the amount of vodka he put away nightly, the rich food for which he had an overwhelming predilection, and the women he debauched with monotonous regularity, he looked damned good to himself.

Fyodor Pavlovich was tall, taller than almost any man in his command. Indeed, the Czar's Fifth Imperial Dragoons looked up to him literally as well as inspirationally. He was the perfect commander for a regiment of young Russian hell-raisers, most of whom were hand picked for this border duty, many of whom were, like Pavlovich, of noble birth.

Every one of his subordinates considered it an honor to serve under him in Brest-Litovsk and labored under the collective delusion that this was select duty. Eyebrows would certainly have been raised and grumbling heard if the truth were known. For Fyodor, Count Pavlovich was, in fact, an outcast in disgrace.

A scant ten months past he had been invited to the Royal Winter Palace as an honored guest and the potential commander of an elite battalion which had since gained glory in the great struggle now raging against Kaiser Wilhelm's Germany. Arrogant by nature as well as birthright, Pavlovich had gotten riotously drunk and obnoxious during dinner on his second evening there. An indignant Alexandra whispered in the Czar's ear, and the next thing Pavlovich knew, he was being ordered to leave the dining table. He threw his napkin down and reeled out of the dining hall and up the great staircase.

Two hours later, with the household retired for the evening, he knocked on the door of Sonya Petrovna, one of the Czarina's ladies-in-waiting, pushed his way into her room, and forced himself upon her. In the morning he left her room, only to come face to face with an angry Czar Nicholas. The result: virtual exile at the head of a forgotten regiment in Brest-Litovsk. What chance for glory, buried here, the ass-end of nowhere?

Daylight was filtering in through the sides of the drawn window shades. A short bracer of vodka, followed by a close shave and a good breakfast, and he would be ready to lead the morning patrol.

o

Count Pavlovich walked briskly to the stables. His horse was saddled and bridled. The beautiful gelding, rust-red in color, sixteen hands high, with the perfectly arched neck and molded head of a pure Arabian, had been meticulously groomed, so that even in the dull light of the stable his coat fairly gleamed as though it had been polished rather than brushed.

Pavlovich's breath exploded in admiration. "*Iisus Khristos,*

Hassan! You are magnificent! Never have I seen you more beautiful."

He looked around and called, "Branyin! Corporal Branyin!"

Several stalls down, the stablemaster, runty and dedicated, leaped out of the enclosure into the center of the stable and came to attention. Pavlovich approached him.

"I want to talk to you about Hassan."

"Yes, Excellency?" inquired Branyin.

"I want to know which of the stableboys attended him this morning."

Branyin's eyes narrowed as he looked beyond the Count, squinting in the dimly lit enclosure. "The one with the feed bucket. There, just going into that stall."

"Call him."

Branyin cupped his hands over his mouth and called, "You! New boy! Come here quickly."

The boy put down the bucket and came toward Branyin and the Count. Pavlovich could see he was fourteen or fifteen, well formed for his age, and though the word "peasant" fit him, there was something about his bearing. Was it pride, or stubbornness, or . . . insolence?

The boy stood before him, head unbowed.

"Do you know who I am?"

"Yes, sir," the boy answered. "You are Count Pavlovich."

"And you are Polish," said the Count, in the boy's native tongue.

"Yes, Excellency, I am."

"What is your name?"

"Jozef Wynocki."

"Why did you take such pains with my horse this morning?"

"I don't know which one is yours, Excellency."

"Come, come, boy, the chestnut Arabian. There!" he pointed with his riding crop.

"Oh. Yes. That one. He is like a king among the other horses."

The Count strode past the boy, to Hassan's stall. He

inspected the Arabian once more, walking around the horse with a practiced, critical eye. He ran his gloved hand along the animal's withers and inspected the glove. Not a speck of dirt, not a grain of dust.

He stepped out of the stall and summoned the boy.

"You will henceforth address yourself to the care of Hassan. Exclusively. You will see to it he is properly fed and groomed at all times. Your devotion to him will become a way of life."

"Yes, sir," the boy answered smartly.

"God help you if Hassan does not look as beautiful *every day* as he does today." The Count amended this. "On second thought, even God will not be able to help you in that event."

Pavlovich led Hassan out of his stall, mounted him, and rode out of the stable onto the parade ground. Horse and rider made a splendid picture of military aristocracy.

Corporal Branyin was secretly pleased. Most of the stableboys hated their lot in life: the constant polishing of leather, the shifting of saddles on and off the horses, the endless manure piles to be shoveled up and disposed of, the bitter smell of equine urine that stung their nostrils and infested their garments.

Jozef Wynocki had *asked* for stable work. He obviously loved horses, and watching him that morning, currying, brushing, pampering Hassan, Branyin, a horse lover and confirmed cavalryman himself, had nodded his approval.

Now, as Jozef watched the Count smartly trot Hassan toward the assembled horsemen of the third platoon, Branyin nudged him and said gruffly, "All right, boy. Just because you got a few words of praise from His Excellency does not mean there is no more work to be done today."

o

As the third platoon moved slowly through the city streets on morning patrol, a sudden icy gust of wind knifed through the protective layer of fur enveloping the person of Fyodor Pavlovich. He was seen to shiver violently by Sergeant-Major Markov, riding directly behind him. Markov turned in his saddle and murmured to Sergeant Zamansky, "Did you see that? Someone just walked over his grave!"

o

Martin, wide awake, pleaded with his father.

"Then what happened, Papa?"

"No more tonight, Martin. Is long story."

"When will you tell me the rest of it?"

"Some other time."

"Tomorrow night?"

"We'll see. You sleep now."

Chapter

11

The New Vista movie theater was barely distinguishable from the "old" Vista theater. Nestled between a bakery and a laundry on Iron Street in that section of South Chicago known as "Steeltown," the New Vista survived as the main source of entertainment for the steelworkers and their families.

Hung just under the marquee, on all three sides, was a white silk banner, fringed in gold, upon which was imprinted the likeness of a dark blue penguin and the legend: "Cooled by Refrigeration." This was a lie. A large, standing fan to the right of the screen hummed in noisy monotony, ineffectually moving the stale air trapped in the theater. The surface of the yellowed screen was smudged and uneven, having been painted over several times and then, finally, left to deteriorate once the Depression set in.

To Mary Frances Wynocki, the New Vista represented Mecca, Paradise, Nirvana, Utopia. She attended the theater with dogged regularity.

As she walked up 13th toward Iron Street, this hot July day, she remembered with pleasure the movie she had seen yesterday, "No Man of Her Own," with Clark Gable and Carole Lombard. They had kissed, she thought, as though they really meant it; she wondered whether something was going on between them in real life. Mary Frances had read in *Screen Romances* that Gable was married to Rhea Langham and Lombard was currently being squired by William Powell, but ... those kisses! It thrilled her to speculate on the delicious possibilities of a secret Gable-Lombard romance.

Today, the new double feature, with an eye toward the weekend family trade, was "Young Eagles" with Buddy Rogers and "Movie Crazy" with Harold Lloyd. Tomorrow she would make Joe take her and Martin to the Century of Progress. She had not yet been to the World's Fair, and it seemed crazy to her that such a great exposition should be less than thirty-five minutes away by bus or streetcar and still not be experienced by the Wynocki family.

She glanced at the little Hamilton watch her father had given her many years ago. Twenty past twelve. She quickened her pace. She did not want to miss the main titles. Movies had become a habit; no, an *obsession*.

She had no friends among the female population of Steeltown; the wives of her husband's fellow workers tended to avoid her. "She thinks she's too goddamn good for us," sniffed one of them upon the occasion of an imagined (or perhaps real) snub by Mrs. Wynocki.

The truth was, Mary Frances had little in common with the average drudge keeping some steelworker's house and spewing brats, one after another, out of tired loins. She had nothing to say to these monosyllabic slatterns, whose idea of a good time was an evening of bowling and beer topped by a slobbering roll in the hay, animal upon animal. She had hoped vainly for one—just one—girl friend with whom she could share her enjoyment of the movies, but no such female existed within the range of her acquaintances.

Withdrawing into herself, she acquired friends from her fantasy world: she laughed uproariously with Jack Oakie and Marie Dressler, suffered empathetically with Garbo, Joan Crawford, and Helen Hayes, related as a sister-to-the-big-brother-she-had-never-had to James Cagney, Pat O'Brien, Bing Crosby, and Warren William, became "pals" with Joan Blondell, Ann Dvorak, Clara Bow, and Jean Harlow, and had

63

restless, disturbing dreams about Gary Cooper, Herbert Marshall, Bruce Cabot, Clark Gable, and innumerable other leading men, all of whom she labeled "swell" or "grand." Once, in her living room, with Martin listening to the table radio in the corner and Joe struggling to read the paper, she had slipped into a kind of daydream and unconsciously began audibly improvising a love scene between herself and Buddy Rogers. Only when Joe looked up from the paper and said "You say something?" did she realize what she had been doing. Not that she really cared what her husband thought.

As she turned off 13th onto Iron an older man nearly bumped into her, and his eyes lit up as he grinned into her face. She elicited that kind of reaction from almost every male.

Mary Frances Wynocki would have more than held her own in any beauty contest; in Steeltown she stood out against the sea of homely females peculiar to the area. She was taller than average, with wide-set pale green eyes, slightly tipped nose, well-defined cheekbones, generously full lips, and long dark hair falling gently over her shoulders; her Irish ancestry fairly cried aloud to be noticed and admired. Her legs were superbly formed, her waist slim, and her breasts, high and full, were a source of wonder to the male contingent in Steeltown. Even Old Man Belanger blushed every time he saw Mary Frances, partly because he feared what might happen should her bodice come undone, partly because he found himself hoping it would.

When the Wynockis moved to South Chicago ten years earlier, she had visited the New Vista during her third week in the neighborhood. Joe was at work. She was newly pregnant and bored. Otto Bomasch, a transplanted German in his mid-fifties, looked up when she entered his theater. His jaw dropped and the accumulated ash from his cheap cigar made gray snowflakes on his vest.

She did not return for over two weeks, and he had begun to think she was not from the neighborhood. When she had again approached the theater, one Friday afternoon in late April, 1923, he had leaped forward from his ticket-taking position.

"Please, young lady. Right this way," Bomasch gestured with his arm toward the entrance. "It is good to see you here again."

"You remember me?"

"Yes, sure, of course. Who could forget such a *gnädige Fräulein?*"

She smiled.

"My name is Bomasch. Otto Bomasch. I own this theater."

"How do you do. I am Mrs. Wynocki."

"You live around here?" he asked.

"Yes. We just moved here from the North Side. My husband has a job at the Belanger Mill."

"I see. You like the movies?"

Her smile dazzled him. "Oh, I love them. Before I was married, I used to go twice a week." Wistfully, she added, "I used to see all the new movies back then."

"Well, you will come to the New Vista often, *nein?*"

"Oh. I'm afraid not." She made a tiny shrug. "You know what a steelworker makes. Just enough to keep a roof over his family's heads and a little food in their mouths."

"You have children?"

"No," she said ingenuously. "Not yet."

There was a pause that made her uncomfortable.

"Well, I guess I'll go inside now."

He seemed to be weighing some decision. It took him all of four seconds to make up his mind.

"Er—Mrs. Wynsocki—"

"Wynocki."

"You come as often as you like to the New Vista. As my guest."

"Free, you mean?"

"I let you in myself, whenever you want."

"I don't understand. Why should you want to—?"

"Ah, please, Mrs. Wynocki, I am a good American now, but German blood runs in my veins. We Germans have a great love of beauty, and, if you will forgive me, you are the most beautiful girl to ever come to the New Vista. I hope I will not offend you if I say it is a pleasure just to look at you."

My God, what a silly old man, she thought. She suddenly

became afraid she was going to laugh in his face. She bit her lower lip, hoping he would not notice her amusement. *I know! I'll play a scene with him. What fun!*

She gave him her dazzler again and said with disarming sweetness, "Mr. Bomasch, I had forgotten how kind some people can be. I accept your offer with gratitude. To be able to sit in your theater and watch movies to my heart's delight would surely be a gift from heaven." She laughed merrily, a Talmadgesque silver peal that caught Bomasch somewhere between the groin and the abdomen.

"*Ach*, I am glad. So glad!" he said.

Mary Frances leaned toward the old man and kissed his cheek with exaggerated tenderness. She smiled at him, and, without another word, moved past him, deliberately brushing her right breast against his shoulder, leaving him standing there, transfixed.

From that day forward Mary Frances had taken full advantage of Otto Bomasch's offer. One day, a few months after she had begun her regular visits to the theater, Bomasch, emboldened by what he felt was now an established relationship, surprised her when she stopped at the entrance to say her usual "hello" and "thank you," by furtively looking around to see if anyone was watching and then placing his right hand on the well-molded swell of her left buttock. She tensed her thigh muscle momentarily, not so much in indignation as having been caught off guard. The way the old man looked at her every day, she had expected a move of this kind. She grinned and slowly allowed the muscle to relax, letting him feel the change from hard to pliantly firm.

If the old duck enjoyed feeling her, what harm was there in it? She was fairly certain his ambitions were limited to getting a cheap thrill.

The pattern was established. She would pause at the entrance, he would explore the curve of her hip, the depth of her breasts, and, on one occasion, the cleft between her legs.

"Not there, Mr. Bomasch," she admonished gently. "Never there. I'm pregnant."

She was in her fifth month and her belly had begun to

66

swell. Bomasch froze, surprised, and rarely touched her again after that day. He would merely smile and wave her into the theater. Occasionally, he would pass his hand over a part of her anatomy almost dutifully, as though he were afraid she might feel slighted if he did not. All in all, the arrangement suited her admirably.

She had decided to get to Hollywood somehow and break into pictures. She was convinced that if given half a chance she could act rings around most of the ladies she had studied and envied on the New Vista screen. Well, maybe "given" was not the word. She had been "given" damn little in this world. You've got to take what you want, she thought to herself. Just like Joan Crawford did in "Rain."

Now, fully ten years later, as she walked under the marquee on this mercilessly hot July afternoon in 1933, she knew the time had come to make her move.

She smiled at old Bomasch, who nodded absently as she walked inside. She took a nickel from her purse, dropped it into the vending machine, and treated herself to a box of Hershey Kisses. As she walked down the narrow aisle, the lights went out and "Young Eagles" began. She barely watched the screen. In a world full of interested men ready to do favors for her, there was no reason to stay with Joe. She would leave him as quickly as possible.

Chapter

12

"Papa. You promised."

"No. I said 'sometime.' Maybe."

"Oh, please, Papa. What happened after you started taking care of that man's horse? What was his name?"

"Pavlovich."

"Yeah. What happened? What did you do?"

Joe sighed. He did not want to speak of the past. Or even think of it. His hatred of the Russian Cossacks had never abated. The senselessness of their behavior was still terrifying. Yet, he had begun to tell the boy what had taken place. Why had Mary Frances pushed him into it? He looked at his son, lying in bed, eagerly awaiting the rest of the story.

"All right," he said finally. "Where I stop last time?"

"You were ordered to take care of the horse. What was his name?"

"Hassan."

"Yes. And you had some kind of a plan."

"Yes. My plan."

Martin waited patiently.

"Well," began Joe. "I wait for first big snow. Three weeks is no snow. Sky is clear. Then one morning I get up. Look at sky. Many clouds. Little snow is beginning. I can tell. Will be heavy snowstorm by nighttime. Lots of snow important to my plan."

"Why, Papa?"

"Shh. Listen. That morning, for first time in three weeks I do not take care of Count's horse. Horse looks terrible. I send another boy with Hassan to Pavlovich's house. Soon I am ordered to come myself. Is what I want. To be inside his house. To see what is in it. Everything."

Martin propped himself up on his elbow, fascinated.

"Martin, you lie down, try to fall asleep. Your mother comes home from movie soon. She is angry with me if you are awake."

"But, I'm not tired, Papa," Martin protested. "Don't stop now."

Joe cleared his throat.

"All right, all right. I go into the Count's house. He is mad. Very mad. He asks me why horse looks terrible. I tell him I am sick. He takes riding whip and beats me. Hard. I don't care. I look around room, see everything. His bed, where he sleeps, his sword which he kills my mother with, his pistol hanging from peg on wall. I look at furniture in room. Then I see where he keeps his clothes. Is big . . . is big . . ."

Joe spread his arms wide apart, intent on showing Martin the shape and size of . . . what?

"A closet?" Martin offered.

Joe shook his head. "No. Not closet. Is piece furniture. Stands on floor, against wall."

"Oh. Like a cabinet, maybe?"

"Yes, is right. Like big cabinet." Once again Joe spread his arms. "With two doors. Both are open. One side is uniforms. Other side is boots. Is good, that cabinet. Perfect. I am on my knees, looking at it as Pavlovich whips me. Like dog he whips me. But I not care."

"Why, Papa? What were you going to do?"

Joe peered at Martin in the semidark. "What you think, son? I am going kill him. That night."

Martin's eyes went wide.

o

Jozef awoke somewhat later than he had planned and went to the stable door facing the parade ground. Gently, he pressed down on the handle. As the door opened, a gust of wind caught it and only the boy's desperate grab kept it from banging loudly and waking the whole place. Jozef eased the door open and looked out into the night. The parade ground was totally deserted and, except for the perimeter lights, the garrison was in darkness. Way down at the main gate, he could barely make out the guard hut, the soldier on duty walking his cold, lonely post, rifle slung over his right shoulder. Jozef calculated the time to be around three A.M., and he noted with satisfaction that while the snowfall had decreased somewhat in volume, enough continued falling to serve his purpose.

He pulled the door shut as noiselessly as possible and looked around. No one stirred. Going directly to Hassan's stall, he wakened the animal, saddled and bridled him, and gave him a healthy ration of oats. Then Jozef returned to his pallet, gingerly stepping over the sleeping forms of the other boys. He dug his mother's blue glass beads out of the straw where he had hidden them and wrapped them in her shawl. Then he fashioned it into a kind of sling that he could wear like a knapsack and hooked it over the cantle of Hassan's saddle.

He walked the horse up the middle of the stable and took him out into the night, tying his reins to a small post, and closing the door quietly. No one had awakened. The wind was gusting, the snow thick and blinding. His shoes sank a good six inches into the drifts, soaking his stockings. He walked straight back to the four-foot-wide drainage ditch located behind the stable and made a running jump over it, landing on his feet with no difficulty.

Beyond the ditch at the perimeter fence, he took from his coat pocket the wire clippers he had stolen from the armorer's hut the week before, and began cutting. When he finished, a five-foot section had been separated from the rest of the wire-bound fence. It was now relatively easy to force each wooden stave in the freed section backward until, minutes later, there was a gap in the fence, five feet wide.

Jozef returned the wire cutter to his pocket and walked along the rear fence, keeping his tracks as close to it as possible, until he stopped just behind Count Pavlovich's house. He turned in his tracks, facing the fence, and once again used the wire cutters. He cut enough wire to release six six-inch staves, then forced them backward until they toppled over. He stepped through the opening, and began to walk away from the garrison, down a snowy slope leading to a small gully, where he had perceived a running stream some days before. He was careful to plant his feet heavily in the thick snow, making deep shafts that came halfway up his calves, soaking them uncomfortably. The distance to the stream was nearly fifteen hundred feet from the fence, and he prayed it was running, not frozen. That was essential to his plan. He was relieved to find it cold and wet, and again he recalled his father saying it never snowed in freezing weather. Then came the most difficult part.

Turning his head as far around as he could, Jozef began to walk backwards, carefully placing his feet in the tracks he had just made. It was a laborious task, not completely successful, but the boy was gambling that no one was going to inspect those tracks too carefully in the confusion that was about to take place.

When he reached the fence, he moved backward, through the opening he had made, and then it became easier. The snow along the side of the Count's house was fresh and unmarked. Jozef began taking long backward steps in it, making a slight arc in front of Pavlovich's house, and stopping three feet in front of the Count's bedroom window. He reached down and removed his shoes. The Count's front door was behind him to his right and, shoes pinched tightly together in his left hand, he raised his right leg, extending it as far as he could to the side, to make contact with the low stoop in front of the door. By inches, the foot wriggled from a·mere toehold to a firmly planted sole upon the slippery cement. Calling upon all the body leverage he could muster, he swung himself sideways and gained the foothold. The toe of his left foot traced a groove in the snow ten inches long beside the stoop, but he doubted anyone would notice it.

With his shoes in his left hand, Jozef reached with his right for the door handle. He had noticed yesterday that the door

had a keyhole, but he had seen no key. The door gave way
easily with a slight squeak. Jozef closed his eyes and expelled
the breath he had been holding. God *was* with him tonight.
Carefully, he backed into the hallway, knelt down just inside
the door, and smoothed the snow on the stoop, completely
obliterating his footprints.

He closed the door with the utmost care. After a moment,
he was able to make out the shadowy forms of the table and
chair he had seen earlier. Stocking-footed, he moved quickly
past them to the Count's bedroom door. Don't squeak, he
prayed. It did, and his heart pounded as he moved into the
bedroom and closed the door behind him. He needn't have
worried. The Count lay in the large bed, snoring. The dregs
of a fire still burned in the hearth, casting a dim orange-red
glow over the lower half of the room.

Jozef went directly to the upright mahogany cabinet. The
boy took one look at the sleeping nobleman and, satisfied he
would not awaken easily, opened the twin doors of the
cabinet. Quietly Jozef moved the six uniforms to the far
corner of the cabinet, and did the same with three pairs of
the boots, lifting each one carefully and placing it down just
as carefully. In the empty left side of the cabinet he placed
his own shoes and, leaving the left-hand door wide open, he
reached over and eased shut the other door.

He blinked once in an effort to improve his vision in the
dark, since the weak firelight had all but expired. The gun
rack; where was it again? He went to the wall on which it had
been mounted, and ran his hand gently along the surface. His
fingers accidentally came in contact with the hanging saber,
and before he could grab it, it banged loudly against the wall.
Jozef felt a hot flash course through his body. Reflexively, he
clutched at the heavy metal sheath, stopping it from hitting
the wall again. He heard the rustling of bedclothes, and
forced himself to look back at the Count. Horrified, he
watched Pavlovich sit straight up in bed, grunt, scratch
himself under the left arm.

The boy stood rooted, not daring to breathe. The Count
yawned prodigiously, belched, and fell back on his pillow,

sound asleep again. It took fully two minutes for Jozef to regain control of himself. He opened his fingers slowly and released the saber sheath and, as he did, he suddenly realized he had been holding the instrument of his mother's death. He looked at his hand as though it were a leper's, quickly wiping it on his coat to erase the taint of the murder weapon.

The holstered revolver had hung from a leather belt on another rack-peg and Jozef counted on that peg being its permanent resting place when it was not slapping against Pavlovich's thigh. His groping hand came in contact with the smooth cowhide grain of the holster. He took the belt and gun to the foot of the Count's bed and laid them on the floor. Freeing the covering flap from its brass stud, he removed the pistol.

The large revolver was heavy and unwieldy in his youthful hand. He had once fired his father's shotgun at a band of marauding crows, and he recalled that by drawing back the hammers, the triggers of that double-barreled weapon were also drawn back. He raised his thumb and, with a bit more effort than he would have imagined it took, he pulled back the hammer of the big double-action revolver to full cock.

He took his finger out of the trigger guard and held the gun by the handle only, the barrel pointing at the floor, not wanting to risk an accidental discharge. He walked to the window alongside the Count's bed, turned the locking handle, and opened it wide. Snow, wind, and cold rushed by him into the room, filling every crevice and corner. Jozef leaned out over the sill and was glad to see the footsteps he had implanted were still stamped into the snow.

The cold penetrated the room quickly. The Count stirred and, awakening, found himself staring into the impressive muzzle of his own sidearm. He recognized the boy behind the gun in the limited light and, looking around the darkened room, he weighed the possibilities. The only defensive weapon now available to him was his saber. At this range, however, he would be shot dead before he could throw the covers off and get to it. He might try leaping directly at the youth and wresting the gun from him. He gave Jozef a

73

sidelong glance. The boy held the gun shakily, but Pavlovich could see from the position of the trigger that the barest pressure upon it would trip the hammer. No good! He would have to think of something else. And when he did (and make no mistake, he would!), he would hang this troublesome young Pole by his thumbs in the forest east of the garrison, and let the wolves pick his bones clean!

"Are you not acting somewhat drastically over a little whipping, Jozef?" he began in quiet, soothing tones.

Jozef remained silent.

"Come, boy, you are obviously harboring a grudge because of the punishment you received yesterday morning. Which," he added, pointing his finger at the boy, "you richly deserved and you know it!"

Jozef stood there, two feet from the bed, training the gun on the Count, who raised his voice slightly, and complained imperiously, "It is cold, you little fool. Must we have the window open while we discuss this midnight visit of yours?"

Jozef said softly, "I want you to know why you are going to die, Excellency. Nearly one month ago, you and your soldiers visited the town where I lived. Podlasz. It is almost eighteen miles from here, across the border. Do you remember?"

"And if I do, what then?"

"On your way into our village, you came upon a boy and a woman."

Jozef paused, waiting for Pavlovich to affirm this. Impatiently, the Count growled, "Yes, yes, continue, for Christ's sake! I am freezing."

"Do you remember? A boy and a woman."

"You know, I have but to shout for my servant, and, in a few moments, your life would be over. Finished. I am being ridiculously patient with you, Jozef."

"A woman and a boy!"

"That day is hazy in my memory. I was drinking vodka, a lot of it as I recall."

"I was the boy. The woman was my mother. You killed her. You laughed when you cut her head off, and you laughed afterward when you rode away."

The Count's eyes slid to the sides of their sockets, remembering. "Ah, yes."

He regarded Jozef keenly, trying to perceive his features in the semidark. "I understand. The special attention to Hassan. You *planned* it all. Very clever! Very enterprising!" He smiled. "It is a shame you are a Pole. You have a gift for planning that is peculiarly Russian."

He extended his hand toward the boy.

"Now, I think it is time we stopped this farce. You should have killed me while I slept. Not that you would have escaped. The moment you fired that gun, every man and boy in this garrison would have come running. They would have torn you limb from limb."

Proudly, he added: "I am Fyodor, Count Mikhail von Klauswitz Pavlovich, cousin to the Czarina, possessor of noble bloodlines that began centuries before you peasants raised yourselves out of the mud and put shoes on your feet! I am sorry for you, but I cannot sink to my knees and pray for the soul of every man, woman, or child who has fallen beneath my sword! It is the *way* of things! Understand? The *way* of things!"

He paused now, taking a deep breath. "Now, give me the gun. You are not going to shoot and you know it!"

He moved his body in the bed, his mouth smiling, his eyes dark and penetrating. Jozef had seen that look before, just once, that misleading appearance of benignity preceding the strike. As the Count raised his open hand toward Jozef, the boy added his left hand to the revolver handle to steady his aim, and extending both arms toward the nobleman, lips compressed, eyes nearly shut, he pulled the trigger.

The Nagant went off, sounding like a field piece in the bedroom. The 7.62-millimeter slug took the complete right side of the Count's face away, and he died taking half his calculatedly benign countenance to eternity with him, half of his mouth still curled up in a semismirk, the remaining eye bulging in shocked surprise, the lid locked open, the eyeball wide and white, as though it had belonged to a thyroid victim.

A wave of relief swept over Jozef Wynocki. His mother

and all the other Podlasz victims were avenged. At that moment he experienced a sudden and altogether impractical desire to be caught and punished, so great was his feeling of accomplishment, his sense of anticlimax. However, he had planned the escape as well as the assassination. Lights were already flicking on all over the garrison. He could hear movement in the rear of the Count's house.

He glanced once again at the dead nobleman, whose shattered head had slumped against the carved oaken headboard of his bed at a grotesque angle. Still holding the gun in his hands, the boy raced past the foot of the bed, directly into the upright mahogany dresser, pulling the door shut in front of him.

The cabinet door had barely closed when Kubalov, the Count's servant, burst into the room, turned on the overhead light, and screamed.

"Murder! Murder! Murder! Murder! Murder!"

Over and over the servant kept shrieking the word, and now the closeted boy could hear doors banging shut, shouts, and the crunch of running feet approaching the house. Through the keyhole he saw Lieutenant Ulanov and Captain Zaroff rush into the room. Moments later, the bedchamber was crowded with officers of the Czar's Fifth Imperial Dragoons.

Lieutenant Ulanov leaned out the open window, saw the footprints there, leading around to the rear of the house.

"Come on," he cried. "Here are the murderer's tracks. Hurry and we can catch him." He leaped out the open window into the snow, several officers following suit, the rest exiting the way they entered.

The room was suddenly silent. Jozef guessed that, by now, the searchers had passed through the gap in the fence and were following his tracks down to the stream.

He put his palm against the door, eased it open an inch, and froze. Corporal Branyin appeared in the doorway of the room unexpectedly. He walked straight to the bed, lifted the covering sheet from Count Pavlovich's head and, staring at the dead man for several seconds, gathered a glob of saliva within his mouth and spit it into what was left of the Count's face. He replaced the sheet, wheeled, and left the room. Jozef could hear the crunch of his boots through the wall, as he made his way to the rear of the house and the telltale fence-gap.

It was now or never. Quickly tying his shoes, which were soggy and uncomfortable, he crawled across the floor to the window. Cautiously, he raised his head until his eyes were level with the sill. The parade ground looked empty, albeit well-lit now. He had been right. Within the space of five minutes, the entire camp had been roused and were now engaging in a massive manhunt.

He left the house by the front door, closing it with gentle finality. Fighting to keep from bolting across the parade ground to the stables, he forced himself to walk at a reasonably normal pace, the Nagant now stuffed into his waistband. The guard at the main gate spotted him, giving him no more than a cursory glance.

Jozef moved as inconspicuously as possible to the side of the stable, then slipped around the corner, gave in to near-panic, and began running. He could hear distant shouts on the other side of the parade ground. *They're at the stream,* he thought as he ran the length of the long building. *They have split into two parties, one searching upstream, one down.*

He rounded the rear corner, fully expecting to encounter someone, but Hassan alone greeted his arrival, his rear feet stamping the cold, snow-covered ground in shivering anticipation.

I am going to escape, thought Jozef headily. *I have killed Pavlovich and I am going to escape.* The overwhelming need for flight overcame him. He rushed at the horse, causing the big Arabian to rear back slightly and nearly undo his tethered reins. Jozef slung his mother's shawl-knapsack over his shoulder, slipped the reins loose, mounted and, kicking the horse's flanks with his heels, urged him into a short leap over the drainage ditch and through the five-foot-wide fence-exit created earlier.

Before them lay the white Russian countryside and freedom.

Chapter

13

Early on the morning of Saturday, July 24, the Wynockis boarded a streetcar in Steeltown, then transferred to a big green-and-yellow double-decker bus and paid their first and last visit to the Chicago World's Fair. The heat of the July day was modified by a brisk, warmish breeze blowing off the lake. Mary Frances, her hair tied back with a ribbon, her dark tresses shifting gently in the wind, caused many male heads to turn and stare appreciatively. She enjoyed the attention, occasionally smiling back at one of her admirers.

They rode the breathtaking Sky Ride, walked through several free exhibits, ate lunch (hot dogs and soda pop) at a concessionaire's awninged booth, stopped in front of Sally Rand's theater to look at the pictures of the celebrated fan-dancer. Large blowups were mounted on either side of the entrance with Rand posed fetchingly in the buff behind two large white fans, her eyes wide, her mouth forming a naughty "Oh," as if to indicate the forbidden pleasures awaiting inside. *I'm prettier*, thought Mary Frances. *And my figure's better than hers.*

She tore her eyes away from the photographs and the Wynockis moved on. Soon they found themselves in front of an exhibit called "Buck Rogers in the 25th Century." The famous comic-strip hero was the idol of every boy in the country. Except Martin. Futuristic ray guns, flying belts, and mockup spaceships held little interest for him.

o

Ever since Joe had bought the boy a secondhand Stromberg-Carlson table model for his eighth birthday, Martin had become as obsessed with the radio as Mary Frances was with the movies. But he did not spend all his time listening to "Tom Mix and His Ralston Straight Shooters," or "Little Orphan Annie," or "Jack Armstrong, the All-American Boy" like the other kids in the neighborhood. He liked to twist the dial until he found a dance band. Or a singing star. Martin would bury his head in his arms and turn up the music. Soon he was able to distinguish the various bands and singers broadcasting from ballrooms, hotels, and radio studios all over the country.

Martin liked them all, for different reasons. He came to understand the disparity between George Olson's creamy, unexciting dance band and the dark, deep richness of the Duke Ellington tonality. He enjoyed the bland, clean sound of the Ted Weems organization, yet would never tap his foot in time the way he did when he tuned in the colored bands from New York's Harlem.

In time, he learned the words to some of the popular songs of the day. One night he tried singing along with Ivy Anderson and the Duke Ellington band. He found that it was not very difficult to stay in tune and to keep up with her as she sang "Stormy Weather."

Soon he got into the habit of singing in unison with nearly every singer, male and female, whose voice came barreling out of the radio. He did duets with Bing Crosby, Russ Colombo, Rudy Vallee, Kate Smith and Gertrude Neissen and Ruth Etting and Connee Boswell. The first and last of these vocalists had something special for Martin. They did not merely sing the words and music to any song "straight." They bent the melody to suit their individual styles, added words to the existing ones, and that gave their renditions

79

something extra. They were the donors of a certain kind of education that he could not get from books or classrooms.

o

As a fitting climax to the afternoon at the Fair, twenty-four seaplanes, led by General Italo Balbo, swarmed over the fairgrounds at a quarter to six that evening. Joe Wynocki looked up and shielded his eyes as the silver-hulled, triple-tailed Savoia-Marchetti monoplanes droned and flashed their way across Lake Michigan to end their history-making flight from Italy. *How wonderful! They are from Europe, too.* And then he thought rather sadly, *I am an American now. No! I am still a Pole and I will never forget Podlasz.*

The day ended and the Wynocki family went home.

"Is too late for stories," Joe protested that night. "Was big day at Fair. Go to sleep, Martin. Maybe tomorrow night."

Martin stifled a yawn. "I'm not tired, Papa. Honest."

"You know he'll just nag you to death if you don't go on," said Mary Frances.

Joe himself was tired. Nevertheless, he sat down in the chair by Martin's bed.

"You just shot the Count, Papa," Martin reminded him. "Everyone was looking for you, but you got away. On his horse. Hassan."

"Yes," said Joe. "I ride on horse for many nights. In daytime I hide, best I can. Soon I am in Rumania. In seaport. Many ships in harbor. I wait till night. Is very late, very dark. I sneak past guards onto ship."

"Papa. What about Hassan?"

"Is cold. Much snow. I not leave him to starve and die. I shoot him. Is better."

Martin looked stricken.

"On English ship. They find me. Next morning. In cargo hold. They are good men. They are on way to America for to get food and er ... war ..."

"Supplies?"

"That's right. Supplies. To bring back to England. They like me. Am good luck for them. All the way across ocean, no trouble. Is first time they not see submarines. By the time we get near America I am what you call ..." He snapped his fingers trying to summon up the word.

"Their mascot," Mary Frances called from the bedroom.

"Yes. That is word they use. Mascot. Now they make plan for me to get into America."

"But how, Papa? Don't you need a passport?"

"Yes. Is true. Supposed to have papers. But I have only money from farm and my mama's glass beads. Nothing else."

"Well, then?"

Joe lowered his voice conspiratorially, as though someone from the immigration service was lurking about. "Captain of ship. Ogilvie. He makes deal with man he knows on Ellis Island. I buy papers and passport from this man."

"Papa! You mean—"

"Shhh. Is only way I can get into America."

"But ... but even when you got the papers. What were you going to do here? Did you know anyone? Have any relatives?"

"No. No one. Captain Ogilvie gives me letter to friends. In Brooklyn, New York. He has already talk to them. Arrange for me to stay with them. Until I find job."

"Oh, you stayed with ..."

"No, little *synuz*," Joe said, using a near-forgotten Polish term of affection. "Never get to Brooklyn, New York." He looked up at the ceiling. "God is watch over me. Is lead me to where your mama live."

o

Jozef Wynocki stood on the deck of the Ellis Island ferry, heading toward Manhattan. A boy, slightly older than Jozef, approached him and looked closely at his name tag. The older boy's clothes stamped him as having come from Russia or Poland.

His face lit up. "You are named Jozef. I am Jozef also. Jozef Zivic." He addressed Jozef Wynocki in Polish and mentioned his birthplace, a small village not far from Podlasz. Jozef was delighted at hearing Polish spoken once again.

Zivic's cousin, twice removed on his mother's side, was a

mine foreman who lived in a big frame house with many bedrooms in a town called Commerceville, Pennsylvania. Zivic had been invited to move in with his cousin's family and get a job in the coal mines.

"What about you, Wynocki?" he asked.

He was dismayed to hear of Jozef Wynocki's lack of a job in the U.S. Was he determined to live with Captain Ogilvie's friends in Brooklyn? Did he not realize New York had millions of people, most of whom spoke perfect English and were, therefore, first in line for the few jobs that were to be had?

Jozef explained to Zivic that he knew no one in America. What could he do?

Zivic smiled at him. The moment the ferry docked, and the big bow chain was dropped, the older boy grabbed Jozef's hand and yelled enthusiastically, "Come on!"

They walked all the way from where the ferry had docked to Pennsylvania Station, and that walk was a milestone in the lives of both boys. Who would have believed such towers of concrete and glass and steel could really exist? It was a miracle. The boys gawked and "oh-ed" all the way to the train station. Within forty minutes, the two Jozefs were on a day coach heading for Commerceville, munching on a pair of delicious apples they had bought from a vendor who moved through the train selling sandwiches, candy and fruit.

And so Jozef Wynocki had begun his new life in Commerceville, Pa., during the cold, wintry months of 1915. Just as Zivic had promised, his cousin, Stepan Koszminski, welcomed the orphaned boy and got him a job in the mines. The two Jozefs became closer than most brothers. After Zivic's marriage to a blond, blue-eyed German girl named Heidi, Jozef Wynocki rented a room in a boardinghouse nearby.

o

"What happened then, Papa?" Martin asked yawning.

"Nothing. Is end of story. I live in Commerceville. Work. Meet your mama. We come to Chicago."

"But didn't anyone ever find out about the Count?"

"Only your mama. And now you, son." He smiled. "You not turn me over to police now, will you?"

"Papa!" Martin laughed.

From the bedroom, Mary Frances called, "Go to sleep now, Martin. It's very late."

"All right, Mother," the boy replied. While he called Joe "Papa," he never addressed Mary Frances in any way other than the more formal "Mother."

"G'night, Papa," the boy murmured.

"Good night, *synuz*."

From the bedroom, Mary Frances called softly, in a seductively low voice Joe had not heard for a long time.

"I'm waiting for you, Joe."

That night Mary Frances gave herself to Joe with complete abandon. Taken by surprise, he experienced the most rewarding night of lovemaking he had ever known. Once he fell into a deep sleep, his face pressed into the pillow, Mary Frances removed herself from the bed and dressed as quickly as possible. She woke Martin, placing a hand across his mouth to keep him from asking foolish questions, dressed him, and silently slid from under the bed the suitcase she had packed the previous afternoon. In the kitchen she slipped off her wedding ring and placed it on the table. She took the boy's hand, opened the screen door, eased it shut, and walked into the black July night and out of Joe Wynocki's life forever.

Chapter

14

Mary Frances headed for Thelma Malloy's boardinghouse
like a homing pigeon. Holding Martin's hand tightly, she
mounted the front steps, lowered the suitcase onto the
porch, and rang the bell. In a few moments a light could be
seen through the frosted glass of the front door.

"Who the hell . . .?"

Thelma snapped the porch light on from inside the hall.

"It's Mary Frances Wynocki."

The door opened wide. Thelma, in a light cotton night-
dress, peered out into the darkness.

"What in God's name are you doin' here in the dead of
night?"

Mary Frances smiled. "Can we come in?"

o

After Martin was packed off to bed, Mary Frances and
Thelma went into the kitchen and sat over a pot of cocoa.
Mary Frances told her about the dreariness of Steeltown, the
ugly little house, Joe's meager salary at the mill, her own fear
of growing old without having done any of the things she had
always dreamed of doing, the sudden decision on Friday
afternoon to break away, once and for all.

"And what about Joe?" asked Thelma.

"He'll be okay. He'll find somebody else and be happy. Oh, maybe not right away, but some day. Anyway, I couldn't take it one more day. In three and a half years I'll be thirty. Is it wrong for me to want to make something of my life before it's too late?"

Thelma sipped her cocoa. Then she smiled and placed her hand over the girl's.

"Ah, what the hell. Where is it written ya gotta stay married if it ain't workin' out? Lissen, when I was young, I had all kinds of dreams about, ya know, gettin' married, havin' kids. Later, I was content to make my livin' on my back. And don't let anyone kid you, baby, sometimes whorin' can be fun." She chuckled hoarsely. "Ever hear of Minnie Dolan?"

"No."

"Well, hon, old Minnie was near as scrumptious as you, in her day. She turned more tricks than you count on an adding machine, hundred bucks a crack. Retired when she was forty. Bought half the real estate on the North Side, out near Irving Park. Lives like a queen, with a chauffeur, a cook, and two personal maids in one of them new tall buildings on Lake Shore Drive." She shook her head wonderingly. "Minnie Goddamn Dolan!"

Mary Frances smiled and stifled a yawn. Thelma caught the look of fatigue on her face.

"Geez, I'm a gabby old bitch, ain't I?"

She snapped off the kitchen light, and the two women, arms linked, climbed the stairs to the bedrooms.

o

Late in the morning Thelma, Mary Frances, and Martin sat around the table in the dining room, enjoying breakfast. The Depression had taken its toll; the Malloy boardinghouse boasted fewer than a half dozen tenants, most of whom were out looking for nonexistent jobs.

"Mother," said Martin. "Are we going back home today?"

"No, Martin, we're not. Look, honey, we'll talk about it later. I'll explain everything and—"

85

"Say, Marty lad," Thelma intérrupted. "Why don't you go upstairs to my bedroom. It's the first door on your left. I've got a nifty little radio on my bureau. You go ahead and play it all you like."

"Thanks, but there's not much to listen to during the day. The stuff I like, the bands and the singers, come on mostly at night."

"Late at night, I might add," said Mary Frances. "He's a regular night owl, Thelm. Stays up all hours listening for dance music from California and New York."

Thelma regarded Martin with curiosity. "That's not very good for your health, is it? What about other kids? Baseball and football?"

Martin did not reply.

"Martin," Mary Frances commanded. "Answer your Auntie Thelma."

"Mother," he pleaded, "when are we going home?"

"Martin!"

His mother looked at him pointedly.

Martin left the dining room and slowly climbed the stairs.

When he was out of earshot, Thelma said, "Take it easy, Irish. You've gone and tore the floor out from under that kid's feet."

"He'll just have to get used to the idea," Mary Frances said. "I'm through with Steeltown. And Joe Wynocki."

"Jesus, hon, that big good-lookin' Polack worships you. I'll bet he's out lookin' for you and the kid right now."

"He's not going to find us if I can help it."

"How much money you got, kid?"

"Ninety-six dollars. It took me nearly ten years to save ninety-six goddamned dollars."

"Won't go far, toots. Even in a Depression."

"That's why I came straight here, Thelma. If Martin and I could just stay with you for a few weeks—"

"Use your head, Mary Frances. This is the first place your old man'll look."

"Oh, God. What am I going to do?"

"Got any plans at all?"

"Just one. To get out of this town and head for California. I want to get into pictures. Do you think I can?"

Thelma Malloy regarded her shrewdly. "I've got a feeling you can do just about anything you set your stubborn little mind to do."

Mary Frances beamed. "Oh, Thelma! I know I can make it out there. I just know it!"

"Wait a minute!" Thelma said. "You get into the movies and get your pan plastered all over the silver screen, and that old man of yours'll hop the first train West."

"I thought of that, Thelma. Quick as I get out there, I'll get a Mexican divorce. A lot of the movie stars do it. In a place called Tijuana, just across the border from San Diego. Even if he does show up, I'll be free and he won't be able to do anything about it!"

Thelma's advice to Mary Frances was to get a room somewhere in the area and look for work. "You're the breadwinner now for yourself and the boy. About the only jobs around these days are waiting tables, and even those are scarce."

"I know, but . . . a *waitress!*"

"Face facts, hon. It's a livin', temporarily at least, till you can put some more cash together and get outta town."

Mary Frances shuddered.

"Got any better ideas?" Thelma asked.

Grimly, Mary Frances shook her head. "I guess not. Where do you think I can find a job?"

"I saw a sign in the window of a Pixley and Ehlers at the corner of Division and Dearborn. You get a job there, who's gonna take care of Marty?"

"You're right. I'm not thinking very clearly."

" 'Course," Thelma said, inspecting her nails, "you could ask your old pal Thelma to keep an eye on him when you're workin'."

"Thelm! Would you really?"

"I gotta hunch Marty and me'll get along. We both like the radio. And music."

"Honestly, you're grand. I don't know how to thank you."

87

"Aw, forget it. I'm a lonely old dame these days. Might do me good bein' around a youngster like Marty."

○

Anxious to be gone from Thelma's boardinghouse that morning in case Joe turned up, Mary Frances found a room in a hotel-apartment building off Division Street. She quickly moved Martin and herself into the small bed-sitting room, which boasted a fraying couch, a dresser with its paint peeling, and a Murphy bed that slammed down like thunder once you opened the doors that hid it from view. The small pullman-type kitchenette was utilitarian, nothing more, but it would do. The room was only temporary anyway, she reassured herself. And it was certainly no worse than that cracker box in Steeltown.

Martin thought it was worse. That cracker box still held his father and his radio, and he missed them both.

Mary Frances applied for a job as a waitress at Pixley and Ehlers and was hired on the spot. She was issued a uniform, informed she would receive twenty dollars and tips for six days' work, eight hours a day, with Sundays off. At nine the next morning, Thelma went to stay with Martin, and Mary Frances plunged into the first day of the first job she ever had.

Her worst fears were soon realized: carrying dirty dishes to the kitchen, stacking trays, wiping up food-splattered tables, emptying ashtrays, it was a job more suited to a bus boy than a waitress. By the time her lunch break came around, she was nearly exhausted, the calves of her legs aching, her feet hurting, her back full of shooting pains.

"You're usin' muscles ya never used before, dearie," said Madge, one of the other waitresses on the day shift. "You'll get used to it."

"I'll never get used to it. I don't want to."

"Oh, I see. You got some rich uncle somewhere gonna leave you a million bucks, huh? Or maybe some sugar daddy to keep you?"

Mary Frances calculated how long it would take to save up five hundred dollars, her financial goal before heading for California. Her rent was thirty-five a month and she and

Martin had to eat. If she was lucky, she might be able to put away—oh, say, fifteen or twenty every month. Let's see. She counted off the months on her fingers. Oh my God, twenty-two months of dirty dishes and dirty napkins and dirty forks and knives and dirty hands and fingernails and mops and pails and ammonia and—Madge! She said, aloud, "Almost two years! Jesus!"

o

"Welcome home. How was the first day on the job?"

Mary Frances rolled her eyes heavenward in answer to Thelma's question. She collapsed into the only comfortable chair in the room, and looked at Marty. "Come here, honey, and give your tired old mom a big kiss."

Marty complied. As he moved away from the dresser, Mary Frances saw Thelma's radio sitting on top of it.

"Aw, nuts, why not?" Thelma explained. "I'm gonna be spendin' most of my days here anyways, so I brought it along. It's good company for Marty and me. Right, kid?"

Marty turned to Thelma and smiled. *Good*, thought Mary Frances. *They really do like each other.*

"Did, uh . . ." Mary Frances asked as casually as possible, "did anyone come by your place today, Thelm?"

Thelma nodded. "Bright and early. Relax. I didn't say nothin'."

"Thanks, Thelma. You're a real friend."

"I ain't so sure about that. You-know-who was awful unhappy." Thelma changed the subject. "Marty and me had a swell time. I took him over on State Street and bought him a hamburger. Then we came back here and played cards a little and listened to the radio."

"Yeah," Marty suddenly brightened. "There was a program with a band I never heard before. What was the name of that band again, Aunt Thelma?"

"Ben Pollack."

"Oh, yeah. Ben Pollack. Gee, it was really good. And it was on in the *daytime!* I was surprised!"

Thelma smiled. "Hey, Mary Frances. This son of yours knows all the hits, and sings 'em in tune! He's really got talent!"

89

Mary Frances beamed. "Maybe I'm the mother of the next Bing Crosby, huh?" she said.

"From what I heard this afternoon, that ain't impossible," said Thelma. "Haven't you ever listened to the kid?"

"I've heard him humming along with the radio from time to time."

Thelma snorted. "What you got to do, young lady, is get acquainted with this boy of yours."

"Oh, Thelm . . ."

"No, I mean it! I think Marty's got a future as a singer."

"Would you like that, Martin?" Mary Frances asked.

"Boy, I sure would."

Thelma stood up. "Come on, you two. I'll treat ya to dinner just this once. I'm not John D. Rockefeller, you know."

Chapter

15

On the third Saturday of Mary Frances' employment at Pixley and Ehlers, the cafeteria was unbearably hot and it seemed she was plagued with far more nose-pickers, and behind-pinchers than she had encountered previously. The smell of cheap food and stale body odor made her feel nauseated, and then she slipped on a wet patch near the kitchen door and dropped a tray of dishes. Naturally, she was informed, the cost of the broken crockery would be withheld from her pay.

On her coffee break at four o'clock, Mary Frances called Thelma.

"Hi, kid," the old girl answered. "Hot enough for ya?"

"Thelma, is Martin there?"

"Of course he's here, silly."

"I mean, is he right there, next to you, by the phone?"

"He's upstairs listenin' to the radio. As if I had to tell you."

"Listen, Thelm. I can't face another day in this damn place. I can't, that's all! Besides, August is nearly over. Martin's supposed to go back to school in September. What am I going to do about that, if I don't get him out of this town before the semester starts? And Joe. You know damn well he's looking for us, every chance he gets. Sooner or later, he's going to track us down if we stay in Chicago. I've got to put some real money together quick!"

"So?"

Mary Frances took a deep breath. "I've been thinking over what you told me about Minnie Dolan and all the money she made. Thelm, do you think I could do that? I mean just until I can make enough to get out to California."

Thelma was silent on the other end for several seconds. "How many men you been to bed with?"

"What's that got to do with the price of eggs?"

"Everythin', toots. You think it's just in and out and thanks for the buggy ride? Not a chance. Not when you're worth a C-note a night. You gotta know how to take care of a man. To give him what he likes. There's more to makin' love than takin' your clothes off and lyin' on your back! And what'd Marty say if he ever found out his mom was a whore?" She whispered this last into the mouthpiece.

"Don't use that ugly word!"

"Well, a whore is a whore. It don't matter whether you're callin' yourself high-falutin' names like 'call girl,' the minute you take money from a guy for lettin' him put it in you, you're a whore."

"All right," Mary Frances said edgily, looking around to be sure no one was listening. "Then I'll be a whore. Just for a while. Until I have enough money to get to Hollywood."

Thelma sighed. "Are you sure you wanna do this, hon?"

Mary Frances looked around. The only customers in the place were a vacant-eyed man, sitting near the front, staring at nothing after another day of fruitless job-hunting, a frumpy, middle-aged woman in white nurse's clothes, her face a powdered mask of indifference, cigarette dangling from the corner of her carmined mouth, and a wino, incongruously clad in a heavy overcoat, a half-eaten piece of apple pie going untouched in front of him as he supported his stubbled jaw with the heel of his hand and his elbow, his eyes half-lidded in a dreamy stupor.

"Yes," she answered. "I'm sure."

o

Marty was in bed, listening to the radio, nearly dozing, when someone rapped softly on the door to tell Mary

92

Frances she was wanted on the hall phone. She left the door partly open as she walked down one flight to take the call.

"Hello?"

"Well, I made an appointment for ya, but it ain't like it's written in granite. Ya don't have to go if you don't want to."

"No, no, Thelma. I want to."

"Okay. Here's the setup. I called my old pal, Minnie. Like I told ya, she's retired now, but she still knows a lot of people—men. It so happens there's a guy just blew into town from K.C. Meat packer, lots of dough. She gave me his room number at the Congress."

"How much can I get?"

"Fifty, baby, but he might want you to stay all night."

"How do I do that? What would Martin think if he woke up in the morning and I wasn't there?"

"Well, I can't do this every night. But this once, I'll stay with the kid. You'll have to find someone to stay with him if you're gonna start turnin' tricks regular."

"I told you I'm not. Just enough times to—"

"Yeah, yeah, I know. Okay. This gee wants you there around eleven. That gives you plenty of time to doll yourself up."

"Wait a minute, Thelm. What am I going to wear?"

"Oh, Jesus, you'll have me tyin' your shoes and combin' your hair next. Awright, jump in the tub and get ready for your big night out. I'll be along soon."

Thelma arrived an hour later with three dresses. Mary Frances liked the red one ("It's certainly appropriate," she remarked), but Thelma chose the dark green velvet gown. Its previous owner had been a somewhat more ample lady than Mary Frances, but Thelma set to work on it with needle and thread and in just over an hour expertly altered the garment until it fit her young friend.

"Now listen," said Thelma, careful not to wake the sleeping Martin as she helped Mary Frances into the gown. "I've warned this guy no rough stuff. I told him you never did this before."

"Thelma!" Mary Frances' voice rose angrily and she immediately modulated it. "Why did you do that?"

"Because, you dope, it'll keep him from expectin' you to

93

do things you ain't ever done or even heard about. And, because he'll be even more excited, knowin' he ain't gettin' a piece of shopworn goods. That's why."

Mary Frances looked lovely and desirable.

"You're worth dressin' up, kid. If they don't put you in the movies out in Hollywood, they're a bunch of jerks, take it from me."

Thelma glanced at the alarm clock on the dresser.

"Right! Off you go, and good luck, honey."

Chapter

16

Mary Frances' fears were dispelled the moment George Thomason opened the door of his suite. He was tall and fit in his paisley silk robe, with iron-gray hair, and a generous mouth that was no stranger to laughter.

She stood in the hallway while he drew in his breath at the sight of her. He caught himself and said, "Oh, I'm sorry. Please come in. Miss Maguire, isn't it?"

She liked his soft, midwestern twang and his gentle blue eyes. "Mary Frances," she said.

"That's a nice, old-fashioned name. Would you think I was pulling your leg if I told you Mary's my mother's name?"

"Why should I?"

"I don't know. Just thought you might think I was handing you a line or somethin.' "

"Under the circumstances," she said, "that's hardly neces-sary, is it?" She colored slightly after she said it. *Remember what Thelma told you: be tactful.*

He was not offended. "No, I guess not," he said.

Lord, he's nice, she thought. And handsome in the bargain. I'm almost going to be sorry to take the money. Almost.

He offered her a glass of Dom Perignon. Mary Frances, who had never before tasted champagne, was unimpressed, but she smiled gaily. He gave her a fifty-dollar bill, for which she thanked him.

"I just don't understand," he said. "You're one of the most beautiful girls I've ever seen. Why are you doing this?"

"Haven't you heard? Decent jobs are scarce. I've decided to use my looks to make some money. Believe me, it's better than scrubbing floors or waiting tables."

He laughed, "My God, you're a breath of fresh air."

He reached into his pocket and removed a twenty-dollar bill. Then, he laughed again, this time to himself. "A bonus! Jesus! I don't even know if you're any good in bed!"

"Neither do I!" Mary Frances admitted. "Shall we go find out?"

Her first evening as a call girl was a resounding success for both her client and herself. Thomason was careful not to make unusual demands upon her, and their session in bed was energetic, albeit conventional.

By the end of the month she had had liaisons with no less than seventeen men, three of whom she serviced in the course of a twenty-four-hour period. Most of them were businessmen, in Chicago for a day or two, lonely and bored, anxious for the company of a lovely young woman to take to dinner and a show. That she ended up in bed with them she accepted as a fact of her new life.

One night she thought she saw Joe just as she was about to enter the Silver Frolics with Hunt Shattuck, a wealthy Texas oil man. She quickly feigned illness, but recovered sufficiently in Shattuck's hotel room to provide him with a memorable fifty-five minutes.

The near miss (imagined or real) caused her great concern. She now had well over five hundred dollars saved, and with Labor Day just around the corner, after which school would commence again, she was anxious to put Chicago behind her and Martin and head for California.

"Thelma," she said on returning home one night. "I want to talk to—"

"Hey, hon!" Thelma interrupted. "Didja see this in tonight's paper? It's made to order for you and Marty."

"Thelma! Will you please listen?"

Thelma thrust the paper at her. "Geez! Glom this advertisement. Talk about perfect timing!"

Impatiently, Mary Frances snatched the paper from the old girl's hand and laid it on the table.

"Later," she said. "First, I want to tell you something."

"Lord, you're stubborn! Will ya just pick up that paper and see what's in it?"

She rose, took the paper from the table, and practically shoved it into Mary Frances' face. With the index finger of her right hand she indicated a large ad in the center of the amusement page.

Mary Frances sighed and read aloud:

SATURDAY ONLY!
A GREAT LABOR DAY WEEKEND ATTRACTION FOR THE WHOLE FAMILY!
UNCLE BILLY BALLEW'S SCHOOL DAZE REVUE!
SEE THE MOST TALENTED KIDDIES IN THE LAND
SING! DANCE! JUGGLE! ACT! PLAY MUSICAL INSTRUMENTS!
ONE FULL HOUR OF GREAT ENTERTAINMENT WITH MASTER SHOWMAN
UNCLE BILLY BALLEW
AND THE MOST TALENTED KIDS IN ALL THE LAND
FOUR PERFORMANCES ONLY!
SEPTEMBER THIRD: CAPITOL THEATRE

Mary Frances laid the paper back down on the table.

"So?" she asked.

"So read the rest of it, dumbbell."

"I read it all."

"No ya didn't. Read what's at the bottom. In the smaller print."

Mary Frances picked the paper up again.

"Let's see. Oh, here. 'Uncle Billy Ballew is searching for talented young performers to appear in a new Hollywood series. If your child can sing, dance, act, or play a musical instrument, come to the Capitol Theatre, Friday morning,

September 1 at nine sharp for the Uncle Billy Ballew School Daze auditions.' Thelma, what's this got to do with me? Or Marty?"

"Just this: you want to get out to the West Coast, right? If you can get Marty set up with this Ballew guy, you can both go for free—expenses paid—and whatever you've put away so far is insurance against goin' hungry once you get there. Look, beauty, there ain't no guarantee you're gonna strike pay dirt the day you arrive at the train station."

"Do you really think Martin's good enough?"

"Hell, Mary Frances, I've been listenin' to your boy warble steady now for over a month. And lemme tell ya, honey, the little squirt can really sing. He ought to be a cinch to cop a place in this dumb little kiddie revue."

"Oh, but how will we ever get near the place? I bet there'll be thousands of mothers bringing their kids to the Capitol Friday morning."

Thelma grinned. "Leave that to me."

Chapter

17

The moment Billy Ballew saw Mary Frances Wynocki, Martin's place in the Kiddie Revue was assured. Ballew had, in his younger days, been tall, with a ranginess that did him justice in well-cut clothes. His fair hair and sensitive white skin had alternately benefited and suffered from exposure to the sun, and since he had gone out for crew in his junior year at college, he often gave the appearance of a towheaded lobster, so white-blond was his sun-bleached hair, so flush-red his skin.

Now, just turned forty, his face was still red, not from the sun but as a result of the not inconsiderable amount of alcohol he ingested daily. His ranginess had blossomed into bulkiness, and his formerly athletic frame boasted several overweight pounds. He drank vodka exclusively, laboring under the general misconception that it was odorless and therefore undetectable by either his troupe of little moppets or their moms. Even so, he was obsessive about his breath and a common joke among the mothers had to do with vying for the Sen-Sen concession.

He showed no sign of losing his hair, which he had allowed to grow well down his neck, giving his whole head a leonine appearance. The color was still straw-wheat, streaked wth runnets of yellow, courtesy of a bottle of peroxide. On the whole, he gave the impression of hulking, good-natured vitality, if you overlooked the eye-glaze and the slight sardonic set to his jaw.

"Come right in," he beamed at Mary Frances. He picked up an envelope from a table and read, "Mrs. Wynocki and, uh, Martin. Is that right?"

"Yes, Mr. Ballew," replied Mary Frances. "We certainly want to thank you for seeing us ahead of all those others."

"Not at all," said Ballew. "Any friend of Sheldon Marcus is a friend of mine."

"Sheldon who?"

"Sheldon Marcus." Billy Ballew held up the envelope. "Marcus Attractions, Inc. He says in this note you're a friend of his and asks me to give your boy a private audition."

"Oh. Oh, yes, Sheldon." Mary Frances moved to mend this fence quickly. "Of course, I can't honestly say we're friends. He's really a friend of a friend of mine. Thelma Malloy."

"Don't know the lady. What does your boy do?" asked Ballew, never taking his eyes off Mary Frances.

"He sings."

"I see," said Uncle Billy, somewhat disappointed. "I had hoped he might do something a little different. Ventriloquism, perhaps. Or acrobatics."

Ballew didn't really give a damn whether Martin Wynocki could so much as carry a tune. This exquisite piece, his mother, was too fantastic to pass up. After some of the mothers to whom he had been giving stud service on the tour thus far, she would certainly be a hundred-percent improvement.

Ballew summoned the rehearsal pianist, who took the sheet music from Martin's hand, propped it on the music board of the venerable old Schnabel upright situated against the far wall of the dressing room, and asked Martin, "What key, kid?"

"Uh . . . I don't know."

The pianist, a wizened little man with a perpetual weary

air about him, grunted and ran his fingers over the keyboard.

"How zat feel?" he asked the boy. Martin thought about it.

"Uh—okay, I think."

The pianist played a four-bar introduction and Martin began to sing.

Am I blue?
Am I blue?
Ain't these tears
In these eyes
Tellin' you . . .

At first, Ballew ignored the boy, concentrating solely on the mother. After the initial eight bars, however, it was impossible not to turn his attention to the son.

Martin Wynocki, age ten, stood next to the piano, singing in a pure, clear voice. Dressed in short pants, white shirt, and tie, wearing his only jacket, his dark hair neatly combed to one side, his eyes shining, he sang the words with more understanding than any child had a right to.

Moe, the piano player, brightened considerably, and executed the accompaniment with nuance and shading.

At the end of the chorus, Moe led Martin back to the bridge and strengthened the rhythmic pattern in his left hand, making the song take on a more urgent, insistent beat. Martin followed Moe's lead perfectly and subtly changed the mood, punctuating certain words for effect, holding some of the notes far beyond where they ended on the sheet music, then catching up with the meter just before Moe modulated a half key up into the last eight bars.

Was I gay?
Till today,
Now she's gone
And we're thru
Am I blue?

Moe's right hand tremeloed as his left created a finger-stretching pattern of chromatic tenths, rising and then descending down the keyboard again. Martin sang the unexpected "tag" as though he had rehearsed it for weeks.

Now she's gone
She's gone
She's gone and we're thru
Am————I————Blue !

He held the last note as Moe improvised an intricate musical ending.

When the singing and the playing died away, there was a kind of stunned silence in the room.

Jesus, thought Mary Frances, Thelma was right! Martin really can sing!

Good, thought Uncle Billy Ballew. The little bastard's got talent. Now nobody'll be able to say I signed him up just to get into his mother's pants.

o

"Gee, I'm sure gonna miss you," Thelma sniffled, wiping her nose with a handkerchief. Mary Frances was busy throwing things into a suitcase, spread wide open on the Murphy bed.

"We'll miss you too, won't we, Martin?" she said.

Marty stood near the window, looking out into the street.

"Martin," his mother insisted. "We'll miss Aunt Thelma, won't we?"

The boy looked at the boardinghouse keeper and smiled sadly. "I will miss you," he said. Thelma went to him and ran her hand through his hair.

"Ah, honey. I hate to see you go, but you'll make me proud of you out in Hollywood." She kissed his cheek and he responded with a hug, burying his face in her bosom.

There was a knock at the door, and they heard the familiar voice of the hotel clerk. "Phone call for you, Miss Maguire."

"Who is it, did you ask?"

"He said to say it was Weldon."

Mary Frances grimaced. One of her "Johns."

"Thelm, get it for me, will you? Say I'm not in."

"Oh no, darlin'," her friend answered. "Do your own date-breakin'. It's your red wagon." Mary Frances sighed and left.

Marty looked up into Thelma's eyes. "Could I ask you for a favor?"

"Of course, Marty. Anything."

He reached inside his shirt and pulled out a sealed envelope. "Please, would you mail this to my father?"

Thelma took the letter from the boy and turned away, her eyes bright with tears. "Don't worry, Marty. I'll send it for you."

"One thing, though, Aunt Thelma."

"Don't tell your ma, right?"

"Please don't."

"Okay, kid. It'll be our secret."

The next morning, after Marty and Mary Frances had gone, Thelma dropped the letter into a corner mailbox. Two days later, Joe Wynocki tore open the envelope and read what his son had written to him.

Dear papa,

I miss you. Mother and I are going out to Hollywood California. I'm going to sing with a kid show. Could you come and be with us? Write to me as soon as you can.

I love you
Martin.

He sat down at the kitchen table, Martin's note clutched in his fist, and wept.

"Where I write?" he cried. "Where I write?"

o

Martin had a hard time falling asleep. The excitement of his first train ride, the prospect of singing with the Kiddie Revue, the dull ache in his heart as every click of the tracks beneath him carried him farther away from his father—all robbed him of his rest.

It seemed an eternity since he had seen his father; actually

103

it had been less than two months. When Uncle Billy added him to the show, Martin had gone to his mother and begged her to contact Joe Wynocki and tell him the good news. Wouldn't it be wonderful if all three of them could go out to Hollywood together? Mary Frances was firm on the subject. Did Martin see any other fathers along with the troupe? No! Mothers only.

He missed his father acutely—the bedtime stories, the good-night hugs, the rough yet gentle hands. Still Martin's happiness had been marred by prolonged fights between his mother and father, fights that had sent him running to the radio in self-defense. A twist of the knob and there was music coming from somewhere, protective and insulating, drowning out his father's weary protests and his mother's harangues.

Martin Wynocki had been a lonely child in Steeltown. He had little in common with the offspring of the steelworkers. His schoolwork had been below average, and at one point his teacher wrote, "Martin is a dreamer—capable of much better work." The boy plodded along, one ear constantly cocked for the three-o'clock bell that meant he could go home and listen to the radio. Maybe tonight he'd get Duke Ellington from the Cotton Club.

Now all that was behind him. He was on a train, heading for the West Coast and a job—singing! He could hardly believe it. He tried to relax and drift into slumber. The upper berth he occupied was cozy, and the pitch and roll of the sleeping car, the occasional clatter of the wheels as they crossed over intersecting tracks, should have lulled him to sleep. Yet here he was, awake and aware of the fact that it was very, very late at night, or rather, early in the dark of a new morning. The pale blue night light glowed dimly above his head, and he experienced an urgent need to urinate.

He threw off the covers and, parting the curtains of his berth, climbed down the ladder into the aisle. He wondered idly if his mother was asleep and, parting the curtains of her lower cubicle, he peered in. The berth was empty! Puzzled, he made his uncertain way up the darkened swaying gangway, past rows of uppers and lowers, all curtained in and silent, toward the dull yellow light at the end of the car where the men's room was located.

He relieved himself, noted the sign above the toilet: *Do not flush while train is standing in the station,* and flushed the bowl. He unlocked the door and began to make his way back to his berth, when the train rounded a curve and he had to grab a ladder to keep from falling into someone's lower berth. From inside it he heard a slight moan. Maybe one of the kids in the troupe was sick. Forgetting that all the children slept in uppers while the mothers were assigned lowers, he took both hands and tried to part the curtains. They were buttoned from the inside, but he was able to see through a crack between the buttons.

His mother lay in the berth naked, her head turned toward him. Her eyes were closed, the brows knitted as though she were in pain. Her lower lip was trapped behind her upper teeth, which were clamped down so tightly they might have drawn blood. Unaccountably, she wore the dark blue glass beads that had once belonged to Martin's paternal grand-mother: Joe Wynocki's wedding present to his lovely young bride.

The blue night light illuminated her face, shoulders, and breasts, her nipples hard, her whole chest and abdomen heaving jerkily up and down as the rate of her breathing increased. Bathed in pale blue also was the equally naked form of Uncle Billy Ballew, massively poised over her, arms extended straight downward as if he were in the upper position of a push-up. With almost brutal insistence he pumped away at Martin's mother, as she now began to shake her head slowly from side to side.

Horrified, yet unable to tear his eyes away, Martin watched open-mouthed. His ears were strangely hot, burning up, in fact, as his mother's head turned toward him, the violent movements of Ballew's body causing the blue glass beads to slip from between her breasts and fall to one side.

Now, Uncle Billy altered the positon of his body slightly and the move caused Mary Frances to open her eyes popping-wide as a vertical crease appeared between her brows. Her breathing became noisy as she gasped for air, and Martin could see she was bathed in perspiration. Suddenly she lifted her head slightly toward the curtain. Could she see Martin? *Oh, no*, he prayed. *Please, please, don't let her see me. I've got to get away from here. Now!*

He could not move a muscle.

At that moment, Billy Ballew came into the "down" position and as his belly came in contact with Mary Frances', she shuddered, issued a long "oooooooohhhh," and wrapped her legs around the trunk of his body. His movements quickened and with every downstroke she whispered, "Yes— yes—yes—yes—yes—." Then, she grabbed a corner of the blanket under her, and stuffed it into her mouth. A huge tremor coursed through her. She arched until she was almost in a dancer's backbend, an amazing feat considering the size and weight of Ballew. She held that contorted position for more than twenty seconds before she relaxed and went limp on the bedding.

Billy Ballew withdrew from her and Martin could see his large, moist penis, veined and uncircumcised. An ivory bubble of creamy-looking liquid clung to the tip. Ballew rolled off his mother's body and lay beside her in the cramped space, his forearm thrown over his eyes, breathing hard, as Mary Frances ran her right hand up and down her body, from her breasts to her pubic hair, murmuring over and over, "Jesus—Jesus!"

Martin's throat was completely dry. He willed himself to get away from there, yet his motor parts would simply not function. He saw his mother, her face once again turned toward him, raise her head and stare with narrowed eyes at the curtain.

And now, because he absolutely had to, his fingers released the curtain and he ran, barefooted, not back to his berth but beyond, to the other end of the Pullman car where the ladies' room was situated. He threw open the door. The lounge was empty. He ran to the toilet and vomited, started to leave, changed his mind, and threw up again.

This time, as he turned to go, he was shocked to see Mrs.

106

Metcalfe, mother of Margorie Metcalfe, the troupe's budding ballerina.

"And what is wrong with the men's toilet, may I ask?" queried Mrs. Metcalfe, a bathrobed, peroxided woman with a perpetual sneer as though she were constantly smelling something.

"It's—it's broken—and I was sick to my stomach—"

"Broken, eh? I'll just go and report it to the night porter."

"Oh no, ma'am. Don't do that! I mean—well, it's so late and everything."

Mrs. Metcalfe closed the door behind her and shook a stern finger at Martin.

"Now listen here, bub. You stay away from the little girls in this show, hear me? If you can't wait till you're full-grown, why then you can just pound your pud. But you lay a hand on any one of these darling little things and *particularly* my own sweet angel and you'll rue the day you were born, understand?"

"Yes, ma'am. Excuse me," he said, as he turned once again to the toilet bowl and had several spasms of dry heaves. His eyes tearing, he ran past Mrs. Metcalfe, slid the door open, and stumbled back to his upper berth. Martin climbed back in and lay there, shivering under the blankets. He found it difficult to swallow, thanks to a lump, real or imaginary, that had formed in his throat.

How could his mother do—*that?* He had turned away in revulsion at the sight of Maggie and Jiggs fornicating on a couch, as portrayed in one of the "dirty books" the boys used to bring to school. He could not fail to notice, though, the exaggerated breasts, the preposterously huge penises, the graphic attention to detail in regard to women's sex organs, surrounded by an absurd overabundance of pubic hair, the insertion time and again of penis after penis in a female character's vagina, rectum, mouth, and on occasion, an orifice that would defy a gnat's machine.

A crude way to learn the facts of life, but by his tenth birthday Martin Wynocki knew about sex. He arose "hard" certain mornings, and on several occasions he awakened after

107

disturbingly erotic dreams to find the bedding between his legs wet and sticky.

He thought about what he had just seen his mother doing and he felt strangely stirred. Why? What was he experiencing?

And then it came to him. In those dirty books, sex had always been portrayed seamily, an ugly act committed by grotesque comic-strip characters. His mother, on the other hand, never looked more beautiful than she had only a few minutes ago lodged under the impressive bulk of Billy Ballew. Did she love him, was that it? Martin thought not. But then—why would she be naked in bed with him—doing *that?* Had she done *that* with Martin's father? *Of course she had. That's how I was born.*

She was not supposed to do it with anyone except Martin's father, that the boy knew for certain. God! How could she?

And yet—he had *never* seen his mother so radiant, flushed with—happiness, he supposed. Even when she had seemed to be suffering—in pain—she had seemed to be enjoying it! Martin shook his head. He did not understand.

An hour later Mary Frances returned to her lower berth, climbing the ladder first to look in on Martin. He feigned sleep, but when she retired to her berth, his eyes snapped open and remained that way for the rest of the night.

o

"Martin, eat your breakfast. What's the matter with you?"

"Nothing, Mother. I'm just not hungry."

Mary Frances was wearing a colorful print dress. Around her neck were the dark blue glass beads, and Martin, looking at them, suddenly felt himself growing hard between the legs. Mary Frances fingered the beads, and he was horrified to find he was growing bigger and harder. Thank God he was sitting down!

"Martin, you've got to eat something. Breakfast is the most important meal of the day."

From the table across the aisle in the dining car, Mrs. Metcalfe smiled poisonously and offered, "He's probably just tired from prowling around last night after everybody else was fast asleep."

Mary Frances looked at her son sharply.

"I—I wasn't prowling, Mother. I had to go to the bathroom, is all."

"Yes," Mrs. Metcalfe said. "The girls' bathroom."

Martin's face turned red. In addition to his embarrassment, he was having trouble with his bulging pants.

"What were you doing in the girls' bathroom, Martin?" asked his mother.

"I—the men's bathroom was—it wasn't working—the toilet wouldn't flush—"

"He's lying, you know," said Mrs. Metcalfe primly. "I checked with the porter. There's nothing wrong with the toilet in the men's room. If you ask me, he was up to no good. I warned him if he bothers any of the girls in this—"

"First of all, I didn't ask you," Mary Frances cut her short. "And second, where do you get off accusing a ten-year-old boy of anything like that?"

"I wasn't accusing anyone of anything," said Mrs. Metcalfe. "I merely said—"

"I heard what you said, lady, and if I were you, I'd keep my mouth shut from here on in where my son is concerned. He's a good boy, and, incidentally—" she paused for effect and in a louder voice added, "—probably the most talented kid in this whole shebang."

Mary Frances addressed Martin. "Eat your breakfast."

Martin's downcast eyes were fixed on his plate. He poked at the food with his fork.

"If you're not eating, then leave the table."

"What? Now?"

"Do as I tell you."

Frantically he appealed to her. "Please. Not now. I—I can't!"

"You heard me. Go and play with the other kids."

"Mother, I—"

"Now!"

Mortified, Martin rose from the table.

"Look! Look at his pants!" crowed Mrs. Metcalfe triumphantly.

The bulge at fly-level was unmistakable. Tears of humiliation sprang to the boy's eyes as he fled the dining car.

"Well!" harrumphed Mrs. Metcalfe.

Before Mary Frances could comment, Billy Ballew burst into the dining car, the picture of robust energy.

"Morning, ladies. Good morning one and all!" he beamed. "And how is my happy family this morning?"

o

Martin was sullen and uncommunicative throughout the rest of the trip. Mary Frances tried on more than one occasion to snap him out of his mood, to no avail. Finally she decided the wisest course was to let him sort out whatever was troubling him. She had her own fish to fry. As the train lumbered its way through the eastern Rockies, she nestled in Ballew's beefy arms. They made exhausting love and, as he lay there, drained, she whispered, "Tell me again, William. You'll really introduce me to Ernst Rauschbauer?"

Ballew groaned. "Jesus, Mary Frances. Do we have to talk about it right *now?*" This young woman was inexhaustible, Ballew decided. She could make love like a wild animal for an hour and then talk your head off for the rest of the night.

"Yes, you'll meet him. I told you before—*several* times. He's a close personal friend."

Ballew had not actually met the famous movie producer. His agent had made a deal for the New Kiddie Revue to appear in a series of Rauschbauer's shorts. It would be a simple matter to introduce Mary Frances to him. And if not—so what? This delectable piece of ass was just another stage-struck mama. There were millions of them, all believing fervently in the sublime talents of their children. All certain they had given birth to the next Jackie Cooper or Mitzi Green. All willing to do anything—*anything*—to get their kids that one all-important break.

Mary Frances, he admitted, was slightly different. She did not give a tinker's damn about her kid or his talent. Oh, she went through the motions of playing mother, but Mary

Frances was wrapped up in Mary Frances, and her self-love overrode all other considerations.

She's certainly good-looking enough to be in the movies. He grunted inwardly. *Christ! Maybe I've been banging the next Jean Harlow and don't know it!*

Chapter

18

Hollywood!

Mary Frances could hardly contain her joy. She was—*here!* Even Union Station had a certain aura about it. Outside, as Billy Ballew was arranging transportation to the hotel, she breathed deeply of the Southern California night air. It was surprisingly cool with a balmy breeze blowing the palmettos at the entrance to the station, and Mary Frances was certain the air was laced with the scent of orange blossoms.

As she and Martin rode in the lead taxi with Billy Ballew, her eyes drank in every detail.

"Is this it? Are we actually in Hollywood, Willie?" she asked at least five times during the twenty-minute ride.

"How should I know?" he grunted. "I've never been here before either."

Shortly, they arrived at their destination, the Bimini Apartment-Hotel on Vermont Avenue near Third Street. Mary Frances was slightly disappointed. It was so unglamorous, so common-looking. Oh well, she thought, as she entered the tiny lobby, it's clean and white and it has a kind of charm, with its potted plants and dwarf palms in the foyer, and the white-iron grillwork on the door of the elevator.

The rest of the troupe came trudging in, the mothers carrying suitcases, the children dull-eyed with fatigue yet excited by the new surroundings. Billy Ballew signed everyone in, tipping the sole bellhop handsomely for helping one and all with the legion of luggage. Conveniently enough, Ballew's suite and the Wynocki room were on the same floor, and, as Uncle Billy opened the door for Martin and Mary Frances, he whispered something in her ear and she nodded.

The next morning, the whole troupe journeyed downtown to rehearse at the Million Dollar Theatre since the Uncle Billy Ballew School Daze Revue was scheduled to open in three days. Martin had been learning the song assigned to him, and when he rehearsed it with Moe, the dour-faced pianist broke into one of his rare grins.

The rehearsal lasted well into the late afternoon, and by the time the caravan of taxis headed back to the hotel, most of the children were tired, edgy, and hungry. When Mary Frances and Martin got to their room, it was nearly six-thirty. Mary Frances complained that he had not eaten all day.

"I couldn't eat a thing, Mother," he said. "I'm still too excited. How did I sound? Was I good? Do you like the song they gave me?"

"It's fine. Listen, Martin, why don't we hop a bus and ride up Hollywood Boulevard? We can see some of the sights, have dinner, and go to a movie."

"Well, gee, I don't know. I'm awful tired."

"Aw, come on." She mussed his hair playfully. "Don't you want to go see the footprints in the cement at Grauman's Chinese? Come on. Just Mama and her big boy, on the town."

Mary Frances would have preferred the company of Ballew, but Billy was having dinner at the home of Ernst Rauschbauer. "Strictly business, baby," he told her earlier in the day. "Got to work out the details on the two-reelers. Why don't you step out with your kid tonight?"

Bewildered by his mother's sudden interest in his company, still angry over her behavior during the train trip, Martin was torn in his feelings toward her. Did she really want him to go? *Bet if old Uncle Billy wasn't busy tonight she wouldn't care two pins whether I stayed home or not.*

"You go ahead, Mother," he said. "I'll just go to bed."

"Okay, okay," she said, suddenly gay. "Be an old stick-in-the-mud if you want to. I'm going to see Hollywood. If you feel like eating, get the bellboy to bring you a sandwich and a glass of milk."

She slipped into a fresh green and white polka-dot cotton dress with a wide white belt encircling her waist and completed the outfit with brown and white spectators and a neutral mannish trench coat.

As she prepared to walk out the door, she said, "Will you be all right?"

"Sure. I'll be fine."

"Gonna give your mother a little kiss?"

Martin blushed as she leaned close and kissed him on the mouth. Her lipstick tasted like strawberries and her breath was clean and warm. He could smell the faint dab of perfume she had fingered into the hollow of her neck, and it stirred him down to his groin. He turned his head away from her.

"That bad?" she laughed. "Some people like kissing me."

I'll just bet they do, thought Martin angrily, and at that moment he could have cried for his father.

When she was gone, Martin turned out the light and sat in the gathering darkness of the room, examining his disheveled emotions. He wished he had never come to California. No, that wasn't true. He wanted to sing. Wanted it so bad. And now he would. On a stage. In front of people, with lights and curtains and an orchestra. He was happy about that part of it, but his mother—! He was ashamed of her! *I'll bet everyone knows what's going on between her and Uncle Billy.*

And what about his father? Would he ever see him again?

o

For the first time in her life, Mary Frances felt that she was finally in her element. Hollywood Boulevard was everything she had imagined and more. The lights, the restaurants, the theaters were thrilling. She had dinner at Pig 'N' Whistle, near the Egyptian, then walked past the Hollywood Hotel at

Highland and Hollywood Boulevards toward Grauman's Chinese Theatre.

Never before had she so fervently wished she knew how to drive an automobile. She longed to cruise around Beverly Hills where the stars lived, to see the Carthay Circle Theatre where so many gala premières were held, to behold the Garden of Allah where the famous resided when they arrived from New York. She knew the names of all the celebrated night spots (had she not read tons of movie magazines?), and she wanted so much to stand in front of the Cocoanut Grove of the Ambassador Hotel on Wilshire Boulevard where the glamorous movie colonists spent their evenings dining and dancing.

God! She was really here! She vowed she would never leave. She would get into pictures any way she could.

She left the forecourt of the Chinese and walked over to the curb looking east down the boulevard. The cars, the lights, the theater marquees, the cool, clear night, the bright, starlit sky with a storybook crescent of a moon, all were a wonderful amalgam of aphrodisia. She savored her feelings to the fullest. To celebrate her first night in Hollywood she treated herself to the current movie at Grauman's: "Dinner At Eight," featuring an all-star MGM cast.

o

The Uncle Billy Ballew School Daze Kiddie Revue opened at the Million Dollar and did excellent business. Mothers brought their children from as far away as Santa Monica to see the famed radio personality and his talented troupe of youngsters, and they all applauded Miss Marjorie Metcalfe as she pirouetted her way across the big stage; they laughed at Warren Burgess as he did impressions of Wallace Beery, Laurel and Hardy, Mae West, and Eddie Cantor; they loved Patty Kalish, who tap-danced to "Wedding of the Painted Doll"; they whistled and stamped for Martin Wynocki's rousing singing of "You're Getting To Be a Habit With Me"; and they cheered the finale: a specially arranged version of "School Days, School Days," in which not only each young performer participated, but Uncle Billy himself did a com-

115

edy-eccentric dance dressed in a royal blue cap-and-gown and ridiculously large horn-rimmed spectacles.

Ten days after the troupe closed at the Million Dollar, they reported for work at Marathon, to begin shooting the first film in the series.

The two-reelers were an attempt by Marathon Studios to try to compete with the Our Gang-Mickey McGuire-Baby Burlesque comedies. The action would center around the Schoolhouse and the mischievous, talented kids under the tutelage of their harried teacher, Uncle Billy Ballew.

In addition to working in the "pretend" schoolroom erected on Stage Four of the Marathon lot, the children put in three hours a day "for real" in a genuine classroom adjacent to the commissary, where a stern disciplinarian named Mrs. Michaelson drummed their lessons into them with all the vigor of a captain of cavalry.

After a few days, Martin found movie-making boring. The incessant waiting around, the cloying smell of makeup as it became stale on your face late in the afternoon, the lack of air on the set, the "extra" kids who were brought in to "fill" the "schoolroom" seats, children who had been in Hollywood for a long time, acting stuck-up and snotty toward the Ballew gang. He couldn't wait for the days to end.

He begged his mother for a radio, and she bought him a used one with part of his first week's earnings from the Million Dollar engagement. She was going out almost every night with Billy Ballew. Martin stopped caring. His world centered around his new radio now, and since many of the dance band broadcasts came from Los Angeles and San Francisco in the early evening, he was able to hear several of his favorite orchestras and vocalists without having to stay up late. On weekends, his mother encouraged him to get out and play ball with the other kids or to go roller-skating with Marjorie Metcalfe.

Martin enjoyed the weekend ball games during the daytime hours, but the nights were his to do exactly as he pleased, and it pleased him to listen to the radio. He knew the theme song of virtually every dance orchestra in the country, as well as the names of the announcers and the singers. There, in the dark of the bedroom, in his pajamas, his hands clasped behind his head, his eyes closed as the strains of dance music filtered softly through the tiny radio speaker— there was Martin Wynocki's real classroom, the only homework he liked.

He was getting very, very good at it.

Chapter

19

Soon after the School Daze cast began making films at Marathon, Billy Ballew invited Mary Frances to a dinner given at the Rauschbauer estate in Bel Air. She spent all day preparing herself, bought a beautiful new evening gown, and when she stepped out of Ballew's rented limousine into the foyer of the Rauschbauer mansion, both men and women turned to stare.

During drinks in the library, she hoped to catch Mr. Rauschbauer's eye, but he stood at the bar, his back to her, caught up in conversation with three serious-looking men in tuxedos. There was, however, no dearth of male attention, and she smiled at all who approached her with a kind of quiet reserve, just as she had seen Garbo do countless times in the movies.

After an elaborate sit-down dinner for forty people in a dining room the size of a basketball court, the guests adjourned to the private projection room for the obligatory movie. No sooner had the lights dimmed than Ballew felt a tap on his shoulder. He turned to see André Bolling, Rauschbauer's right-hand man, hanging over his shoulder. "E.R. wants you," he whispered. Ballew excused himself and followed Bolling out of the projection room into

Rauschbauer's private study, adjacent to the billiard room in the right wing of the house. He entered alone and closed the door behind him.

The motion-picture magnate sat behind his huge, carved desk surrounded by the accouterments of his profession: Oscar statuettes, plaques of merit and congratulations, myriad photographs of the beautiful people he had known and helped up the ladder of fame, golf trophies, and assorted desk-set gimcracks. Leather-bound copies of scripts lined the shelves behind him. His likeness in oil glared down from an ornate gold-framed wall painting.

Ernst Rauschbauer was a singularly ugly man, entirely bald with thin, arching eyebrows, full lips, and pointed ears that were positively Mephistophelian. In his early fifties, he was built like a bear, with a large chest and powerful, short arms. He wore a wine-colored dinner jacket, dark gray pants, a white shirt, and a narrow black bow tie. A heavy gold watch gleamed on his left wrist. The solitary light in the room came from an exquisite Tiffany twin-tulip desk lamp, and when Rauschbauer looked up as Ballew came in, the effect was chilling; the producer looked positively evil.

Rauschbauer sighed and sank a little more deeply into his leather desk chair.

"Who is she?" he asked quietly.

"Come again?" ventured Billy Ballew.

"The woman you are with. Who is she?"

"Oh. Mary Frances. Well, it just so happens she's the mother of one of your newest contract players."

Rauschbauer's eyebrows arched a little higher. "And who might that be?" he inquired.

"Kid named Martin Wynocki. Sings. Not bad."

"And the mother? What does she do?"

Ballew smiled. "Would it surprise you to know she wants to be in the movies?"

"Nothing surprises me, Mr. Ballew," said Rauschbauer, his speech faintly tinged with a Prussian accent. "I am beyond surprise. Has she any talent?"

Ballew's smile turned to a smirk. "In one department."

"Please." Rauschbauer held up a hand. "Do not be crude. Can she act, do you know?"

"Mr. Rauschbauer, she's acting all the time, every minute of the day."

"Really, Mr. Ballew. You do not seem to be able to answer a simple question. Can she act? In front of the cameras?"

"I wouldn't be a bit surprised if she could."

Rauschbauer took a Havana from a humidor on his desk. He did not offer one to Ballew. He picked up a small scissors and cut the end off the large cigar, placed it between his generous lips, and lit it with a lighter fashioned like a small automatic pistol. He blew a cloud of blue smoke ceilingward and leaned back in his chair. He was not a tall man, and the desk seemed to dwarf him now.

He puffed at the cigar in silence, removing it from his mouth twice to regard it with pleasure. Ballew waited for him to speak. He was still standing. Rauschbauer realized this and motioned toward a comfortable-looking chair into which Ballew now lowered himself.

"I'm interested in this young woman. What is her name?"

"Mary Frances Maguire, she goes by."

"What do you mean?"

"Oh, there's a husband somewhere back in the Midwest, name of Wynocki. She wants to get rid of him or so she says."

"Do you think she is telling the truth?"

"Yes I do. All she wants is her chance on the silver screen."

"I see."

"Look, would you like me to go get her, bring her in here to meet you?"

"No, no, no, no. Not here. Not tonight." Rauschbauer cleared his throat. It didn't make much difference. His voice had a natural rasp to it.

"Ask her to come and see me at the studio tomorrow. Around five-thirty in the afternoon, yes?"

"Yes, indeed," Ballew grinned.

"Thank you very much. Please forgive me for making you miss part of the picture."

"Oh, that's all right, Mr. Rauschbauer. I noticed it wasn't a Marathon picture. How good can it be?"

120

Rauschbauer smiled. "I think you will do quite well in this little community of ours."

"Why, I'm counting on that, Mr. Rauschbauer," said Ballew, rising from the comfortable leather armchair.

"Oh, Ballew. One more thing."

"Yes?"

"This Maguire woman. Have you some sort of—special relationship with her?"

Ballew gave him his wisest smile. "Would it make any difference if I had?"

Rauschbauer puffed on his cigar.

"Not a bit," he said.

o

Mary Frances Maguire walked into Ernst Rauschbauer's outer office at precisely 5:29 the following afternoon. After a short wait, she was ushered into his commodious office, a room done in maroon leather furniture and maple paneling. Rauschbauer greeted her cordially, offering her a drink, which she declined. He poured himself three fingers of Scotch from an antique cut-glass decanter resting on a small white rolling bar cart.

Mary Frances wore a green chiffon dress she had purchased in Chicago when she had been selling her body, and it was more suited to the later hours of the evening. She had a touch too much eye shadow on, and the shade of lipstick she had chosen for this interview was a trifle too dark and too red. Even given these detractions, Rauschbauer could see she was quite stunning.

They made small talk for a while and he was amazed to discover how much she knew about movies. This young woman apparently lived, ate, and breathed motion pictures. The phone interrupted their conversation several times and finally he held his hands up in mock despair.

"Ah, this office. These phones. I must get away from them by this time of the day or they drive me insane. I wonder— would you like to have dinner with me at my flat in town?"

Mary Frances lowered her eyes. "But, Mr. Rauschbauer, you're a married man, aren't you?"

"Yes," he admitted, "I am. And you are a married woman. So?"

Mary Frances considered this. Then she rose and said, smiling sweetly, "I would be delighted to dine with you."

They suppered by candlelight in a spacious apartment the producer kept on Fountain Avenue near Crescent Heights Boulevard. Afterward they sat in a small alcove, sipping brandy from huge snifters as the sweet sad strains of Brahms Third Symphony floated in from the phonograph in the living room. Rauschbauer encouraged her to talk about herself and she held forth for the best part of half an hour. Her dream was to *contribute* to the motion-picture industry in whatever small way she could by acting in films. She was loving Hollywood, she was deeply flattered that Mr. Rauschbauer ("Call me Ernst")—all right—that Ernst had taken notice of her, my what a lovely apartment, all those paintings. They must have cost a fortune. Might she have a bit more brandy. Goodness, it burns going down.

Oddly enough, this mundane small talk did not bother Ernst Rauschbauer. This lovely creature was enchanting, in her outrageously naïve way. She was typical of the many who came West looking for the merry-go-round's brass ring. Most of her kind wound up as cocktail waitresses or doing extra work in films or getting married or going back where they came from, badly disillusioned. Something told him that this girl was different. Whether she had any acting talent remained to be seen, but he recognized a certain quality about her, a kind of toughness beneath her glossily beautiful exterior that stamped her as a survivor. She was willful, this one. And very desirable.

Rauschbauer rose from his chair opposite her and interrupted her babbling with a kiss. She responded and when the kiss ended he backed away from her, all the better to really see her. A small fire burned in the alcove fireplace and the flames danced across her face and hair, the shadows accentuating the fine cheekbones, the thrust of her lovely chin, the hollow of her throat.

"I am going to test you. Tomorrow or the next day at the latest. I make no promises. If you have one grain of acting talent, if you photograph as well as you look tonight, no, *half* as well, I will place you under contract to the studio."

She started to interrupt him with her thanks but he waved her off with a slight gesture.

"Wait. Please. I am not finished. I find you a most exciting young woman. I have no illusions about myself. Women have thrown themselves at me as if I were John Barrymore. I understand their motives."

He looked away from her, into the fireplace flames.

"I wish to make love to you. If you do not wish me to, it will make no difference at all in the matter of your screen test. Be assured. That is foregone. If you reject me, I will have my chauffeur drive you home immediately. I will not degrade myself by chasing you around this apartment."

He looked at her. "However, if you accept my proposal, please go into the bedroom at the end of the hall and remove your clothes. I shall join you shortly."

She rose, went to him, put her arms around his neck and kissed him passionately on the mouth, a long, lingering, open-mouthed kiss. The she drew back, searching his face with her eyes. She unwound her arms from his thick Prussian neck and, without another word, turned and headed straight for the bedroom.

o

Mary Frances' screen test for Marathon Studios was barely passable. Her acting was precisely that: acting. She did not have a gift for underplaying, and every line in the scene she had memorized and worked on with the studio's acting coach, Mrs. Holloway, came out bigger than life. Rausch-bauer screened the test in his private projection room and was disappointed. When he questioned Mrs. Holloway as to the advisability of giving Mary Frances acting lessons, the drama coach shrugged. Rauschbauer insisted there was a place for Mary Frances in the movies, and, over the mild objections of his production heads, he placed her under contract to the studio at $100 a week. Besides, he had plans for Mary Frances and $100 a week would lend their association a certain respectability.

Mary Frances' fringe benefits from her relationship with

Ernst Rauschbauer were manifold. He set her and Martin up in an attractive apartment on Crescent Heights in Hollywood. She was conspicuously exhibited at a large number of important premières, dinner parties, and social functions. She accumulated one of the choicest, most expensive wardrobes in town. And she learned the rudiments of acting, so that, ultimately, Rauschbauer was not ashamed of having put her under contract.

At thirty-one, Mary Frances' soft lines had hardened somewhat, and the pigeonholing element of the motion-picture industry type-cast her as The Other Woman. She accepted the image unquestioningly. She was, in fact, the other woman in Ernst's life. She became one of that small, select group of actresses adroit in playing the bitch, the home-wrecker, the *femme fatale*. Consequently, whenever Claire Dodd or Helen Vinson or Gail Patrick or Astrid Allwyn were unavailable, Mary Frances Maguire got the part.

When she and Rauschbauer finally severed their relationship, she acquired an agent, Manny Binder, and she did well. The crews liked her breezy manner, cameramen remarked that she was eminently photographable from almost any angle, and she took direction intelligently. Her life was in order, except for one small item, and she rectified that one weekend in late 1935, on a trip to Tijuana with Gareth Grae, a leading man in "B" pictures and acknowledged stud-about-town, when she obtained a quickie Mexican divorce from Joe Wynocki.

o

By mid-1936, Marathon Studios had ground out twenty-three "School Daze" two-reelers. The series ranked second only to the Our Gang comedies in nationwide popularity polls and was a consistent money-earner. Martin had grown into a not-so-miniature version of his father, strongly made and as handsome as any thirteen-year-old had a right to be. He was far and away the most valuable asset Billy Ballew had in his burgeoning cast of young characters, and had become the leading juvenile in each of the short films, opposite Marjorie Metcalfe. The studio sent them to motion-picture premières together, and the various fan magazines featured spreads on the "two youngest heartthrobs in Hollywood-land."

Martin realized it was part of what he was being paid for and suffered patiently. In the past couple of years he had learned reams of songs. He had worked for hours with the pianist, Moe Stein, who marveled at the youngster's natural instinct for a lyric.

One night in July of 1936 Moe called him and told him about a phenomenal new band playing the Palomar Ballroom on Vermont Avenue. Would Martin like to hear this orchestra in person that evening?

The boy and the pianist arrived just after nine-thirty. As they bought their tickets, the rhythmic strains of the Benny Goodman aggregation wafted through the open inner doors, audibly aromatic, thrillingly relaxed, and different from anything they had ever heard before. Martin and Moe made their way past the throngs of dancers and listeners and positioned themselves directly in front of the bandstand. The band was playing "Blue Skies," and Martin's heart beat faster. The ensemble sound was so loose, loose in a different way from his favorite band, Duke Ellington. The saxophones weren't nearly as jerky in their execution of the figures. They were voiced much closer together, almost like a modern barbershop quartet might be, and they ran the eighth notes unbroken, in silken unity.

Now a thickset young man stood up in the trumpet section and began to play a fiery, driving solo to the delight of the onlookers, who shouted his name and clapped fiercely, "Go Chris! Swing it! Yeah!"

Moe leaned over and said into Martin's ear, "Get a load of this guy, kid. Name's Chris Griffin. He's tremendous!"

When the trumpet player finished his solo Martin was among the most enthusiastic applauders. Now the band played a short interlude, leading into the final chorus, which began with the leader, a bespectacled, placid-looking man in a dark blue suit, making the initial statement on clarinet, a solo that began quite simply with only the rhythm section sustaining him. The saxophones contributed to the second eight bars, weaving in and out with variations on the original melodic structure of the tune. Goodman played the middle or bridge of the chorus against a driving rhythmic background, and finally the whole band emerged for the final eight bars, with the leader's clarinet sailing above everyone, like a kite, high and fluttering in the wind. As they added a short coda, the drummer, a gum-chewing, darkly handsome man, buried behind an assortment of gleaming brass cymbals and white pearl-and-chrome tom-toms, came into focus with a short exciting break. Noticing the "GK" on the bass drum, Martin turned to Moe and asked, "What's his name?"

"Gene Krupa. One hell of a drummer, huh, kid?"

The number finished and the crowd emitted a collective roar that Martin felt down to his toes. He spent the rest of that evening in a kind of happy daze, learning the names of all the musicians from Arthur Rollini to Allen Reuss to Murray MacEachern. For the next week he wheedled his mother's permission to allow Moe to take him to the Palomar every night and, at week's end, he was singing the ensemble figures to "Organ Grinder's Swing," "When Buddha Smiles" and "Goody Goody" along with the band.

Now Martin's musical education began to escalate. He started spending his allowance on phonograph records. Goodman had broken the dance band business wide open, and a whole slew of swing orchestras was emerging: Count Basie out of Kansas City, Jimmie Lunceford, Tommy and Jimmy Dorsey, Charlie Barnet, Wiley McKay, Chick Webb and, of course, the omnipresent Duke Ellington.

The more he heard of the "new" music, the fledgling bands, the great soloists, the more Martin hated what he was doing. He felt the School Daze two-reelers were a terrible waste of time. He was sick of the simpering kid actors, the conniving mothers, the grinding sameness of each interminable day. Most of all, he was sick of Marjorie Metcalfe. Mrs. Metcalfe's little ballerina was no longer little. In the past several months, she had started getting distinctly grown-up ideas. One day, on the set, between takes, she had placed her mouth close to Martin's ear and whispered, "Have you noticed, Marty? I'm growing bosoms."

Martin flushed to his ears and had trouble saying his lines

in the next scene. Marjorie was highly amused at his obvious discomfort, and the very next time the crew moved to a new "setup," she sidled up to him again and said, demurely,"Don't you think it's about time America's youngest sweethearts found out about lovemaking?"

He could only stare straight forward and walk rigidly away. What had gotten into her? He had never heard her talk like that!

Most of the other kids in the Ballew troupe had lost their virginity, of that Martin was reasonably sure. I'm too young, though, Martin thought, and just as quickly knew that was not the reason. If he were to be honest with himself, Marjorie was a darn good-looking girl and—yes, sexy!

Yet he had rejected her.

What is the matter with me? he wondered despairingly.

Chapter

20

By 1938, the School Daze two-reelers had run their gamut and faded into the huge tapestry of forgotten films. Not until two decades later were they dusted off and sold to TV to become a Saturday morning institution.

The cast scattered. Carmine Fusco enrolled in Harvard Law School with the money he had earned in the series; Warren Burgess took a step backward and joined a vaudeville unit touring the Midwest; Patty Kalish discarded her tap shoes, applied herself to the study of film editing with Marathon's chief editor, and went on to win an Academy Award in the early sixties. Marjorie Metcalfe became one of Hollywood's most legendary call girls.

With his earnings (which his mother doled out rather tightfistedly to him), Marty bought himself a second-hand Ford coupe, and proceeded to drive the length and breadth of Los Angeles, drawn like a magnet to the small clubs where music was being played and sung by the greats, the near-greats, and the yet-to-be-discovereds.

Moe Stein, always in demand as a rehearsal pianist, spent his days working in the studios and his nights accompanying Marty on his rounds, steering him to this club, that theater, numerous out-of-the-way *boîtes*, where everything from small jazz combos to large orchestras could be found. Marty heard a variety of singers, mostly good; a few, outstanding. He gleaned a little knowledge from every one of them. No law school or film-editing career for him; he was going to be a real singer, like Crosby, like Bob Eberle, like Jack Leonard.

"Not like *any* of them," counseled Moe. "Like yourself. That's the secret, Marty. To be an original. Sure, use what you hear those guys do, but that's all. Don't copy it."

"Moe, when do you think I'll be ready to sing professionally?"

The pianist's eyebrows raised. "What the hell you think you been doin' all those years at Marathon?"

"Oh, yeah, but that was different."

"You were singin', weren't you? And gettin' paid for it. That makes you a professional singer. And you got a little edge to boot. You got a name, kid. Okay, so you hated doing those crappy little School Daze shorts, but, what the hell. When you start workin' as a singer, it ain't gonna be like you're some unknown."

"Well, when do you think I'll be ready to start?"

"Christ, you're sixteen. Have you shaved yet? Gotten your ashes hauled? Don't be in such a goddam hurry. Look, I know you're impatient, but think how lucky you are. You're listenin' and learnin' and your SAG card is still current. So get some jobs in movies for a while. Bide your time. Keep practicin' with me. I'll let you know when you're ready to fly."

Marty continued the learning process. He listened to records until they were worn through; sat, bleary-eyed, in smoke-filled rooms until all hours of the morning. He plugged away with Moe month after month, refining what came to him naturally, listening to Moe's comments, sometimes disagreeing with him violently, since, as he grew older, he began to develop a mind of his own.

To sustain himself and enjoy a modicum of independence, Marty sought work in films. His mother, in a rare fit of interest, persuaded her agent to represent him, and soon he was in modest demand at the studios, playing high-school boys, military school cadets, and a variety of other roles appropriate to his age. He enrolled in Hollywood Professional School, an institution designed to educate child actors and to work in and around motion-picture schedules. He dated several young actresses, went to parties, in general fell into the standard social scheme of things.

o

Marty and Mary Frances became a pair of ships passing in the night. The taller he grew, the more he filled out, the more frequent were her sessions in front of her vanity mirror. I'm nearly forty, she thought, even though she had only just turned thirty-seven. She took to spending time in beauty salons, submitting herself to endless facials, mud packs, pluckings and tweezings, massages and exercises.

After two abortive Hollywood marriages, each of which lasted less than five months, Mary Frances Maguire had sworn off. Between alimony and the cash flow from occasional acting jobs, she found herself in a state of reasonable solvency by the late 1930s. Though she had not attained stardom, she was a popular guest at select dinner parties, premières, and nightclub openings, always escorted by some well-known Hollywood male.

She had become less profligate. As time deepened the lines around her mouth, sharpened her nose, tugged at her skin, and generally conspired to dissipate her beauty, she became convinced that the one true preservative of beauty was sleep, and she indulged in long bouts of it, sometimes lasting fourteen or fifteen hours at a clip. Actually, the few lines she had acquired imbued her countenance with a character it never before had, and the result was more interesting to prospective employers.

In the autumn of 1940, she played the title role in a modestly budgeted film called "Woman of the World," which opened to good reviews at the Pantages on Hollywood Boulevard. There was some talk of a nomination for Mary Frances when Oscar time rolled around, but the picture died aborning, not having even earned its black-and-white negative cost back, and Mary Frances' chances of earning an Academy Award died with it. She accepted well-meaning expressions of condolence and bitchy left-handed compliments with an air of unconcerned insouciance, but the loss of the gold statuette, which had been so close, ground at her insides.

Christmas Eve she got falling-down drunk at a party. She woke up four days later in a hotel room, stumbled to the door, and found it locked. From the outside.

She was naked and, looking around for her dress or a robe, was surprised to find neither. The room was empty, save for furniture and a mirror, and as she moved unsteadily to the dressing table, what greeted her in reflection was so shocking as to cause her breath to leave her body.

Her left eye was black and blue, with a two-inch cut just above the eyebrow, blood-crusted, scabbing. What appeared to be a cigarette burn marred the pink beauty of her left nipple, staining the blossom near the tip, orange-brown and ugly. Her whole body was a mass of welts, black, blue, and green-yellow.

Oh my God, she thought. Where the hell am I? What have I done?

She went to the phone on the nightstand and jiggled the receiver.

"*Si, a sus ordenes?*" the operator answered.

Why was she speaking Spanish?

"This is Miss Maguire in room—" She looked on the telephone dial for a room number but found none. "I don't *know* what room this is."

"*Numero cuatro,*" came the reply.

Spanish again.

"Please. Let me talk to the manager."

"*El administrador? Un momento.*"

After a brief pause, the manager came to the phone.

"I am Señor Garcia."

"Listen, *por favor.* I am—I am Señorita Mary Maguire, *comprende?*"

"I speak English, Miss Maguire," came the smooth reply.

"Oh, thank God. Please, can you tell me—Where am I?"

"You are in Room Four of the El Mirador Hotel in Acapulco."

"You're joking? What am I doing in—"

131

"You have been our guest for nearly four days now."

"But how did I get here? Who did I come with?"

"A man, señorita. A large man with graying hair. Perhaps fifty years old."

"Where is he now?"

"Gone. Yesterday afternoon."

She tried to marshal her thoughts. Her head was fuzzy, her tongue thick. I've been taking barbiturates, she thought.

"Please, Mr.—Señor Garcia. Where are my clothes? Why is the door locked from the outside?"

"Just a precaution, Miss Maguire."

"I don't understand," she said.

"Miss Maguire," said Garcia, his voice a trifle weary, "you ran through our halls yesterday without a stitch of clothing, screaming obscenities, annoying our guests, making a spectacle of yourself, trying to kill this man you came here with."

"I—*what?*" Mary Frances exclaimed.

"Oh, yes," the voice on the other end of the phone went on. "You tried to stab him at the end of the hallway on the first floor. He apologized to the other guests, picked you up, and carried you back to your room."

"Oh, my God!"·

"I called and asked you both to leave immediately. He promised you would. Then, yesterday, around four in the afternoon, he checked out. He said you would pay the bill."

"I see," she said, slowly regaining her wits. "And how much would that be?"

"Just a moment, please," said Mr. Garcia, moving away from the phone. When he returned he said, "Your bill comes to about eleven hundred dollars in American money."

"That's incredible! For four days?"

"*Señorita,*" said Garcia, lowering his voice. "We have been discreet. I should have called the *policia,* but your friend told me you were somewhat well known in your country, and—"

"All right, you blackmailing bastard."

"Pardon?" came the polite query.

"Forget it. Where's my purse?"

"Ah. Yes. Well, that's the problem. You had no purse when you arrived. Just the clothes you were wearing."

132

"I see. And that's why the door is—"

"*Exactemente, señorita.* I assume you have funds across the border. If you could call there and—"

"Yes, yes, I'll do that. Señor Garcia, I—Is there a doctor in this hotel?"

"We have no doctor in attendance here, but I know of one. He is a personal friend of mine. But he is not inexpensive."

"I would have bet on that. All right. Please call him. And ask your operator to give me long distance."

"Er—one thing, Miss Maguire."

"Yes?"

"You will reverse the charges, won't you?"

Mary Frances called her agent. Within four hours she had paid her bill, had her bruises, cuts, and contusions treated by a Doctor M. Sanchez, and booked a flight to L.A.

When she arrived at Lockheed Air Terminal in Burbank, she was met by a gaggle of reporters and photographers. While she was relatively small potatoes in motion pictures, the papers smelled something juicy in the sketchy report they got over the telephone from an anonymous male caller.

Mary Frances walked into the air terminal blithely and announced that she had taken a sorely needed vacation in Mexico after a wonderfully hectic, financially fruitful year of appearing on the screen.

Had she gone down alone?

Of course.

What about this mysterious caller?

"What caller? I thought you boys just came out to welcome me back?"

"Come on, Mary. What about this guy who called the papers and claimed he had gone down there with you, that you had been drunk and on drugs most of the time and that, before he left, you tried to knife him and he had to beat you up?"

"Oh, my God" (laughing), "Bud—it is Bud, isn't it? From the *Times*?"

"Yeah, that's right."

"Ah, honey, I think you had a little too much Christmas

133

cheer. Here it is nearly New Year's and you're still hungover. Now let me see. As I recall, there was a nuisance of a jerk—said he was from Texas, aren't they all—"

(General laughter.)

"Well, anyway, he kept calling me, asking me to dinner, to the track. I told him I had gone down there to rest and that, anyway, I didn't date strange men—"

(A few chuckles.)

"So, this character keeps calling and sending me flowers and notes, telling me about his oil wells and his cattle and his millions of acres of ranchland and a lot of other crap—oops—like that. Anyway, he's the reason I left early."

"And he didn't beat you up, Mary Frances?"

"Look me over, boys. Do I look like a battered broad?"

She had taken great pains with her makeup and her hair, combing it over her cut eye and hiding the scab. Since most of the bruises she had suffered were on her body, the black, high-necked sheath covered them amply.

Bud of the *Times* clucked, "Okay, princess. I guess this was a wild goose chase." .

"Not at all, Bud. I'm always flattered when you fellas take an interest in me. Tell you what. Stop in at my place on New Year's Eve and we'll all have a drink together and welcome 1941 in."

o

Mary Frances threw a New Year's Eve party for well over a hundred people in the house on Miller Drive in which she and Marty had lived for the past two and a half years. She hired a small group of musicians to play for dancing, and the house, smartly decorated and lit for the occasion, resounded with laughter and music. Marty had invited Amelia Carson, a young film hopeful, and they made an attractive couple; the girl in a brocaded black and gold party frock, Marty in a dark blue suit.

Nearly eighteen, he stood a shade under six feet, moving with a grace that one saw mainly in athletes. He was clearly handsome, with an easy smile and a self-effacing manner. His eyes and nose he could thank his mother for. The firm jawlines, high cheekbones, and curly hair, dark blond with lighter strands glinting here and there, he owed to his father.

Mary Frances glanced at him as he walked by her, carrying a drink to Amelia. Who was this tall, good-looking young man, she thought. She wondered whether he was still a virgin and decided he was not.

She was in error.

There was absolutely nothing wrong with Martin Wynocki, of that he himself was sure. Oh, perhaps he had a foolish, romantic streak in him which precluded sex for sex's sake. Possibly all the love songs he had been singing in the little club on La Brea for the past seven months had colored his thinking on the subject of women. Certainly he felt there was something cold and mechanical in bedding down a girl purely for pleasure, with no emotions involved. He was well aware of such behavior on the part of most of the young people he knew and ran with. It just did not suit him to do the same. On top of which none of the young women he knew, Amelia included, moved him sufficiently in that direction. They moved him, yes. But not sufficiently.

Many of the pressmen who had met Mary Frances at the airport had accepted her invitation and now, a minute before midnight, flashbulbs once again popped as several members of the film community set about kissing each other in celebration of the brand-new year about to unfold.

Mary Frances had purposely avoided inviting a date for herself. She wanted to give her attention to her guests. Now, as the band played "Auld Lang Syne" and the crowd sang it and blew whistles and horns, she watched as Amelia Carson wound an arm around her son's neck and kissed him. Mary Frances smiled and, as she turned away, a large male form blocked her vision. She looked up into the face of a darkly handsome man, with iron-gray hair and a thin mouth. She had never seen him before although, having spotted him earlier in the evening, she had assumed he had squired one of the decorative women present.

She opened her mouth to wish him a Happy New Year and suddenly found herself enveloped by the man, his arms around her, trapping her own arms at her sides, his mouth wet and hard and open against hers. She was so startled that, momentarily, she was immobilized. Then, when it was obvious he intended to prolong the kiss, she struggled to break free.

Someone had turned out the lights, and she and the stranger went unnoticed in the dark, noisy confusion. The more she struggled, the tighter he held her, forcing her to move backward by virtue of his own bulk. Her eyes were wide open and, as she tried to pull her lips away from his, he took his left hand from around her waist and placed it at the back of her head, preventing her from terminating the kiss. At the same time, he pushed her back toward her bedroom.

She was moving her head vigorously from side to side, trying to free her mouth in order to protest, but the man held her fast. Now they were in her bedroom, and he kicked the door closed behind him, without releasing her. His left hand, at the back of her head, grasped her hair, painfully pulling her head back until she was looking at the ceiling.

"All right. I'm gonna let you go now. One peep outta you and I'll wreck your face, get me?"

She nodded and he released her. She immediately struck him in the face as hard as she could. He slapped her back fiercely, knocking her onto the bed.

"I'm gonna say it once more. Don't give me any shit or it's your funeral. Do I make myself clear?"

Her eyes teared as she nodded again.

He reached into his inside breast pocket and she recoiled reflexively. Was he going to shoot her? Why?

He removed a manila envelope from his jacket.

"I got some pictures to show you."

He took them out of the envelope and spread them on the bed beside her.

She glanced down at them, saw what they contained, bolted from the bed into her bathroom, and threw up savagely. The man came and stood in the doorway as she knelt beside the toilet bowl, retching. Finally, when her vomiting ceased, he took her arm and brought her to her feet.

"Come on, Mary," he said, moving her back into the bedroom. "I want you to take a good look at them."

He shoved her onto the bed, beside the pictures. She tried

to avoid looking at them but he took her head in his large hand and forced it downward so she couldn't avoid the photographs.

There were twelve of them, slightly oversize, black-and-white. In two, she was performing fellatio upon a well-muscled, swarthy Mexican; in three she was engaged in cunnilingus with two other women, both Mexican, one rail thin, the other rather full blown; in yet another, she sat upon a bed, smiling dreamily into the camera, while on either side of her the Mexican women sat, fondling her breasts; in another, a close-up, the women's hands spread the lips of Mary Frances' vagina for the benefit of the camera, and she sat, open-legged, smiling the same dreamlike smile; in another, she lay on the bed, with the thin woman stretched out on top of her in the opposite direction. She was eating the woman who, in turn, busied herself by inserting a banana into Mary Frances. In another, the two women stood in the background, watching rather clinically, as two men, both Mexicans, kept Mary Frances busy, fore and aft. And then, she saw the one with the dog—

She began to gag, tried to get to the bathroom again, and fell to her knees on the carpet, fighting the convulsions that wracked her body. The man knelt beside her.

"I think we ought to talk about a financial arrangement, don't you?"

She shook her head violently.

"Don't be stupid. You either cough up or I'll print enough of these to paper every wall in your house."

"I—I haven't got any money. Not—not a lot of it."

"You've got jewelry, fur coats, a house."

"This house?"

"Yeah. You got equity in it, right? Sell it."

"You're crazy. Where are my son and I supposed to live?"

"I don't give a shit. That's your problem. Now what I got on that bed there are a bunch of salable items. If you don't want to buy them, I know plenty of people in this town who will. These photos'll make you more famous than you've ever been before."

"I'm drugged in them. Anyone can see that."

"Oh, yeah, baby. You're drugged, all right. But nobody's gonna care. They're just gonna have a good time watching you go down on those broads, not to mention the guys. And how often does anyone get to see pictures of a movie star fuckin' a dog?"

Mary Frances was crying softly. "Why? Why are you doing this?"

The man laughed. "For money, stupid. I gotta live, don't I?"

In a burst of rage, she leaped upon him, clawing and scratching, raking her nails across his face. They rolled around on the floor, a bull and a wildcat. She avoided screaming, since the thing she most feared was an unwanted visit by one or more of her guests with those pictures spread all over the bed. He grabbed her hands and pulled her to her feet. He trapped both wrists in his huge left paw and, with his doubled right fist, he slammed her hard in the stomach. Her eyes rolled in her head, and she went down, barely conscious.

"You dumb cunt!" he said, taking a handkerchief out of his pocket and dabbing his bleeding face. "Didn't you have enough in Mexico?"

He walked to the bed and gathered up the pictures, placing them once again in his breast pocket.

"Now, let's quit screwin' around. For fifty thou, you get the pictures and the negs. Not one penny less. And don't give me any more crap about how you ain't got it. You got it. Or you can get it. I wouldn'ta wasted my time pickin' you up at that Christmas party, gettin' you stoned, and flyin' you across the border if you didn't."

"Fifty thousand!" she moaned breathlessly.

"That's right. Hey, I don't get it all. I had expenses, get what I mean? All your playmates down there had to be paid for their services. Although," he chuckled, "I think the skinny broad woulda done it for zip. She really liked workin' on you."

"Stop it. Please."

"Okay," he said placidly. "Look, I'll contact you in a couple of days. You start figurin' out, in the meantime, how you're gonna put this dough together. And don't try stallin' me. I'm a patient man, but you fuck around with me and I'll put you in the hospital and these goodies—" he patted his breast pocket—"in circulation."

He stood by the bedroom door for a moment, looking at her. "You wouldn't do somethin' dumb, like call the cops, would you?"

She shook her head. She was crying, the mascara black-tracking down her cheeks.

"Just in case you get any ideas along those lines, remember—poor is better than dead."

Chapter

21

She sounded desperate on the phone.

"Sally," she implored, her voice shaking, "I've got to see you. Please."

"You got to be kiddin', puss. It's New Year's Day! I'm goin' to the Rose Bowl game. I got a bundle laid off on it."

"Please, Sally, please. This is an emergency. You once told me if I never needed your help—"

"Yeah, yeah, I know. But New Year's Day, for Christ's sake!"

"Sally!"

"Awright, awright. Relax. Where do you want to meet?"

They rendezvoused at a fish restaurant in Santa Monica, one of the few open on the first day of the year.

"Sally" was Salvatore DeMarco, a top-echelon kingpin in organized crime throughout Southern California. He was a much-sought-after escort by many of the beautiful women of the town, and had frequently dated Mary Frances. His connections were said to extend to the Governor's mansion and beyond. He carried with him an air of danger, not to mention a certain acquired overlay of class, and to be in his presence was insurance against boredom.

He and Mary Frances sat facing each other. She looked wan and pale, her eyes puffed from lack of sleep.

"That must have been some party you had last night at your place," he commented.

"It was," she answered quietly. "Why didn't you come?"

"I had something going. Thanks for the invite, though."

She regarded him with open admiration. She had wakened him out of a sound sleep. Yet here he was, a man nearing sixty, an hour and a half later, freshly shaved and powdered, immaculate in a camel's hair jacket and dark brown slacks. He was a big man, bigger than her would-be blackmailer of the previous evening, with craggy, irregular features. His large nose was cocked crookedly on his face, his eyes dark brown. A small scar on his left cheek added character to his countenance.

Slowly he buttered a breadstick, as he asked, "So what's it all about, Mary Frances?"

She told him, omitting nothing.

When she finished, he said, "What's this crumb's name?"

"I don't know. He never told me."

"But he's going to call you in a few days, huh?"

"That's what he said."

"What do you want me to do?"

"I want you to stop him."

"Oh ho, now wait a minute. That could get kinda complicated."

"What do you mean?"

"Honey, this guy sounds pretty well organized to me. He's got your little ass in a sling, and he knows it. He's not about to fold because I put a little pressure on him."

"Oh, Sal, what'll I do?"

He broke another breadstick. "Okay. The minute this guy contacts you, call me. I'm not guaranteeing anything, but he might be persuaded to give up the pictures and the negatives. Out of goodwill, you know?"

A frown clouded her face.

"What if he won't?"

He patted her hand. "Hold your water, kid. Let's wait and see."

o

As she drove up Benedict Canyon, she glanced at the clock on the dash: 11:17. The man had given her explicit instructions on the phone. Just before the summit, a dirt road to the left. Drive until the dirt road terminated in a dead end. Douse the lights. He would be along shortly.

She found the dirt road, turned, and drove as far as she could, till it ended in a tangle of weeds and overhang from several trees. She turned out the lights and waited.

By 11:50 she began to think he wasn't coming. She fought an impulse to start the engine and back out onto Benedict once again. A hand tapped on the window.

She rolled it down, and the extortionist said, "I see you found it okay."

He opened the door on the driver's side. "Move over," he said, as he pushed in beside her. "This used to be a lovers' lane. I copped a lot of cherries right in this very spot, baby." He put his hand on her knee. She moved away from him, up against the passenger door.

"I get it. Strictly business now, eh? You weren't this touchy in Acapulco."

"I was doped, you prick!"

"Ah-ah. Temper. Remember what you got last time you bad-mouthed me."

"I don't want any trouble with you," she said tiredly.

"Right. Down to business. What about the money?"

"Well," she began, her eyes not meeting his, "I've sold what jewelry I had that was worth anything. I'm trying to find a buyer for my coats. But I'm telling you right now, I can't raise fifty thousand. Nowhere near it."

"What about your house? How much equity—"

"God damn it! I'm not going to sell my house. I have a son—"

"Hell, he's almost a man now—"

"—who lives with me and I can't just move him and myself into the street."

"Take an apartment. You don't need that big a house anyway."

She battled her rising anger.

142

"Isn't there anything I can say to make you change your mind? Oh, I don't mean not pay you. I want those negatives. But fifty thousand. Be reasonable."

"I went to a lot of trouble to set you up. Fifty thousand is cheap, considering."

She smothered her disgust with what she hoped would pass for a coquettish smile. "Well then," she said softly, "you'll just have to give me time to get it."

Without warning, he took her jaw in his large hand and squeezed her cheeks together. "Hey, you trying to con me? Stop that fluttering eyelash shit! You start acting like you want me to take it out in trade, and I'll get very nervous. Like you're planning to cross me. I wouldn't like that." He released her face and pushed her back into her corner with the heel of his hand. "Be yourself, princess."

Realizing she had nearly overplayed her hand, she tightened her mouth and said, "You're right. You're a no-good son of a bitch who's taking away everything I worked for for the last eight years."

"So what? You're still famous and beautiful. Marry some rich jerk and get well all over again. The easy way. On your back."

She didn't answer him. She had read enough scripts to know about pacing. It was time for a pause in the conversation. He lit a cigarette, content to let her think about things.

Finally, she spoke. "All right. I'll do my best. Maybe I can borrow it from somebody. I'll see what I can do."

"Don't see what you can do. Do it. Period."

He opened the door and got out of the car.

"Where are you parked?" she asked.

"None of your business," he replied. "I'll call you day after tomorrow. You better have some good news for me."

She played her trump card. "Wait," she said, reaching into her purse. Had she brought a gun to this meeting? His hand darted inside his coat jacket to the .32 automatic he had shoulder-holstered there.

"Here's twenty-two hundred from the jewelry I sold. A down payment."

"Keep it," he said. "It's chicken feed." And he left.

She shrugged and put the money back into her purse. She snapped on her dashlights and smoked a cigarette. Five minutes passed. From in front of the car emerged the large figure of Sal DeMarco, making his way through the under-brush beyond the dead end, accompanied by another man known to her only as "Buzzer."

DeMarco walked to the driver's side and got in.

"Well?" asked Mary Frances. "Do you know him?"

"Oh, yeah. I know him all right. He's one of my *paisan.* Name's Ritchie Palermo. And he's tough. Him and me, we got into it one night, back in the old days. He tried to heist a gambling ship I used to run off Catalina. One of his men gave me this scar," he added, touching the indentation on his left cheek.

"Ritchie Palermo," he repeated softly. "So that's his racket now. Setting up foolish women."

"Now wait a minute, Sally—"

"Sorry, kid, I didn't mean you. You were just in the wrong place at the wrong time on Christmas Eve."

"Well. Do you think you can help me?"

"Only one way, Mary Frances," he said, looking her in the eye. "The crumb needs banging in the head."

"You mean—"

"There's no other way. I didn't scare him in the old days and I'm not going to scare him now. He'll suck you dry, like a leech, and you can be sure he's got a double set of those negatives and prints. Honey, he'll bleed you for the rest of your life. You'll never get off the bubble."

"But—"

"Listen, babe. You asked me for help. I can furnish it. I'm not going to pay for it myself; it's your headache. But I can supply the Bromo for a price."

"How much are we—"

"Five grand. Hell, that's a whole lot better than fifty. And you'll be done with the bastard for good."

"I don't know Sally. I'm afraid."

"Don't decide right now, Mary Frances. Think about it."

"The thing is, I can't stall him too long."

"Then you better think it over in a hurry, right?"

Sal DeMarco got out of the car and beckoned the impassive "Buzzer." He leaned into the open car window and said, "Let me know." He and "Buzzer" disappeared back into the underbrush.

o

Palermo called her three days later. The conversation was short and to the point. She begged, he threatened. She stalled, he pressed. And threatened again. When he hung up, she was in a state of near collapse from fear.

She called Salvatore DeMarco.

o

Ten days later, a dark gray 1939 Cadillac sedan was fished out of the ocean, near the Santa Monica Pier. Inside was the body of Ritchie Palermo. He had been strangled with piano wire and shot in the head. The papers gave the murder wide coverage and reported to the public everything they could. What never got into newsprint was the fact that Palermo's genitals had been cut off and his penis shoved into his mouth.

Initially, the Ritchie Palermo killing was written off as gangland business. Then, a young, eager crime reporter for the *Herald* began digging into Palermo's background. He came up with, among other things, an old story in the *Herald*'s files regarding a fracas aboard the *S.S. Lucky Star*, a gambling ship belonging to Salvatore DeMarco. In addition to other articles on underworld characters (a series assignment he wangled by pestering his city editor), he chronicled the enmity between the late, unlamented Palermo and the influential Mr. DeMarco.

The Santa Monica Police Department followed his lead and began a serious investigation into DeMarco's activities, particularly his whereabouts on the night of January 10, 1941 when, according to the coroner, the Palermo murder had occurred. Of course, DeMarco had an airtight alibi: he had been in Tijuana all day and overnight, attending the bullfights and enjoying the town's diversions.

His well-known lieutenant, Frank "Buzzer" Falzone, was

also able to account for his movements on that day. But "The Buzzer" had made one fatal error. He had invited his nephew, Ralphie Falzone, to accompany him on the occasion of putting out Palermo's lights. The L.A.P.D. picked up young Falzone on the ludicrous charge of jaywalking. The fact that he was carrying a concealed weapon (a .380 Colt automatic) interested them. When a ballistics check was made on the weapon, it was found to be the gun which had pumped an unnecessary *coup de grâce* slug into the head of the already-strangled Ritchie Palermo.

After a round-the-clock interrogation by some of L.A.'s (and Santa Monica's) finest, Ralphie, who lacked his uncle's fiber by several thousand degrees, broke and told the whole story of the Ritchie Palermo killing.

Why was Palermo killed at this point in time? What had he done to DeMarco recently?

Ralphie hunched his shoulders up. "It was a paid hit, that's all I know."

"Paid by who?"

"I dunno. A broad. I think she's in the movies."

Suddenly every woman who had ever stepped in front of a motion-picture camera and had, at one time or another, dated Sal DeMarco, came under suspicion. Several detectives were assigned to the case, mainly as interrogators. Naturally, Mary Frances was one of those questioned. She remained cool under the fire of the inquisitors and was considered to be innocent.

Falzone and DeMarco were arrested and charged with Murder One. Mary Frances prayed Sal DeMarco would beat the rap. He did not. Both he and Frank Falzone were sentenced to die in the gas chamber.

One day in late February of 1941, Mary Frances' front doorbell rang. She opened the door to find a stranger with a briefcase standing there. A Mexican. He walked past her, placed the briefcase on the coffee table in the front room, and opened it, withdrawing an envelope. He threw the envelope on the table and said nothing. She opened it. The twelve slightly oversized black-and-white photographs screamed up at her. The man was the photographer who had captured the Acapulcan orgy on film.

He was less greedy than Ritchie Palermo had been. He demanded only thirty thousand dollars. He added that he was certain Ritchie had been killed on her orders and that he would go to the police if she did not pay. She told him she would think it over.

She packed her bags, walked into Marty's room, and told him she had to leave town for a few days. Badly frightened and desperate, she got into her car and allowed herself to be swallowed up by the vast, sparsely populated Southwest. She had had the foresight to take what cash she had in the house with her. She drove like one possessed, stopping only once at an auto court in Kingman, Arizona, to fall, exhausted, into a lumpy bed and sleep. When she got to Santa Fe, New Mexico, she stopped. It was remote, scantily settled, small. It was reputed to be a haven for artists and craftsmen. She took a room, unpacked her bags, went to a drugstore, bought a bottle of peroxide, cut her hair, and dyed it blonde.

She got a job almost immediately in a real estate office, giving her most recent married name: Mary Frances Toland. Now she thanked God she had never been a high visibility movie star. She walked the streets of Santa Fe unknown, although not unnoticed. The male citizens eyed, with appreciation, the "new girl in town."

After a month of residence in Santa Fe, she placed a long-distance collect call to Marty, who had been worried about her. Had he reported her disappearance to the police? Of course he had, when she had not returned home after ten days. Had anyone come around to see her? Any strangers? Yes, as a matter of fact, a man. Looked like a Mexican. Didn't believe she was gone. Marty had to practically run him off the property. He seemed furious over Mary Frances' absence. Say, where was she anyway? When was she coming home?

"I'm not coming home, Marty. Ever. Look, I can't explain, and I can't tell you where I am. I'm all right, though. I'm fine. I'll call you collect every other week or so. Please, Marty, don't ask me any questions right now. Just trust me. Maybe when—if—things straighten out, I'll be able to tell you—" She bit her lip. She could never tell him. "Look, are you all right? Can you manage there, in the house, alone? Do you need anything?"

"No, Mother, I'm fine."

"How's your job going?"

"Just fine. I like singing at the Buccaneer."

"That's good. Listen, Marty, I'll say goodbye now. Be good and I'll try to call you next week."

"But, Mother, I don't understand. When will I see you?"

"Soon, I hope. Real soon." She knew better.

Well, at least the house was completely paid for, thanks to her last divorce settlement, so he wouldn't have to worry about anything but the taxes. He was making a living, of sorts, at the nightclub, and he could always supplement his income with movie work.

Marty, bewildered beyond words, hung the phone up, filled with a strange and unsettling sense of loss.

The Mexican photographer, Antonio Jiminez, vented his frustration on the fender of the old car he had driven across the border. He knew he could not go to the police with the photographs; he was a visitor in this country and they would ask him how he came by the pictures. How could he tell them he took them himself? They would throw him into the *calabozo* and throw away the key. Who, then, would pay for the trouble he had gone to in bringing his set of the prints all the way from Acapulco? The young man who had answered the door at the woman's house? Hardly. Probably one of her lovers. Women like that liked young boys. And girls. And dogs.

God damn it to hell, somebody would have to pay him for his pains. He found a buyer. The editor of a sleazy magazine, with offices in a dingy building in East Los Angeles, gave him five hundred dollars. Señor Jiminez beat it back across the border.

The editor knew he could never publish the photographs, but he did have negatives made off the prints, and proceeded to peddle the pictures quietly to "select" customers at fifty dollars a set. They sold very well, and one well-known male star, whose sexual prowess was fodder for every newspaper column, had the shot of Mary Frances and the dog blown up to poster size and framed above his bar. It became one of the best-known conversation pieces in Los Angeles.

Chapter

22

The "Maguire Shots," as they came to be known, enjoyed brisk circulation in the Cinema Capital of the World, and it was inevitable that Marty should be seared by them. He was questioned several times by detectives as to his mother's whereabouts and her possible involvement in the murder of Ritchie Palermo. He told them, truthfully, that he had no idea where she was. Had he heard from her? Yes, he admitted, but he had the idea she might be moving around.

The police were satisfied. Two of the investigating detectives had seen the snapshots, and neither of them blamed Mary Frances for getting out of Hollywood.

Marty quit his job and kept to the house. He answered the phone, when it rang, in a phony Japanese houseboy accent because he did not wish to hear one more expression of concern from his mother's friends, or the snickers from total strangers who called at all hours. He thought of disconnecting the phone altogether, but that would sever his only link with Mary Frances. He stayed home, played records, and brooded.

o

The phone rang.

"Herro? Who call, prease?" said Marty.

"Can it, kid. It's me. Moe. Returning your call.?

"Oh. Hi, Moe."

"That's the worst Japanese accent I ever heard."

"Yeah? Maybe I better switch to Chinese?"

"Maybe you better stop sittin' there lookin' at the four walls and rejoin the human race."

"That's why I called you. I need your help."

"So ask. So I'll help."

"Didn't you tell me once you worked with Wiley McKay?"

"Yeah. In the twenties. We both worked for Des Pomfrey. You should've seen Wiley back then. Arms barely long enough to work his slide. But by God, he did, and pretty soon Kid Ory and Teagarden and all the rest were sitting up and taking notice."

"Moe, listen. Do you think you could get to him? On the phone, I mean?"

"Who? Wiley? Sure, but why?"

"He and Denny Mason aren't getting along. It's in this morning's paper. Mason got drunk last night and told McKay off. It looks like Mason could get fired."

"Hmm. I doubt it, kid. Wiley's not only a great musician, he's a good businessman. Mason's too big an asset to the band to—"

"Moe, I want that job."

"What, Mason's?"

"If Wiley McKay fires him, he's going to need a new boy singer, right?"

"Sure, but—"

"I want that job, Moe. I'm ready. Besides, I've got to get out of here."

"Things getting you down, huh kid?"

"Yeah. But mainly, it's because I feel I could do the job and do it damn well."

Moe was silent for a moment.

"Look, kid, I'm just finishing up at Fox. I'll be over in an hour."

o

As Martin and Moe entered the McKay suite at the Hollywood Knickerbocker the next afternoon, two photographers, armed with Leicas and Rolliflexes, were busily snapping pictures of the famous trombonist, who stood in the center of the sitting room, dressed in a tailored Western-cut suit, complete with neckerchief, hand-tooled boots, and cowboy hat, doing incredible things with an old Colt six-gun.

Marty watched in amazement as McKay juggled the revolver deftly, twirling it, balancing it on one finger, changing it from hand to hand with lightning speed, placing it behind his back and flipping it up, over his shoulder expertly, the pistol describing a perfect arc and coming back into his hand right side up, as the flashbulbs popped.

McKay became aware of Moe's and Marty's presence.

"Okay, fellers?" he asked the photographers, in the rich, sonorous baritone that had become famous over the radio airwaves in recent years. "Will that git 'er?"

"Yeah, thanks, Wiley. I think we gotcha covered."

The two men made their goodbyes and shouldered past Marty and Moe, nodding as they went out the door.

Wiley McKay flung the six-shooter onto the couch and made for Moe, a big grin on his face.

"Christ, hoss, how the hell are you? Been a dog's age since I last saw you!" he said to the little piano player as he embraced him. Moe beamed, returning the embrace, slapping the lanky McKay on the back repeatedly. Next to the band leader, Moe looked positively dwarflike.

"Hey, Wiley," Moe said. "You gettin' taller or am I standing in a hole?"

"Aw, hell, pardner, you know me! I'm a growin' boy, is all." They both laughed.

Marty stood apart from them, feeling a little awkward and nervous. Moe broke Wiley's bearhug and indicated Marty.

"Wiley, say hello to Marty Wynocki. Marty, Wiley McKay."

McKay extended a huge hand toward the young man. "Mighty glad to know you, Marty."

"Same here, Mister McKay."

"Whoa, Nellie! Nobody calls me 'Mr. McKay' 'cept my accountant."

"Well—okay. Er—glad to meet you, Wiley."

"Now you're talkin'. Come on in, you two, and set. Get you a drink?"

Marty declined the offer, but Moe accepted.

"I've been on the recording stage all day on an Alice Faye epic. She's a great dame, but some of the other people on this show! I need a drink."

As McKay poured Moe a gin and tonic and himself an astonishing amount of straight bourbon, Marty said, "That stuff with the gun! That was great!"

McKay grinned, walked over to the couch and sat down next to the discarded Colt. He picked it up and twirled it once, affectionately. "This here belonged to my grandpappy McKay. He was a Texas Ranger, one of the first and, believe it or not, my ol' daddy carried this hogleg on his hip for twenty-six years when he was town marshal of Wimberly, Texas. Never drew it once in anger either. I grew up ridin' horses and shootin' guns almost before I could walk proper." He grinned. "Aw, hell, that's an exaggeration. But I am fond of this old thumbbuster. Been in my family a long time. Sometimes when we're on the bus, like in Texas or Arizona, I shoot jackrabbits with it. I'm a fool for rabbit stew," he hastened to add. "No sense shootin' anything you don't aim to eat."

"Where were those guys from?" asked Moe.

Wiley took a long pull from his glass before answering. "*Collier's* magazine. Want to do a big story about me and the band. And when it comes to publicity for my band, you know me: Born on Wednesday, lookin' both ways for Sunday."

Moe laughed and said, to Marty, "Talks funny, don't he? When I first worked with him, I couldn't get over how he never ran out of quaint phrases like that."

"Aw, hell. That's everyday talk where I come from."

Marty was fascinated by Wiley McKay. The bandleader was tall and lean, with an almost sorrowful countenance. His hair was darkish blond, and he wore it unfashionably long, the back curling around his neck. He sported a mustache that drooped down both sides of his mouth, Old-West-fashion, and when he smiled the hairy appendage framed a mouthful of white, even teeth. His eyebrows, sandy brown, seemed to have been glued on in a perpetually quizzical slant, low at the far corners of the eyes, high at mid-brow. His nose was bony and strong, evidence of his quarter-Cherokee bloodline. Only his chin left something to be desired, slightly underslung, receding. Marty couldn't decide whether he looked like General Custer or Gary Cooper.

Now, as he watched McKay lovingly handle the old revolver, he observed the bandleader's hands. They were perfectly formed, with long, tapering fingers ending in well-cared-for nails. They seemed to have a life of their own as they caressed the blued barrel and frame of the Colt.

McKay took another great gulp of his drink. That he was a prodigious imbiber was no secret in and out of show business. His binges had been chronicled by the press on numerous occasions. Marty watched him consume his bourbon, slightly amazed, and the bandleader looked at him and read his mind.

"Don't ever get started on this stuff, hoss. It'll rot your guts, sure as shootin'!" said McKay, looking remorseful. He put the drink on the coffee table. "Well," he said, rising, " 'm I gonna git to hear you sing or not?"

"That's what we're here for, Wiley," said Moe, moving to a little spinet near the far windows of the room. "C'mon, Marty. Let's show the man how songs should be sung."

He sang.

"Deep In a Dream" and "Day In, Day Out" and "Jeepers Creepers" and "The Lady's In Love With You," while Wiley sat near him, on a high bar stool, his forefinger through the trigger guard of the six-shooter, the gun slowly turning in his hand, his head cocked thoughtfully.

When Marty finished, Wiley shook his head slowly and said, "You can sing, boy."

"Thank you."

"I told you, Wile," put in Moe. "I'm not going to bring some schloomp in for you to hear."

Wiley smiled and looked at his watch. "I've got an appointment in about ten minutes, fellers." He looked at Marty. "I'll let you know."

Surprised, Moe said, "That's all? 'I'll let you know'?"

154

McKay smiled tolerantly. "You're forgettin', Moe. I still have a boy singer with my band. Two's one too many."

"Yeah, but from what I hear—"

"Moe," interrupted Marty. "Wiley said he'd let me know. That's good enough for me." He looked at McKay. "Just singing for you was an honor. Thanks for the kind words."

"Meant 'em, pard. Like I said, you'll hear from me, one way or the other."

"I'll be waiting." Without another word, Marty took Moe's elbow and steered him toward the door of the suite. As they reached it, McKay called out, "By the way, Marty. Wha'd Moe say your last name was?"

"Wynocki. It's Polish."

"Hmmm," said McKay. "So long."

Outside the hotel, Moe seemed disturbed. "What the hell's he waitin' for? Christmas? He liked you, goddammit, I know he did. Otherwise you'd a never got past the first tune." He addressed the "No Parking" sign at the curb. "He sat and he listened and he liked the kid. So what the hell is this 'I'll let you know' dreck?"

They drove back to Miller Drive in silence. When they pulled up in front of the house, Marty opened the door wordlessly and got out. He closed the car door and leaned in through the open passenger window.

"Moe, I want to thank you. I've never had a better friend."

He waited for an answer, but Moe merely sat there, staring straight ahead. "Well," said Marty finally. "See you."

He turned and started up the short walk toward the house.

"Marty," called Moe unexpectedly. Marty turned.

"You may just be," said Moe slowly, "the best friggin' singer I ever heard. If Wiley doesn't fire that idiot Mason and hire you, he's a prime asshole." With that, Moe stepped on the gas and, tires squealing, drove off.

o

A week later, the phone rang.

"Marty, it's Moe. Can you be ready to leave in three days?"

"What do you mean?"

"To go on the road. With Wiley McKay. He finally canned that prima donna of his and he wants you."

"God, Moe. That's great! Listen, can you move into my house for a few days? I'll get in touch with a rental agent and see about leasing it to somebody. But when my mother calls, you can tell her I've gone with McKay, and get a number where I can reach her."

"Okay, *shagitz*, leave it to Moe. So long, and congratulations."

"Wait a minute, Moe. What do I do now?"

"Simple. Call Wiley at the Knickerbocker and tell him thanks and that you would be delighted to join the band."

Marty hung up the phone, slightly dazed. Wiley McKay? To go on the road with one of the greatest bands and probably *the* greatest jazz trombone player in the world? Yes, he'd do anything to get out of town, away from wagging tongues and amused glances, but this job was more than he had dreamed of.

Three days later, Marty showed up at the Knickerbocker Hotel. Parked in front was a chartered Greyhound whose side panels proclaimed in dark blue letters: Wiley McKay, The Texas Trombone and his Orchestra.

Marty boarded the bus and headed east.

Chapter

23

METRONOME MAGAZINE
Denver, Colorado, April 13, 1941, by Ray Krauss:

The Wiley McKay behemoth slayed the locals here with a knock-down-drag-out one-nighter March 13 at Elitch's, the first of a series of one-night stands that will take the band across the country to the Apple and a three-week stint at the Café Rouge of the Hotel Pennsylvania.

The individual efforts of such stalwarts as Cisco Contreras on alto, Dave Schindler blowing up a storm on tenor, and Fats Deidrich handling the "ride" trumpet chores all made for a great evening of jazz.

Bitsy Munro is by way of being astounding. While he lacks the blinding speed and technique of TD's great tub thumper, Buddy Rich, it will be interesting to see these two young men go at it, mano a mano.

"Concerto for Trombone," unveiled here, is perhaps the most exciting "extended" work to come along since Goodman's "Sing, Sing, Sing."

McKay's new singer, who has replaced the popular Denny Mason, is a real find. He sings with poise, excellent phrasing, and faultless intonation and surprised everyone with a rendition of "Chicago" that bespoke the vocal influences of Louis and Ella. Unfortunately, on this, his first date with the band, the newcomer became involved in an ugly incident that threatened to turn Elitch's into a battleground. However, keep your eye (and your ear) on this young man.

"Hey, kid, have you seen this?" said George Pachmeyer, the band's bass trombonist, as he handed the copy of *Metronone* over his shoulder to Marty, who sat directly in back of him on the bus. Marty was alone in his seat, not yet having "buddied up" with anyone in the band. He read the article and flushed. Why did it have to happen on his first evening with the band? Dammit!

He had been happy, if a bit reserved, when he had boarded the bus in Hollywood. Would the band resent his usurping Mason's position? He was, after all, a newcomer, audaciously trying to fill the shoes of one of the top singers in the country.

Wiley McKay, who always traveled on the bus with his band, walked back to where Marty was sitting and introduced him to various members of the band, most of whom welcomed him. By the time the bus had reached San Bernardino, the newest addition to the McKay aggregation was able to relax somewhat.

"Hey! Wynocki! Yeah! Weren't you the kid in all those movie shorts? You know, like in a schoolroom or something?" asked Cisco Contreras.

Marty smiled. "Yeah, I'm afraid so. Don't hold 'em against me though."

Contreras, known in the band as the Cisco Kid, smiled broadly. "Oh, no, man," he said, with his slight Mexican accent. "They were great. I really liked 'em. And I remember how good you sang. For a kid, I mean." Contreras was not quite twenty.

"That's if you happen to go for kids," remarked Sherm Becker, one of the trumpet players, who sat across the aisle. Becker's complexion was sallow and pockmarked. His hair was thinning rapidly and he looked more like a *mafioso* than a musician. He was one of the band's few malcontents and had been a drinking buddy of Denny Mason's.

"I mean," he continued, "at this rate, maybe our noble leader will replace Dede with Shirley Temple and we can all wear funny hats and sing 'On the Good Ship Lollipop.'"

Wiley, hearing Becker's comments from up front, leaned out into the aisle.

"Mind your manners, Becker. You ain't even heard the young feller sing yet."

Becker grunted. Then he mumbled just loud enough to be heard, "So what. He looks like a loser to me."

Dede Farmer, McKay's girl vocalist, who had been sitting in the middle of the vehicle, rose and made her way back to where the conversation had been taking place. Her blonde good looks and friendly smile warmed Marty's heart, as she reached over and put a hand on his shoulder. When she spoke, however, Dede was "one of the boys," and she could outswear any male member of the band.

"Sherm," she said to the trumpet player, looking directly into Marty's eyes, her voice soft, her manner sweet. "You are completely full of shit! I haven't heard Marty sing either, but I'll bet you a week's salary he's a winner!"

Marty had heard women, his mother included, use vulgar language before and had found it unpleasant. But somehow, he was amused by Dede's offhand use of the crude expression. Perhaps, he thought, it was because of her college-girl appearance.

"Well, come on, man," Cisco now goaded Becker. "Take her up on it. Put your money where your mouth is."

"Yeah," joined in Milt Engle, the band's pianist, who sat alongside Contreras. "You say he's a loser. When the hell did Tex ever pick a loser?" Many of the sidemen called McKay "Tex." "I think he's a winner, like Dede says. And I'll back my hunch with some geets too, just to make life interesting."

Braced, Becker could only grouse and squirm out of the challenge. Who the hell knew what this punk kid sang like? He lapsed into silence and immersed himself in *Down Beat*.

Dede grinned at Marty, winked, and made her way back to her seat on the swaying Greyhound.

During the ride to Denver, the band's first ballroom date on its way east, Marty and Milt Engle huddled on the existing arrangements for the male vocalist slot. Marty felt strange, going over vocal sheets that had the name "Denny Mason" printed in bold, black ink strokes in the upper left-hand corners.

As the bus headed up into the Rockies, the temperature grew chillier. Outside, all was stygian darkness. Marty opened his eyes just as sunlight peeked over the rim of a summit, announcing the dawn. In the seat directly in front of him, a brown face, wiry black hair, a broken-at-one-time nose, and a mouth tenanted by large, irregular, yellow-ivory teeth greeted him.

"Hey, now. What's shakin'?" came the slightly hoarse query, whistling through the large space between the twin central incisors.

Marty rubbed his eyes and sat up straighter.

"What'd you say?"

The mouth grinned broadly.

"I axed you 'What's shakin'?' And you supposed to answer: 'Ain't nothin' shakin' but the bacon and that's taken,' dig?"

It was Marty's turn to grin. "I dig."

A hand was proffered in Marty's direction. "Bitsy Munro."

Marty smiled and shook hands. "I know. I sure like your playing."

Bitsy looked at him sideways. "Yeah? You ain't jivin'?"

"No, I'm not—I ain't jivin'. I must've played your record of 'It's the Drummer in Me' till I wore it out."

"Oh, man," said Bitsy, embarrassed. "It ain't my record. It's Wiley's. I just play on it."

"But you're featured. It's a great drum solo."

Bitsy beamed. "Aw, shoot. I don' know why Wiley makes me play them solos. Drums is meant to keep time, hold the band together, you know? Ain't but a handful o' cats have anything to say when it comes to solos, anyways."

Bitsy held onto the seatback, bracing himself against the

roll of the moving vehicle, too shy to intrude upon Marty by sitting down next to him, uninvited. Munro was the only Negro member of the McKay aggregation, tiny, with slightly hunched shoulders, and strong, supple hands, and a habit of covering his gap-toothed mouth self-consciously when he laughed or grinned.

Benny Goodman and others had pioneered hiring talented black musicians. Yet, in 1941, it still took courage on the part of any bandleader to allow a colored musician to sit among the sea of white faces on the bandstand, especially in the South. Wiley had aborted several lucrative Southern dates because club owners objected to the inclusion of Munro on the band's roster.

McKay did not care. Bitsy was worth it.

Wafer-thin, he exhibited a driving force that was astounding once he seated himself behind his drums. If Wiley was the dynamite, Bitsy was the detonator, and together they sparkplugged the band.

Marty indicated the empty seat next to him. "Have a seat, Bitsy."

Bitsy, looking grateful for the invitation, came around and joined him.

"What drummers?" asked Marty.

"Huh?"

"You said there were only a few drummers who can play solos."

"Oh yeah. Well, like I said, they's some cats that er—uh, got a whole lot of chops, don't you know. And when I hear them play solos, then I know how, er—uh, bad I really play."

Was Munro putting him on? Marty looked closely at the little drummer. He did not think so. Was it possible Bitsy did not know how great he was?

Bitsy was warming to the subject. "Now you take Chick Webb. You ever heard of him?"

"Are you kidding? 'Liza.' 'Whacky Dust.' 'Spinnin' the Webb'?"

Bitsy laughed delightedly, covering his mouth with his hand. He held his other hand out to Marty, palm up.

"Hey, man. Gimme some skin!"

Marty slapped his hand in the popular fashion.

"Well, er—uh, you know, he died a while back but, man, he could play some drums. I mean he played 'breaks' like Ella sings. Like melodies."

"Yeah. You're right. I never thought of that."

"You know, he was no bigger than me, 'cept that he had a humpback."

"Who else?"

"Well, then there's—Hey, man. You sure this don't bore you?"

"Bores the shit outta me," commented Sherm Becker across the aisle.

Bitsy waited for Marty to answer.

"No, I'm interested in your opinion."

The young drummer looked pleased. This new ofay singer was all right!

"Well, like I was gonna say, there's Jimmy Crawford with Lunceford, plays great press rolls and er—uh, Sid Catlett with Louis, and lemme see. Oh yeah, Cozy Cole with Cab, 'cept his solos are kinda stiff, ya know?"

"So far you've only mentioned colored drummers," Marty interrupted, hoping the comment would not offend Bitsy. "How about Gene Krupa?"

"Oh, he's a champ," said Bitsy earnestly. "He just like Chick. I mean, they started a whole lot of stuff that everybody copies now. Course, they's one cat makes all the rest look sick."

"Who's that?"

"Buddy Rich. With Dorsey. He's a killer! Better'n Chick. Better'n Gene. And a whole lot better'n me. I mean, er—uh, that cat's a whatchamacallit—a genius!"

Diplomatically, Marty said, "Oh, he's tremendous. No way around that. But I think you're every bit as good, if not better."

"Well, man, you gonna get a chance to see for yourself." Marty thought Bitsy's voice quivered just a little.

"What do you mean?"

"Aw, ol' Wiley's gone and arranged a 'Battle of Bands'

162

between us and Dorsey while we're in New York. Man, I get sick just thinkin' about it. Buddy gonna wipe up the floor with me that night."

"I'll bet you'll more than hold your own."

Bitsy shook his head.

"Ain't no way. Ain't no way."

The band played the first set of the evening at Elitch's Gardens and neither Dede nor Marty had gotten to the microphone. Wiley called a gently swinging, rather subdued group of instrumentals as the ballroom slowly filled, first to capacity and then to overflowing.

Now the second set of the evening was in progress. Dede Farmer made her way to the microphone and sang "Could Be" to the delight of the crowd who had heard and loved her recording of the tune, a record which was currently in great favor on most of the jukeboxes all over the country. Wiley then unleashed his Texas Trombone and, as the mass of young faces beamed up at him, he introduced a new *tour de force* called "Concerto for Trombone" that left the multitude limp with stamping, whistling, clapping, and cheering.

Marty felt uncomfortable, sitting next to Dede, aware of the curious eyes of several members of the audience, all fans of Denny Mason, resentful of this usurper. Could he even sing? Why didn't Wiley McKay bring him forward so the Mason cultists could hear him and judge for themselves? (Although, for God's sake, how good could he be? There was, after all, only one Denny Mason. Poor, stupid Wiley McKay, letting Denny get away from him!)

When the second set ended, Marty had still not yet sung a single note.

Backstage, during intermission, he avoided everyone's gaze, particularly Sherm Becker's smarmy looks. Bitsy came up to him and patted him gently on the arm. "Stay cool, Marty. He gonna let you sing for sure this next set."

"I don't know. Maybe he's changed his mind about me."

"Don't be silly, Marty," Dede said. "I know Wiley. Shit! He's just waiting for the right time. It's showmanship, that's all." She smiled and moved away.

Milt Engle was back on the stand before anyone, plunking

his usual chime chords to indicate the intermission was ended. The band filed back onto the stand.

Wiley was the last to return to the bandstand, and the huge throng of youngsters standing twenty deep against the rim of the stage greeted him with a roar. He waved in gratitude, his lanky frame clothed in a powder blue, Western-cut suit, stitched pockets, hand-tooled cowboy boots and all. The kids loved it.

He leaned over the saxophone section and communicated something to the band. Then he turned and walked to the mike.

"Guys and gals," he drawled. "We'd like to start this here set by introducing you to our latest recruit, a young feller who hails from out California way and who has a real big future as a singer."

There was a perceptible rumbling in the room. Here, finally, was the upstart who foolishly thought he could supplant Denny Mason.

"I know," continued McKay, over the slight hubbub, "that you nice folks here in Denver are gonna give a real friendly Rocky Mountain welcome to my brand new buddy—MARTY WYNNER!"

The crowd applauded as Marty, stunned, rose and made his way toward center stage. Marty WYNNER? Had Wiley forgotten his name? The tall trombonist gave the downbeat for "Chicago," one of Denny Mason's best-known vocals, and, as the McKay band's newest addition prepared to sing it, Wiley leaned over and whispered in his ear.

"I agree with Dede and Milt, boy. I think you're a winner. But we'll spell it with a 'y' just so you don't forget who you are. Okay?"

Marty could only grin and say, "Okay, Wiley."

"Right. Now show 'em what singin's all about."

Marty Wynner "showed 'em."

When he finished "Chicago," the crowd treated him to a loud and sustained round of applause, accompanied by several shrill whistles. Wiley McKay's uncanny knack of discovering new talent was still right up there! (My God, this Wynner guy's almost as good as Denny Mason—Almost?

164

Hell, he's better. He swings like Mason never could. —Denny Mason? Who's Denny Mason?)

There were, however, a few holdouts.

During the fourth and final set of the evening, as Marty was called upon to sing a current ballad, several young toughs pushed their way up against the bandstand. The ringleader bore a startling resemblance to James Cagney, his hands hooked in the belt loops of his flared, pegtop pants, unruly mop of red hair crowning a freckled, Irish mick of a face, upper lip curled back over his teeth.

Marty finished the chorus of the song, and stood waiting for the band interlude that would take him through the modulation into a slightly higher key and the final eight bars.

Irish tugged at his pantsleg.

"Hey. Where's Denny?"

Marty ignored him.

Irish tugged harder.

"You deaf or somethin', jagoff? I said, 'where's Denny Mason?'"

Marty heard his cue and began singing again.

Irish eyed his companions, and they exchanged smirks. Then the ringleader reached up and around the back of Marty's pantsleg and pinched the singer's calf as hard as he could.

Marty felt as though a red-hot poker had been inserted into a raw wound in his leg. Reflexively, his foot shot out in front of him. The toe, as though guided by a string, connected squarely with Irish's mouth, and suddenly that young man was sprawled over the dance floor, spitting teeth and blood.

Everything stopped.

Marty, in pain, shot an agonized glance at Wiley and limped off the stage. Within seconds, the security guards were on the scene. One of them escorted Irish to the manager's office in search of first aid. The other guard questioned Wiley, who explained what had happened. The guard nodded in understanding. They had had trouble with Irish and his gang before.

Wiley got the band going again, and the sprightly instrumental he chose, a crowd-pleaser full of Bitsy Munro drum breaks, diverted the dancers, most of whom did not know what had happened, so quickly had the incident taken place.

Martin Wynocki, a.k.a. Marty Wynner, had to be escorted onto the Greyhound by the two security guards, amid a great amount of pushing, shoving, yelling, and threatening from the gang of young hoodlums.

As the bus pulled away, Marty sat alone in the rear seat, pondering the vagaries of the band-singer business.

The musicians were silent for the most part. It had been a harrowing experience. Only one of them made any comment as the bus rolled out of the city limits.

"A winner, huh?" snorted Sherm Becker. "Some fuckin' winner!"

Marty sank deeper into the seat, wanting nothing so much as anonymity at that moment. Wiley had not said a word about the fracas. Was he disgusted with him? Would this be his first and last night with the band? As soon as they reached their next destination, Des Moines, would Marty receive a few dollars and a one-way ticket back to L.A.?

And now he thought about the evening. The crowd had liked him! And to sing in front of the McKay band, backed so superbly by sixteen fine musicians! Never had he been happier than in those few platinum moments on the stage of the Elitch Garden ballroom. *I don't want to be fired*, he thought. *I want to stay with this band.*

Bitsy Munro sat, looking out the window, chewing gum rhythmically.

Doc Weldon read *The Satyricon of Petronius Arbiter.*

Wes Williamson, Dave Schindler, and Chuck Lindell played cards.

Dave Rasmussen watched them, thinking to himself: Isn't it funny how saxophone players stick together.

Dede Farmer slept, her head rolling from side to side with the movement of the bus.

Gordon Read and Vern Sales played chess.

Sherm Becker ogled the naked girls in a magazine he had bought that afternoon in downtown Denver.

Wiley McKay sat in the front seat of the bus, opposite

Mack, the driver, getting quietly drunk, as was his custom every single night. He thought about the newly named Marty Wynner. He realized the kid had been a victim of reflex action, that he had involuntarily kicked out at his tormentor. Weren't no big thing. Lots worse had happened on the road. And the young man could sing his ass off! He raised the pint of Early Times to his lips and took a long, satisfying pull.

Chapter

24

Now began the most exciting time of Marty Wynner's young life.

From Denver the band traveled in a jagged line eastward—the Val Air in Des Moines, a prom at Kansas State University, St. Louis and the Tune Town Ballroom, a week at the Riverside in Milwaukee, Hennepin's Orpheum in Minneapolis, the Circle in Indianapolis. They broke records at the Stanley Theater in Pittsburgh and the Earle in Philly. After several college dates in New Jersey, a date at the Adams Theater in Newark was made memorable by an audience of young toughs who catcalled and hooted throughout most of the shows.

Marty: learning new songs, gaining confidence, making friends within the band (and at least one enemy, Sherm Becker); in awe of the band's soloists; moved by the power of the combined brass section, the fluid grace of the saxes, the relentless drive of the rhythm section, with Bitsy creating a surging pulse that never let down; feeling new respect each evening for his singing female counterpart as, more and more, he came to realize how perfect were her intonation, phrasing, and concept, even with the most inane melodies, the most banal lyrics; openly amazed at Wiley McKay's skill with a trombone.

o

New York City. The fabled island from which emanated the music that had shaped his childhood, nurtured his ambitions, aroused his dreams. The Blue Room of the Lincoln, the Café Rouge of the Pennsylvania, the Strand, the Paramount. Fifty-Second Street with the Onyx and the Famous Door and the Hickory House and the Three Deuces, they were all here, in Babylon.

The band checked into the Forrest, and Marty spent his days ingesting Radio City, Rockefeller Center, Broadway and 42nd Street, Lindy's, Jack Dempsey's, the Brill Building, home of all the music publishers. At night, he and Bitsy traveled to Harlem: to Dickie Wells and Minton's and the Savoy and the Cotton Club and the Apollo. Everywhere they went, Bitsy was greeted with enthusiasm and, because Marty accompanied him, he was immediately accepted.

In the four evenings he had off before the McKay band opened at the Café Rouge, Marty Wynner met many of his heroes: Count Basie, Coleman Hawkins, Barney Bigard, Andy Kirk, Al Cooper, Benny Goodman, Bunny Berigan, and countless others who were either visiting Harlem to listen and perhaps sit in or actually appearing there.

Marty assimilated a great deal in those few days. The night before they opened at the Pennsylvania, Bitsy again led him uptown, this time to hear Billie Holliday.

He sat in the hushed room, listening to the diamondlike notes, shaped by hard times. She wore a white, low-cut dress, and a gardenia in her blue-black glistening hair; and Marty thought, as she sang "Loveless Love" that, next to his mother, she was the most beautiful woman he had ever seen.

Riding back to the Forrest in a cab, he could only shake his head in wonder. Bitsy laughed and pounded him on the arm.

"S'matter, baby? Somethin' you ate?"

"Hell, no, Little Bit, something I heard. Christ, she's fantastic. I feel—I don't know—excited and depressed at the same time."

169

"I don't dig you."

"She's an inspiration. I wouldn't have missed hearing her sing for anything. But it depresses me to think I'll never be anywhere near that good."

Bitsy put his arm on Marty's shoulder.

"Hey, man," he said seriously. "You damn close to bein' as good as Billie."

"Aw, come on, Bits."

"I ain't no shucker. Man, you got somethin' rare, dig? You been with the band how long now? 'Bout four months? And all them cats and chicks that er—uh, hated you for takin' Denny's place—why, shoot, man, they forgotten all about him. That's 'cause you special. I mean it. Man, you a real *jazz* singer. And that's the truth!"

Marty looked glum. "I wish I believed it."

"Shoot, man, I'm gonna prove it to you, once and for all. You'll see."

o

The McKay orchestra's opening at the Café Rouge came within twenty patrons of breaking Glenn Miller's record. Marty sang several numbers with the band, including "Chicago," on the remote broadcast at 11:30, and the evening for him was hugely exciting. By the time the weekend rolled around, the customers and fans in attendance had clasped Marty Wynner to their collective bosoms.

On the band's off night, Sunday, Bitsy, like a tiny Pied Piper, led Marty once again into Harlem, beelining for the Chez where Lady Day was appearing. Marty seated himself at a small table while Bitsy disappeared for a moment. He returned to the table just as Billie went on and Marty, for the second time in seven days, listened in jaw-opened wonder.

"Fine and Mellow," "As Long As I Live," "Any Old Time," and the bitter litany of "Strange Fruit," all were haunting, pungently exhilarating. She stood, regally beautiful, barely moving, the familiar gardenia in her severely combed-back hair, her full lips framing the words, her body swaying almost imperceptibly to the rhythmic patterns laid down by the drums, bass, and piano.

170

Near the end of her performance, she paused.

"Ladies and gentlemen," she said, in that strange, husky speaking voice, "We have with us, tonight, a young man who is creating quite a sensation downtown at the Pennsylvania Hotel." Several people, having seen Bitsy enter the club, applauded. A few yelled, "Yeah, Bitsy. Git 'im up to play!"

Billie waved her hand for silence. "I'm talkin' 'bout a new guy who, they tell me, is a fine singer. Now, you know, I never get to go anyplace because the boss here is such a *slave* driver." (Hoots and catcalls.)

"Anyways, I guess the only way I'm goin' to get to hear this man is right here and now. His name's Marty Wynner. Let's get him up."

The audience clapped as Marty, in a daze, rose. Oh, Jesus, God. To sing in the presence of Billie. His throat felt dry and he was certain he would not be able to produce a single creditable note.

The crowd quieted as Marty approached the microphone and Lady Day. She put her arm around his waist.

"You're not half bad-lookin', baby. For an ofay." The audience laughed appreciatively. "Now if you sing as good as you look—"

"He does, Billie," yelled Bitsy.

"How 'bout it, stud?"

Marty found his voice. "You'll have to decide that for yourself, Miss Holliday."

Billie laughed. "*You* may call me 'Lady,' good-lookin'."

From behind the periphery of small spotlights that ringed the ceiling over the stage, someone suggested, "Hey, Billie, get him to sing 'Chicago.'"

"Good as any," replied Billie. She squeezed Marty's waist and said, "I'll be listenin'." Then she walked to the sidelines and sat at an empty table.

Marty peered at Bitsy, shading his eyes with his hand. "I'd sure feel a lot better if you'd come up here and help me out, Little Bit."

The crowd agreed and, shyly, Bitsy stood and made his way

171

to the stand. Someone yelled, "Hey, Bits, sing it with 'im."
And before Bitsy could demur, the musicians improvised an
intro to the song.

Marty began to sing. Very simply, no frills. As he came to
the middle of the first chorus, Bitsy interjected a "scat" fill
that brought cries of approval from the audience. Marty,
relaxing, continued, his phrasing looser, extending word
patterns, falling behind the meter of the song, then catching
up in time to end a couplet perfectly. Now the trio of
musicians moved into a higher key, and Bitsy sang the
melody in a style strongly influenced by Louis Armstrong.
Marty darted in and out, between phrases, singing his own
brand of improvisation. He had never "scatted" before, but
had always wanted to try. His style was reminiscent of "Bon
Bon" with a touch of Leo Watson and a soupçon of Ella
thrown in for good measure.

At the end of the second chorus, the crowd shouted and
stamped. Bitsy turned to Marty with a wide grin and held
both his palms, facing upward, toward him. Marty slapped
them stingingly. Someone shouted: "Put it in yo' pocket and
lock it!" and Bitsy jammed both his hands in his pockets to
the customers' delight.

Suddenly, there was Billie between them, smiling at Marty.

"You're right, Bitsy. This here man's a killer! You think we
could make like the Andrews Sisters?"

The audience approval was deafening. The pianist modulated into Billie's key, and now it was her turn to sing
"Chicago" in long, strung-out phrases, as Marty and Bitsy
sang riffs, like a saxophone section, behind her. When
they came to the last eight bars, Marty and Bitsy jumped
into melody with Billie, and when they came to the end of
that chorus, the crowd screamed, "One more," so loudly
that Billie nodded and again the pianist took them up a
key.

For the final chorus, all three of them sang their own
personal versions of the song, all uniquely different, all
dovetailing beautifully. When it was over, the crowd was on
its feet and cheering.

Billie kissed the blushing Marty full on the lips and said in his ear, "Baby, you're welcome uptown anytime."

That night, Marty Wynner had trouble getting to sleep; his mind simply would not turn off. He had sung with Billie Holliday! God damn! At that moment, he was certain he would never be happier.

Chapter

25

Roseland was jammed for the Battle of the Bands between Wiley McKay's orchestra and the Tommy Dorsey crew. Eager patrons of all ages had laid claim to their dance-floor turf the moment the door of the famous ballroom had opened. On hand were critics, press agents, record company executives, and musicians all savoring the double-barreled event in store.

The plan for the evening was five sets, two each for the rival orchestras, then a final joint set in which everyone would participate. The Dorsey band started the evening with a roar. The trombone-playing leader dispensed with his usual moderately swinging opener, and rocked the place with "Hallelujah," with Ziggy Elman reaching for high notes that threatened to break the revolving mirror-ball in the center of the dance-floor ceiling, and Buddy Rich driving the band on drums. Dorsey extended the final chord as Rich underscored it with a snare-drum-mauling burst of triplets. When he finally bashed a cymbal in termination, the crowd went berserk. Dorsey, normally a master of pacing, then called another ear-breaker, "Swing High." Again the fans applauded their approval. Throughout the forty-five-minute set, only two ballads were played, one a Frank Sinatra vocal, the other a standard sung by Jo Stafford.

Backstage, listening to the first Dorsey go-round, Wiley commented to Tom Rockwell, his agent, "Ol Tommy's trying' to wear 'em out 'fore we git on the stand."

Wiley stood leaning against a wall, a pint of bourbon in one hand, his gran'pappy's six-shooter in the other.

"Tex," said Rockwell, "you shouldn't bring that gun into New York with you. We got the Sullivan Law here. If the cops catch you with it, they're going to lock you up and throw away the key."

Wiley drank from the bottle, a long, gurgling belt. "Don't worry about it," he said.

The Dorsey band ended its set with "Hawaiian War Chant," which featured a center duet by the redoubtable Ziggy Elman and the dynamic Buddy Rich. And again, the extended ending with Rich supplying a barrage of rim-shotted triplets, concluded by a cymbal-snare-drum-bass-drum explosion. The cheering lasted for nearly a minute.

Tommy went backstage to say hello to Wiley. As they shook hands, the Sentimental Gentleman's wry grin seemed to say, "All right, Tex. Top that!"

The McKay band's first appearance on the stand drew cheers only slightly less vociferous than the initial Dorsey reception. Wiley called the first tune.

A ballad?

Was McKay losing his marbles? The band should have come out roaring, as Dorsey had done. Instead, Marty Wynner stepped up to the mike and sang "I Didn't Know What Time It Was." The arrangement, an intricate one, required attention from the listeners, and Marty sang against the complex Eddie Sauter backgrounds with taste and understanding. When the song ended, there were no whistles, no shouts; just good, strong, long-lasting applause.

Next McKay called for Dede Farmer, who sang a moderately tempoed novelty tune in her usual fetching style. She was treated to noisy handclapping at the finish.

Tom Rockwell, watching from the side of the bandstand,

nodded to himself. The audience had spent itself emotionally and physically on the Dorsey side of the ledger. The lanky Texas Trombone was giving them breathing room.

After the third tune, a Lunceford-like treatment of "Show Me the Way to Go Home," with a memorable solo by McKay himself, the large mob of devotees whistled with delight. The tempos began to accelerate. A recent addition to the McKay library, "The Duel," featuring several tenor sax choruses by Wes Williamson and Dave Schindler, was followed by a rhythmic pastiche titled "Little Bit" that not only spotlighted Bitsy on the vocal and the drums, but showcased the little drummer's tap dancing. Even the jitterbugs gave up their gyrations to cheer along with the rest of the audience.

Wiley then summoned Marty to the microphone to do "Chicago" with a newly scored four-way trumpet interlude that added fresh excitement to an already outstanding arrangement. Marty sang the old standard superlatively, noting that Frank Sinatra was standing near the far edge of the bandstand, listening. When he sang the last note of the song, the response genuinely shook him.

Wiley ended the set with "Concerto for Trombone," playing it as he had never played it before. *McKay*, thought Tom Rockwell, *is loaded for bear tonight.* The Texan's psychology had been correct. At the end of the set, it seemed as though the crowd would never stop cheering. Tommy Dorsey good-naturedly jumped up on the stand and shook a fist in Wiley's face in mock anger, and the press photographers had a field day.

Dorsey's next group of tunes, and Wiley's subsequent ones, more than satisfied even the most discerning listeners. Finally, the moment had arrived when the two bands would play as one. Thirty-four superlative musicians, jammed together on Roseland's stand, began by playing Sy Oliver's version of "Rose Room," adjusting for volume, phrasing, intonation. Where solos were indicated, sidemen from both bands would stand and share the honors, never before having played the arrangement, yet performing with professional

176

mastery. A romping ensemble chorus in the best Oliver tradition ended the number.

Next, all of Dorsey's singers and both of Wiley's headed for center stage, music in hand, to sing something Freddy Norman had put together called, "Merely the Blues," which drew on nearly every blues lyric known. With Sinatra and Wynner and Connie Haines and Jo Stafford and Dede Farmer and the Pied Pipers, the result was sensational.

When the tumult died down, the final tune of the evening began. Sy Oliver's "Horns O' Plenty" was an up-tempoed rocker, complete with a slew of solos. Tommy Dorsey made the mistake of trying to trade eight-bar chunks on his trombone with Wiley, and was badly outclassed by the Texan.

Toward the end of the instrumental, the spotlight shone on Bitsy and Buddy, who held forth for better than eight minutes in a drum duet that was a work of art, a testing of champions: Rich, a forceful drumming machine, seemingly incapable of error, Bitsy playing with less strength but great nuance. Late in the drum challenge, Bitsy initiated a delicate press roll that was almost inaudible. Slowly he built it, with accents on the bass drum, to an open, drubbing sound resembling an airplane engine in flight. Rich joined in with his own version of the press roll and the combined effort was stunning. As if by some secret signal, the drummers broke the roll and began to play their own climactic solos, wonderfully intertwined. Tommy, on one side of the stand, and Wiley on the other, waited for the percussive climax and gave simultaneous downbeats, bringing their orchestras together for one last chorus.

And then there was sheer bedlam, an explosion of applause and cheering that lasted fully two minutes. On the stand, musicians from both bands exchanged compliments, although not much could be heard over the din. Sinatra walked across the stage to congratulate a beaming and grateful Marty Wynner, while Buddy Rich, in his pseudo-gruff manner, paid homage to a shy, happy Bitsy Munro, who nervously covered his mouth with his hand.

Afterward, there were drinks for all the band members in

the star dressing room (which Wiley had graciously surrendered to Dorsey). The noise, laughter, and conversation proved unnerving to Marty, who walked out into the ballroom as the last of the crowd moved through the exits. On the stage, both band boys were breaking down their respective orchestras, collapsing the music stands, putting away the books, dismantling the drums sets.

Marty sat off to one side, content for the moment to be quiet. He had been with the band for nearly five months and had proved his worth on several occasions. Yet, tonight had been a milestone. He (and the band) had performed under stress, competitively, and there was no doubt about the outcome: no one had come off second best. The evening had ended in a dead heat, with both orchestras and all the singers coming in for shares of glory.

He felt a tap on his shoulder and turned. A young girl, no more than seventeen, stood there in a skirt and sweater, bobby-soxed and saddle-shoed. Her honey-blonde hair cascaded around her shoulders and her pretty face wore a sober expression.

"My name's Ginny," she said. "I think you're wonderful, Mr. Wynner."

Marty laughed. "Hey, I'm not much older than you. The name's Marty."

She smiled. She had a wide mouth, hazel eyes, and budding breasts beneath the fuzzy wool of the angora pullover.

"I came here with my girl friend tonight. Her name's Wanda. We go to school together. In the Bronx. She's a Frank Sinatra fan. I was too. Till tonight. Gee, I think you're swell. Honest. You're the best singer I ever heard."

Marty could detect the Bronx accent now, and the girl's attempt to disguise it by carefully enunciating her words.

"Well, thanks, Ginny, I think Sinatra's the best there is."

"No, you are. I'm just a high-school student, so maybe my opinion doesn't count for much, but I mean it."

Marty smiled. "What can I say except thank you?"

"Well," she said, "you could say 'Let's go have a Coke somewhere!' "

"What about your girl friend?"

"We had a fight. Over you and Sinatra. She just walked away from me."

"How are you going to get home?" said Marty, looking at his watch. It was ten minutes to two.

"Oh," she said airily. "I'll manage, don't worry. Right now, I could sure use a Coke."

"Okay. I'll go in back and find you one. They're having a party and there's all kinds of things to drink."

"Tell you what," she said, as though the idea had just come to her. "Why not get us a couple of Cokes and maybe some bourbon to make them interesting and then we could go back to your hotel. You staying at the Forrest?"

"Yeah. Hey! How old are you? And how did you know I was staying at the Forrest?"

"I'll be eighteen in three weeks. And all the musicians stay at the Forrest."

Marty looked at her with new interest.

She laughed, and quite suddenly sh seemed older than her seventeen years. "I'm not a virgin, if that's what you're worried about."

That night, following some awkward moments, Marty came alive sexually for the first time. After they made love the girl leaped out of bed, ran to the bathroom, and closed the door. When the sound of running water stopped, she emerged and plopped on the bed next to him.

"I had to douche out," she explained. "Gee, don't you keep rubbers around?"

"I'm—I ran out of them."

"Do you swing with a lot of girls?"

"Enough."

"How was I?"

"Oh, you were fine."

"I thought for a while there that something was wrong. I mean, it took you such a long time to get hard."

"Yeah, well, I'm kinda tired, Ginny. It's been a pretty long evening."

"Oh, sure, I understand. Say, do you know Georgie Auld?"

"Not personally. He's a great tenor man, though."

"Next time he plays in New York, I'm going to try and meet him." Her guard was down now, the Bronx accent more pronounced. Once again, she changed the subject. "Do I give good head?"

"Oh, come on."

"No, please. I really like to suck, and I want to be good at it. Am I?"

"Look, Ginny, it's very late. Don't you think you'd better be getting home?"

She crawled over him onto the other side of the bed and drew the sheet over her nakedness. "Can't I stay? It'll be easier to go home in the morning. I mean, more buses running and stuff."

"What about your parents?"

"I told them I was sleeping over at Wanda's."

"Well, I'd like to let you stay, but I've got a roommate."

"Oh? Who?" she asked, interested.

"Bitsy Munro."

She sat up. "You room with a jig?"

"Hey, watch it! He's not a 'jig,' he's a Negro."

She wrinkled her nose in distaste. "I balled a spade about a year ago. He smelled."

"Hey, baby," said Marty angrily. "Put your clothes on and get out of here."

Without another word, Ginny dressed. As she was ready to leave, she took a pencil and a penny postcard out of her purse and wrote on it, then placed the card on the table. "That's my address and phone number," she said matter-of-factly, as though there had been no words between them. "Call me next time you're in town. If you want to, that is." She opened the door and walked out.

Jesus, thought Marty. *Seventeen years old.* Suddenly he wanted a cold glass of water and a vigorous toothbrushing. He was about to get out of bed when there came a soft knocking. He slipped on his shorts and went to the door, opening it to find Ginny standing there.

"Please, could I ask a favor? Don't be mad."

Marty sighed. "What is it?"

"Well, if you should happen to meet Georgie Auld on the road sometime, would you tell him about me and give him my phone number?"

Chapter

26

The band headed west.

It was June, the height of the prom season and, between ballrooms and college dances, life for Wiley McKay and his players was a round of bus rides, auto courts, packing and unpacking, catch-as-catch-can meals, signing autographs, and a weariness brought about by the rigors of trying to sleep in a swaying, bumping Greyhound.

Marty loved it.

He was liked by the band for his self-effacing qualities, his talent, and his willingness to use criticism to better himself. Even Sherm Becker had begun to come around. Marty felt he belonged.

He stayed in touch with his mother, writing to her weekly once he had her address. His letters were full of news about his job with the band, the people he had met on the road, the new songs he was learning. He never referred to the life they had lived in Hollywood, and he never asked her what she was doing with herself in New Mexico. The letters were signed "All the best, Martin."

After a month of back-breaking one-nighters, the band halted in Chicago for a three-week stand during most of July at the Panther Room of the Hotel Sherman. The McKay group shattered the attendance record formerly held by the Gene Krupa orchestra and generated a high level of excitement.

Marty couldn't help wondering about his father. Perhaps the old man had gone back to Poland. He had not had any contact with Joe Wynocki since 1933. But if his father were still living in Chicago, wouldn't someone see or hear Marty and let the old man know?

See or hear Marty *Wynner?* How would anyone connect Jozef Wynocki with Marty Wynner?

Marty called the Belanger steel mill and got the personnel manager on the phone.

She studied her payroll records and said, "Jozef Wynocki. Yes, here it is. Oh, I see he hasn't worked here since August of 1933. As a matter of fact, we still owe him a week's pay. Apparently, he just disappeared one day."

"I see. Thank you." He hung up and looked in the phone book. Plenty of Wynockis, but not one Joe or Jozef.

Marty tried to put the thought of his father out of his mind but it dogged him like a toothache that came and went.

During the Chicago engagement there was a decided escalation in Wiley's drinking. The band worried about it. McKay had never made any "fluffs" during working hours till recently, when, well in his cups, he had muffed several notes in key solos, once while a broadcast was in progress.

The tall Texan had gotten roaring drunk with Tommy Dorsey at the party after the Battle of the Bands and had stayed on a binge right through subsequent one-night stands. During the Sherman Hotel gig, old buddies from his youth, musicians who had played with him at the inception of his career, sought him out, took him out, kept him out till morning, drinking.

He missed appointments with columnists and critics. He'd stagger to the bathroom, look in the mirror, shudder, and root around his room for some "hair-of-the-dog." After he tossed down three fingers of Early Times, neat, his shaking would stop and he would be all right. For a while.

He followed this routine virtually every day he spent in Chicago and, by the time the second set of each evening

183

began, Wiley would be well on the way to another night of carousing. On the stand, he would nod dreamily at his young admirers.

On the next-to-closing night of the engagement, from behind the door of his seventh-floor suite in the Sherman, came a wall-rattling *bang*, followed by another explosion. Guests came running out of their rooms.

Bitsy and Marty had rooms on that floor, and it was Marty who got to McKay's suite first and pounded on the door. McKay, in his cowboy boots and undershorts, beamed when he saw Wynner and several band members behind him.

"Hey, y'all. Come on the hell in."

In one hand he held a telegram. In the other, he clutched his gran'pappy's old Colt revolver. A blue haze of powder smoke drifted through the room.

Musicians crowded into the suite. Wiley slammed the door shut, held the wire in the air, and pointed his six-gun toward the ceiling.

"Wa-hooo!" he bellowed, as he fired the gun. It sounded like an artillery piece.

George Pachmeyer advanced on Wiley, very carefully.

"Wiley," he said. "Give me the gun. Please."

Wiley's eyes narrowed. "Whoa, now, hoss. You wouldn't try to take my ol' gran'pappy's hogleg away from me?"

"No, no, Tex. Just want to keep it for you."

" 'Cause you know damn well, pardner, if anybody—" He looked around menacingly. "—ANYbody tried to take this here gun away from me, I'd—"

"No, Wiley. Nobody wants to do that. I'd just like to look at it for a minute, okay?"

Wiley squinted at George, then suddenly cocked the revolver and pointed it at Pachmeyer's breastbone. No one breathed. Then the gun wavered and Wiley, a stupid grin on his face, let the barrel fall in a little half-spin and presented the butt end to George, who carefully removed it from the bandleader's fingers.

"Be careful, Georgie boy. It's loaded," warned Wiley, his speech slurred. "Hey! I got great news!"

He held up the telegram. "See this here little goodie from

Western Union? Well, it says we're goin' out to Hollywood to make a picture. For MGM. How 'bout that! And we're gonna be the main stars, too. It's goin' to be a movie 'bout the band business. And you kin bet your ass it'll be the best damn band movie ever made."

"Hey, Wiley, that's really great," said Milt Engle. "Now how about a nice cup of hot coffee."

Wiley put one hand on Milt's shoulder. "Milton, mine boy," said the Texan in a poor imitation of a Jewish accent, "it vouldn't help!" He turned to the others. "I, gennulmen, am drunk as a skunk. Ain't no way I'm gonna play my horn tonight. Tonight, ol' Vern can play all my solos in one of my outfits. Nobody'll know the difference." Wiley threw back his head and laughed wildly. "Oh man. Won't ol' Vern love that."

They put Wiley to bed and played the evening's music without him. It was the first time ever that he had missed a performance, but not the first time he had to pay a hotel manager for the damage he had done.

o

The band closed at the Sherman Hotel without further incident and headed westward in its own private railroad car, which had been added to the Super Chief. It was late, and everyone had retired.

Wiley had smuggled a case of bourbon on board and secreted it in his drawing room. At one o'clock in the morning, he invited Fats Deidrich, Tony Sylvestri, Dave Rasmussen, and Chuck Lindell to join him and, together, they began to kill the case of Early Times. By two-thirty, they were, to a man, drunk and smitten with a case of the "sillies," their raucous laughter keeping many of the band members awake.

Wiley had a great idea. He got up and went to his lavatory, pulled down the stainless steel washbasin, took a paper cup, and filled it with water. Then, very carefully, he walked over to Lindell, who was sitting by the window, peering out into the dark vacantly, and threw the water into the alto saxophonist's face. The rest of his pals roared with laughter.

Lindell looked up at Wiley and grinned. He downed what

185

bourbon was left in his glass, slowly rose, went to the basin, and filled the glass to the brim with water. He walked back and stood in front of Tony Sylvestri, who regarded him with drooping eyes. Lindell stood there for a full ten seconds and then threw the water onto Tony's shirt, soaking him. More uncontrolled laughter, with Wiley leading it.

From out in the darkened corridor came several shouts.

"Hey, you guys! Pack it in, will ya?"

"For Christ's sake! We're trying to sleep!"

The happy drinkers paid no attention. There began a good-natured round of pushing and shoving to get to the basin. Soon the drawing room's occupants were soaked to the skin. It was getting more hilarious by the minute.

A new idea occurred to McKay. He poured himself a full glass of bourbon, made as if to drink it and, instead, doused Dave Rasmussen's head with it.

"Aha!" cried Rasmussen, following suit and dumping his nearly-full glass of whiskey directly into Fats' lap.

Fats stood up, looking miserable, and regarded his soaking crotch. He looked as though he were going to cry. The rest of his drinking companions were sick with laughter.

Once again, from the corridor, George Pachmeyer's booming voice issued, "Hey, you friggin' idiots! Have some consideration for the rest of us, will you?"

Wiley stood up and put an index finger to his lips.

"Georgie-Porgie don' like us to make noise," he stage-whispered. "Got to get his beauty sleep."

"Fuckin' pain in the ass little old lady!" grumbled Fats.

Wiley winked. "Got an idea." He sat down heavily and began removing his boots.

"Ever'body. Take off your shoes."

They all followed suit.

Wiley took the bottle next to him and filled his tumbler to the brim with bourbon. He stood and beckoned with his free hand. "Follow me, *compadres.*" Once again, he put his finger to his lips. "*Pianissimo,* fellers. We're goin' to give ol' Georgie a surprise." With exaggerated care, Wiley opened the door of his drawing room and stepped into the dark corridor, his sidemen following like cows after a bull. They

186

tiptoed past the rows of berths, hands over their mouths to keep from laughing out loud. Wiley stopped without warning and the rest of them bumped into him and each other, a chain-reaction-Keystone-Cop comic routine. The bandleader turned and whispered into Lindell's ear, "Which one is Georgie's?"

Lindell looked around stupidly, trying to distinguish the numbers on the curtains. Standing on tiptoe, he put his lips against Wiley's ear, and whispered, "I think it's number 13."

Wiley nodded and proceeded down the aisle to Lower 13. He stopped and grinned at his cohorts. Fats guffawed once, uncontrollably, before Sylvestri, right behind him, stifled him with a firmly placed palm over his mouth.

Wiley stood back and got set. He looked at his men once more, all of whom nodded "Go!" He pulled the buttoned curtains apart to reveal the horizontal form in the bunk.

"Happy New Year, hoss!" Wiley roared. He threw the contents of his glass into the berth just as the occupant turned around. Dede Farmer got the glass of bourbon full in the face. As the whiskey blinded her, she let out a horrifying scream. Lights went on, heads poked out of curtained berths. Dede was sobbing, great rending gasps shaking her body. The stinging pain of the alcohol was unbearable. "Help me," she cried. "Oh God, it burns!"

Pachmeyer was the first to reach her.

Wiley stood there, in shock, too drunk to function.

"Nice going, Wiley," said George to his employer, disgustedly.

"Aw, shit, it was an accident. We thought it was your bunk," said Fats, without a sign of contrition. Pachmeyer slammed him in the stomach and the rotund trumpet player went down.

"Shut up, you son of a bitch," roared the enraged bass trombonist. "You're lucky I don't knock your friggin' teeth out."

He reached into Dede's berth and helped her sit up.

"Take it easy, Dede. Try to open your eyes."

She tried. And screamed again. "Oh, my God! I can't see. I'm blind!"

187

"Quick," he said to Marty, who stood next to him. "Let's get her to the washroom at the end of the car."

Marty led the way, as George carried Dede into the lounge-lavatory. The band members clustered in the doorway as Pachmeyer soaked a towel in cold water, folded it and placed it across her eyes. Dede was shivering now, not so much from cold as from shock.

Pachmeyer patted her shoulder as she held the compress against her eyes.

"You'll be all right, Dede," he said, trying to soothe the frightened girl.

He looked up at Wiley, who was standing in the doorway, swaying slightly.

"George," McKay said apologetically. "It was jus' a joke. Hell, we were just funnin', and—"

"McKay," George growled. "Get the hell back to your goddam compartment and stay there or, so help me God, I'm going to beat the living shit out of you."

McKay regarded him blearily for a moment, then turned and made his way through the crowded aisle, back to his room.

"Go on, you guys," said George to the assembled men in the doorway. "Get back to bed. I'll stay with her till we reach Kansas City. We'll find her a doctor there."

Reluctantly, the bandsmen dispersed. All except Bitsy and Marty, both of whom insisted upon staying with Dede and George.

Dede, in pain, but slowly regaining her composure, reached out with her hand and found Bitsy's.

"Who's that?" she asked.

"It's Bitsy, Deed."

"Little Bit? Hey, man, what's shakin'?"

Bitsy smiled sadly. "Ain't nothin' shakin' but the bacon, and that's taken."

"Marty?" Dede called. "You still here, handsome?"

"Right beside you, beautiful."

Dede lowered herself to a prone position on the bench-seat of the lounge, keeping the cold towel pressed tightly against her eyes. No one said anything for a while.

Finally, Dede spoke. "I will be all right, won't I, guys? I mean, I will be able to see. Won't I?"

They were silent for a moment.

"Won't I?" she repeated, more urgently.

"Of course you will," said George. "You're just temporarily blinded by the booze. When we get into Kaycee we'll get a good eye doctor to wash your lamps out and they'll be fine."

"You wouldn't bullshit a gal, would you, George?"

"Absolutely not, Dede," he said, looking at Marty and Bitsy. "I know you're hurting, but if you could try to sleep, it would do you good."

"What time do we get into Kansas City?"

"Around two-thirty. Not too long from now."

Dede laughed.

"Jesus," she said. "I wonder if there's a market for a cute blind girl singer."

Chapter

27

Work on the movie began on August 11, just ten days after the McKay organization arrived in Hollywood.

With the band ensconced in the Hollywood Plaza Hotel, on Vine near Hollywood Boulevard, they would all rise daily at 6:30 a.m., and be in the bus by 7:30, rolling out to Culver City and the MGM lot. Slated for filming first were two instrumentals and a Dede Farmer number, to be choreographed by Nick Castle.

Dede had been examined by an ophthalmologist in Kansas City. She had had to buy extremely dark glasses and wear them day and night until she began shooting the picture, but by the time the first day of filming rolled around she was able to face the strong lights on the set without flinching. She did a great amount of God-thanking. So did the boys in the band. Especially Wiley McKay.

When they had arrived in Hollywood Wiley, who always stayed at the Knickerbocker, canceled his rooms there and moved into the Plaza with his players. Next, he rented a large double suite and called a luncheon meeting of the whole band. The spread was delectable, with a conspicuous absence of spirits on the tables. When the boys and Dede had eaten their fill, Wiley rose from his table and addressed them.

"Hey, lookee here," he began. "Speechifyin' ain't my long suit and you all know it. But, damn it, here I go makin' a speech. Well, no. More like an apology, I reckon. 'Pears like my drinkin' got way out o' hand lately. I mean, hell's bells, I got me the best bunch o' people in the whole business, and there I've been, actin' like some dumb-ass school kid havin' his first whingding with a bottle."

He paused. Pachmeyer cleared his throat. Bobby Van Allen coughed.

"Well, sir," Wiley continued, looking at Dede, "my foolish ways was nearly the cause of this little lady's blindin', and don't you think I won't thank God ever' day of my life that He seen fit to spare her eyesight. Aw hell, what's the use o' my getting windy about it."

"Git 'er said, Texas," said Dave Rasmussen, encouragingly.

"All right, then, I will," said McKay. "I quit booze. I ain't had a drink since that night on the train, and I don't aim to ever again. I mean it! If a full-growed man cain't exercise some control over hisself, then he ain't got a right to be boss over nothin', no less the best goddam band in the world!"

He looked at George Pachmeyer. "George, I may've been skunk-drunk on that Godforsaken night, but I recollect you telling me to git out o' your sight or you'd beat the livin' shit out o' me. Well, now I'm tellin' you in front of one and all—if you see me take a drink—ONE drink—ever again, you do just that. And don't go hittin' me anyplace but the mouth. I mean it! 'Cause if I ever touch a drop again, so help me God, I want my chops all busted up so's I cain't play my horn any more!"

The boys and Dede applauded, whistled, cheered, went to their leader, and patted him on the back and congratulated him. Then he said, in passing, "Only wish Marty'd been here to hear what I said."

o

As the McKay train had entered New Mexico, Marty had gone to Wiley's road manager and requested permission to detrain at Albuquerque so he could visit his mother. He knew the band had a week and a half off upon arrival in Hollywood, and he could catch a later train for California.

191

Wiley told his manager, the only person he would open his door to, that Marty's request was perfectly in order.

o

Marty looked for his mother when he got off the big, hot Trailways in Santa Fe. The late afternoon sun was subsiding as he stood, duffel bag in hand, wondering if she had received his telegram. The bus pulled away with a spewing of airbrakes and a swirling of dust, causing Marty to raise a shielding hand. Through the cloud of agitated sand, he saw a big man coming toward him. The giant smiled and held out his hand. When he spoke, his voice came from deep in his barrel chest.

"You're Marty," the man said, smiling. "I'm Clint Sonenberg."

Marty stared at him blankly.

"Clint Sonenberg," the man repeated. "Your mother sent me to get you."

"Oh," said Marty. "Where is she?"

"Out on the desert, riding a new horse. We raise 'em, you know."

We? thought Marty.

"Didn't your mother write you about me?" He pronounced his name carefully, as though Marty had not understood it the first two times.

"Well, Mr. Sonenberg, maybe. I don't remember."

Clint laughed. "Just like your mother. I'm the man she came to work for when she first arrived in Santa Fe. I'm in real estate."

"Oh, yes. Of course. I'm sorry."

"No need to be. Car's right over here."

They headed out of town, toward the setting sun, in Sonenberg's wooden-bodied station wagon. Marty marveled at the fact that the huge man's head did not break through the roof every time the car lurched over a rut in the road.

Clint Sonenberg was a robust forty-five, blond-headed, gentle-faced with a large, flat nose, eyes of pure Scandinavian blue, and the most infectious grin this side of Wiley McKay. His physique was positively Bunyanesque, with arms that threatened to burst out of his plaid cotton shirt, the chest of a bull, and the slim lower torso of a good running back.

Marty was about to speak when Sonenberg beat him to it.

192

"Your mother and I are getting married."

Marty opened his mouth and shut it again.

"No comment?" asked Clint, looking at him.

"No, sir," Marty replied. What was there to say?

"Do you approve?" Sonenberg pressed him.

"Does it matter?"

"A question with a question, eh? Okay, Marty. No. It doesn't matter. I want nothing so much as to make your mother happy. She deserves some happiness after what she's—Well, anyway, I'm glad you're here. Stay with us as long as you like."

"Thank you. I can't stay more than a few days. I've got to be in L.A. next Tuesday."

"To rejoin McKay, huh?"

"That's right."

"One hell of a trombone player, McKay. Mind you, I don't know if I put him in the same class as Teagarden. Or even Miff Mole, on one of his good days. But he's sure getting there."

Marty looked at Sonenberg in surprise. Clint laughed.

"We may be out in the boondocks but, honest to God, we have electricity, and indoor plumbing and radio and records and a few other home comforts. It's not a bad life out here at all. Done wonders for your mother. She's a changed woman."

Really? thought Marty, not believing him.

They rode in silence for a few moments. Then Clint Sonenberg said, "You see, Marty, I know everything."

Marty turned to look at the big man.

"What do you mean?"

"Your mother and I have had long talks. Sometimes until the sun came up. I know about your father. And Ernst Rauschbauer. And her other marriages. And her affairs. Marty, I know everything."

Strange, thought Marty. It wasn't like his mother to run off at the mouth to a prospective husband.

Clint grinned at him, reading his thought.

"I guess you'll have to see for yourself.

o

The Sonenberg ranch lay thirteen miles due west of Santa Fe, a complex of low, sprawling ranch houses, corrals, and covered stables. Dozens of horses milled about inside the main corral. In a smaller enclosure, two cowhands in checkered shirts and leather chaps had looped their lariats around the neck of a magnificent dun-colored stallion, and were speaking softly to the bewildered animal, calming him, gentling him. In the distance a dust cloud could be seen, several working hands rounding up strays. A few Mexicans busied themselves hanging a new gate on what appeared to be a stock pen. The chimneys of both the main house and the bunkhouse poured forth smoke, a sign of approaching dinnertime.

As they pulled up to the house, a large white adobe structure with red-tiled roofing fashioned in the manner of a Mexican *hacienda*, Clint said with a touch of pride, "We raise Arabians here. Some of the best in the world. Started out as a hobby, but it got so damn big and time-consuming, I had to hire a fella to run my real-estate business for me. And believe me, it's doing all right. Santa Fe's booming. If we keep out of this war and things stay reasonably normal, why, you're going to see—"

Clint grinned self-consciously. "Hell, I do go on sometimes."

Marty followed Clint into the house. The walls were hung with colorful Indian tapestries, and the floors were devoid of rugs, dark hardwood and hand-pegged. The ceiling of the main room sported large, rough-hewn beams, and the furniture that graced the large central living room-dining area had been selected for comfort rather than show. Marty thought of his mother's house on Miller Drive back in Hollywood, with its super-feminine decor, and it occurred to him that if she was living comfortably in a house such as this, she must be a changed woman indeed.

Clint indicated a passageway off the main room. "Your room's right down that hall. Why don't you settle in and I'll find out when dinner'll be ready."

Marty entered a comfortably decorated bedroom, free of frills yet warm and inviting. The bed and walls were covered with Navajo blankets. Off to one side was a modern bathroom with a tub-shower combination. Marty suddenly felt tired and dirty. He slipped off his clothes, went to the

194

tub, and turned on the hot water tap. He soaked for the best part of half an hour, then dried off, and permitted himself the luxury of lying down on the old-fashioned brass bed. Within minutes he was sleeping.

And dreaming.

He was seated in a theater. Alone. Empty seats and usherless aisles. Before him hung a wide silver screen. Blank. Suddenly pictures began to flash upon the screen. Pictures of his mother. Pictures he had never seen but had heard about. Pictures from Acapulco. His mother, naked, involved in a variety of sexual positions with a variety of partners. Enjoying it. Reveling in it. He strained to turn away, to avoid watching. Something held him fast, immobile. The photographs, blown up to theater-screen size, were horrible, stupefying, morbidly fascinating. Again he tried to tear his eyes away. He attempted to rise from his seat and run. To no avail. His subconscious kept producing picture after picture upon the big screen, in rapidly increasing succession. Soon they were just a blur, as if the loop in the projector had slipped and the film was running free and aimlessly through the gate. *I want this to stop,* he thought. *I want it to stop right now.* Still his eyes remained glued to the screen. The images fused: a flash of breast, a glimpse of thigh, the impression of a penis being thrust into—

o

Marty wakened sweatily. He lay naked on the bed. A sheet had been pulled over his body, and under it he was aware of a painful erection. The room was dark and, as he adjusted his eyes, he became aware of a figure standing near the bed, in silhouette, framed by the light coming from the hallway, beyond the open door of his room.

"Hello, Martin," said Mary Frances.

He sat up in bed and strained to make out her features. She was dressed in a long white terrycloth robe. Marty suddenly felt cold. He shivered.

"It gets quite chilly here in the evening," she said.

"How long have I been—"

"About an hour. I hated to wake you but dinner's ready now. Are you hungry?"

He thought about it. "I could eat."

195

She made no attempt to kiss or embrace him, merely stood there looking at him.

"I'm sorry I couldn't meet you in town, but—"

"It's all right."

"It's good to have you here, Martin. I must change. See you in a few minutes."

Marty dressed and pondered his mother's greeting. He had not seen her in well over six months. She had greeted him not as a sorely missed son, but as a guest in the house. He thought about Clint's words earlier: *Your mother's a changed woman.*

Marty doubted it.

He was, therefore, rather startled to see the difference in at least in her appearance, when he joined Clint and his mother at the dinner table.

She wore a simple summer print dress, white with vari-colored patterns. Her hair, dark and lustrous once again, was tied back with a white scarf. She wore no makeup whatsoever, and her face was richly tanned. Around her neck were those blue glass beads. Marty remembered when she had worn them on the train going out to Hollywood.

"You're looking well, Martin," she said, interrupting his thoughts. "Life on the road seems to agree with you."

"It does," he replied.

"Are you happy?"

He thought about it. "Yes. I am. Are you?" he asked, shooting a look at Clint, who sat eating his soup slowly.

"I've never been happier in my life," she said with some conviction. "I love New Mexico. I love raising horses." She reached out and placed her hand on Clint's. "I love Clint." She patted his hand (rather patronizingly, Marty thought). "We're getting married soon."

Marty sipped his soup. "That's nice," he said, not looking at her.

"Well, Clinton, what do you think of my big boy?" she asked.

"I think," said Clint without abrasiveness, "that your big boy is a man, Mary Frances. An adult making his way in the world and doing a damn good job of it apparently. I think he probably resents being talked down to. And," he added, "I think maybe he resents me just a little bit. Guess I don't blame him much."

Mary Frances actually blushed. "Well, Clinton is nothing if not direct."

Marty looked at Clint. "I like that. And, just to get the record straight, I don't resent you, Clint."

" 'Preciate that, Marty. I'd like us to be friends."

"How long can you stay, Martin?" asked Mary Frances.

"Like I said in my telegram, just a few days. The band begins shooting a picture next week and I've got to report for work Tuesday."

Mary Frances fingered the glass beads at her throat. "Shooting a picture," she said thoughtfully. "I haven't thought about movies or Hollywood in—Do you know how long it's been since I've even seen a movie? You won't believe it. Not since I left Hollywood. Six months! I think I'm cured!"

"And it's not as if we didn't have a movie theater in town," Clint added. "Matter of fact, until recently, there were two. I ought to know. I hold the deed on the lot one of 'em sits on. But your mother—well, she's gotten used to a different kind of life here. There's no need to escape to the movies any more. She's got her hands full running the ranch and raising horses." He looked at Mary Frances proudly. "She's developed into one hell of a horsewoman."

Marty looked at his mother. She sat, straight-backed, picking at her salad, her eyes downcast. Was Clint's evaluation of her accurate?

Mary Frances and Marty got through dinner engaging in small talk, carefully skirting the subjects of their former life in Los Angeles, her ex-husbands, Martin's father, and the events that led to Mary Frances' exodus from Hollywood.

While a stout Indian woman cleared the dining table, Clint, Marty, and Mary Frances adjourned to the veranda in front of the main house. A thin red strip of daylight underlined the darkening sky, dimly lighting the western horizon. The August stars were already in evidence, cold, white, and profuse. It was a time of the quarter moon, ivory-tinged, lifting slowly over the mountains, chasing what remained of the day. Marty surveyed the panorama thinking: How peaceful and beautiful. If his mother was merely playing at being happy in her New Mexico way of life, she was a fool.

He stood off to one side, watching, as Mary Frances shivered and Clint put an arm around her shoulders.

Sonenberg seemed like a good man. Certainly in love with Mary Frances. In *worship* seemed more accurate. Obviously, she could do no wrong as far as he was concerned. Perhaps, knowing what he knew about her past life, he was obsessed with the idea of the reconstructed "bad woman." Yes, but was his mother "reformed"? Or was she acting? Marty realized he did not care either way.

"Getting too chilly for your mom, Marty. Come on inside. I want to show you something."

Clint steered Marty toward a long, low wooden cupboard against one of the white adobe walls of the commodious living-room area. "Looks like nothing much besides a storage cupboard, right?"

Before Marty could reply, Clint opened the doors to reveal a complicated-looking radio-phonograph combination. Sitting on the base of the unit was a squat, black collection of tubes and dials. Clint reached down and flipped a switch, and the tubes slowly came to life, glowing dull orange. Marty heard a humming from above and noticed, for the first time, two enormous speakers hung at each end of the room, just below the ceiling joints.

"That," said Clint proudly, pointing to the amplifier, "and those," indicating the speakers, "are what make this the best goddam record player in New Mexico. Hell, Marty, I don't mean to brag but this just might be the best record player in the United States."

"Or even the world," added Mary Frances, seating herself on the sofa.

Was she being snide? Marty wondered.

Now Clint opened another door in the cabinet and Marty could see hundreds of records stored neatly. Clint looked at him and grinned.

"You'd never figure a big, dumb Swede horse rancher to be a music lover, would ya? Well, I am. We've spent some great evenings right here, your mother and me, listening to some of the finest recordings ever made, haven't we, dear?"

Mary Frances smiled slightly and nodded. *Yeah*, thought Marty. *I'll just bet she's loved every minute of it.* Still, she looked composed and utterly lovely, sitting there, unmoving, her hands clasped in her lap, waiting, listening, noncommittal.

"Got everything from Coon-Sanders to Lunceford. What's your pleasure?"

Clint started a fire in the fireplace and, as the logs sputtered and popped, they listened. To Duke. And Lunceford. And Goodman. And Teagarden. And Basie. And Tatum. And Django. Clint changed needles to preserve the records as well as enhance the sound. And the unit was magnificent. Under Clint's expert twisting of dials and turning of knobs, this phonograph offered a fidelity of amazing quality.

"Impressed?" asked Clint.

"I never heard anything like that in my life. It's like being there."

"It's better. All that great music, right in your own home. Perfect playback."

Marty went over to the record storage cabinet and bent to examine the records. "I'm really impressed with your collection, Clint."

Sonenberg smiled at Mary Frances, then said to Marty, "You haven't seen or heard the best part of my collection."

"There's more?"

"Oh, much more. Look," he said, pointing to a separate cabinet a few feet away from the main one. "That's where the really fine stuff is."

Mary Frances rose from the sofa. "Fellas, it's late. Maybe you two don't need your beauty sleep but I do." She went to Clint and allowed him to kiss her cheek. She turned to Marty and kissed his cheek. Her lips were cool and soft on his face.

"I've got to be up early," she said. "Stevens will be here in the morning about the stallion."

199

"Aw, for God's sake, Mary Frances. I forgot to ask you about it. Been so busy making Marty welcome. What do you think?"

"I think we should buy him. He's sound and beautiful, and he'll be a great breeder."

"You're the boss," said Clint as if he meant it.

Mary Frances smiled. "Good night, you two. Don't stay up till all hours, for heaven's sake. I'd like to take Marty out riding in the morning and show him some of the countryside."

"Don't worry. We won't be too late," Clint assured her.

o

For the next several hours Marty sat, dumfounded and enlightened, while Clint played the works of Stravinsky, Ibert, Bach, Milhaud, Rachmaninoff, Prokofiev, and Ravel. Clint Sonenberg really was a music lover, and the music he chose to play opened up a new world for the young singer. Marty felt as though, all his young life, he had been partially deaf, hearing only a fraction of what was available to be heard. That night, Clint, like some miraculous ear surgeon, unblocked his auditory senses and made him aware of the magnitude of classical music, the sheer beauty, the force, the brilliance of a symphony orchestra.

As the last crashing sounds of Ravel's "La Valse" died away, Clint turned to Marty.

"Well, what do you think?"

"I—I don't know what to say."

"You've never listened to classical music before, have you?"

"No. God, what I've been missing."

"Mind you, Marty, I love jazz as much as you do. But this kind of music—the music of the masters, I call it—sticks to my ribs a lot longer. Sort of like the difference between Chinese food and a good T-bone steak. With composers like Ravel and Stravinsky, you're not hungry an hour later."

"I see what you mean. Say, how did you get interested in classical music?"

"My mother was a pretty famous concert pianist in Sweden. I grew up listening to her practice the piano for

200

hours on end every single day. I guess I just became a lover of fine music by osmosis." Clint looked at his watch. "Jesus, your mother's going to kill me. It's nearly two o'clock."

"I'm not a bit sleepy," Marty said, stifling a yawn.

"Like hell," Clint grinned. "Look, think you can stay awake for just one more album? A short tone poem, really."

"Sure," Marty said. "Absolutely."

Clint had carefully and lovingly put each of the fragile records back in their respective cardboard sleeves once they had been played. Now he stooped low, peering into the vertical racks, searching for a specific album. He found it, brought it back to the player, and laid it on the turntable, gently placing the tone arm at the outer edge of the record. The he sat down in a chair facing Marty and watched the singer's face.

As the bittersweet strains of Delius' "On Hearing the First Cuckoo in Spring" issued quietly from the speakers, Marty realized it was the single most beautiful piece of music he had ever heard. The only other time he had been so moved was when he had first heard Duke Ellington's sad, dirgelike tribute to his dead mother, "Reminiscing in Tempo."

After the last chord of the tone poem died away, Marty, his eyes grown misty, alluded to the Ellington composition and his similar reaction.

Clint nodded in understanding. "I'm not surprised, Marty. Did you know that Duke's favorite composer is Frederick Delius?"

Marty had not known this but it made sense. Both had patently beautiful souls, he thought, and were able to translate that beauty onto music paper.

"Have you any more music by Delius?" Marty asked hopefully.

"Tons, Marty. We'd better get to bed. I love your mother dearly, but when she loses her temper, I want to be in another state. Like Vermont, for instance."

They said goodnight. Marty went to his room, undressed, and got into bed. He was tired but stimulated. As he drifted off to sleep, the haunting theme of Delius' tone poem tripped across the meadows of his mind.

o

Marty had never ridden before. His mother, on the other hand, was everything Clint had said she was on a horse: commanding, accomplished, graceful. She must have ridden hours every day for the past six months to have gotten that good, Marty thought. She led him carefully over the New Mexico topography, skirting clumps of cactus and avoiding the hillier mounds of desert sand.

Mary Frances rode a beautiful big dappled-gray gelding, her favorite mount, while Marty was astride a smaller, rangier animal his mother had chosen for sure-footedness. At one point, without warning him, Mary Frances spurred her horse from a lazy lope to a full gallop. Marty did the same, trying to keep up with her.

She turned abruptly, neck-reining the gray over a small sandy hillock and down into a chalky wash that had been a river when dinosaurs roamed New Mexico. Marty followed bravely, clutching the saddle horn. They sped along the dry riverbed, the saddles creaking, the horses blowing, Mary Frances poised and at home on the gelding, Marty grunting with every blow to his groin. Now she left the riverbed and turned into a box canyon, craggy and beautiful, with high walls of reddish rock thrusting skyward. In one well-coordinated movement, she reined in her gray and dismounted. Marty tried to imitate her and fell off his horse, skinning the palms of his hands painfully as he thrust them forward to break his descent.

Mary Frances laughed. "I hope you sing better than you ride," she said.

"You're a show-off, you know that?" he said, getting up and dusting himself off.

"Don't be angry. Are you all right?"

"Do you really care?"

"Of course, silly."

"I'm not so sure about that," he said, his anger fading slightly.

"Grouch," she said, making a face. "Wait till you see what I brought along for us. Then you'll smile."

She reached up behind her saddle and undid two leather thongs which held what looked like a carpetbag. "Come on," she said, as she led her animal over to a clump of needle pines and tethered him to a stout branch. Marty followed her and tied his horse to the same tree.

She sat down on a large, flat rock, reached into the bag, and brought out a small hamper from which she took several sandwiches and a bottle of white wine.

"*Voila!*" she cried triumphantly. "Lunch, m'lad."

She sat there, bottle raised in one hand, a sandwich in the other, daring Marty not to grin with pleasure. He smiled in spite of himself. She laughed.

"Am I forgiven?" she asked.

"All I can say is, those sandwiches better be damn good," he answered.

It was close to eleven in the morning as they sat, sipping and eating. The sandwiches were superb. Or maybe it was the fresh air and the openness of the countryside. Or seeing his mother again.

She had on chocolate-brown riding breeches with matching jodhpur boots, a yellow blouse with a thin brown overcheck, and once again she wore the blue glass beads at her throat. Her hair was tied back with a yellow ribbon and, as she bit into her turkey sandwich, flicking away a morsel that clung to her lip, she seemed content and self-possessed.

And unsurpassingly beautiful.

She read his thoughts. "I look great, don't I." It was not a question.

"Yeah. Terrific."

"Are you glad to see me?"

"Sure."

"How did you like Clint?"

"I don't know. I just met him. He seems very nice."

"He is."

"And very rich?"

"No, not very rich. Rich enough. And he'll be richer when—"

"When you're through with him?"

"As a matter of fact, yes. His business increased more than thirty percent since I went to work for him six months ago. Then, when he and I—Well, you can see he adores me. Do you know I can tell the value of an Arabian as well as any horse breeder in this state? I've become an expert, Martin. Clint knows it and respects me for it. I think he wants to marry me as much for my knowledge of horses as for my—"

She nearly said "body," but amended it to "self."

Marty nodded, without commenting.

She poured some wine into a paper cup and handed it to him. He sipped it as she asked, "And what about you? Do you like the road? Working with the band? Is my son going to be famous?"

Didn't she read his letters? Or hear about the Battle of the Bands on the news? "I *am* famous. And after this movie I'm doing with Wiley, I might just be even more famous."

"My, don't we love ourself."

"Why not? If I don't, who will?"

"Sad, little deprived boy."

"Not any more. People pay a little attention to me these days. I sign autographs when I get asked. Some girls in New York started a fan club for me. Young ladies want to get in my bed."

"Am I supposed to be shocked?"

"Why were you so cold to me last night?"

The question caught her unawares. "What do you mean?"

"Come on, Mother. You acted as though you wished I hadn't come."

Peevishly, she said, "I was afraid you might bring up unpleasant things. Unhappy memories. Martin, I won't let anything or anyone spoil what I've got here."

"Who wants to? I'm glad you're happy."

"You don't hate me? Just a little?"

"Of course I hate you a little. You left my father to sweat away his life in a steel mill. You went out night after night and left me alone. I can't recall one single evening when you and I stayed home together. I used to play a game. I would bet myself that once, just one time, you'd come home early, walk into my bedroom, and kiss me goodnight. Or sit down on the bed and talk. I lost every one of those bets while you were out with men like Rauschbauer and that creep who took you to Tijuana and your quickie husbands and all those jerks you 'dated' on your merry old way to 'B' picture stardom."

"Martin!"

"And there I was. Me. Your pain-in-the-ass kid. In the way. Except my being around never even fazed you. The Invisible Boy. How can an invisible boy be in the way?"

Mary Frances took a long drink of her wine, closing her eyes, no longer sipping daintily, but gulping it down.

"Ah, yes," she said after a bit. "Poor Martin. Saddled with this horrible mother, this—this mad seducer of men, this whore who—"

"All right, that's enough!"

"No, it isn't. Not nearly enough. You never met your grandfather, the great Thomas Maguire of Commerceville, P.A. He and his goddamned sanctimoniousness drove me out of that town when I was younger than you. He called me once from Commerceville, after he saw 'Woman of the World.' Butter wouldn't melt in his mouth. My mother had died. All was forgiven. Would I please come and visit him, he was so lonely. I said two words to him. The second word was 'you.' "

"Jesus Christ! Did you ever love *anyone*? Your mother? Me? My father? Did you ever give one good goddam about him?"

"No. I just wanted to get out of Commerceville. And he was handy. We had absolutely nothing in common. He was no more than a—a *coal miner*. I wanted to make something of myself, to be somebody. And for your information, I'm not ashamed of a single solitary thing I've ever done!"

"Really? Not even Acapulco?"

Mary Frances flushed, her eyes wide with surprise and fury. "Shut your mouth!"

She was trembling. It was the first time Martin could remember her crying. She reached into the carpetbag for a napkin and made sharp, jerking stabs at the tears that rolled down her cheeks. He said nothing.

She cried for some time, then took out a mirror and comb and set about placing herself back in order. When she finally spoke, it was in a calm, precise tone of voice.

"Well," she said, looking into her hand mirror, turning her head first this way, then that, to inspect herself. "I have certainly spawned a prime bastard. Is this the thanks I get for taking you out to Hollywood so you could start this career you're so proud of?"

"You didn't take me—you used me as your meal ticket."

"I didn't know you were that good! I took you with me because I couldn't leave you to rot in Steeltown. If I'd left you, you would have grown up to be just like your father. Is that what you wanted—to be a common laborer?"

"I'm sick of this. Let's go back."

"God damn you! Can't you see? I was the strong one. Your father was weak. I made the move. Changed our lives. And if I'd had the breaks, no, just *one* real break in Hollywood—"

"What about Rauschbauer? He gave you every opportunity to become a star."

"That's not true! He held me back!"

"Bullshit! The simple fact is, you didn't have it! Whatever the hell it takes you just plain did not have!"

Mary Frances threw the wine bottle at Marty's head. He dodged and it broke on a rock beyond him. He laughed mirthlessly.

"That's typical of your whole life. 'Mary Frances Maguire—Just missed!' "

She mounted the gelding.

"When did you say you had to be in L.A.?" she asked coldly.

"Sooner than I thought."

"Good."

"By the way . . ."

"Yes?"

"Why are you always wearing those cheap old glass beads Papa gave you?"

"I wear them," she answered, "as a reminder of the time of my life I hated the most!"

"Did you hate Uncle Billy Ballew that night—on the train going to Hollywood?"

Mary Frances spat out one rude expletive, spurred her horse, and bounded away. Marty realized there were tears on his cheeks. He did not know where he was, but he would find the way back.

Chapter

28

Marty made a lame excuse about getting out to Hollywood sooner than he had planned because he had to learn several new songs for the film, only a half-lie. Clint seemed genuinely disappointed, but his mother was clearly relieved. They both drove him into town and saw him off, Mary Frances waving cheerily, a frozen smile etching her features, as the bus pulled away from the terminal. As the big Trailways bounced out of town, he wondered whether he had been too rough on Mary Frances. He had said what had needed saying for a long time; why did he feel guilty about it? He had said it for himself and Papa.

Papa! He'd have been proud of Marty out there in that box canyon.

He wondered when he would visit his mother again. Maybe in another six months. Or maybe six years would be soon enough. Why, then, did he have a feeling of emptiness?

o

During the making of the McKay film, Marty found himself in the center of a minor social whirl. The band had its insanely enthusiastic followers, among civilians and movie stars alike, and Marty wound up attending several parties in honor of the McKay orchestra as well as a spate of studio screenings and even a première at the Carthay Circle Theatre.

He enjoyed being on the big MGM lot and rubbing elbows in the commissary with the likes of Clark Gable, Spencer Tracy, and Lana Turner. "Serenade in Swing" was finished three days over schedule, just after Halloween, and was capped by a huge cast party, to which many Metro stars were invited. Stage 22 was converted into a large ballroom with red-checkered-cloth tables and the band alternately ate, drank, and played to the delight of Lana Turner, Edward Arnold, Judy Garland, and Mickey Rooney, Hedy LaMarr, Robert Taylor, and George Murphy, among others.

Marty had his hands full with a young contract player named Mitzi Mullins, whom he had dated on and off during the past two weeks. Despite the fact that he had less than satisfied her on the studio couch in her apartment, Mitzi had decided he was "too cute for words" and that they really ought to get married. It was a relief, therefore, when somebody asked him to sing and he was able to break away from Mitzi's frequent allusions to imminent matrimony.

As he got up on the bandstand, Bitsy Munro yelled from behind his drums, "Hey, what's shakin', good buddy?"

"Ain't nothin' shakin'," answered Marty with a grimace, "but your good buddy. Mitzi Mullins keeps trying to steer me toward a minister."

"Whoo-ee! That's a bad kick! She looks like a handful!"

"I *mean!* Hey, why don't you grab hold of her? Take her off my hands?"

"Off your back, you mean. You a real pal, pal."

"No, really. That's a great idea. Bitsy and Mitzi. A match made in heaven."

Bitsy laughed and lobbed a drumstick in Marty's direction. Marty ducked and the dancers laughed. Wiley punched Marty affectionately on the arm and, as the electricians up in the catwalks dimmed the colored lights and targeted Marty in a lavender spot, he began to sing "Wait Till the Next Time Around," the ballad he had sung in the picture. Lana, dancing with Robert Taylor, smiled up at him appreciatively; Judy Garland stood in front of the stand, her hands clasped in front of her, listening dreamily; Hedy LaMarr sat at a table nearby, her coldly chiseled beauty softened by the food and the wine and the romantic music. Best of all, Mickey Rooney had seated himself at Marty's table and was engaging Mitzi Mullins in earnest conversation and she was listening intently, ignoring Marty on the stand! Thank God!

During a brief instrumental interlude in the arrangement, Marty turned and looked at Bitsy, who looked at Mickey and Mitzi. The little drummer winked and threw a drumstick into the air, waiting for it to describe two complete arcs before catching it in perfect time, without missing a beat.

Marty smiled and sang the rest of the song. It was one hell of a nice party.

o

The large, ultramodern dining and dancing facility called the Palladium had opened in Hollywood in the fall of the previous year. It had kicked off its roster of name bands with Tommy Dorsey and company and showed every sign of becoming the most popular place of its kind, outshining the Coconut Grove, which catered to older people and featured rather tame dance bands for the most part.

After a short string of one-nighters in Northern California, Wiley McKay brought his brood into the big Sunset Boulevard ballroom for a two-week stand commencing December 2nd. On the heels of much ballyhoo in the press about the band's forthcoming Metro musical, the McKay orchestra set an attendance record that stood for two years until Harry James' Music Makers broke it.

The band had never sounded so crisp, so clean, so fiery. Perhaps it was because the audience was liberally peppered with the most famous of Hollywood's leading lights every night of the week and the McKay men, flattered by the patronage of so many stars, rose to the occasion.

Maybe it was because Christmas was on the way and Wiley was always generous with bonuses during the holiday season.

Or possibly it was Wiley himself who inspired the band. He had kept his promise and stayed away from alcohol. He had been kind and thoughtful and patient and had played (and acted!) superbly during the making of the movie.

Or was it the huge crush of youthful humanity, filling the ballroom to overflowing, fighting for a place directly in front of the bandstand where they could hear and see, close up, the swingin'est band in the land and get a look at Marty Wynner? Was he really as good as Haymes and Sinatra?

While the news of the war in Europe was for the birds, there seemed to be no indication that America would become involved. From backstage Marty could see several military uniforms in the over-capacity crowd. They were peacetime soldiers, and there was something about them that Marty envied. You never saw one that looked fat or sloppily dressed. They looked like they could take care of themselves. They seemed to be mingling easily with the defense workers and college students and the would-be musicians and people in the movie industry, all with paper money jammed in their pockets. The economy was booming, the big bands were thriving, what the hell!

The crowd cheered and applauded as, at eleven-thirty on this first Saturday night in December, 1941, the band returned to the stand and Wiley McKay held up his hand for silence. Another man approached the microphone, placed one hand over his left ear and read from a script.

"From the heart of America's most glamorous city, the movie capital of the world, Hollywood, California, at the crossroads of Sunset and Vine, the Mutual Broadcasting System is proud to present the Band of the Year, the Texas Trombone himself—Wiley McKay and his orchestra!"

The crowd responded noisily as Wiley led the band into the opening strains of "A Texas Serenade." After eight bars had gone by, Wiley softened the volume of the band with a wave of his hand as the announcer continued.

"Ah, yes, boys and girls, ladies and gentlemen, from the Palladium ballroom, America's newest and most beautiful dining and dancing nitery, home of the biggest of the big-name bands, Mutual is proud to present a half hour of joyful sounds. And, folks, I wasn't kidding when I said 'Band of the Year,' because now it can be told. Wiley McKay and his famous orchestra have been named by *Swing* magazine as 1941's most popular big band! How 'bout that?"

A torrent of applauding and cheering went up. Wiley stepped to the microphone, smiling, and said "Thank you" to the crowd.

"Well, Wiley, what'll it be to start the proceedings this evening?"

"Art, I reckon we'll jes' have to kick things off with a new Freddy Norman arrangement that features a talented young man named Wynner and an equally talented youngster named Munro!"

Bitsy immediately addressed his hi-hat cymbals and the band swung into a rocking new version of "The Lonesome Road." After an instrumental chorus that featured a give-and-take bridge between Bitsy and Wiley, Marty rose and approached the mike.

The crowd clapped loudly.

As he sang, he looked out into the sea of faces, pretty young co-eds, sharply dressed youths in pegged pants and saddle shoes, men and women in service uniforms. As far as he could see, people were looking up at him, bouncing and swaying in time to the music. Marty could feel the waves of admiration and affection sweeping over the bandstand from the upturned faces in the audience. Maybe he had never been in love, he thought, but surely this was close. He responded with special vibrations of his own, to every face in the Palladium. He loved the feeling and hoped it would go on and on.

Beyond Marty's range of vision, at a table near the rear of the ballroom, an older man sat, alone, his presence there plainly incongruous. His suit was cheap, ill-fitting, shabby. His face was relaxed into a satisfied smile as he watched Marty Wynner. His hands were resting on the table, folded.

Large, thick-knuckled, covered with a fine layer of dark-blond, curly hair, these were hands that had been bruised and cut and scarred.

The hands of a coal miner.

Or a boxer.

Or a steelworker.

212

Chapter
29

The early war years for Marty were filled with the exhilaration of new fame, being applauded by enthusiastic audiences demanding more-more-more. And as those audiences were increasingly peppered by uniforms, men his age or older who were having one last good time before going off to Asia and Europe, Marty felt the guilt of not being one of *them*. The men were leaving; why was he staying behind?

Wiley got deferments for every member of the band, entreating them not to enlist. An old friend in Washington practically assured Wiley that the band would be posted to active service as a unit with the Air Corps. As a unit, that was the thing! When the Air Corps decided on Glenn Miller, Wiley's friend sought a deal with the Army, the Navy, the Marines, and the Coast Guard. In the end, all the services made other arrangements.

First one and then another key sideman slipped away, called up and shipped out. Two McKay men, feeling a bit disloyal, landed with Artie Shaw's Navy Band. It got harder and harder to stay behind. In the street, Marty thought that soldiers in uniform sometimes looked at him derisively. Older women—mothers of servicemen?—occasionally looked askance at the tall, well-built singer. Was he imagining this? In Omaha one evening, an Air Corps noncom hailed him outside the stage door. "Hey, 4-F," the man said. "Got a light?" The airman was drunk, but did that matter?

Months later, overwrought, Marty confessed his concerns to Wiley. The bandleader replied, "Hey, hoss, you are doing your job just like you would be in a defense plant. You are entertaining the servicemen, you're good for their morale!"

But their morale wasn't Marty's morale. He was the right age. He was in good health. If his number didn't come up, he had to make it come up.

"Wiley," he said, announcing the decision, "I'm off to Fort Benning."

Wiley just shook his head of hair sadly. Then he put his arms around Marty and said, "Kid, just promise me one thing."

"Sure, Wiley."

"Keep your ass down. Don't get yourself killed."

o

Marty's enlistment was under his real name, Martin Wynocki. When asked, he said he was from Commerceville, not Los Angeles. But, inevitably, some of the other trainees recognized him, and the word spread.

"Get a lot of tail in Hollywood?" they'd ask.

Or, "What was screwing Dede Farmer like?"

"Do all you band people smoke weed?"

"How does it feel to have all those gals screamin' over you?"

Marty fielded the questions with a shrug or a smile, which the men accepted as modesty.

"Come on, sing for us," they'd say.

"I'll sing when this fucking war's over," he said. They respected him for it.

At first, in basic training, Marty had a hard time of it. A tour bus is no place to get physical exercise. And the junk he'd eaten at the bus stops hadn't helped. He had to get into shape. Fortunately, he was tall and strong, and pretty soon the rigors of training had his arms and shoulders and chest looking more like his father's had in Steeltown. On the forced marches, he picked up endurance. And in the evening bull sessions, he found himself projecting a different quality than

214

he had on the bandstand. Some of the men began to look up to him. He coached several of his new-found friends who had trouble following the manuals. In field exercises, his leadership began to show. By the time he started jump training at Fort Benning, he was the kind of soldier the others didn't easily pick a fight with. Mary Frances, he thought, would never have recognized him. He had to put the memory of her out of his mind.

For a while his weak spot was marksmanship. With the M-1 rifle, his scores were so-so. With the carbine he was somewhat better. With the .45 automatic he was as lousy as everybody else. But with the Thompson submachine gun, he got the second highest score recorded at the base. You are my baby, he would think about the Thompson, stick with me.

On a weekend pass with two buddies, he ended up in a tavern in Phenix City, Alabama, crowded with B-girls, troopers, and overage drunks.

"Where're all the civilians," he asked one of his buddies.

"Screw civilians," said the soldier.

The other two ordered boilermakers. Marty settled for beer.

The smoke in the place smarted in Marty's eyes and made his throat feel raw. He thought, this is as much a part of the training as what we get all week.

He caught the dark-haired young paratrooper at the next table watching him. Finally, the drunken trooper yelled across. "Hey, ain't I seen you in the movies?"

Marty shrugged his shoulders.

"Ignore him," said his buddy.

"You are a movie star or something?" the trooper yelled. The men at his table tried to shush him unsuccessfully.

"What's your name?" he yelled.

One of Marty's buddies said, "His name's Wynocki. Why don't you shut up?"

"Wynocki my ass," the kid yelled, "he's Marty Wynner. Hey, Polack, you're the singer, aintcha? How come you're here? I thought all you faggot singers were 4-F."

Marty could feel the arteries throbbing in his head as the kid stood up, weaving. He was glad he didn't have the

Thompson in his hands, he would have blasted the kid's head off. Marty smashed the neck of his beer bottle against the side of the table, leaving a jagged-edged weapon in his hands. He saw the bartender coming toward him from one direction, the kid from the other. Then his buddies grabbed the kid by his arms. All eyes in the place were on Marty as he put the broken bottle on the table. "I'll sing at your funeral," he said to the soldier and stalked out of the tavern to the sound of whistling and stomping.

Marty waited on the sidewalk outside, blowing on his hands. His buddies came out. They clapped him on the back.

"Just a drunk kid," he said.

"Right," said a buddy.

"Asshole," said Marty, and both of his buddies laughed so hard and long, he had to laugh too, but he was faking it. He had discovered the capacity for violence in himself, and it was frightening.

o

Back in the barracks, Marty lay awake for a long time, thinking. What was he doing here, getting into booze-hall fights? What was Mary Frances's little boy doing with a broken beer bottle in his hand?

He fell asleep knowing the worst was yet to come.

o

Marty did not break an ankle in jump training, as he sometimes thought he might. He was graduated fourth in a class in which most of the fellows came from places like Steeltown. Shipping out to Europe was a relief. He was getting as far away from Chicago, and Hollywood—and New Mexico—as possible. He made corporal quickly, then sergeant, in the 101st Airborne, and he was so good at his job, his platoon leader made two concessions to him. He let him use the Thompson as his primary weapon and he didn't bug him to sing at company parties.

Chapter
30

At the beginning they would have had trouble remembering the name of Bastogne if it didn't start the same way "bastard" did. Who'd expected the Germans to launch this whole goddamn winter offensive and pull it off? Years later Marty would remember a lot about that day on the road to Foy. He had awakened to see the damn snow coming down again endlessly like a ton of bad news. That evening they had seven men fewer than had awakened when he had that morning. Including the lieutenant who had made him a sergeant.

Marty had seen it happen twenty yards ahead of him. When the machine guns opened up, they all hit the snow and rolled, some left, some right, just so they didn't get up in the same place they'd gone down. But the lieutenant must have had his mind on other things. *Roll,* Marty screamed at him inside his head, *roll.* He saw the lieutenant look over his right shoulder directly at him and then, without rolling, get up in a half crouch. The German machine gunner must have been waiting for him. *You stupid shit,* Marty wanted to yell too late, as the lieutenant caught one right in the mouth.

Cradling the Thompson in the crook of his arms, Marty crawled forward through the snow. The lieutenant was still alive when Marty, keeping close to the ground, slipped the morphine needle into his arm. Out of the corner of one eye, Marty saw somebody else start to rise and yelled, "Stay down!" and then yelled it again as a warning to all the restless men in the snow around him. When he turned back to the lieutenant, blood was coming out of his ear and it was over.

Sergeant Wynocki slipped, slid, and crawled through the snow more than a hundred yards to the woods at the rear before he felt it was safe to run. Holding onto his Thompson as if his life depended on it, he zigzagged until, breathless, he got to the shell-shattered farm building that housed the company command post.

Gulping air, he told Captain Hamilton the situation in his sector. "The medic," he said, "was one of the casualties. And the lieutenant."

"You sure?" asked Captain Hamilton.

Marty nodded.

"Ammo?" asked the Captain.

"Low."

"Which of the noncoms do you trust the most?"

"Me," said Wynocki.

Hamilton registered a laugh. "Besides you."

"The southern kid. Corporal Talman."

"Well, get your ass back there without getting it blown off and tell Talman he's in charge. If the Krauts move, tell him to start pulling back in this direction. I don't think they'll move tonight. Take a few of your men—no more than four—and head over to where the trucks are. You know where that is?"

Marty nodded.

"I want you to get a truck to battalion and load up with whatever they can spare, ammo, BAR ammo, grenades. Tell the Major we can try to stay here if our firepower is impressive. We've got to bluff the Krauts or we're dead. And Wynocki . . ."

"Yes, sir."

"As of now you're acting second lieutenant. The platoon's yours."

"Me, sir? Oh no, I'd rather not—"

"Wynocki! The Krauts are breaking our balls! You gonna stand there arguing with me?"

"No, sir."

"Good. Get out of here."

Two shells bursting nearby caused everyone in the command post to press themselves against the wall or ground.

When Captain Hamilton brushed himself off he said, "Anything else, Lieutenant?"

"Er—no, sir."

"Then get going. The password tonight is 'Carl Hubbell.'"

o

The truck rumbled along the snowy road, Battaglia and Liggett in the rear, Zimmer driving, Wynocki in the passenger seat with the Thompson. As they neared Foy, Zimmer said to Wynocki, "Hey! Wanna give those guys a lift?"

Wynocki peered through the snowflakes plastering themselves against the windshield and made out five soldiers, slogging their way toward Foy. Their leader, a master sergeant, turned when he became aware of the lights of the truck and waved his arm as a signal for the vehicle to stop. Zimmer skidded the truck to a halt.

"Let me do the talking," said Wynocki.

Battaglia stuck his head through the front flap into the cab.

"What's up? Are we there?"

"Get back in there, Battaglia, and keep quiet."

Battaglia ducked back into the truck's innards.

The Master Sergeant walked up on the passenger side and addressed Marty.

"Hi, Sarge—"

"Lieutenant. Wynocki."

"Oh. Sorry. Didn't see any bar."

"Haven't had time to get one yet."

"Uh huh. Well, Lieutenant. We are good and lost. This the way into Foy?"

"You were heading in the right direction."

"My men are awful tired, ya know. We got separated from our unit and—"

"What unit's that?"

219

"We're with the 82nd Airborne and—"

"The 82nd?" muttered Zimmer.

"What'ja say?" asked the Master Sergeant.

"I said it's a piss poor night to be walking this lousy road."

"Not much choice, soldier. We're all that's left of Able Company. Krauts cut us to pieces."

"That's rugged. Where'd this happen, Sarge?" asked Wynocki.

The Sergeant jerked his head in the direction from which Wynocki had traveled.

"Back there. Past Noville. Krauts everywhere."

"Yeah, I know."

Wynocki looked around the windshield to try and see the four other soldiers better. They stood off to the side of the road, just beyond the perimeter of the truck's light, unmoving.

"Any chance of a lift into Foy, Lieutenant?" asked the Sergeant.

"Sorry, Sergeant," replied Wynocki. "We've got seriously wounded men inside. Truck's full up."

"Oh, that's all right, sir. We wouldn't mind riding on the fenders. Or even the hood."

Wynocki studied the Sergeant, trying to make out his face in the dark and the swirling snow. He was lean, bristle-bearded, blue-eyed. He chewed gum doggedly, his jaw rotating with each grinding motion. Wynocki thought he looked like any one of thousands of dogfaces he had seen.

"All right, Sergeant," Wynocki said at last. "Have your men climb aboard in front there, on the hood and the fenders. You better come up here with me."

"Thanks, Lieutenant," said the Sergeant. He ordered his snowy band to clamber aboard, accepted the helping hand of Marty Wynocki, who pulled him up out of the snow, onto the seat.

Zimmer shifted into gear and the truck started up again.

"Sure appreciate this, sir," said the Sergeant. "My name's Wilson. Gonna try to find out how to get back to the 82nd once we get into Foy."

Zimmer could not contain himself. "Pardon me for askin', Sarge, but wasn't the 82nd diverted over to Werbomont to help stop the Krauts from gettin' to Bastogne?"

"That's right," answered the Sergeant. "But we were reinforcements, up at the last minute. We missed going with the 82nd by three hours, so we were lumped in with everybody else to defend Noville."

"Oh," said Zimmer and concentrated on keeping the truck on the treacherous road.

Sergeant Wilson turned his head slightly toward the flap in back of Wynocki's head.

"Wounded, huh?" he said. "Lot of casualties in your outfit?"

"Enough," Wynocki replied.

Wilson made as if to part the flap with his hand and look inside. Wynocki shifted his weight and blocked the move.

"Uh-uh, Sergeant," he said. "Let the poor bastards suffer in peace."

"Oh. Sure. Sorry, sir."

They inched along the road in silence for a few moments, the truck barely making steerageway at five miles per hour.

"Know what'd warm up this night a lot, Zimmer?" said Wynocki.

"No. What?"

"Some good, hot music."

"Yeah, man," said Zimmer.

"You like jazz, Sergeant?" Wynocki asked Wilson.

"Sure do, sir," answered the Sergeant. "Benny Goodman. Glenn Miller. Tommy Dorsey."

"Tommy Dorsey," said Zimmer. "Hubba hubba."

"Gee," said Wynocki. "Wonder if Carl Hubbell is still playing tenor sax with Dorsey?"

Zimmer opened his mouth, then clamped it shut. Wilson sat quietly, watching his men bounce gently on the front end of the truck.

Softly, Wynocki said, "How about it, Sarge? Hear anything about my favorite tenor man, Carl Hubbell? He still with Dorsey or did he get caught in the draft?"

The sergeant looked out into the night and said, "Dunno, sir. I think he's still with Dorsey. At least, that's the last I heard."

Wynocki's body tensed, his jaw muscles tightening. At the same time, he felt Zimmer stiffen in the driver's seat.

"How about the spade bands?"

"Come again, sir?"

"What's happening with the shines? The spooks? *Der Schvartzers?*"

"*Ach, ja, der Schvar—*"

Wynocki slammed the butt of the Thompson into "Sergeant Wilson's" gut. The man emitted an "oof" and tumbled out of the truck, shouting to the men riding on the front of the vehicle, "*Achtung, Schisse! Schisse!*"

One of the men riding the hood turned and fired his M-1 directly into the windshield, spiderwebbing the glass and killing Zimmer instantly. Marty ducked as the rifleman brought his piece around quickly and fired a round into the passenger side. The slug passed through the canvas behind him.

Battaglia poked his head through the flap.

"Hey! What the—!"

"Krauts!" barked Wynocki, as the driverless truck rolled slowly to the right. Marty tried to straighten the wheel, but Zimmer's body swayed across the seat, blocking him. Marty leaped out into the snow just as the truck lurched sickeningly into a ditch. He gained his footing, his head on a swivel, looking for "Wilson." He heard firing, muffled in the heavy snowfall, and turned to see flashes of gunfire coming from behind the truck. Running in a low crouch, his Thompson held by its pistol grip, he headed into the field beyond the ditch, where he thought he saw a figure moving rapidly.

The falling snow all but obscured his line of sight as he crunched on in pursuit of the infiltrator.

He rounded a clump of barren-branched bushes and suddenly from behind, a great weight was upon him. An arm clamped around his throat as a second arm was raised high in front of him with a dagger. He tried to block the descending knife but the Kraut was too fast and Marty suddenly felt a

222

white-hot poker sear his left side, just under his ribcage. With his right hand, he tore at the arm around his throat to no avail. He felt warm for the first time in days, then realized his own blood was supplying the warmth, soaking the left side of his body.

He saw the hand with the dagger raised again, and with all the strength that remained in his body, Marty forced himself to topple forward, at the same time twisting violently to the right. The pain was staggering, but the maneuver worked. The assailant went over Marty's back and head, crunching into the snow. Marty raised himself on all fours, panting heavily. Where the hell was the Thompson? There it was, lying in the snow a few yards to his right. He got the vague impression of sporadic machine-gun fire coming from some-where far off, behind him, back near the truck. He raised his left arm to wipe his eyes, and the pain caused him to cry out as he got to his feet. Where the hell was that son of a bitch?

Twisting around, he saw "Wilson" slowly crawling on the ground, his face contorted with pain. *He must have twisted an ankle. Or maybe broken his leg. Please God, let me be right.* But the bastard still had his knife and was turning around, trying to get up. Marty's heart pounded against his ribs as he bent for the Thompson.

The burning on the left side of his body was hurting him. His fingers closed on the Tommy gun, just as "Wilson" got to his feet, his dagger raised. *The hell with the pain and this fucking Nazi bastard. I'm not ready to die yet!*

Marty aimed his weapon in the general direction of his advancing adversary, and pulled the trigger. The last thing he remembered before losing consciousness was the gun, buck-ing in his hand, spewing ball ammunition—please God!—at the impostor.

Chapter

31

Marty opened his eyes. "Where am I?"

"Very unoriginal. I'm disappointed in you."

He lay on his back in a bed. The ceiling above him was high, its mottled yellowing plaster cracking in places. Someone near him was moaning. He could hear people walking, their footsteps echoing through the room he lay in.

"Where am I?" he said again. His own voice sounded odd to him, like a croak.

"You are at Neuilly-Sur-Seine, in a hospital just outside of Paris, sponging off the United States Army."

Marty adjusted his eyes to where the voice was coming from. At the foot of his bed stood a tall stringbean of a young man in a doctor's white coat covering what looked like Army fatigues. Around his neck dangled a stethoscope. In his hands he held a clipboard.

"Who—who are you?" Marty asked. It was difficult to talk.

"I," said the young man, "am your friendly neighborhood medic. Martin Zachariah Wiseman at your service."

Martin Wiseman was tall, nearly six feet, and skinny, weighing one-thirty dripping wet. His skin tone was light olive, that shade peculiar to certain Italians, Greeks, Arabs, and Sephardic Jews. His thick black hair defied brush and comb. There was a distinct bump in his rather large nose, and his moist brown eyes, under heavy brows, resembled a cocker spaniel's. The effect was such that several Army nurses attempted to mother him, and he was known to have taken full advantage of their succor. His success with the ladies was just short of astounding, since he always looked as though his uniforms were hand-me-downs from some distant Army relative.

"Listen—what happened?" Marty asked the doctor.

Dr. Wiseman raised his eyes to heaven. "Oh, boy. 'Where am I?' 'Who are you?' and 'What happened?' all in less than sixty seconds of conversation. It's going to be one of those days."

Marty tried to turn over in bed. The pain was stupendous.

The young doctor moved to him quickly.

"Don't do that, Sarge. Lie flat on your back. We don't want that side of yours to open up again."

Gently he straightened Marty onto his back again. Then, looking up, Marty noticed the inverted bottle of something on a high stand beside his bed, with a tube that came from the mouth of the bottle down into his right forearm, secured there with surgical tape.

"Sleep, Sergeant," said Martin Wiseman. "We'll talk later."

"Lieutenant," Wynocki muttered hoarsely. "I'm a lieutenant."

o

"How do you feel?" asked Dr. Wiseman.

"What day is it?"

"It's Tuesday."

"Tuesday the what?"

"Tuesday the eleventh."

"The eleventh? That's impossible. We didn't get to Noville until—"

"It's Tuesday, the eleventh of January. Happy 1945, Lieutenant."

"Nineteen For—I don't believe it."

"Believe it, believe it. You nearly had it, chum. You lost enough blood to satisfy Count Dracula for a month. It was touch and go there for a while."

225

"What did I lose besides blood?"

"I hope not your sense of humor."

"Come on, Doc. All I remember is being jiggled around a lot, and the pain."

"You were operated on in a field hospital in Belgium."

"Filled me full of plasma?"

"You must have had a lot of plasma at the aid station or you wouldn't have made it to the field hospital. That knife got your gut and your spleen. Your gut was sewed up, but you developed complications. There was still some internal bleeding. You were flown here for your second operation."

"You mean I've been cut twice?"

"So far."

"What the hell do you mean so far!"

"I was kidding. I hope the complications are a thing of the past."

"What about my spleen, how is it?"

"It isn't."

"Out?"

Dr. Wiseman nodded.

"What the hell do I do without a spleen?"

"You'll be all right. You don't need it."

"You're going to give me a guarantee?"

"Sure. I figure you'll live."

o

On the fifteenth of January, Marty asked Dr. Wiseman, "Did I get the Kraut?"

"How the hell would I know? It's not on your hospital record. Why don't you forget it?"

"I can't forget it."

"You've got other things to think about."

"Like what?"

"Like getting your strength back. Like recovering your voice."

"What's wrong with my voice?"

"Listen to it."

Marty had thought it sounded croaky only to himself.

"It's not going to stay like this, is it?"

"What's so important about a voice, you expecting to be a

226

politician when you go home?" Dr. Wiseman's grin turned sober. "The guy that stabbed you, did he have his arm around your throat?"

"I think so."

"Hard?"

Marty nodded.

"It'll be okay. After a bit."

"You're sure there's no permanent damage in there?"

"You want another guarantee?"

o

January eighteenth.

"I feel like sitting up."

"No dice. Not yet."

"Shit, Doc. I'm getting bed sores."

"Fill out a card and see the chaplain."

"Oh, Jesus, now who's unoriginal."

"What do you want from me? I'm a tired, overworked, underpaid Jew-boy doctor. Get me outta the frigging Medical Corps and I'll show you 'original.'"

"Look, Wiseman, please. Tell me what happened. What about the men who were with me?"

"I haven't a clue except for the word that they're giving you a medal."

"Oh, shit."

"My sentiments exactly. But who am I to argue with the Army?"

"Are you serious? A medal? For what?"

"Well, now, I suppose it's because you're a gen-u-wine, fourteen carat hero."

"That's the most ridiculous—"

A wave of pain flooded him. Fine little white sparks seemed to shoot out of his retinas, like fireworks going off behind his eyelids.

"Enough talk. Sleep," said the gangly young doctor.

o

One day Dr. Wiseman pulled a chair up to Marty's bed and leaned close to the wounded man.

"I know who you are," he said cryptically.

"Really?"

227

"Hell, yes. Your name had me stumped—Wynocki. When they first brought you in here I knew I'd seen you before. Took a while"—he tapped his forehead—"to figure out where."

Wiseman beamed and sat back in his chair.

"Well? Are you going to tell me or just sit there and sneer?" asked Wynocki.

"The Val Air in Des Moines. My hometown. With Wiley McKay. Back in—oh, I guess it was forty-one. You're Marty Wynner."

"Who?"

"C'mon. Drop the act, kid. I'm a fan of yours. I saw you again at Roseland, the night of the big band battle. You guys versus TD. Christ, what a night! I'll never forget it."

"I don't know what you're talking about."

"Hey, what's the matter with you? Ashamed?"

Marty remained silent.

Wiseman rose, his manner abruptly professional. He took Wynocki's pulse with his right hand, reading his watch at the same time.

"Okay, kiddo, you want to play games, it's fine by me. I still think you are one hell of a singer."

o

Two days later, Dr. Wiseman sat down alongside Marty's bed again.

"Do you know I have the best—and I mean the *best*—record collection in Des Moines? I shipped 'em all to New York when I went to study at Columbia. That time I saw you I was only in Des Moines for a few days, visiting my folks. My old man's a doctor. What else? So naturally, Martin had to follow in his footsteps. Tell you a secret, Marty. I have no desire to spend the rest of my life sticking needles into fat ladies' asses, swabbing throats, and writing prescriptions. Know the only reason I agreed to go to Columbia?"

"I'll bite."

" 'Cause it's in Mother Gotham, goddam it! The Big Town. Fifty-Second Street, Roseland. Shit! HARlem, man!"

"Whoopee!" Wynocki said with a grin.

"Yeah, daddy. Whoop-fuckin'-ee!" Wiseman looked

228

around suddenly to see if he had startled any of the other patients.

"So," he continued, "I packed my bags, wrote *Down Beat* to send my subscription to my new digs in Manhattan, and I was off and running."

Martin Wiseman was perhaps five years older than Martin Wynocki. At that moment, however, he was beaming like a ten-year-old.

"Do you know I can name every single member of the Lunceford band, the Basie band, the Artie Shaw band—aw, hell, just about every band there is. I've got every issue of *Swing, Metronome, Orchestra World,* and *Down Beat* ever printed, all bound and catalogued. I used to move like a hummingbird between the Meadowbrook, the Paramount, the Strand, and the Apollo, not to mention haunting the record stores every week for the latest disks."

"Yes, but do you like music?" asked Marty.

"Loathe it," said Wiseman, straight-faced.

Marty laughed.

Encouraged, Martin Wiseman rambled on. "You know, you were the only singer who really fit in with a big jazz band like McKay's. I must have seen 'Serenade in Swing' five times the first week it came out. I really dug you. I mean, beyond the singing, your acting was, I don't know—real. Believable. And then, those few records you made with the band came out and, honest to God, man, they were *so* damn good!"

"When do you think I'll be ready to get out of this prison camp?"

"You're not going to continue with this jive about not being Marty Wynner, are you?"

"You're starting to bore me, Doc."

"Talk about an ungrateful bastard! Here I minister to his every need, practically save his life single-handed, throw myself at his feet in adoring supplication, and the prick won't even give me a straight answer. God save me from *goyim.*"

"It's a tough world, all right."

o

"I think it's fate," said Martin Wiseman.

"What are you raving about now?" asked Martin Wynocki.

229

"Oh, the fact that we both have the same first name, the same initials."

"Yeah. I'm sure there aren't more than several million guys with the name 'Martin' plus a last name that begins with 'W'."

"Jesus, Wynocki, where's your sense of predestination?"

"Come on."

"No, seriously. You and me meeting, it's fate, gate! I don't want to be a doctor. I've got one life. I want to live it my way."

"And what way is that?"

"Don't laugh."

"All right."

"I want to be in show business. You're laughing."

"Christ, Wiseman, are you nuts or something?"

"I don't mean as a singer or actor or anything. I just want to be—associated with show businesss."

"That's easy. Finish your medical training after the war, move to Beverly Hills, and specialize in abortions. You'll find yourself associating with some of the biggest names in show business."

"Quit kidding."

"You quit kidding."

"I'm not, Marty. Really. Look. What are you going to do when this is all over? Rejoin McKay?"

"Maybe. Maybe not. I've got a few other ideas."

"Well, you should have. This war's going to come grinding to a halt any day now. You've got to think about your future."

"I am. Now that I know I've got one."

"Thanks to your friend and savior, the good and noble Doc Wiseman."

"Amen."

"You know, Marty, I've got a hunch about the band business. I think it's seen its best day. Now that Sinatra's busted loose from Dorsey and made it big on his own, I think solo singers are going to be the thing. Maybe I'm crazy, but I've got a feeling that Glenn Miller's death—"

"What? Glenn Miller? Dead?"

"That's right. You didn't know? In a single-engine plane from England, coming here to Paris. Plane went down in the Channel. Never found a trace of him."

"Jesus."

"Yeah. Shame, isn't it. His band's here, though. Ray McKinley's fronting it. Hey, they're going to give a concert right here at the hospital in a couple of weeks."

"Gee, I can't get over it. Glenn Miller."

They thought about it in silence for a few moments.

"Listen, Wynocki," Wiseman said suddenly. "Let me be your manager."

"Cut it out."

"I've never been more serious in my life. Goddammit! You can make it as big as Sinatra, I know it. I feel it."

"Yeah, maybe so. But I'll need a real manager to do it. Look, I'll call you when I need to have my appendix taken out, okay?"

o

On the first Saturday afternoon in February, the Glenn Miller Air Force Band arrived at the hospital for a concert. Wiseman insisted on wheeling Marty Wynocki into the large recreation hall over violent protests from the injured paratrooper. Wynocki fought a losing battle with Wiseman to make it to the rec hall under his own power.

The big room was jammed with patients, hospital personnel, and visitors. A makeshift stage comprised of several risers had been thrown together and, as the Air Force-uniformed musicians made their way onto the irregular platforms, a cheer arose from the audience.

Once the band was settled into place, the leader, tall, thin, bespectacled Ray McKinley, an excellent drummer who had once powered the old Jimmy Dorsey band and had, before the war broke out, co-led his own popular orchestra along with trombonist Will Bradley, stepped in front of the ensemble and held his hands up for silence.

"Glenn Miller," he began, "would have loved to have been here with all of you today. But as you know, that is not possible. Even though he's gone, he left us a style and a sound that will go on as long as there are musicians to play it.

We hope you like our show and we're honored to be entertaining you great guys and fine doctors and pretty nurses. And," he concluded, "that's enough outta me. Let's get on with it."

Another cheer burst the silence as McKinley moved to the drums and the band broke into "American Patrol." From then on, there was an almost constant stream of audience reaction as the large orchestra segued from "In the Mood," to "Goin' Home" and on into "Bugle Call Rag," "Poinciana," "Holiday for Strings," and "Juke Box Saturday Night."

Outside of a vocal on "Juke Box" by the Crew Chiefs, the band's vocal group, the program was devoid of singing. At one point, an amputee on a stretcher called out, "Hey! Where's the Creamer?"

The Creamer, otherwise known as Sergeant Johnny Desmond, was the prime vocalist with the Miller Air Force Band and had, thus far, been conspicuously absent.

McKinley grinned and yelled back, "He's down with the flu. Can't sing a note right now."

There was an audible groan throughout the hall. McKinley left the drums and came to stage center again.

"However," he added, "all is by no means lost. How many of you guys and gals out there are Wiley McKay fans?"

Another king-sized response filled the room. Marty Wynocki shot an over-the-shoulder glance at Wiseman, whose face wore a smug look.

"Well, sir, I've got a surprise for you. There's a patient right here in this hall who used to sing with Wiley McKay. He was making a big name for himself, too, until he joined the Hundred-and-First. Some of you know him as Lieutenant Martin Wynocki, but back in the States, he was killing the people as Marty Wynner! Where are you, Marty?"

The audience emitted a gasp of delighted surprise, followed by applause and whistles. McKinley placed the palm of his hand over his forehead horizontally, searching for the singer.

"C'mon, Lieutenant Wynner, have a heart. We need a singer."

The crowd shouted its approval.

Marty turned around in his wheelchair and barked at Wiseman, "You cute son of a bitch. Very clever."

"Temper, temper. Your public awaits."

Marty sighed, rose from his chair, and made his way to the stage. McKinley greeted him warmly with a pumping handshake, and all the men in the Miller band applauded as well. When the applause and cheering died down, McKinley said, "We never met back in the good ol' USA, but I admire your work, Marty. I've been told what you've been through and I want you to know that in addition to the U.S. Army being proud of you, everyone in the business of making music thinks you're one hell of a guy!"

Marty wanted to drop through the floor.

McKinley laughed and said, with a twinkle, "Lookee here, gang! I do believe this man is blushing."

"Give me a break, Ray," Marty muttered to the drummer.

McKinley got the message and held up his hands to quiet down the friendly laughter.

"Lieutenant," he said into the microphone, "we'd sure be happy if you'd sing something with us."

Marty now experienced his first case of genuine stage fright. Would his throat work? He imagined he was having excruciating pain in his side, that he had a sudden attack of laryngitis, and that if he did not sit down immediately, he would fall down.

He turned to Ray and said, "I'm sorry, Ray. But I haven't sung for an audience in a couple of years."

Ray grinned. "It's like riding a bicycle, Marty. Once you learn, you never forget. How about 'Serenade in Blue'?"

Wynocki nodded, mute.

Ray's downbeat set in motion the lovely quasi-classical introduction, written by Billy May years earlier. The Crew Chiefs gathered at the microphone to Marty's right and the rest of the Miller classic, arranged by Bill Finnegan, unraveled.

When the instrumental portion had ended, the vocal group sang the first line of the song:

When I hear that Serenade in Blue,

Marty answered:

I'm somewhere in another world
Alone with you.
Sharing all the joy we used to know,

And the group sang:

Many moons ago.

Strange to be singing again. There he was, on a stage, like so many others he had stood upon, performing with a superb orchestra. He had never heard the arrangement amplified with strings before, and the effect upon him was exhilarating.

When he finished, he received an ovation, led by Martin Wiseman, who put two fingers in his mouth and produced a shrill, piercing whistle. "More!" he shouted. "More," and the crowd took up the chant.

McKinley smiled and put an arm around his shoulders. "Looks like you're stuck, kid," he grinned. "They love ya!"

So Marty sang "Ida," and "Stairway to the Stars" and "Kalamazoo" and finally, "A Nightingale Sang in Berkeley Square."

Pandemonium! Doctors and nurses and those patients who could walk charged the stage, shaking his hand, smiling, shouting words of praise. He was nearly moved to tears. Never before had he experienced such a wave of—love. Of appreciation. Of respect.

Like a bicycle, McKinley had said.

Chapter

32

Marty still had intermittent periods of pain. "Just how close did that Kraut come to doing me in?" he finally asked Martin Wiseman.

"Do you want it in medical terms or should I keep it simple?"

"No frills," Wynocki implored.

"Okay, pal, it's like this. If it hadn't been cold, if you hadn't had your heavy sweater on under your good old army greatcoat, if his aim had been a little truer, just a little, mind you, if your dumb Polack luck hadn't been working overtime that night—"

"It was the luck of the Irish, Wiseman. I'm half mick."

"Don't interrupt. Like I was saying, if all the 'ifs' hadn't been 'iffing,' you would now be singing with that great orchestra in the sky. That answer your question?"

He walked the corridors and the hospital grounds with a cane to alleviate the pressure on his side. He chatted with by-now-familiar faces: orderlies, nurses, doctors, and fellow patients, many of whom had been far less lucky than he. Ever since the Glenn Miller concert, he had been addressed by one and all as Marty Wynner. No one thought of him as "Wynocki" now, and he accepted the inevitable; from that point on, the "Wynocki" side of his life was a closed book. Only once, in the next few days, was he to hear himself called "Wynocki" again.

Martin Wiseman came up to him as he was having lunch in the mess-hall. "C.O. wants to see you."

"Who?"

"The Commanding Officer of this fair institution. You're still in the Army, pal. Or had you forgotten?"

"What's he want?" asked Wynner.

"Search me."

Wiseman led him out of the mess hall and up the stairs to the second floor, past his own ward, down a long corridor jammed with fresh casualties and medical personnel, to an office at the end of the building. A sign on the door read:

Lieut. Col. G. Westerman
Commanding Officer

Wiseman opened the door and ushered Marty into an anteroom, where a prissy-looking male clerk was pecking away at a bulky old Smith-Corona. He stopped typing long enough to look up and acknowledge the presence of the two men.

"The Colonel is busy at the moment. Come back later," he said, in a surprisingly deep, masculine voice.

"The C.O. sent for this man," explained Wiseman.

The clerk looked at Marty and nodded. "Oh, yes. Lieutenant Wynocki, isn't it? I'll tell the Colonel you're here." He rose and disappeared behind a door labeled Commanding Officer. In a few moments he returned.

"The Colonel will see you now, Lieutenant," he said.

Wiseman gave Marty a little pat on the back. "Catch you later," he said and went back out into the corridor.

Colonel Westerman was in his early forties. He sat straight-backed in his chair behind a nondescript G.I. desk. The room was barren of furniture or decoration of any sort. The only picture present to relieve the monotony was one that sat on his desk, framed, presumably of his wife and child.

The Colonel was balding prematurely. He had thin lips which gave his face a perpetually grim look, and a prominent Adam's apple that bobbed up and down when he spoke.

Marty came to attention in front of the desk and saluted smartly.

"At ease, Wynocki," came the reply, along with an offhand return salute. The Colonel regarded him and said, "I believe your convalescence is just about complete, is it not, Lieutenant?"

"I feel it is complete, sir."

"Then why the cane?"

"Oh, just to keep from doing something dumb, sir."

"Yes, yes. All right."

Was the Colonel angry with him? He seemed to be locked into a constant frown. What the hell was wrong?

The Colonel now seemed at a loss for words. Before him, on his desk, was a sheaf of papers. He studied them for a moment, his brows knitted. Then he reached into the lower left-hand drawer, removed something, and laid it on the desk, alongside the papers. It was a brown-handled dagger, with a gleaming chrome blade and a swastika embedded in the hilt.

"Know what this is, Wynocki?" the Colonel asked, and Marty froze.

"I think so, sir."

"It's the knife that German stuck you with." He picked it up and felt the tip of the blade with his index finger. Marty fought to keep from turning away. The Colonel seemed to be enjoying his discomfort. *Prick!*

"Want to keep it?" the Colonel asked, his eyes narrowed slightly. "Souvenir?"

Marty had never wanted anything less, but he was determined not to show his distaste and thereby give the C.O. any satisfaction.

"Yes, sir," he said, as casually as he could. "Thank you, sir." He reached out and accepted the dagger, bringing it down to rest along his right pant leg.

The Colonel resumed studying the papers on his desk. After a minute or two, he looked up at Marty and said, "I see you list your mother as being Mary Frances Maguire. Not Wynocki?"

"No, sir. When she divorced my father she began using her maiden name again."

"Where is your father?"

"I don't know, sir. I haven't seen him since I was ten."

"Um-hmm." The Colonel hesitated, then asked, "Is your mother the same Mary Frances Maguire who appears in movies?"

"At one time she did, yes, sir."

"I want to get this straight. Mary Frances Maguire, born in Commerceville, Pennsylvania?"

"Why—yes, sir."

The Colonel rubbed his jaw reflectively, and grunted. "I'll be damned! You're *her* son."

"Yes, sir," said Marty, puzzled.

"I'm from Commerceville," the Colonel said. "Born and raised there. I worked as a delivery boy for your grandfather, Thomas Maguire. Is he still living there?"

"I guess so, sir. I've never met him."

The Colonel touched his abdomen near his left kidney. "Your grandfather kicked me once—here. Never been quite the same since."

"I'm sorry to hear that, sir."

"Your mother, when she was a young girl, growing up in Commerceville—she was very pretty. Beautiful, actually. She was my first real crush, and I think I was hers."

Marty did not know how to respond to this, so he kept silent. The Colonel did not seem to notice. He went on speaking, as though to himself.

"We had to meet in secret. Your grandfather was a stern old cuss. Strict, mean as hell. But we managed to see each other as often as we could, your mother and I. And then . . ."

"Yes, sir?"

"Your grandfather caught us."

"Caught you, sir?" Marty asked, sounding as innocent as hell, yet imagining under what circumstances the young lovers had been discovered.

"Er—yes. Found us together. He kicked me so hard, I hurt for a month!" His eyes flashed angrily as he recalled the incident. "Put her in a convent, the old bastard. Locked her away with the nuns. Mary Frances—" he smiled, reminiscing—"was high-spirited, full of life. Can't imprison someone like that."

238

"No, sir."

"I couldn't stand it. I left home. Ran away. Lied about my age and joined the Army." For the first time, the Colonel smiled the thinnest of smiles.

"Didn't mean to tell you my life story."

"I understand, sir."

The Colonel rubbed his nose brusquely, and his attitude at once grew more formal.

"Yes. Well. Enough of that. If Wiseman and Colonel Nolan concur and you are, indeed, fully recovered, I'll discharge you and make arrangements for you to go home. Would you like that?"

"Yes, sir."

The Colonel rose. He was tall, well over six feet.

"That'll be all, Lieutenant. Dismissed."

Marty snapped to attention and saluted simultaneously with the Colonel.

"Thank you, sir." He made an about-face, and reached for the door handle.

"Oh, Wynocki," said the Colonel.

"Sir?" said Marty, turning back.

"When you get back to the States, if you remember, would you give your mother regards from George Westerman of Commerceville?"

Marty's face went blank.

"I can't, sir," he said tonelessly. "She's dead."

o

Like all bad news, it had arrived with total unexpectedness. The McKay band had been playing a one-week engagement at the Missouri Theatre in St. Louis. It was July, and the city was suffering a severe hot spell. The temperature, however, did not deter Wiley McKay's fans. Nor the stream of young girls who sat through five shows a day to hear their new favorite, Marty Wynner, notwithstanding the horrendous Universal musical they had to endure again and again.

Although the personnel of the band had changed radically, McKay's popularity coupled with that of Bitsy Munro, Dede Farmer, and Marty proved to be potent box office and, as the curtain came down on each performance, cheering could be heard right through the titles of the Abbot and Costello epic unfolding with monotonous regularity every other hour or so.

Marty had gone to his dressing room to change clothes and go to dinner with Bitsy between shows. He felt some apprehension about going to the same restaurant they had patronized the previous evening. As they had sat in the booth, studying the menu, two sailors with thick Southern accents had slipped into a booth across the aisle. One of them had glanced over at the two McKay performers and the slurs began.

"Shit, Crocker. Wouldn't see that kind of thing in Alabama."

"Hell, no. Ain't no way a fuckin' nigger goin' to sit in the same restaurant as a white man, no less the same table."

"Goddam! Is this what we're fightin' for?"

At first, the insults were delivered *sotto voce*, but after a few drinks under their summer "whites," the sailors had become more insolent. Instead of covert looks at Bitsy and Marty, they took to staring boldly at them.

The little drummer was tight-lipped and perspiring. His shiny, dark face had actually gone gray. Marty wondered how much more his friend could endure before bolting from the restaurant. The words "nigger" and "white trash" were being repeated with infuriating monotony. Marty pondered the situation. There was, after all, one more performance to give that evening.

He rose and walked across to the sailors' table, a pleasant smile on his face. As he bent to talk to the servicemen, he looked positively embarrassed and apologetic. He cleared his throat as if to speak confidentially to the young Southerners. Swiftly, he grabbed the neckerchief of the one sitting on the outside of the booth. He pulled him half out of his seat and delivered a stunning blow to the side of his head that made the sailor's eyes glaze over. Before the other man could react, Marty grabbed the dazed victim of his blow by the collar with both hands and slammed the man's head directly into his shipmate's face. Blood spurted from the second sailor's nose, staining his issue blouse. He howled with pain and tried to throw a looping right hand at Marty, but the singer was

240

already out of range, having pulled back and up. Now the first man attempted to rise and do battle. Marty picked up the large glass sugar container which sat on the table and smashed it against his skull. The dispenser shattered, cutting a deep gash in the hapless Navy man's head. The man called Crocker wiped his bloody nose and tried once again to reach out for Marty with a haymaker. Marty caught his fist in his hand and held it in midair, immobile.

"Don't try it, you bigmouth redneck, or I'll twist your goddam hand off."

All conversation in the restaurant had come to an abrupt halt, and the owner, a worried-looking little Italian who catered to the bands and the stars that played the Missouri Theater on a near-weekly basis, had three of his waiters from the adjoining bar drag the sailors from their booth and escort them out into the street.

"We'll be back, you little wop bastard. Don't you worry," yelled Crocker, shaking his fist defiantly as he was ushered through the door.

Things had quickly settled back to normal, the bloody booth and table spotlessly cleaned, profuse apologies offered to Bitsy and Marty from the management. But the drummer had been badly shaken. They had skipped dinner and gone back to the theater, where Bitsy had broken down and wept out of a combination of humiliation and gratitude.

Now, Marty knocked on the door of the dressing room they shared. Munro opened the door and smiled at his best friend.

"Hey, man, what's shakin'?" he said.

"Ain't nothin' shakin' but the bacon, and if we don't hurry, all the tables next door'll be taken!" Marty said, with a laugh.

Bitsy frowned. "Next door? Oh, man. I don' know."

"Hey, Little Bit. You gonna deprive me of the only exercise I get all day? Slugging sailors?"

Bitsy grimaced. "Sheeet! I'm sick of white bastards lookin' cross-eyed at me. Makin' remarks, callin' me names. Fuckin' white pricks!"

Marty was slightly astonished. He had never before heard

241

Bitsy express himself so vehemently. "Hey, man," he said with mock belligerence. "Watch it! I'm as white as they come. Pure white. White as snow."

Bitsy flinched, and an almost tangible veil of hatred clouded his eyes. Marty thought, Oh, Jesus, I've gone too far.

Suddenly Munro grinned and said, "No, you ain't, baby. Tha's just the color of your skin. When you sing, you a nigger!"

Marty laughed and batted his eyes. "Aw, gosh. That's the nicest compliment I ever got."

Bitsy snorted. "Shucker!"

"Tha's right, baby. Solidtoody! When I sing, I'm black. Black. From my toes right on up my back."

Bitsy picked it up, laughing. "You from Hackensack?"

"Now you on the track."

Bitsy held out his hand, palm up. "Hit that jive, Jack," he sang.

Marty gave him some skin and chirped, "Put it in your pocket till I get back."

"I'm goin' downtown to see a man," Bitsy countered.

They both sang, "And I ain't got time to shake your hand."

"Hey," said Marty. "Maybe we should team up and do an act."

"Sure," said Bitsy, ruefully, slipping back to his former mood. "We'll call it 'Blackie and Whitey.' "

"Fine," smiled Marty. "If I can be 'Blackie.' "

Bitsy laughed. "Jive artist."

"Guilty! Now can we please go get some dinner before I dry up and blow away?"

They made their way downstairs, Bitsy rapping drumbeats on the handrail, Marty "scatting" some riffs from a current Lunceford record. The elderly doorman, called "Pop" by one and all, stopped Marty.

"Long-distance call for you, Mr. Wynner."

"Who from?"

"Didn't say. Left a number for you to call back." He looked at the slip of paper in his hand. "New Mexico. Santa Fe. Operator twenty-four."

Marty took the slip and thanked the doorman. Well, well,

well. Mother dear was favoring her son with a call. Why? he wondered. It wasn't his birthday, or Christmas, or even St. Patrick's Day. And it sure as hell wasn't because she missed him. Of that he was certain. Oh, well, what the hell. He and Bitsy would eat, and if he had time afterward . . .

When they returned from dinner, Pop stopped Marty again.

"They're calling again. From New Mexico. Want to take it now?"

Marty looked at the clock above Pop's little table. Twenty minutes till showtime. "All right, Pop. I'll talk to them."

Pop rose and handed the phone to Marty. Bitsy waved to him and started up the stairs to the stage level to retighten the calf heads on his drums, variable in the hot, humid weather. Marty sat on Pop's stool.

"Hello," he said into the phone. "This is Marty Wynner."

"Marty?" came the broken-voiced response.

"Who is this?" asked the singer with a slight frown.

"Marty, it's—it's Clint. Clint Sonenberg. Marty, I—I have very bad news. It's your mother. She's—"

Oh, Jesus. Poor Clint. Mommy's had enough of sunshine, sagebrush, and sheep-shit, and has cut out on him.

"Yeah?" said Marty, trying not to sound too disinterested.

"Oh, God, Marty. She's—she's—" Sonenberg was crying. "She's dead."

Marty knew he had not heard the rancher correctly.

"I'm sorry, Clint. Say that again. I didn't—"

"She's dead, Marty. Mary Frances is dead."

Marty took the phone from his ear and looked at the earpiece. He could hear Sonenberg crying on the other end, the sobs far off and metallic-sounding, like some old-time Edison cylinder being played on an ancient gramophone. He put the receiver back to his ear and managed to speak.

"How did it happen, Clint?"

"It was an accident. Please, Marty, can you come here? Right away. The funeral's day after tomorrow."

Marty felt as though the world was spinning. His mouth was unaccountably dry. So were his eyes. He felt no grief, not yet. Only shock. Terrible surprise.

When he did not answer Sonenberg's question right away,

243

the rancher said, disconsolately, "Marty. I know you're busy—working—but—"

"I'll be there. Tomorrow."

"Thank you, Marty. She's being laid to rest here at the ranch. She loved it so. I thought—rather than the cemetery—Marty, is that all right with you?"

"What? Yes. Of course."

"How are you coming?"

"Beg pardon?"

"How will you get here?"

"Oh. Uh—I don't know. Try to catch a plane. Have to—uh—call—and—" He was in a daze, having trouble functioning.

"Listen, if you can't get a seat on a plane, charter one. I'll pay for it on this end. Just get here. Please."

o

Mary Frances lay in the satin-lined casket which had been placed on a large table in the living room of the ranch house. Her hands were folded across her breast, her features calm. She was dressed in the dark blue gown in which she had been married to Clint Sonenberg. The gold wedding band gleamed dully on her left hand. A small procession of neighboring ranchers, businessmen, artists, writers, friends, filed past the coffin to pay their last respects. More than one man shook his head slowly. Most thought she had never looked more beautiful. A few reflected silently that she had, indeed, been one choice piece.

Clint Sonenberg sat in a large chair near his wife, accepting the condolences of his guests. He looked haggard and his bleary, red-rimmed eyes were evidence of a sleepless pair of nights and the shedding of many tears. He rose when he saw Marty come in and went to greet him. Marty held out his hand, looked at Clint, and was astonished. The big man seemed stooped, hunched over, and all the vitality Marty had so admired on his sole visit to the ranch, months before, had disappeared. Sonenberg looked as though he had aged twenty years.

"Marty," he said brokenly, trapping the singer's hand in both of his big ones. "I loved her. I loved your mother."

Tears sprang out of the rancher's eyes and he bowed his head. "It's all my fault. All my fault."

Marty freed his hand and walked over to where his mother lay. He had never before seen her face in such an attitude of total repose, even when he had observed her sleeping. A noxious cliché came to mind: she looks at peace. He had not, ever, had more than ten cents' worth of affection from her. And yet, now, as he looked at her, his throat constricted and he felt that if he allowed himself to, he could shed tears. He stood before the makeshift bier for a long time. Abruptly, he turned away from the coffin and walked past Clint toward the rear of the house, opened the kitchen door, and went in. The same Indian woman he had seen on his first visit stood before the sink, slowly wiping dishes. Clint came into the kitchen and with a slight movement of his head dismissed the Indian. Now they were alone, Clint and Marty.

After a brief silence, the rancher said, "My fault, my fault. We bought a new horse, a stallion, wild, unstable. Bought him mainly for breeding purposes. Mary Frances—she insisted on trying to ride him. I begged her not to."

"So what happened?" asked Marty. "The horse threw her and she was—?

"Yes, yes, that's right. But she didn't die from the fall. Oh, God, Marty. I—" Clint sat down heavily on a kitchen chair and buried his face in his hands.

"Take it easy, Clint," Marty tried to comfort him.

Clint wiped his right eye with the forefinger-knuckle of his right hand and continued.

"You see, she fell from the horse and hit the ground hard. It must have stunned her. And—and while she was lying there, trying to get her breath, a—a snake bit her. Diamondback. If she could have gotten back home we might have—But the horse ran off and left her there. Over four miles from here. She started walking, but—she didn't make it."

Marty was silent. He was horrified to think his mother had died in such a manner, alone and most probably in terrible pain. A freak accident. Just like his mother to go out in so bizarre a fashion. And then he was ashamed of himself for

245

thinking thoughts like that in front of this large, lonely man who had obviously loved and been proud of her.

"I'm sorry, Clint," he said, reaching for the right words. "Sorrier for you than for me. I know what her—leaving means to you."

Clint shook his great head from side to side violently. "I'll never love anyone else. Never!" He looked into Marty's eyes, imploring him to believe it.

"I know, Clint. Take it easy."

Clint Sonenberg put his hands to his face and once again wept for his lost love. Marty sat quietly, moved by the distraught, broken man before him.

Later, Clint said, "Your mother's things are in her room."

"Her room?"

"Well, you know, she was a nervous sleeper, so we each had our own bedroom."

"I see."

"Anything you want, Marty. Of hers, I mean. You're welcome to."

"No, Clint. There's nothing I want," Marty said, but later in the evening he went into her room and sat in the dark for a long while. Eventually, he turned on a table lamp and looked around. The bedroom had been done in pale pink, with lace curtains at the windows, a mirrored vanity table, and a high-canopied fourposter bed. He rose and moved idly to her dresser. It was glass-topped and sported several pictures of Mary Frances with horses, with Clint, with other men, presumably friends or business associates. A small antique music box adorned the dresser top, as well as a sterling silver brush and comb set, with the inscription: "I'll Always Love You: Clint" engraved in the handle of the brush. Marty stood there for a moment and opened the lid of the music box. Tinkly tones issued from it. Inside was a single item of jewelry: his paternal grandmother's blue glass beads.

He slammed the box shut and the music halted abruptly. He quickly left the room, closing the door behind him. Minutes later, he entered again, walked to the dresser, opened the music box, removed the beads, and dropped them into his jacket pocket.

o

The funeral was mercifully brief. Clint's tear ducts ceased to function and, as Marty's mother was slowly lowered into the ground, the rancher's eyes were dry, though his grief was clearly visible.

A ranch hand drove Marty into Santa Fe, where he caught a bus. As the big Trailways swayed and jounced its way toward Albuquerque, Marty, seated near the front, watched the driver manipulate the huge steering wheel in much the same fashion as Mack, the band bus driver, did. The singer felt drained of energy. Clint's grief had been enervating, far greater than his own. He felt guilty about not feeling guilty about it, disconnected.

He turned and looked back into the darkened aisle. Servicemen cluttered the seats, dozing, smoking, reading. He made up his mind. He'd be one of them soon.

Chapter

33

What could Ray McKinley want with him? Marty reported to the Hôtel Des Olympiades as ordered on the 17th of February. The entire Miller Air Force band was billeted there and, as he walked to the desk to ask the *concierge* where he might find the famous drummer, McKinley came up to him and extended his hand.

"How you feelin', Marty?"

"I'm fine, so they tell me. I can't sleep on my left side for a while, and this wet weather isn't doing the wound any good."

"Do you feel well enough to sing with the band?"

"But I thought Desmond—"

"He is. Our prime, number one man in that department. However, we've got a lot of concerts, benefits, and a few more broadcasts to do before they send us home. We could use you, Marty. What do you think?" Ray asked him.

Marty frowned slightly, "Well, what does Johnny Desmond think?"

"He's all for it! Heard those things you recorded with Wiley. Thinks you're great."

"You sure?"

"Sure I'm sure. Listen, Marty. Johnny Desmond is the absolute prime top G.I. favorite. But you're a comer. And if you're not in a blazin' hurry to be stateside, we'd like to have you. What do you say?"

o

Marty Wynner sang with the Glen Miller Air Force Band on the very next evening during a concert the band gave at the Paris Opera House. His dual offering was greeted with as much enthusiasm as Johnny Desmond's brace of ballads. The orchestra shone brightly for the next few months in Paris. During June and July, the Miller men entertained thousands of servicemen in concerts throughout France and Germany, including a show at Nuremberg Stadium, scene of earlier gatherings of another sort.

Finally, the band was processed and transported to Le Havre, where they boarded the *S.S. Santa Rosa* and embarked for the States, landing in New York on August 12, just five days after Hiroshima. Everyone was immediately given a thirty-day furlough. Marty decided to stay in New York, particularly when he saw an ad in the *News* announcing the appearance at the Paramount of Wiley McKay and his orchestra.

It was raining as he caught a bus to the famed theater at Broadway and 44th. The marquee, swirling with all those yellow and white electric "chase" bulbs that had displayed so many great names in its illustrious history, now proclaimed that in addition to the latest Alan Ladd epic, one could, for the low price of a dollar and fifty cents, see, on stage, in person, Dick Haymes plus the Wiley McKay band. Marty saw that Martin Wiseman had been correct; the big bands had seen their day as the prime headliners.

Marty found a seat in mid-theater. The place was packed, mostly with very young girls. The Step Brothers finished their dazzling tap routine and the band played them off the stage to strong applause, but the minute they disappeared, the clapping ended abruptly. Wiley McKay, resplendent in a white Western-style suit and cowboy boots, smiled at the girls in the front row, lifted his trombone off its stand, and launched into the current favorite, "Give Me the Simple Life."

Marty thought some of the excitement of the old band was

missing until the orchestra played Bitsy Munro down from his perch at the drums to center stage. Bitsy punctuated his move with a hip-jiggling, finger-popping dance that drew a shout from the crowd, then launched into "Out of This World," singing it with that same infectious jazz conception that Marty remembered and admired.

The band picked up the tempo of the song slightly, and Bitsy treated the audience to a lesson in tap-dancing that brought forth howls of delight from the basically pro-Haymes partisans. Finally the diminutive drummer made his way back to his pearl-and-chrome Slingerlands, and kicked the band into a breathlessly paced "Diga Diga Do," which culminated in a dazzling display of drumnastics. When Bitsy ended the number with a flashing smile and twirling drumsticks, the theater erupted in a barrage of applause and whistles. Marty joined in, clapping till his palms hurt.

Dick Haymes was greeted with squeals and sighs and screams when he made his entrance on stage, but Marty felt Bitsy had left a residue of brilliance that would not be quickly dispelled. He was right. It took Haymes a full seven or eight minutes of superlative singing to capture the audience fully. Tall, good-looking, possessed of a deep, rich baritone, Haymes exemplified, in Marty's eyes, what a singer of popular songs was all about. He talked little, preferring to make his points vocally, but when he did say a few words he exuded a casual charm and a wry sense of humor.

Marty watched the bobbysoxers around him. Their response to Dick Haymes seemed orgasmic. Many girls stood up, hands clasped, eyes closed in ecstasy, shouting his name. When he sang, "The More I See You," several girls cried and a few seemed to faint. A large group off to Marty's right wore red slipovers with the legend "Haymes Dames" emblazoned across their chests. Marty envied the singer his admirers, although it disturbed him that during the entire performance, their screaming filled the Paramount.

When the show was finished, the house lights dimmed and, once again, the myriad young females squiggled in their seats, prepared to endure Alan Ladd's histrionics several more times in order to see Dick Haymes throughout the afternoon

250

and on into the evening. Marty used a side exit to get to the 44th Street stage door.

o

Wiley greeted his former singer with a whoop and a holler, bear-hugging Marty and shouting out his dressing room door for Bitsy, who came running down the stairs from his room, letting out a joyful yell at the sight of his former roommate.

At Sardi's the three of them ate lavishly and talked about old times. Marty discussed with reluctance his adventures with the 101st. Wiley commented that Marty seemed a little pale, and he was right. Wynner explained haltingly about the effect a drizzly day had on his wound.

The strongest thing Wiley drank during the meal was apple juice. He appeared more saturnine than ever, with his long, lean face and Wyatt Earp mustache.

Bitsy seemed far more assured than he had been when Marty had sung with the band. His importance with McKay had grown considerably, and Marty was somewhat startled by a few things the drummer said during dinner. Bitsy seemed to be having a love affair with himself.

After dinner Wiley seduced his ex-vocalist away from Munro and steered him to a quiet bar on East 54th Street. Marty entered the little bistro with some concern; was this Wiley's secret drinking hideout? He relaxed when they sat down at a table near the rear of the long, narrow bar and Wiley ordered ginger ale.

"Well, hoss," said Wiley, after draining nearly half his glass in a thirst-quenching gulp. "What're your plans?"

"You'll have to ask Uncle Sam," replied Marty.

"Aw, hell, Mart. You'll be outta that soldier suit in jig time now. Any interest in comin' back with me once you're free and clear of the Army?"

"Gee, Wiley. I think I might have a crack at the 'solo' bit."

"Can't blame you." McKay smiled and sipped his ginger ale more slowly. "Handwritin's on the wall for anyone to see. Singers. It's their turn now. Hell, it was bound to happen. Whole damn business is built on cycles. And right now, it's the singers comin' up to bat."

"Hmm. That's what a doctor in Paris told me," said Marty.

251

Wiley made a face. "I need a drink." He signaled the waiter. "Bring me a Coke. A double!"

Marty laughed. Wiley joined in, adding, to the waiter, "In a dirty glass!"

o

Several weeks later, Marty found himself out in the cold December air, his severance pay in his pocket. He made his way, by invitation, out to Long Island and had dinner with Wiley and a quiet, pretty woman whom the bandleader introduced as Doris, "My intended, Marty. Ol' Cupid snuck up and winged me with his six-gun! How 'bout that?'

After dinner, they sat in Wiley's paneled den, listening to records. Marty stood back a bit in the shadows, the drink in his hand untouched, watching Wiley and Doris with equal amounts of happiness and envy.

Wiley was a lucky man; he had Doris. Marty had—no one. It had dawned on him when the band had disembarked in New York the previous August. The Miller men were all coming home to wives, sweethearts, families. Marty Wynner was merely coming home.

He shook his head vigorously to wipe away the memories of the past three Christmases he had spent overseas. He was back in America. Where would he go? The paratroops and then the Glenn Miller band had been like large families to him. Now that was over. He swallowed hard.

The record finished. Wiley looked at Marty and, reading him, said, "Why don't you stay on here as our house guest, at least until after the first of the year?"

"Thanks, Wiley, but no thanks." Marty felt that to intrude upon them would be selfish.

"We'd love to have you, Marty. Really," added Doris.

"Hell, hoss," said Wiley. "Who's likely to make you a better offer?"

Marty smiled. "Nobody. That's for sure, but I've got something important to do. In Chicago."

o

Steeltown had changed little since Marty had been a boy. the same small wood-frame and shingle houses, the dimly lit streets, the narrow sidewalks. The only thing that softened its

252

stark simplicity was a thick layer of fresh snow and the occasional glimpse of a gaily lit Christmas tree, giving the neighborhood the appearance of small-town-picture-postcard quaintness it did not deserve.

Marty stood in front of the house where he and his father and mother had lived. He had gone right to it like a homing pigeon, this unhappy little structure where he had spent much of his childhood. As the sky grew darker, casting a twilight blue on the snow, he watched a group of youngsters noisily carrying their Flexible Flyers down the sidewalk, picking up speed, then belly-flopping onto their sleds, the runners making fresh tracks in the snow.

Marty approached the door of the house and knocked. A big man with a nose and belly to match opened the door. He wore pants with suspenders hanging down, and a grimy white undershirt.

"Yeah?" he said, upon seeing Marty.

"Good evening. I—I—"

"What do you want, soldier? C'mon. It's cold as hell out here."

"I used to live in this house."

"Oh, yeah?"

"Yes. A long time ago. My father worked in one of the mills. I think the man's name who owned it was Barringer. Or something like that."

"Belanger?"

"Yes, that's right. Belanger."

The man grunted. "I work for the cheap bastard."

"Look, mister," Marty said. "I'm looking for my father. I haven't seen him since I was a kid."

"Yeah? What's his name?"

"Wynocki. Jozef Wynocki."

The man thought about it, slowly shaking his head. "Polack, huh?" The man had a slight Irish brogue. "Naw, never heard of him. Tell you what. Go on down the street to 18th and turn right. Guy lives there, lessee, I don't know the number, but it's the only house in that block with a little iron fence in front. He's been with Belanger since the early twenties. If anybody knows your old man, he will."

"Thanks. What's this guy's name?"

"Kosko. Tony Kosko."

"Well, thanks again. And Merry Christmas."

"Yeah," said the man, and shut the door.

o

"Joe Wynocki? Naw, it's been years. Lessee, musta been nineteen thirty-four when he got outta here. Yeah, Thirty-four, it was."

Tony Kosko had grown fat and prosperous during the war. He had been promoted to assistant superintendent of the Belanger Mill in 1943, and the interior of his home boasted a new Frigidaire, a large Zenith combination radio-phonograph, and a green-cloth-covered table for Saturday night poker sessions.

The heavy-set man sat on his sofa, drinking Pabst out of a can. He shook his head, remembering. "Joe Wynocki. And you're his kid, huh? I remember you. You and your mother left here in—uh—"

"Nineteen thirty-three."

"Yeah. Yeah. Broke your old man's heart when she ran out on him."

"I guess she was just unhappy here."

"Hmm. Sure you won't have a beer?"

"No, thank you, sir."

"Okay. Well, anyways, I haven't got the slightest idea where your old man went."

"Didn't he leave any kind of forwarding address? Anything?"

"Kid, the only thing he left was his house. And everything in it. He just went home one day from work, and didn't show up the next morning. I went over to his house to see if he was sick or something. Lots of drawers open, empty hangers in the closet. He just disappeared. You ain't heard from him all these years, huh?"

"Not a word."

"Think maybe he was in the service?"

"I don't think so. Someone I knew at Camp Shanks got in touch with Washington for me. Checked all the service records. No one named Jozef Wynocki listed."

"Well, maybe he joined up under a—whatchacallit—an assumed name."

"Yes, sir," Marty said, with a resigned droop of his shoulders. He extended his hand. "I want to thank you, Mr. Kosko, for seeing me."

They shook hands. Marty picked up his army greatcoat and put it on. Tony walked him to the door.

"Listen, Marty," said Tony in parting. "I want you to know somethin'. Your pa and me—at first, we didn't like each other. Hell, I was rough as a cob in the old days. But your old man—he was a gentle guy, see? After your ma walked out on him, we got to be friends. Matter of fact, I was just about the only one he had anything to do with, after—. Well, all he did was work, and eat and sleep and look for you and your ma. He was, like, empty inside after you two went away."

Marty looked at the gruff man, suddenly feeling he was lonely living by himself in Steeltown. Slightly uncomfortable, Marty said, "Well, I'd better be going. I want to wish you a merry Christmas, Mr. Kosko."

The heavyset man gripped Marty's hand tighter, as though he would like to delay the young man's leavetaking.

"Call me Tony, kiddo. Hunnph! Just thought of somethin'. Your old man. Never called me that. It was always 'Anton.' Never could make him understand that, in America, the old ways were—"

He released Marty's hand and placed his own on the ex-paratrooper's shoulder. "I liked your pa, kid. I miss him."

o

The telegram had reached Marty through Wiley McKay, whose agent had forwarded it from Los Angeles. "Get out here. Call me on 31st. Want to spend New Year's Eve with you. Have good news. Don't goof, Lieutenant." The wire had included Wiseman's telephone number.

Crazy bastard. A miracle I got the damn thing.

Still, Marty realized, he was footloose, unattached. California was as good as any place to pick up the pieces. And what the hell, he liked that stringbean of a would-be manager who had coaxed him back to health in Paris.

255

So, here he was in Lotus Land again. He would call Wiseman. On the 31st, not before.

He slept at the Hollywood Plaza. He ate. He wandered aimlessly during that limbo-week between Christmas and New Year's, seeing movies, sitting quietly in Billy Berg's or the Hangover or Mickey Scrima's underground jazz club, absorbing the music. He purposely avoided calling anyone he had known prior to the war.

Chapter

34

"Hi ya, keed! Happy New Year!"

Martin Wiseman stumbled toward Marty, nearly falling over a chair, and embraced him happily. "Hey, you're just in time, soldier. Big party here tonight."

"Looks like you're starting early, Doc."

"Nix on that 'Doc' jazz. Jus' plain old Martin Wiseman. Artist's representative. And you're the artist, pal, like it or not." He squinted at Marty as he held him at arm's length.

"I don't know. How much faith can I place in a drunk?" said Marty, narrowing his eyes dramatically.

"Awwwww," said Wiseman, mussing Wynner's hair. "Cut it out, Lieutenant. I'm just a little shicker 'cause I'm happy. Happy to see you. Happy because we're going to be together, happy—"

"Now, hold on. I didn't say definitely that—"

"Bullshit! You're stuck with me, hero. Would you have me sent back to a life of drudgery in some hospital, slaving over a hot operating table? Have you no feeling? No soul?"

"Wiseman, you're—

"The cream in my coffee," Martin sang, as he led Marty into the spacious living room of the Pacific Palisades home of his uncle. He steered Marty to the semicircular wet bar in the corner of the room, and poured a large amount of Johnnie Walker into a water tumbler, offering the drink to Wynner. Marty declined. "It's a little early for me."

"Never too early," advised Wiseman as he took a long pull on the Scotch. He put the glass on the bar, held his hand up to Marty's face, and crooked an index finger beckoningly. "Follow me," he ordered. He guided Marty through the living room, down a pastel-painted hallway, and up a short flight of thickly carpeted stairs to the second level of the house. He went to an ivory-colored door and opened it, beaming.

"Your quarters, *mon ami.*"

Marty walked past him into a large, modern bedroom, done in a soft shade of sea-foam green, with slightly darker green drapes framing the windows and an off-white thick-pile carpet spanning the room. The furniture was finished in ivory, and the bathroom to the right sported pale green tile, with the sink, tub, and toilet a glossy hunter's green. Marty lowered his suitcase and whistled. Wiseman was pleased.

"This all belongs to Uncle Ben Rosensweig. My mother's brother. A little nicer than that shitty hospital ward in France, huh?"

Marty laughed. "I've stayed in worse fleabags."

"O-kay, chum," said Wiseman. "Tonight we shall make merry. Or Molly. Or—heh-heh—" he rubbed his hands together villainously—"maybe even Rosalie."

The party was noisy and wild, filled with laughter and horn-tooters and balloon decorations that constantly popped; peopled by a wide variety of types and ages; sustained by every conceivable kind of alcoholic beverage. In the corner a mariachi band played loudly and badly.

As they made their way through the crowd toward the bar, Wiseman waved his hands in the air offhandedly. "I won't bother to introduce you to all these peasants. You'll probably never see them again after tonight."

"Whatever you say, doctor."

"Hey! I told you to cut that 'doctor' jive, man."

"Oh, sorry. A thousand pardons, gate."

Wiseman grinned. "Well all reet."

They reached the bar and managed to get a pair of drinks. Wiseman stood on tiptoe, looking over the heads of the jostling, dancing guests. "Want you to meet somebody. Trying to spot—"

As if on cue, an extremely pretty young woman emerged from the crowd and asked the bartender for a vodka martini.

Martin scratched his head, almost unsettling his droll little party hat. "I'll be damned. You reading my mind or something, Rosie?"

"What?" the girl asked, turning toward him.

"Never mind. I'm drunk. Marty, say hello to my cousin, Rosalie Rosensweig. Rosalie, this is Marty Wynner the best singer in the world as if you didn't know from my talking about him nonstop you two get acquainted because I gotta go pee." Glass in hand, Wiseman dropped into a Groucho Marx crouch and bobbed and weaved his way through the crowd toward the guest bathroom in the front hallway.

Marty laughed and looked at the young woman. She was almost beautiful, with wide brown eyes, dark brown hair, worn shoulder-length, and sensuous-looking full lips that could seem faintly derisive when they formed a smile. Her shoulders were attractively broad, her breasts high and astonishingly fulsome. If her figure was flawed at all, a thinness of shank, thigh, and calf could be blamed.

"It's a trait in Jewish girls," she said casually. "Big tits and thin legs."

Taken by surprise, Marty could only say, "My God! You *are* a mind reader."

"Did I embarrass you?"

Marty considered. "I don't think so."

"Good," she said. "My dear cousin has been talking the pants off me for the last few weeks, mostly about you. Mind if I speak my mind?"

"I doubt if I can stop you."

"Bright boy. Look, do him a favor, will you? Talk him out of this show business crap. His father thinks he's lost his marbles. So does my father."

259

"How about you?"

"Oh, hell. Don't ask me. I've been doing exactly what I wanted since I was seven. But I promised Uncle Morrie, Marty's father, that I'd talk to you."

"So?"

"So—I've talked to you. What time is it?"

Marty looked at his watch. "Nearly time. About a quarter to twelve."

She scanned the crowd, looked toward the front door.

"Looking for someone in particular?" he asked.

"Yes. Somebody was supposed to be here before midnight. To see the New Year in with me."

Marty smiled at her. "Well, in case he doesn't show, I'll be glad to stand in for him when the clock strikes twelve."

Her mouth twisted into a derisive grin. "Don't kid yourself, junior." Junior! She looked to be all of twenty-five or six!

Suddenly up popped Martin Wiseman, still doing his Groucho impression. He took the plastic stirrer out of his glass and struck it in his mouth like a cigar. Then he removed it, wiggled his eyebrows up and down and said, "I always wanted to screw her, Marty, but what the hell, she's my first cousin and if she got knocked up, the kid would probably wind up being an idiot, like Horse Kennelly. Remember?"

They both doubled up with laughter. Kennelly was a subcompetent army career doctor, whose labored breathing and moronic laugh, during operating-room sessions, had kept the staff of the hospital near Paris in a state of constant hysterics.

Rosalie sipped her drink, unperturbed. "I'm sure," she said acidly, "I am missing some brilliantly conceived pearl of humor, comprehensible only to geniuses like yourselves. Why don't you two rodents go find appropriate holes in which to celebrate the coming of the New Year?"

Wiseman roared and quickly disappeared. Rosalie's friend did not arrive. When the large grandfather clock in the foyer chimed twelve, and the lights dimmed, and the guests sang "Auld Lang Syne," Rosalie and Marty Wynner were locked in each other's arms, mouth upon mouth, tongues probing.

o

Martin said, "Would you be surprised if I said, 'Oh, my aching head'?"

Marty said, "I'd be surprised if you didn't. The amount of booze you put away last night, you'll probably be hung over until Valentine's Day."

"Well, what the hell. Why not?"

"Who were all those people at the party?"

"Oh," said Martin. "An assortment of total strangers."

"What?"

"Well, we couldn't just celebrate the New Year by ourselves, could we? You and me and Cousin Rosalie? I ran into most of those freeloaders at a party in Bel Air last week, so I went around that night collecting phone numbers, and next morning I called and invited them to come over and see the New Year in with us. Nifty, huh?"

"Wiseman, you need help."

"Which is more than I can say for you, Wynner. Looks like you had everything under control last night with my nubile little cousin. I noticed you disappeared right after midnight. Did you and she do feelthy theengs to each other in the pool house?"

"About your mind . . ."

"No, seriously."

"Seriously what?"

"How was she?"

"Christ, Wiseman, the lady's your cousin!"

"So? What are you, a religious fanatic or something? Screwing is screwing, and believe me, she needed it. She's been going with this jackoff associate professor from USC. One of those schmucks whose idea of giving a girl a good time is to park up in the Hollywood Hills and spout Freud and Jung at her. I was glad he didn't show up last night so you and Rosie could get together and make beautiful music."

"Now, wait a minute. I never said we—"

"Oh, bullshit! You laid her. I can tell from that tired hangdog expression, you got into her pants. Bravo!"

"Wiseman, you bastard! I'm—"

"Shut up and pass the toast. Oh, Jesus. My poor head."

261

○

Later that day, Wiseman sought out his cousin in her room. Closing the door behind him, he leered at her.

"Aha! So this is where you're hiding. For shame!"

"Hiding? This is my room, remember?"

"Oh, yeah. Cozy. The scene of the great debauch last night"

"Run that by me again?"

"No need to be coy, Cousin Rosie. You and the 'Swinger.' "

"The *what?*"

"That's what the G.I.'s used to call Marty when he sang with the Glenn Miller band. Johnny Desmond was the 'Creamer,' Marty was the 'Swinger.' "

Rosalie Rosensweig treated her cousin to one of her wry smiles. "Well, I've got news for you, cuz. You'd better dream up a new nickname for him."

Martin was surprised. "Are you kidding?"

"Would I kid the kidder? We slipped out just after midnight and drove to Santa Barbara. We were all over each other in the car. God, it's a wonder we didn't have an accident. But once we got into the motel room, zilch! Oh, he tried, I'll say that for him. And I did all I could to help him, which, if I do say so myself, was considerable."

"I'll just bet it was."

"We finally got together, in a manner of speaking. But the 'Swinger'? Oh, Marty! I've had more fun all by myself."

Wiseman sat down on the bed next to his cousin.

"Listen, Rosie. This guy is going to make it. And I'm going to help him go all the way. I know the family thinks they've got a complete meshugenah in their midst, but I can't help that. The music business interests me more than the doctor business. I've tried to tell my dad, but you know your uncle. He's got this dream: Wiseman and Son, General Practitioners.

"Goddammit, Rosalie, I hate practicing medicine. Where is it written that as the father goes, so shall the son? This son is going to be Marty Wynner's manager.

"So. Keep what you just told me to yourself. If it gets around that he's a dud in the sack, it could be the kiss of death. You know how females are about boy singers. Jesus! I can't believe it. I would have thought Marty was the prime stud of all time."

"Not hardly. And don't worry. I'm not going to run through the streets naked yelling 'Marty Wynner's a lousy lay.' "

Chapter

35

"Where are we going?" Marty wanted to know.

"You'll see," Wiseman grinned. He sat slouched at the wheel of his uncle's Buick, Wynner beside him, as they drove along the Sunset Strip toward Hollywood.

"What's the big mystery?" Marty persisted.

"No mystery, Lieutenant. Just a little surprise, that's all."

Wiseman pulled up to a small building a few blocks east of La Cienega, near Miller Drive, where Marty and his mother had once lived. The lanky ex-doctor got out of the car and ushered Marty into the building. Its interior was neat and modern. When Wiseman proceeded to climb the stairs, Wynner fell in and followed him up to a door labeled in block lettering:

W W II

"I don't get it," said Marty.

"God! Are all singers dumb?"

"Am I supposed to know what the hell 'WW II' means?"

"Double U, double U two. World War Two; Wynner and Wiseman, two. The two of us. We got together during double U double U two, right? So I opened offices under our

264

new company name: Double U, Double U two. Two guys named Wynner and Wiseman."

"Very clever, Doc. Thanks for the top billing."

"You deserve it, keed. You're the artist. I am merely Svengali. The molder. The shaper."

Marty smiled at his friend. "You, O wheeler-dealer, are something."

"That is precisely what I've been telling you. Come on in."

Wiseman opened the door. The office was unexpectedly large, with a spacious reception area and an inner sanctum that boasted a desk and a chair and nothing else.

"Furniture arrives tomorrow. So does my secretary. Big blue eyes and knockers to match."

"Wiseman, where are you getting the money for all this?"

"Not from my father, I can tell you. He's just about disowned me. My Uncle Ben, who still thinks I'm a nut, kicked in with a loan. We gotta do it right, Marty. Start in style. Look important or we'll be small potatoes from the word 'go.' Agreed?"

Marty held up his hands. "I'm just the singer around here. I'll swab the deck, you run the ship, Cap'n."

Wiseman's features assumed a faraway look. "Gee," he murmured. "I wish I'd said that. By the way, I've changed my name. Martin Wise, from now on. Shorter. Easier to remember. Dignified and to the point. What do you think of it?"

"I think you should finish your doctor's training."

Martin actually looked hurt. You're joking, Marty," he said. "I thought you were sold on the idea of me and you going down the road together. Dammit, Marty! I love show business and—and you, you dumb Polack mick."

"All right, all right, save the hearts and flowers. It's you and me, truckin' on down. Okay, Doctor Wiseman?"

"Wise. Martin Wise. A name to conjure with."

o

A flood of letters began arriving at "WWII." Most of them, forwarded by Armed Forces Radio Service, came from discharged servicemen and women who had written to ask about the "Swinger's" whereabouts, plans, and aspirations.

There was also a healthy correspondence from overseas personnel, who still heard airchecks of Marty with the Miller band on Radio Luxembourg.

Martin Wise made an appointment with the program director of NBC, and, armed with a briefcase full of such ammunition, unceremoniously dumped its contents on the astonished man's desk. An hour and a half later, Marty Wynner had a firm offer to star on his own fifteen-minute-thrice-weekly radio show, providing, of course, he agreed to sign with RCA records, the owner of the National Broadcasting Company. Martin Wise, sensing his client's potential, demanded and got a large piece of "front money." He practically skipped out of the large green building at Sunset and Vine and made his way through the parking lot to Uncle Ben's Buick. His high spirits would have nosedived, however, if he had known how high NBC had been prepared to go to obtain Wynner's services.

Martin Wise and Marty Wynner bought a pair of cars. A cherry-red Buick Roadmaster convertible became Marty's pride and joy, a familiar sight, parked in its own designated slot in the NBC parking lot on Vine. As rehearsal pianist for the new radio show, he sought out Moe Stein, who had long since terminated his employment with Twentieth Century-Fox.

After five weeks on the air, NBC elected to change the name of the show from "The Marty Wynner Show" to "Swingtime With the 'Swinger' Starring Marty Wynner." The ratings zoomed. Marty possessed the unusual ability to attract the male contingent of listeners along with the obvious feminine idolators. Thus a rarity in sponsorship occurred: on Mondays and Fridays, a famous women's cosmetics firm subsidized the show; on Wednesdays the largest men's toiletries company in the country pushed their products during three separate one-minute intervals. After the first thirteen weeks, the program was extended to a half hour, with a larger budget for guest stars. It climbed to the second-most-listened-to radio show in the nation, surpassed only by Jack Benny.

During the sixth week of the "first thirteen," Marty made

his initial sides for Victor. The first record raced to the top of the *Cash Box-Billboard-Variety* charts and threatened to remain there permanently.

Martin Wise renegotiated with NBC-RCA, and the new deal was sweeter to the tune of tens of thousands of dollars.

Marty Wynner traded in his near-new Roadmaster on a shiny white Coupe de Ville.

Fan letters continued to pour into "WWII." Did the Swinger have a steady girl friend? What was his favorite color? Was it true he liked to drive too fast? Marty soon outgrew his initial delight in such mail and allowed Martin Wise's secretary to handle the flood.

One week a particularly dog-eared envelope was among the hundreds forwarded by NBC. The address appeared to have been printed laboriously, and inside was a short note in the same painstaking hand:

Martin,
I am here.
Papa
1309 Cedar Avenue

Two weeks later, Joe Wynocki received a printed reply:

Dear Fan,
Marty Wynner appreciates your taking the time to write him. Since he gets hundreds of letters each week, we have to use this form to thank you. We are enclosing an autographed photo for your collection.
The Marty Wynner Fan Club

By the end of the 1940s several of Marty's records were topping the top ten. He played several of the most famous nightclubs and hotels in the country, smashing attendance records and carrying away spectacular percentage proceeds. NBC renewed his radio show for another season and entered into serious conversations with Martin Wise about the coming monster, television.

During the rainy seasons, the old knife wound on his left side gave him moments of great discomfort. He resisted taking pain pills for a while, but Martin Wise convinced him they were invented to be used, as long as one did not make a habit of them. Marty took them only when the pain was unbearable. Otherwise, he enjoyed good health.

He moved out of his Hollywood apartment near the end of the first cycle of broadcasts and rented a small but rather luxurious house in Brentwood. The longish drive to the studio was easily offset by the heated pool and badminton court and, while Marty had always been a loner, he now found himself host to some of Hollywood's best-known luminaries. Sundays became a habit at the house on Mandeville Canyon Road, with impressive amounts of food and liquor consumed, new acquaintances made, compliments dispensed like change tossed upon a counter, and, best of all, some of the most talented people in the world letting down their professional hair and performing in the cozy living room, alongside the polished ebony Wurlitzer Grand presented to Martin by the president of NBC as a bonus for re-signing with the network.

In 1949, hc got an offer to play a series of movie theaters in the Midwest and the East, and while he knew the five-and six-a-day schedule would be rigorous, he loved the idea of it. He insisted on, and got, Wiley McKay and his orchestra to accompany him.

He had long since signed with MCA for agent representation, and before the tour began they advised him of the billing status: "The Marty Wynner Show" starring Marty Wynner (100 percent), Billy and Betty Sutton, tap dancers (50 percent), Wiley McKay and his orchestra (50 percent). The MCA agent who explained this to Marty was a simpering, patronizing little man absurdly dressed in a Brooks Brothers suit, the front buttons of which threatened to explode from the pressure of a well-fed stomach. Marty informed him in precise terms that Wiley McKay was to receive 100 percent equal billing.

"Kiddy," the little man said. "He doesn't deserve it. He's lucky to get work right now. So why should you—"

268

"Don't argue with me. McKay gets equal billing and that's final, understand?"

The agent's manner became ingratiating. "Well, certainly. If that's the way you want it. I mean, I don't agree with you, and I think you're hurting yourself, kiddy but . . ."

"Wiley McKay's an institution, and don't you God-damn-well ever forget it. Now stop the shit and do what I tell you!"

The agent straightened up to his full five feet, five inch height and tried to maintain his composure.

"There is no need," he said, his voice trembling slightly, "to get abusive."

"And one more thing, friend," said Marty.

"Yes?"

"My name isn't 'Kiddy.' "

o

The moment the tour began, Marty, Wiley, and Bitsy started acting like long-lost alumni of some extinct college fraternity. They took most of their meals together, sat around the dressing rooms between shows, talking about old times, and spent many post-performance hours seeking out small clubs with good jazz to listen to.

One night, while they were in the middle of a two-week stint at the New York Paramount, they made their way up to Harlem and found a fairly new establishment called Ginchy's, where the likes of J.C. Higginbotham, Henry "Red" Allen, and Sid Catlett were purveying their musical wares. They listened in rapt attention as these giants of jazz wove their way through "Sweet Lorraine," "I Found a New Baby" and "How High the Moon." At the end of the set, Wiley jumped up and ran backstage to see Higginbotham. Marty and Bitsy were left at the table. A pianist wandered up onto the stage and began to tastefully explore the world of Ellington.

"Er-uh, Marty," Bitsy said. "I want to ask your advice 'bout somethin.' "

"Sure, Little Bit, ask away."

"Well, er-uh, you seen this here Sammy Davis, Jr. yet?"

"Yeah. Talented guy."

"He's really beginnin' to make some noise, ya know? Any-

269

ways, I been thinkin'. Maybe I ought to put away my drumsticks and try to get up an act."

"Yes? Go on."

"Well, tha's about it. I sing good and I can do a few impersonations. 'Course I been dancing and drummin' all my life so I guess I'm pretty damn good in those departments."

"Not pretty damn good, Bits. The best."

Bitsy nodded. "Yeah, so they tell me. Thing is, with Sammy bustin' loose now, I think I got a chance, too."

"What does Wiley have to say about it?"

"I ain't told him yet. He's liable to think I'm runnin' out on him. I mean, er-uh, I'm the last survivor from back before the war, dig?"

"Bitsy, I'll betcha ol' Wiley'd be the first person to encourage you."

"I do' know. With Dede married and out of the business, I kind of feel like a deserter or somethin'."

"No, you're not, Little Bit. Honest. Look, you want me to talk to Wiley about it?"

"Nnn—no. I better do it myself."

"Got an agent or manager in mind?"

"Yeah. This here guy—his name is Walsh—Burt Walsh. Wants to manage me. And GAC said they like to be my agents."

"Do it, Bitsy!"

"Yeah? Really?"

"Really!"

"Well—all right, then. Guess I will."

"Good. Anything I can do—"

"Thanks, Marty. Hey. Maybe someday I'll get to be as big as you."

o

When the theater tour was over, Marty returned to Hollywood and began his next cycle of radio shows. Martin Wise came to see him with a proposal from NBC regarding a television series. Marty thought it might be somewhat premature to jump into the new medium, but when he saw how enthusiastic Martin was about the offer, he changed his mind and accepted. After the first three telecasts Marty's ratings began peaking the Neilsen and Arbitron charts.

A series of beautiful young women passed in and out of Marty's life. Several of them moved into his house, but in every case the tenancy was short-lived. His sexual performance left a lot to be desired; and anyway, he didn't feel like getting into anything too serious. Eventually, he called a halt to the stream of feminine house guests, preferring, instead, to date at random, to be lionized in print as the town's most eligible bachelor by the gossip columnists. His hit-or-miss record in bed never became common knowledge, probably because he always parted with these women on the pleasantest of terms.

All through the early 1950s, he lived the good life. Premières, parties, women in abundance, work of his own choosing, an outrageous amount of money earned, invested in oil, land, cattle, apartment buildings, securities, and a few inventions. He had unquestionably become one of the biggest names in the business.

Chapter

36

In the mid-fifties, when teenage music fans began turning more and more toward their own peer group in search of young idols with whom they could identify, the record business changed.

All at once, the new songwriting oracles were high-school students, college kids, and, in a few cases, pre-teens. The songs were juvenile, based on three or four chords, sophomoric in lyrical content, puerile in harmonic and melodic structure. It did not matter. Slowly, surely, "rock" made inroads, until the music of the young became the mainstream of American popular sound, and all those not privileged to dwell in that twelve-to-twenty-five-year-old age range could swim in it or sink and be damned!

To Marty, the new trend was mindless, and, despite urgings from "wiser" heads around him, he resisted the transition. He still did reasonably good business all over the country and, despite his lack of current hit records, Martin Wise negotiated a lucrative multiple-year deal for him at the newly built Arabian Nights Hotel and Casino in Las Vegas. When the Scheherazade Room was ready to open in that plush castle on the desert, Marty was its première performer. Nate Kaner, the principal owner of the hotel, had a framed oil painting of the singer mounted just outside the entrance to the beautiful showroom. It bore the brass-plated legend:

MARTY WYNNER

FIRST OF THE GREATS

SCHEHERAZADE ROOM

ARABIAN NIGHTS HOTEL

1958

In early 1959, he was overjoyed to find himself again in Vegas, this time while Bitsy Munro was appearing in support of Danny Thomas at the Sands, and Wiley McKay was leading a pickup band (he had disbanded his traveling orchestra in '58) in the Lounge at the Flamingo.

The three old friends spent many nights together, and once Marty feigned illness and skipped a show so that he could go see Bitsy perform. The little man was a marvel, positively scintillating on the Copa Room stage, and Marty found himself moved to tears by his performance. He was going to be big. Unquestionably. One night, Bitsy came by the Arabian Nights, and together with Marty they made their way down to the Flamingo to catch Wiley's last set of his final evening.

At the urging of the smallish audience, Marty got up on the stand with Wiley and performed. Bitsy declined, rather poutishly, Marty thought. Marty and Wiley gave the patrons something to remember, and the trombonist's eyes shone with pride when, at the end of the performance, Marty thanked him publicly for all he had done for him. When the cheering died down, everyone agreed the set had been memorable.

It also, unfortunately, marked the twilight of whatever glory Wiley had left. He had not done business in the Flamingo Lounge. Never again would he play Las Vegas as a star attraction. Never again would he assemble a big band or even a pick-up group. He would settle in Hollywood, scene of many former triumphs, and eke out a living as a recording

273

musician, an employee, in some cases, of arrangers whom he had once hired to fashion scores for his famous orchestra during the halcyon days of the Big Band Era.

o

Martin Wise left a message on Marty's answering service:

Please meet me at Mr. Rauschbauer's office,
Supreme Studios, Four P.M. Important.

Rauschbauer? Jesus! Was that old bastard still alive? He had not heard the name in years. Apparently his mother's ex-lover was still producing. Amazing. He had to be three years older than God by now.

Martin ushered him into a rather small, unpretentious office in the Producer's Building on the Supreme lot. A brisk young secretary announced them, then waved them through a door leading into the inner office. Martin blinked. The man behind the desk was young, stout, and rather tall, with curly blond hair and a round, almost cherubic face. His eyes were pale blue and his handshake was firm and warm. When he motioned toward a pair of chairs, his smile was friendly.

"I'm Willie Rauschbauer," he announced, seating himself behind his desk. He grinned and looked around the room, which was small and somewhat cheerless. "Not exactly in the tradition of my father when he owned this lot." Only then did Marty realize he was on the site of the old Marathon Studios lot. "I believe," said Willie Rauschbauer, with a touch of amusement, "that your mother and my father were—friends."

Marty grinned right back at him. "Something like that."

Willie continued to smile. "Beautiful woman, your mother. I remember her very well." Willie appeared to be around Marty's age. "She's, uh, she's dead, isn't she?"

"Yes. She died a long time ago. During the war."

"I know. On a ranch in New Mexico. I just wanted—I didn't know how you felt about her passing."

"You don't have to walk on eggs. My mother and I didn't get along. It was no secret. She's gone and that's that."

274

"I see, Marty," said Rauschbauer, digesting Marty's words. "May I call you 'Marty'? Thank you."

"How about your father, Willie? May I call you 'Willie'?"

Rauschbauer looked at Wise for a moment as if to ask whether the singer was mocking him. Wise's face betrayed nothing. This was Rauschbauer's party. He would have to fend for himself. Willie turned back to Marty. "He's still alive. He's had two strokes in the last year and a half. Can't talk. Paralyzed completely on his left side. But he understands everything you say to him. He's as good as can be expected. Answer your question?"

"Comprehensively."

"Good word. You obviously read a little."

"Better than watching the boob tube."

"Don't even mention television. No offense. I've seen your show. Several times. It's good. But I'm in the motion-picture business. Film. Images twenty times larger than life, not ten times smaller. You know what made the great stars gods? I'll tell you. The motion-picture screen. Close-ups of Gable the size of a four-story building. Goddam awe-inspiring! TV! You have to get up close with a magnifying glass to make out who's who!"

Martin Wise cleared his throat and said, "Would you tell Marty what you spoke to me about over the phone?"

"Of course," said Willie, his ire quickly dissipated. He reached into a drawer and removed a thin, leatherette-bound synopsis.

"I have a hell of an idea for a picture," he said.

When Marty finished reading the synopsis, he threw it on the floor of Rauschbauer's office and jumped to his feet.

"This is sick. Sick! What the hell do you think I am, anyway?"

Willie said mildly, "I think you're the only man to play the male lead. I think the picture will be a very big hit and do your career a lot of good. I think we need each other."

"Christ! I thought your old man was weird, but you top him!"

"Come on, Marty, let's get off on the right foot. Look. My

275

father lost this studio years ago because of bad judgment and—well, philandering. Your mother wasn't the only woman he ever kept. No offense. Women were his greatest passion, greater than making movies. His obsession with beautiful faces and big tits finally did him in. Now he's nothing but a broken, lonely old man. Well, let me tell you something— here's one Rauschbauer who won't end up like that.

"I don't give a flying fuck about women. I care about making pictures. Pictures that make money. I don't mean crap. I mean good stories, like the one you just threw on my rug. I'm sorry if that synopsis struck a raw nerve, but I'm going to make that film, with or without you. I just know it would be better with you."

"You—you," Marty sputtered, "really believe in this piece of shit?"

"Marty," interjected Willie. "Just because it's close to the bone where you're concerned doesn't make it a piece of shit. Dalton Trumbo is interested in doing the screenplay, Bennie Herrmann is signed to write the music, and I think—I'm not sure but I think—I can lock up George Seaton to direct, if you give me the green light."

Marty tried to compose himself. "And who," he asked through slightly clenched teeth, "do you have in mind for the woman?"

Willie opened a leather folder on his desk, picked up an eight-by-ten glossy, and spun it around on the desk top for Marty to see.

"Lola del Rey," he said. "She's perfect for the part, and I can't think of a hotter property right now. She's ready to break through in a very big way. This role can do it for her, and for you as well, Marty. I know it!"

o

The film was called "Mother and Son," and was one of the box-office sleepers of the 1959 winter season. Strategically released in mid-December, it earned a "Ten Best" in *Motion Picture Herald,* won second place in the New York Film Critics Choice Awards, and was nominated for four Oscars including Best Actress and Best Actor.

The story, at which Marty Wynner had initially bridled,

276

was a fictionalization of his own past, with Lola del Rey playing his ambitious mother, a child actor named Mick Fairley playing the "Marty" character as a boy, and Marty playing "himself" as a man.

Marty began the project with misgivings, but the quality of the direction, the camera work by Harry Stradling and the acting, principally by Lola, imbued him with a competitive instinct. His natural acting abilities came to the forefront and far outweighed his objections to what he felt was an invasion of his privacy. He was able to step back mentally and look at the role of "Tony," his fictional name in the picture, dispassionately, and as filming progressed he threw himself into the part as though the entire plot line were pure fiction. Sieger and Kroll wrote six new songs for the production, which was basically a drama with incidental pop tunes, and one of them, "Love Found Me," was among the nominations.

On the evening of April 4, 1960 Marty, with Lola del Rey on his arm, rolled up to the Pantages Theatre on Hollywood Boulevard in a chauffeur-driven limousine. The massed fans cheered as they made their way to Army Archerd, waiting in the foyer to have a few quick words with the arriving luminaries. Marty and Lola were ushered to their seats and sat through the next two and a half hours of film clips, Bob Hope quips, presentations, speeches, production numbers and envelope-openings until their categories were announced. Marty lost out to Charlton Heston's "Ben-Hur" portrayal. When the festivities ended, the orchestra struck up "Love Found Me" as the Anointed and the Disappointed made their way up the aisles, back to their waiting cars and the various parties being held that evening.

Marty and Lola emerged from the theater lobby, and a great cheer went up. It was a true polyglot crowd of movie fans: teenagers, housewives, mailmen, clerks, stenographers, soda jerks; someone from virtually every walk of "ordinary life," ranging in age from the very young to the nearly infirm. Dozens of cameras flash-popped blindingly, and several spectators shouted, "Hey, Marty! You were robbed!" Marty smiled warmly, knowing that this film had initiated a brand-new career in films for him, in much the same way "From Here to Eternity" had done for Frank Sinatra. He saw his limousine pulling up to the curb.

To the right, a gray-haired, Slavic-looking man was making his way down the steps of the bleachers set up for the curious. It was a chilly night and he wore a faded raincoat and a worn cap. He was, in every sense, nondescript, unobtrusive, one of the faceless throng.

When Marty stepped to the curb and opened the door of the black Cadillac for Lola, the old man was about thirty feet away, pushing people aside in his attempt to get through. "Martin! Wait!" he called, but his voice was lost in the general uproar.

A cop blocked his path. "Come on, buddy. Get back!"

As Marty Wynner's car pulled away, the old man waved frantically after it. When it was gone he turned and walked slowly eastward on Hollywood Boulevard. He crossed Hollywood at Gower and stood waiting for an approaching bus that would take him back to downtown Los Angeles.

Chapter

37

Lola del Rey was one of those unique young women who became the envy of her peers, the delight of her co-workers, and the object of varying degrees of admiration, love, and lust.

Born Hilda Delgado in Globe, Arizona, she had determined, at an early age, to escape the monotony of the small desert community and make something of herself. Like thousands of pretty girls before her, she beelined for Hollywood and attracted immediate attention by virtue of a compact, perfectly proportioned figure, a lustrous mass of rich, dark hair, framing an oval face that boasted wide-set near-black eyes, sensually flaring nostrils, a nose that turned up slightly, and a generous mouth that could laugh easily or turn cruel upon a director's request.

When success came, she remained gracious and good-natured. She joked with the gaffers and grips, played cards with the extras between shots, and firmly assured interviewers she was merely one of the "lucky ones," at the same time making certain everyone understood that she took her profession seriously.

One day, just after they had begun shooting the picture,

Lola and Marty were having lunch together in the studio commissary when a contract player named Luke Brainard walked up to the table and greeted Marty effusively.

"Marty, how the hell are you, *amigo?* Jesus, I haven't seen you since, let me see, since Oskar's party, back in, Christ, it must have been February. My God, the months get away from you, don't they?"

Marty had met Brainard for the first and only time at "Oskar's party" and had exchanged less than a dozen words with him. The young actor pumped Wynner's hand like a long-lost pal as he looked admiringly at Lola.

"Aren't you going to introduce me to the lovely lady?" he asked.

"Oh. Sure. Lola del Rey, Luke Brainard."

Luke beamed at the actress, turning his back on Marty. He took her hand in his, made a courtly bow, and kissed it.

"Miss del Rey," he said, dropping his vocal register nearly a full octave, and affecting an English accent. "There are some rare beauties in this little village of ours who, unfortunately, cannot act."

Lola resumed eating her soup, giving Marty an amused glance.

"And," Brainard continued, "there are those ladies whom God did not endow with loveliness but who are superb at the art of emoting. And then, there is Lola del Rey, who has the complete package, beauty, talent, charm. I can't tell you how much I've looked forward to this meeting."

Lola placed her spoon carefully upon the soup saucer, dabbed at her lips with her napkin, looked up at Brainard, and said sweetly in a loud voice, "Do you suck?"

Several chairs were heard to scrape in the immediate area. Marty fought to keep from stuffing his napkin in his mouth. Brainard, a notorious climber, went red in the face, mumbled a word in parting, and fled the dining room as Lola, unruffled, turned her attention back to the bisque.

When Marty stopped laughing, he impulsively reached over and took Lola's hand. "You're terrific," he said.

Lola smiled. "You better behave yourself too. Remember I'm supposed to be your mother."

o

Lola was fanatically selective where men were concerned. Usually, she shunned her leading men as potential lovers ("How can a man love you when it's obvious he loves himself more?"), and consequently the town was more than a little surprised when she began showing up in public with Marty Wynner. "A new romance?" the columns blared. "We're simply great friends," replied Lola. "Who's kidding who?" the columnists persisted. "You're kidding yourself, if you think we're kidding," Marty assured them.

The simple truth was: Marty had found a friend. Martin Wise had long since gotten married (to an old school chum of his cousin Rosalie), and had settled into a nine-to-five-thirty pattern that precluded "hanging out" with his client. Wynner did not belong to the Friars Club or any of the Los Angeles area's country clubs that boasted a roster of movie and show business celebrities. He was essentially a loner who could be gregarious on occasion.

With Lola, however, he found himself having fun, exchanging jokes, sharing special moments. On the set he called her "Mother" and their co-workers roared. He asked her to move in with him. She said no, she needed her privacy, but that did not preclude their seeing each other on a more-or-less steady basis. Sex was never discussed. Why louse up a perfectly wonderful relationship by thrashing around naked on a bed? It seemed to work. Whatever she did on those nights when they were not together went unquestioned. Marty, likewise, spent an evening or two a week out of her company with no questions asked.

Weekends were spent together in a house she had leased in Benedict Canyon. Many a rainy night they spent sleeping in each other's arms, she in pajama tops, he in bottoms. One night, they fell into a siege of prolonged kissing that left them both exhausted and slightly shaken, but they were loath to break their tacit understanding. He had desired her that night and had come close to being forceful with her, but their relationship had passed the point of no return.

Rauschbauer wisely signed Lola to a three-year exclusive term contract. Marty was somewhat miffed that Willie had not offered him a similar deal, but his anger was short-lived. Scripts were pouring into the "WWII" offices, which now employed two young agents, a receptionist, and a "go-fer."

One of the screenplays was the story of an ex-G.I. in Europe, looking vainly for a comrade who had saved his life and disappeared before the war ended. They had both been in love with the same English girl before going to fight in France. It was a tale of search and despair and guilt and love, with a surprise ending calculated to send the audience out of the theater shaking their heads and exclaiming "Whew!"

Martin Wise accepted the project for Marty. It was an English-Italian-French co-production to be filmed on location in part as well as at Borehamwood and Cinecittà. Marty desperately wanted Lola to play the English girl, but the director, a hard-nosed Scot, would not hear of it. And even if he had okayed her, Willie had no intention of lending her out.

Marty wanted Lola to do the film mainly because the thought of leaving her for four months was painful to him. He was not able to reach her on the telephone from England despite daily attempts to make contact. After a month of frustration, he gave up calling, thoroughly mystified.

Coincidental with the end of his telephonic efforts was the arrival of a letter from Lola. In it, she stated simply that she still thought of him with fondness, but after all, they had merely been like brother and sister, and now that he had gone away for a period of time, she felt it was the right moment to call their relationship to a halt. Fondest regards and good luck on the movie. Marty crushed the letter into a ball and threw it at the wall of his Dorchester suite.

o

On a Saturday night, he went to the Royal Opera House in Covent Garden to see a performance of "Swan Lake" by the Royal Ballet Company. There, on the stage, was the most beautiful, the most graceful creature he had ever seen. While she did not dance the prima ballerina role, she stood out in striking contrast to the rest of the *corps de ballet*. She moved with a fluid ease that one found in great athletes, a sense of coordination that pleased the heart and charmed the eye. Marty, who had been dragged there by Eve Mayfield, a young, pretty English actress, had never been interested in ballet. The music, yes; the dance, not really. That night changed Marty's opinion.

He excused himself at intermission and sent a note backstage, asking to speak to the company manager. The man, a short, harried-looking fellow named Prather, met him in the Dress Circle bar. They had a drink and Marty, whom Prather recognized immediately, explained why he had sent the note: he wanted to meet a certain young ballerina in the company.

Prather smiled and said, in a voice that betrayed his deviated septum, "It'll be Anne-Marie."

"Well, I don't know her name, of course. She's one of the dancers in—"

"Anne-Marie," Prather sniffed positively. "One of your countrywomen. They all want to meet her."

"Oh?"

"Ah, yes, Mr. Wynner. I can arrange it, of course. But I might as well tell you, meeting her is one thing, taking her out is quite a different matter."

"Why is that?"

"She's what you Americans call a loner."

Marty smiled. "People have called me that from time to time. Maybe two loners might find they have a lot in common."

Prather sighed. "Have it your way, sir. Would you like to come back right after the performance and meet her?"

"Nnno. I'm with someone. I'll have to get rid of her. Look. I'm seated in Row E, in the aisle seat. Would you tell her I would like to take her for a late supper at, oh, say Rule's? Have her meet me there at eleven-thirty." Marty had arranged many dates in this manner and, despite what Prather had told him, he had no reason to believe the ballerina would not join him for supper. He was surprised, therefore, when an usher pressed a note into his hand during the second half of the performance. He opened it and leaned over the aisle to make out the writing.

The lady says no. Sorry. Prather.

Marty's sense of self-importance was dented. How dare she turn him down? A goddam little (well, tall) toe dancer, a nobody. Fine, so she was pretty (well, beautiful) and graceful (all right, all right, damn talented), but those attributes did not give her license to snub movie stars. I mean, who the hell did she think she was?

After tactfully getting away from his date, he went backstage and asked for Prather. Several young dancers recognized him and flashed bright welcoming smiles. He spotted Anne-Marie as she began to climb the stairs to the dressing rooms. She turned for a moment to see what the furor was about, looked right at him without the slightest sign of recognition, and continued to climb the stairs.

Prather appeared, and Marty once again expressed his desire to meet the young American dancer. Prather shrugged and asked him to wait. In a few moments he returned with the message that she was dressing and would be down in due time. The waiting seemed interminable. He had never before been cast in the role of Stage Door Johnny, and the image pinched him like tight shoes. He kept nodding goodnight to the departing members of the ballet company as they disappeared through the stage door. Finally, it seemed as though everyone had gone and the theater was deserted. Marty looked at his watch. He had been waiting over forty minutes. A thought occurred: Had the girl been playing games with him? Was it possible she had long since gone, using some other exit, leaving him to wait, alone, like some poor stage-struck fool, embarrassed, humiliated?

He looked at the doorman, who was obviously waiting for Marty to leave so he could lock up and go home. Marty gritted his teeth and turned to go, when he heard footsteps.

She descended the stairs slowly, wearing a trenchcoat tightly belted around her tall, svelte torso. She had somehow escaped the curse of most ballerinas, whose legs usually resembled a linebacker's. Hers were slim and long, full in the calf, but supple, not muscle-bound. She wore low-heeled shoes, which pleased Marty because she was tall and high heels might have made it uncomfortable to walk alongside her. As she stepped into the light, he was once more shaken by her beauty. Her features were in the classic mold, almost Nordic in character. She carried herself perfectly erect, with that posture peculiar to professional dancers. Her green eyes regarded him with curiosity, once again betraying no sign of recognition. Damn her!

"Are you waiting for me?" Her voice, he noted, was low and cultured.

"No," he replied flippantly. "I'm flying the mail to Pittsburgh."

"Is that supposed to be a joke?" she said.

"Is keeping me waiting for nearly an hour supposed to be a joke?"

"I didn't ask you to wait, Mr.—?"

"Wynocki. Martin Wynocki," he said sarcastically.

"Oh. I thought Mr. Prather said your name was Wynner."

"In that case, why did you pretend not to know who I am?"

"I wasn't pretending. I don't know who you are. Should I?"

"Yes, unless you've been living on some other planet."

"You're famous, are you?"

"Quite."

"What do you do?"

"I'm in the same business you're in."

"Oh. You dance?"

Marty was getting angry. "No, stupid lady. I sing."

The girl's face tightened. She stepped past him, said "Goodnight" to the doorman, opened the stage door, and left. Marty stood there for a moment, undecided. Then he also went through the door into the night. He looked both ways. She was walking swiftly down the darkened street. He ran and caught up, falling into stride alongside her. She said nothing and he matched her silence. Finally, he asked, "Have you had supper?"

She continued walking. "Please go away."

"I asked you a question. Have you eaten?"

"I never eat before a performance."

"Would you like to come with me for a bite of food?"

"No, thank you."

"You have to eat anyway. Why not with me?"

She stopped walking and looked him in the eye.

"I don't," she said coldly, "have to do anything. And as for having a meal with you—what's the point? I don't like you and you're plainly offended because I don't know who you are. Why prolong the agony?"

"Because," he replied, "I think you're the most attractive girl I've seen in years as well as the most talented. I like the way you talk and look, and I'm sure I'd like the way you smile if you'd let yourself. I can't say I don't give a damn about your not knowing who I am, but I don't think that should be a stumbling block to having supper together."

She considered. Then she said, "I'm not hungry," and Marty's hopes fell momentarily until she added, "But I will have a drink with you. Just one. Would that please you?"

"Well," he said, "it's a beginning."

"There's a small pub just along here," she said. "It isn't very plush but I like it."

"Lead the way."

"Incidentally," she said as they walked. "I hate being damned by faint praise. I am not 'attractive.' I am beautiful."

They had a drink together and Marty found he was able to amuse her. When she threw her head back and laughed, an invisible finger prodded at his heart.

Later, when he dropped her at her flat, he persisted until she agreed to see him the next evening. As she climbed the steps to her front door, he poked his head out of the taxicab window and said, "You were putting me on, weren't you. You really know who I am."

286

"Of course. Marty Wynner."

Marty grinned, self-satisfied. "I knew it."

She smiled dazzlingly. "You did say that was your name, didn't you?"

Chapter

38

For the first time in his life, Marty set out in earnest to win a woman. He called for her every evening after her performance and treated her to sumptuous meals in London's finest restaurants. Several nights they walked through Hyde Park or along the Embankment talking of their respective vocations. He had never met anyone so obsessed with a career as Anne-Marie, and he told her so.

"Not 'career.' I don't like that word. 'Art.' That's what I live for. The art of dancing."

"Fine," he said. "Tomorrow night I'll take you to the Savoy and we can dance till dawn."

"I don't appreciate your making fun of what I do. It's a lot more demanding and creative than singing popular songs."

He laughed. "Wait. I think I see a soapbox. If we can hold out till noon, you can make that speech right over there, near Marble Arch."

"I'd like to go home now."

"I love you."

"Don't be silly."

"Well, that's a charming reaction."

"I think you've sung too many romantic ballads."

"I do love you. And I don't, for one moment, take your

talent lightly. I don't know much about ballet, but I know when someone is special. You're really something. I wish you could see yourself."

She made no reply.

A light bulb went on over Marty's head.

"You could see yourself, you know," he said. "So could millions of other people."

"My, you do babble on."

"Listen, beauty. I'm famous. Like it or not, there it is. I make movies. In that place you probably think of as a cesspool of cultureless souls, Hollywood, I know Gene Kelly. Very well. He's also a dancer, in case you haven't heard. So is Cyd Charisse. And Leslie Caron. And Vera-Ellen. And they display their art on film. It isn't Sadlers Wells or the Royal Ballet, but how many people know the name of their current prima ballerina? How often is she recognized in the street?"

"What difference does that make? She has her share of admirers."

"What do you think of Moira Shearer?"

"She's a great artist, of course."

"Well, she made more fans by appearing in just one movie—"

" 'The Red Shoes.' "

"—than by dancing in every theater in Europe."

"Are you saying I could dance in films?"

"Why not? You're nearly as good as Shearer and even more beautiful. And besides, a very popular singer with clout to spare is in love with you."

o

Never had Marty been so taken with a woman. To say he was in love with Anne-Marie might strain the bounds of accuracy. Certainly, he was madly infatuated with her, and when he learned, after a week of nightly rendezvous, that she had been orphaned at the age of eight, he had to have her, to protect her, to make her secure. The fact that Anne-Marie Pacelli was the most self-contained, coolly controlled young woman in the world was beside the point.

They fought from the inception of their relationship, and he discovered she had a cruel side that bordered on the

289

gothic. She had been born in June and, while Marty had never given the slightest credence to the mumbo-jumbo surrounding astrology, he had to admit she was prototypically Gemini, the possessor of the kind of dual personality that could wither you with a glance or melt you with a smile. Since the withering glances far outnumbered the melting smiles, her infrequent moments of kindness seemed to him like golden rays bursting through an essentially cloudy existence.

Marty wondered if there had always been a deep streak of latent masochism within him that had finally surfaced when Anne-Marie came into his life. She resisted his marriage proposals daily, and the more she resisted, the more he pressed the issue. He knew that much of his zeal to rush to the altar with the glorious Anne-Marie had to do with going home to California and parading her in front of Lola.

And so they were married. On their wedding night, she came to bed in pajamas, her hair pinned and her face white and makeupless. The effect was jarring, but Marty did not care. He had wanted her for a month, never having been able to turn his sexual drive for her into a *fait accompli.* Until now.

He came to her eagerly, but she would not allow him to enter her. They fought. Finally, she accommodated him by taking him in her mouth, but her efforts on that score were lacking in expertise. He tried to reciprocate, but she turned over, snapped out the lamp on the nightstand, and went to sleep.

Marty got out of bed and walked over to the window. He looked down at Park Lane and thought: Maybe I should jump. Or get her out of bed and throw her down to the street. He thought about books he had read concerning temptresses, sirens, witches who worked their wiles on men and filled them with rapacious desire. Had he been bewitched all these weeks? Was he the victim of some high order of gamesmanship in which the gently snoring woman in the bed there had contrived a kind of chase-me-till-I-catch-you ploy? No, he decided, the mastermind of this charade was none other than himself. What to do? Was it nobler in the mind to suffer the slings and arrows of this outrageous, cold-blooded woman, or simply end the farce and walk away?

That's too easy. The film's completed. She has ten more days before the Royal Ballet season ends. I'll take her back to California, show her off, shower her with things she's never had before, give her a large helping of the good life. Goddammit, she's bound to respond. He began embellishing the rationale: *She's been without parents since she was a little girl. She's had to make her way in the world alone. It's a tough go, any way you look at it. And then there's the dancing.*

Hours of rigid application to one's art. Study. Practice. Attention to diet. Long hours. Low pay. The only true rewards came during the relatively short time one spent on a stage, performing. And how many young women of the corps de ballet ever made the transition to prima ballerina? Damned few.

He looked at his new wife, his compassion for her greatly expanded. She had been sparing in the detailing of her personal history. Marty was certain now it was because she had been through unspeakable trauma, pain she could not share, even with her bridegroom.

o

Anne-Marie Pacelli, Marty learned, had been eight when her parents were killed in a private-plane crash just outside Tarrytown, New York. Her father had managed a paper-box factory in Utica, and when he and her mother were laid to rest, Anne-Marie went to live with her mother's brother in a large, comfortable house in Shelbyville, Indiana.

She hated her schoolmates, hated her uncle Harold and his wife Sue, hated her cousin Paul, who was two years older than she. Most of all, she hated Shelbyville, and she said so, again and again, until Harold and Sue and Paul and the entire third grade of Shelbyville Grammar School got the message. She was peremptorily shipped to a rich but distant maiden aunt in Philadelphia.

Aunt Wilhelmina found living with the willful young girl difficult. Anne-Marie staged a number of hunger strikes and threw countless tantrums, until Aunt Wilhelmina decided the child needed something to keep her busy. When her aunt enrolled her in a local ballet class, Anne-Marie accepted the gesture with all the stoicism of a brave soul being led to the guillotine. She misread the move on her aunt's part as a means of getting rid of a nuisance child for a few hours a week. Actually, her aunt had observed Anne-Marie in an unguarded moment, dancing improvisationally to a record, and the young girl's instinct for movement delighted Wilhelmina.

Anne-Marie had a natural affinity for music and rhythm and, within a few years, she was performing in amateur recitals. As she grew, in ability and experience, she became something of a celebrity in the City of Brotherly Love and, by the time she was twenty, she fled Philadelphia and joined the Royal Ballet Company. She knew how talented she was, and that her eventual transition to prima ballerina was a certainty. The dance to her was everything.

o

Marty threw a large party when they arrived in Los Angeles. Chasen's catered the event, and Marty's little house was crowded with well-wishers. Lola del Rey waited until nearly eleven to make her entrance. On her back was the newest Balenciaga creation, and on her arm was Pedro Calveras, Mexico's latest export to the motion-picture industry, who maintained a properly bored expression throughout the evening.

When Marty introduced Anne-Marie to Lola, they flashed their individual smiles at each other, these two distinctly different feminine types, and exchanged guarded pleasantries. Marty had boyishly indulged in an everything-out-in-the-open evening with his intended just prior to the wedding ceremony, and had told his new-found love about his former relationship with Lola. Anne-Marie did not believe him initially and, after meeting Lola, that disbelief was strengthened.

The Wynners soon moved out of the Brentwood house, which Anne-Marie found "confining," and purchased a large white elephant of a place on Rexford Drive in Beverly Hills. Marty bought her an Alfa-Romeo and a sable coat as wedding presents and tried to keep her amused. He soon discovered he had taken on a thankless and unrewarding task. His wife was a born malcontent, and nothing he tried to do for her found favor.

He called upon his reserve of friends and associates in the movie industry to meet with his wife and see her dance. In virtually every instance, the reaction was the same: very talented, undeniably beautiful, if somewhat cold-looking, a good prospect for musicals at a major studio.

Unfortunately, musicals were "out" and showed very little sign of making a comeback. How could Anne-Marie's abilities be shown off to the best advantage? Marty called a producer at Columbia who owed him a favor. The man agreed to test the dancer for a straight dramatic role in his upcoming film.

Anne-Marie accepted the offer with disdain. She was a dancer, a ballerina. Cheap little movies were beneath her talent. She need not have worried. The test was a failure, her acting ability minuscule.

After a few more incidents of this kind she gave up the idea of a film career. She spent long hours in a variety of beauty salons, bought shameful amounts of high-fashion clothes, and indulged in whatever whim caught her fancy. The Rexford house boasted a giant living room as well as a spacious den and projection theater. It also contained separate bedrooms.

One day he found her sitting in her room, looking at pictures of Mary Frances. "She was a very beautiful woman," Anne-Marie said admiringly.

"I suppose she was," Marty answered.

His wife lifted her hand and dangled the blue glass beads. "By the way," she said, "I found these in your drawer."

Marty reached out and said, "Don't touch those. Ever."

They were rarely at home alone. If a party at the house was not in progress, they would usually be at someone else's home, having cocktails, exchanging tedious compliments and vicarious gossip. Marty wearied of this constant, almost manic thirst for activity on Anne-Marie's part, but he continued to feed himself an unstrained diet of rationale: *I seduced her away from a budding career. She's substituted her present activities for her former ones. Who can blame her?*

In his heart of hearts, though, he suspected she rode the social merry-go-round as a means of avoiding being alone with him. The suspicion badly damaged his ego. He joined a health club, even walked some golf courses, in an effort to ward off a depression that stemmed not only from his unlucky choice of a wife, but from his lack of activity as a singer-actor.

o

He had recently made the rounds of guest-shot, talk-show television, played a few weeks in Vegas, and cut two singles for a neophyte record company, but his career had waned badly since his second movie, which had been a critical success but hadn't recovered its costs. His funds were diminishing slowly but inexorably. His current business manager had made some imprudent choices in investments and in one instance had been the victim, along with the rest of his clients, of a downright swindle perpetrated by a land company in Arizona. Marty's loss on that particular fiasco ran into six figures.

Martin Wise continued to call him daily and report what little progress he was making in setting some nightclub dates and concert appearances but, more and more, Marty was becoming irritated with a stock remark he was hearing from his manager, as transmitted by his agents, the William Morris office. "We're getting a lot of resistance to Marty Wynner from buyers" was the phrase, and no matter how gently Wise tried to soften these truths, they hurt and angered the singer. So did the fact that Martin Wise now handled several young rock singers.

"So you're in a little slump," Martin comforted him. "It happens to everybody. Relax and enjoy your life a little. The pendulum will swing back our way, just watch." Marty found it difficult to believe.

"Music," he would storm. "What the fuck happened to music?"

"Music," Wise would reply sadly, "is not what the kids are

interested in today. They want to relate to their own kind. We're just going through a phase right now, that's all."

Marty tried "hanging loose." Daily he visited the gym, working himself into better shape than he had ever been in before. Anne-Marie, on the other hand, was deteriorating physically. Rich foods and no exercise were taking their toll. She grew wide in the hips and heavier in the arms. A slight suggestion of double chin began to mar her once sharply defined jawline. She slept until noon, had breakfast, dressed leisurely, and got down to the daily business of spending Marty's dwindling cash reserves.

o

He went to Detroit on December 23 to appear on a telethon for the United Way. A lymph node popped on the left side of his neck during the evening, and he flew back to California discomfited by a severe sore throat, having aborted most of the time in which he had been scheduled to appear on the program.

He arrived at the Rexford Drive house by taxi after one-thirty in the morning. Since he knew he was not expected, he considered ringing the bell and waking his wife rather than entering the house and perhaps frightening her in the middle of the night. But since she occasionally used sleeping pills, he took a chance and quietly opened the front door with his key, closing it gingerly behind him. He removed his shoes and tiptoed through the hall toward his bedroom.

As he passed Anne-Marie's door, he heard movement and muffled laughter coming from her bedroom. Perhaps she had fallen asleep and left the TV on. He opened the door.

One nightstand lamp was burning, the shade tilted toward the bed, bathing it in light. Two empty wine bottles lay on the floor. A third dead soldier was poked, upside down, into an ice bucket on the nightstand. The bedclothes were in wild disarray. Lola del Rey sat propped up against the headboard, naked. Lying flat on the bed, equally unclothed, stomach down, her head planted directly between Lola's open legs, was Anne-Marie.

Marty blinked.

Anne-Marie turned away from her work and regarded her husband with equal amounts of surprise and insolence.

Lola, who was very drunk, said with amusement, "You're just in time, Marty. I'm having my Christmas duck—whoops, I mean 'suck.'"

Marty's fists doubled and he started toward the bed with double murder in mind. He swallowed once and the swollen lymph node felt like an apple in his throat. For no apparent reason, he experienced a flash of pain under his left arm where his old wound had lain dormant for many months. Without a word he whirled, slammed the door behind him, and ran out of the house.

o

"Divorce," said Marc Rabinowitz, "is, unfortunately, my business. My duty, however, is to try to find a path toward reconciliation, Mr. Wynner."

"Not interested," said Marty.

"Why be inflexible, Marty," advised Lester Brendel, his lawyer. "Listen to the man."

"I'll listen, but it won't do one bit of good."

"Your wife," continued Rabinowitz, "is desirous of a reconciliation. Why aren't you?"

"You really want me to tell you?" Marty said.

"Yes, sir, I really do," the lawyer replied.

He looked at Anne-Marie, sitting calmly across from him at the conference table in Rabinowitz' plush suite of Beverly Hills offices. She looked as though she were listening to stock market reports.

"That goddam bitch lady," Marty said savagely, indicating his wife, "is a—"

"Careful," counseled Brendel. "Don't say anything you'll regret, Martin. And I do mean financially."

"That's good advice, Les," said Rabinowitz. "You know, sometimes I think there should be stricter laws about getting married. It should be as tough to get hitched as it is to get unhitched. Now, perhaps both of you made a mistake, believing you were meant for each other, but you're seeking the easy way out. Why not try to resolve your problems and stick it out? There's a lot of time invested in this union of yours, you know. A lot of time and, I might add, considerable cash and property. Isn't it worth giving it a go one more time?"

Sweet shit, thought Marty. Where the hell did she dig up this orator?

o

They tried again. Anne-Marie swore she had never indulged in sex with a woman prior to the night he had found her with Lola. They had gotten very drunk on wine, she explained, and before she knew it she was seduced by Marty's old girl friend. Marty fought to believe her and, in fact, once they had reconciled and he had moved back into the house, he found her to be more considerate than he had ever known her to be.

Well, what the hell, a lot of women probably had a latent strain of lesbianism in them. And Lola was a forceful, dominating creature, capable of anything.

Chapter

39

Anne-Marie began going out alone again at night. Marty became suspicious and hired a private investigator to follow her. The detective reported back to Marty, who rode in the car with him one evening to a house on the corner of a quiet street in Santa Monica.

"She's in there," he informed Marty. "Want to bust in? It's illegal but it's the only way you're gonna see for yourself. You handle the costs if they sue for breaking and entering, understood?" Marty nodded.

They got out of the car and walked to the house. The detective drew a snub-nosed .38 from his coat pocket.

"Is that necessary?" Marty whispered.

"Never can tell," the man whispered back.

He kicked in the door and they bolted up the stairs. In the front bedroom they found five women, engaged in various forms of lovemaking. One of those women was Anne-Marie, and what sickened Marty most was the sight of his wife, straddling a thin blonde woman, a dildoe strapped around her naked hips.

He wisely kept the divorce from becoming messy, making a settlement out of court. So soured was he on marriage that he vowed never to repeat that mistake as long as he lived. He engaged, for a time, in a practice he had heretofore found odious; he bought the time and talents of a variety of call girls. The one-hundred-dollar-a-night companions were uniformly pleasant, trouble-free, clean, attractive, and gifted. Their job was to please him. What difference did it make that he was not an insatiable lover, that he did not fulfill their image of him as the "Swinger," a nickname that still served to identify him to the public at large? They were there to service him and service him they did, in a variety of ways. Marty found he liked most of these breezy, candid ladies and invariably presented them with a bonus.

o

Through the remainder of the 1960s and on into the early 70s, Marty Wynner's career figuratively resembled a faulty hourglass, with the sand pouring smoothly from one container to the other at intervals, only to have the tiny center tube clog and halt his progress.

He would sit around for weeks, waiting for the telephone to ring. He forced himself to vocalize, to keep his singing muscles in shape, but as the days and weeks went by with no word from his manager or agents he would lapse into inactivity. He would become morose, certain he had sung his last note professionally, acted in his final film, feeling totally rejected, and the result was corrosive to his personality and appearance.

He went for days without a shave, wearing the same faded jeans and Adidas tennis shoes, his hair uncombed, his eyes bloodshot from lack of sleep. He took to not answering his phone. He was certain it could not have anything to do with work. Nobody wanted him. Why answer?

His finances were perilously low from time to time, but just when he was down to what could be described as near-bankruptcy, Martin Wise would turn up at the little Malibu residence he had rented and suddenly the clouds would part and the sun would shine again. An offer for six weeks in Australia, a Far East tour, a picture in Italy, a swing through Scandinavia. Martin Wise, the Roto-Rooter man, the unstopper of the hourglass. The sands would flow smoothly again for a time, and Marty would clean up, begin vocalizing, exercise away the bloat, and go out into the world again. His faltering bank account would beam with fresh funds.

On one of these windfall tours to Australia, he performed at the Leagues Clubs in Sydney, private gambling establishments that made a practice of hiring American entertainers. He did well with the customers and even better at the tables. For the first time in years he was in possession of a really sizable chunk of money.

When he returned to America, the undisclosed winnings were used to buy the Malibu cottage. There was enough left over, along with Marty's three-year-old car as a trade-in, to place in Marty's carport a shiny new Jensen. What was that old saying? You separate the men from the boys by the price of their toys!

He began to date again, old flames and some new ones he met at the beach. The columnists mentioned him sporadically, usually because of his association with some current popular lady of the silver screen or the 19-inch tube. He did some dramatic guest shots on television, and his natural acting ability caught the attention of a producer, who offered him a TV series. It was essentially cops-and-robbers, with Marty playing a fifteen-year veteran of the Los Angeles Police Department. It ran successfully for a full year and, as a result of Wynner's excellent acting, he was pegged for a key role in an all-star multimillion-dollar extravaganza at MGM. Two days before he was due to begin filming, he contracted pneumonia. The plum acting assignment went to Robert Lacey (who later won the sole Oscar for the film).

Marty was furious. Once he was out of danger and back on his feet, he chose to drop out of sight. He took to taking long, solitary drives in the Jensen along the coast highway late at night, traveling at dangerous speeds on fog-shrouded patches of roadway.

To have a base in town, he rented a house in Hollywood on Sunset Plaza Drive, not the most fashionable location these days, but one he could almost afford. Money matters were pressing again. He thanked God for an upcoming three-week stand at the Arabian Nights in Vegas, the residue of an old, unfulfilled commitment he had had to postpone twice before because of conflicts in television.

He tried renewing a few old acquaintances, but he had kept to himself too long. Invitations were hard to come by, and most of the women he had dated were involved in new situations with other men. Several people he had known, liked and disliked, had died:

Moe Stein (heart attack).
Dede Farmer (breast cancer).
Billy Ballew (cirrhosis of the liver).
Ernst Rauschbauer (massive stroke).

One late afternoon, as he sat at the bar in Cock and Bull having a quiet drink, the waiter handed him a note:

"Have a drink with me for old times' sake. Lola."

He looked around and saw her sitting at a table near the buffet board. He got up and walked over, seating himself opposite her. It had been years since he had last seen her. She had weathered the time well, looking trim as ever. Marty had read she had gotten a facelift and he believed it. Her face seemed wrinkle-free and smooth from what he could see in the dimly lit interior of the restaurant.

He took his drink from the bar with him, and as he raised it to his lips he said, "Well, well, well."

She smiled and lifted the drink in front of her in salutation.

"Absent friends," she said and sipped at her white wine.

"I suppose it's superfluous to say you're looking good," he said.

"A lady always likes to hear nice things. Wish I could say the same for you, Marty. My God, you look awful. You've got to start taking better care of yourself."

"I thought you wanted to have a drink, not preach a sermon."

"Sorry. Frankly, I didn't know if you'd come over or not."

"What the hell, why not? Bygones and all that crap. You working?"

"Haven't done a movie in five years. I'm—"

"Got some broad keeping you, huh?"

"Now, Marty—"

"Some bull dyke lapping at your cunt and paying for the privilege, no doubt."

"I'm getting married."

"No shit! Who's the lucky girl?"

"The man's name is Collins. He's meeting me here."

"Ohhhh. If he only knew what I know."

"Just what do you know? Or think you know?"

"Come off it, Hilda. My charming ex filled me in on your sexual—what's the word—proclivities." He emptied his glass and called the waiter for a refill. He did not offer to buy Lola a drink, so she had to order another glass of wine for herself.

She lit a cigarette and sat back in her chair, eyeing him speculatively. "Just what did Anne-Marie tell you? I'd really like to know."

"Oh, nothing earth-shaking. Just the sordid details of America's gift to men, Lola del Rey, and her—proclivity—for making it with ladies. Listen, in a way, I'm glad you picked on her. She was colder than the iceberg that sunk the *Titanic*. Took a les like you to get her started on the road to eating cunt. Congratulations."

Lola's famous nostrils flared and two flaming spots appeared on her cheeks. She stubbed out her cigarette in an ashtray. Her eyes blazed, then cooled, and she leaned forward, touched Marty's hand, and laughed.

"Oh, Marty. My poor old buddy Marty. Think for a moment. Have you ever known me to lie to you?"

"Of course. When you pretended to be a woman. You were a man all the time. Damn good impersonation."

"No, Marty, you're wrong. I am a woman and I always have been. The one time, the *only* time I ever strayed away from what I am was the night you found me with your wife. Let's get this straight. I didn't pick her; she picked me! She called and pleaded with me to come over. You were out of town, you had quarreled bitterly before going—"

"Quarreled? That's a goddam lie!"

"You had quarreled bitterly," Lola repeated. "Would I

please, *please* come over and talk with her; counsel her, is the way I believe she put it. Well, I bought it. I drove over and she played quite a scene. She was a cunning bitch. I tell you, Marty, she hated you. My God, how she hated you. She was sick with it.

"Anyway, out came the wine bottles. I hadn't eaten dinner, and after a few glasses of wine I got so drunk I didn't know which end was up. I vaguely remember her suggesting I lie down until the dizziness went away. She helped me upstairs and I fell asleep on her bed.

"When I woke up I was still drunk and dizzy. I was also naked and your wife was having at me with her tongue. Look, I suppose I should say the whole thing repulsed me. But I'd be a liar. I was drunk and I liked it. I even reciprocated. She opened more wine. It was Christmastime and what the hell, once a year and all that. I was absolutely pissed out of my mind when you walked in. I remember saying something stupid to you before you made that dramatic exit. I regret that, Marty. I regret hurting you."

She looked into his eyes earnestly. "I always liked you. You were good to me and for me. I don't know, we got off on the wrong foot from the beginning, I guess. Every man in town seemed to want to get into my pants in those days. You were the only one who seemed to like me for myself. Maybe— maybe if we *had* made love, early on, things might have taken a different turn."

The waiter brought their drinks, and she quickly downed hers with a nervous gulp.

"That's no way to drink wine," said Marty.

"Marty," she said imploringly. "I know it's late in the day to say this, but I'm really sorry. For everything. I'm getting married to a nice guy. When I saw you at the bar, I was happy. I'd like to go to Minneapolis—" She laughed. "Believe it or not, that's where we're going to live. He has a stock brokerage there. I'd like to leave this town with a clean slate where you're concerned." Once again, she reached over and touched his hand. On the third finger of her left hand she wore a large diamond engagement ring.

Marty raised his glass and downed his drink in one swallow.

303

He stood and said, "Good luck, baby," and walked out of Cock and Bull into the fading afternoon light.

o

Marty Wynner was getting a bad reputation around town. He was drinking heavily, and he engaged in several embarrassing scenes at restaurants from Beverly Hills to Malibu. He was in a great deal of pain. No one knew that. For some unaccountable reason his wound had flared up. One doctor said it had to do with his accelerated drinking; another that it was psychosomatic, brought about by anxiety over his flagging fortunes as an entertainer. He did not care much about the cause, just the effect.

A long period of time went by until he was offered any work which he felt was not demeaning. The harsh turn in his life puzzled and angered him. It was incomprehensible, this rotten run of bad luck. Smart-ass agents used to smirk: *Luck, hell! People make their own luck!* To an extent, that was true. But he had been to bat several times in the past few years in what should have been winning situations. Instead, he had experienced minor triumphs, pyrrhic victories. He had won several small battles but he was losing the war.

Chapter

40

It had been raining in Southern California for nearly four weeks, heavy sheets followed by intermittent drizzles, followed by even more violent torrents. In the gray chill of the early morning, it was splattering on Marty's roof, spanging in his gutters, splatting into the foliage of his landscaping. He could hear the water running down his driveway into the street, gurgling in rivulets along the curbline, rushing toward the Strip below.

He turned slowly onto his side and gasped as pain cut him. He grimaced as he thought: cuts like a knife. Naturally. That's what made the pain in the first place. He looked up at the mantel of his bedroom fireplace and regarded the Nazi dagger with its chrome hilt and swastika emblem. *Why do I keep it?*

The old wound had been hurting him for nearly a month, and he had been counteracting it as best he could with Percodan, but it was a depressant and he went around with a constant feeling of short-windedness and a peculiar ache around the heart that he could not shake.

He reached up and turned on the bedside lamp. The bottle of pills sat on the nightstand on top of yesterday's *Los*

Angeles Times, open to the entertainment page. He looked at it again.

WYNNER A LOSER ON TWO COUNTS

Singer Marty Wynner lost two separate battles today, both of which are going to be costly for different reasons. In Las Vegas, Superior Court Judge William G. Mardigan ruled against the singer, who was represented by Arnold Best of Best, Finer, Severson, in a civil suit that stemmed from an incident last January in the Scheherazade Room of the Arabian Nights Hotel. Wynner was held responsible for punitive and compensatory damages.

In Hollywood this morning, Paramount Pictures, Inc., announced that the role of Lindemann in "Sacred and Profane" had gone to British thespian Brian Markham. Wynner had mounted a much-publicized campaign in recent months to secure the part. When asked why Wynner was passed over, Jack Bream, vice-president in charge of production, had no comment. Shooting will begin November 27 in Spain.

Marty lifted the bottle of Percodan, slid the offending newspaper into the wastebasket alongside the nightstand, and went into the bathroom. He turned on the light, twisted the cap off the bottle, lifted the glass out of its holder above the sink, ran the cold water tap, and washed a capsule down. Peeling off his pajamas, he stood naked before the full-length bathroom mirror and regarded himself.

Fifty-one years old. He was still well-muscled, with a minimum of flab. None, really, unless you counted the barely perceptible "love handles" just above the waistline and the slight softening of tissue on his abdomen. He had all his teeth and most of his hair, now turned an attractive iron-gray at the temples. *I'll bet I look a lot like Papa now.*

Papa.

The pain he felt when he thought of his father hurt more than his old war wound. He had fallen into the habit of thinking about his old man every morning when he opened his eyes. He would stare at the ceiling and try to remember Joe Wynocki, but it was difficult. So many years!

Marty reached over with his right hand and fingered the knife scar, just under his ribcage on his left side. Funny how some days he had to peer into the mirror to make it out; on other days it turned a livid pink, an angry four-inch gash that looked as if it were only weeks old and still healing. He pressed it with his fingers, winced, and withdrew his hand. He looked at his limp penis in the mirror. *If that frigging Kraut's aim had been a little better he could have cut my cock off. Might as well have, for all the good it does me. Could have learned to piss through my navel.*

He was conscious once again of the dark-brown taste in his mouth. He wanted a drink badly but decided against it. He had appointments today with his prune-faced psychiatrist, with Marty Wise at the Brown Derby, with his lawyer, Arnold Best, and he did not want to smell of fear, failure, and liquor. He removed the cap from the Colgate tube, put the nozzle in his mouth and squeezed out a quantity. He snapped on the Broxodent and gave his teeth and gums a vigorous electric massage. Then he stepped into the shower and let the needle spray slam into him, regulating the temperature from lukewarm to ice cold with slow deliberation. He shampooed his hair, shaved right there in the shower stall, and treated himself to a final stinging soak before shutting off the water.

As he opened the shower door and stepped out, his knees buckled slightly and he felt lightheaded. Shooting stars appeared in the retinas of his eyes, a phenomenon that had been occurring with increasing frequency in the last few weeks. He clung to the shower-door handle and steadied himself. *Christ, that time I actually saw red. What the hell is that all about?*

In a moment he felt better. He wondered if he was seriously ill. Heart disease or cancer, perhaps. *Who knows? Might be the best thing that could happen to me.*

What would he miss? Women? He had desperately sought out a variety of women over the past several months, only to fail with so damn many of them. His career? *What* career? A club date here and there, a dramatic guest shot on TV at absurd money, a tightly closed door in Vegas, where, after all, it was at.

And then just as quickly he thought, That's ridiculous. So I lost the lawsuit. And the movie. I'll still get another cut at the ball.

He dressed in a pair of conservative black-and-white houndstooth-checked slacks, a bright red wool polo shirt, and black cashmere sports jacket, with dark gray cashmere socks and freshly shined black Gucci mocs. He applied a discreet amount of Atkinson's Royal Briar to his cheeks and felt braced enough to face the world.

The digital on his dresser announced it was 9:23. It would be three hours before his luncheon date at the Derby. He had not eaten anything since yesterday afternoon, having preferred, instead, to drink his dinner on the previous evening. His stomach was crying for food. Better whip up a light breakfast.

Marty suddenly remembered he had forgotten to do his customary pre-weekend shopping and the goddam cupboard was almost bare. He would have to grab a quick bite at Nate 'n Al's.

He walked into the moderately large living room, with its attractively modern furniture, floor to ceiling bookcase, ebony grand piano (left over from early NBC days), framed against the sullen light of the dreary morning now sneaking its way through the latticed picture window. A floor lamp with a leaded glass shade burned dully next to the piano and several picture-frame lights, rheostatted down to a dim glow, still shone in their gleaming brass cylinders over the few paintings and lithographs Marty had managed to salvage from the Rexford house.

Compared to his former Beverly Hills residence, this Hollywood house was modest, but the condition of his finances dictated his present life style. At least he had managed to hang onto the little beach house in Malibu.

And now he brightened even more. This was Friday. Tonight he would head for the beach. He would swim early the next morning, while the November fog still shrouded the whitecaps, have lunch at one of the seafood restaurants along the coast highway, and in the evening, who could tell? A quiet party somewhere in the colony with the kind of nitty-gritty people who populated that part of Malibu: writers, artists, musicians, even a couple of airline pilots, all reasonably friendly folk.

He reached into the hall closet and slipped the Burberry trench coat from its hanger. He put it on, tied the belt in a single cross-over and tucked it into itself, raised the collar, and stepped out of the house into the wet.

It was unfortunate this little tract house of his did not have an enclosed garage, only a woefully inadequate carport. The Jensen seemed out of place squatting under the open-sided shelter, its superb hand-rubbed factory paint job beginning to look decidedly tatty and dull thanks to weeks of exposure in this lousy weather. Marty clucked in sympathy as though the car could hear him. He ducked under the eaves of the carport and got a cold, wet trickle down his neck. He opened the left-hand door and "sat" into the low-slung automobile, tucking the skirt of his trench coat under him and closing the door solidly. He sat there for a moment, his hands on the leather-gloved wheel, smelling the cowhide interior, the damp air, absorbing the chill of the morning, letting the Percodan do its work and ease the pain. Somehow, he rejected the idea of starting the car. Turning the key and bringing the engine to life meant beginning the day in earnest. Why this feeling of foreboding?

It's the Percodan. Now stop the crap and start the engine, Wynner, and let's see what kind of a day this is going to be. He pulled the car out of the driveway, started down the hill, and approached the intersection that would set the pattern for the day.

He was about to play The Game Of The Lights.

Chapter

41

Marty Wynner did not have a lucky number, nor did he believe in astrological signs. He placed no significance in broken mirrors, hats on beds, or whistling in dressing rooms. In short, he had no superstitions save one.

The Game Of The Lights.

For some strange reason, if the fates and good timing combined to allow him to "make" all or most of the traffic signals on a given day, then invariably that day was a banner one, personally and professionally for him. On the day he was nominated for an Academy Award, the traffic patterns of the city seemed to open wide for him, and throughout the afternoon not a single red light delayed his progress. But when Academy Award night rolled around, so seemingly against him were the signals at each intersection that he knew he would not be a winner.

Now, as he approached Sunset Boulevard, wipers swooshing away the heavy blobs of rain on the windshield, he could see the traffic light was green. A good omen. He depressed the accelerator and the car spurted toward the intersection. Then, without warning, a beige Fleetwood Cadillac emerged from a driveway into Marty's path, causing the singer to brake hard and turn his wheel sharply to the left. The rear end of the Jensen slewed around on the wet pavement as Marty fought for control. The car shuddered to a stop facing backwards, its right rear fender scant inches from the massive chrome bumper of the Fleetwood.

Marty threw open the door and ran up to the Cadillac. With a whirring sound, the electric window slid down to reveal an attractive matron, who smiled apologetically. "Are you all right?" she asked and then recognized him. "Aren't you—?" But Marty was already on his way back to his car. *Goddam woman driver.* He slammed the door closed, started the engine, and brought the Jensen back to its correct direction just as the traffic light, which had turned red and then green again moments ago, turned red.

Great. Beautiful beginning.

The Pirellis squealed as Marty tooled around the corner and headed for Beverly Hills. A yellow caution signal awaited him as he approached Clark Drive, and for an instant he thought he might run the light, just to increase his chances down the line. Then he spotted a black-and-white Highway Patrol car, parked in the Tower Records lot, facing Sunset, and he decided against it.

Red light number two.

Now the string of traffic standards before him stretched up the Strip beyond Cock and Bull, into the residential area.

Doheny Drive. Red light.

He snaked into the left-turn lane and used the green left-turn arrow to head down Doheny toward Santa Monica Boulevard. The traffic was light and once again Marty booted the Jensen, but Santa Monica was a solid stream of backed-up traffic, moving with exasperating slowness. Marty slammed the steering wheel with the heel of his hand.

o

He had been experiencing an alarming lack of self-control for the past three months. Which is not to say he had exactly been master of his emotions for the past few years. Take the Vegas incident:

As he had stood on the broad stage of the Arabian Nights' Scheherazade Room, facing a noisy convention audience, a woman sitting ringside had poured a drink on his right shoe.

He had made a great joke of it ("That's a hell of a waste of liquor, lady. My toes don't drink. Now, if you had poured it on my kneecap—")

No one laughed. Marty had continued his song, and this time the woman's burly escort lit a Zippo lighter and moved it toward Marty's tuxedo pant leg. (Shades of Wiley McKay and that memorable night in Denver.)

Marty had kicked the lighter out of his hand, reached down quickly, and dumped the woman's mixed green salad (with Roquefort dressing) all over her Dynel wig. That made her fella mad. He climbed up on his chair, and just as his right foot gained a purchase on the stage, Marty coolly kicked him in the groin. The man screamed and fell back in a faint.

Marty shot his right arm forward in the direction of the audience and placed his left hand on his right bicep in the well-known rude Italian salute. He walked off the stage to mass booing.

The joker with the Zippo had sued, and now a judge in Vegas had declared Marty responsible for damages (the victim of Marty's attack would have a severely limited sex life thereafter). Three weeks after the Vegas incident, Wiley McKay killed himself.

o

McKay's wife, Doris, had been ailing, and when her illness was diagnosed as cancer, Wiley needed every cent he could scrape up to continue her cobalt treatments.

The McKays had been married for nearly thirty-one years, and Wiley depended on Doris for moral sustenance. She had been one of the main reasons Wiley had stayed dry. To his great credit, McKay did not fall off the wagon when Doris died. She had taught him to fend for himself, and he proceeded to do so. At first.

Then, in a freak fall down his front stairs, he broke his right wrist. It was a compound fracture that healed tenuously. For months the injury affected the manipulation of his trombone slide. When Wiley began to hold up record dates and ruin good "takes," he found himself regretfully replaced by the friends and admirers who had sustained him for years.

312

He haunted the musicians' union, called old friends, at first for an opportunity to work, then for the return of money he had lent them when he had been king of the music mountain and they had been struggling hopefuls. A few paid their old debts, but most felt the statute of limitations had run out. Marty did what he could, spending time with his old mentor in the one-bedroom apartment in Studio City McKay had moved to shortly after Doris' death.

They sat there, many evenings, listening to McKay's vast collection of 78s, reminiscing about old times, the music they had played, the places they had been, the friends they had known. They discussed one in particular: Bitsy Munro.

The one-time McKay sideman had become one of the great names in show business: singer, dancer, drummer, comic. He had toured with his own revue, won an Emmy for a dramatic portrayal of a runaway slave in the Civil War, broken attendance records all over the world with his one-man show, and then taken it into a Broadway theater where it ran for two years to standing room only. Bitsy's legendary energy exceeded itself when, during the one-man show engagement, he also doubled at the Copa, packing the east side showroom night after night. New York could not get enough of Bitsy Munro; neither could the rest of the world.

Marty had run into him several times, and Bitsy's greetings had been strange. He had hugged Marty, and kissed him, and called him "baby" during the course of each encounter, and Marty went away from those random meetings bemused and disturbed. Granted people changed, especially when incredible success was theirs, but the metamorphosis that had taken place in Bitsy's case defied comprehension. Stranger yet was the very last time Marty had run into his old friend and former roommate.

They had both been performing at a benefit for Israel at the Beverly Hilton. Bitsy closed the show and stopped it handily. When the cheering had died down and he had returned backstage, Marty greeted him with a smile. Bitsy had shaken Marty's hand limply, and was hustled off to a waiting limousine by a startling number of blacks who formed his current coterie of advisers, bodyguards, well-wishers, sycophants, and hangers-on. Marty stood there feeling foolish and angry, and his reaction did not go unnoticed by Hank Grant, who mentioned the whole scene the next morning in the *Hollywood Reporter*. The blurb in his column was a slap in the face to Bitsy, who could not have cared less. Bitsy Munro was beyond piddling criticism.

Ah, the hell with the little bastard, thought Marty. I'm worried about Wiley.

McKay had become terribly run-down, and all the good habits he had practiced for so many years had gone down the drain. One day he discovered his teeth were loose, a deadly condition for any brass player. The dentist confirmed that Wiley had an advanced case of pyorrhea and that, in the near future, he would have to plan on getting false teeth.

Marty had been singing in Cincinnati at the time. When he returned to Los Angeles, Martin Wise had met him at the airport, with a grave look on his face. They left the airport complex in Wise's Mercedes and headed for Beverly Hills on the San Diego Freeway.

"New car, isn't it?" Wynner remarked.

"Yeah. I always swore I'd never buy a Nazi car, but Sheila talked me into it. She says we can't go on hating and, besides, it's a great car, so I figured what the hell—"

"What's wrong?"

"Why should anything be wrong?"

"Come on. You show up unexpectedly at the airport looking like you lost your best friend."

Martin Wise drove in silence for a moment. Then he said sadly, "You got it wrong, kid. I didn't lose my best friend. You lost yours."

"My God! Wiley?"

Wise nodded.

"Oh, Christ. What happened?"

"It was sad, Marty. And weird. He went on a real bat. Didn't bother anybody. Just bought a case of booze, took it back to his apartment, and locked the door. 'Member you told me about his great record collection? All the old, hard-to-get stuff on 78s? The way they figure it, he'd play one, then take it off the machine and break it. Play another and do the same thing. Can you imagine? He broke every single record he had, all the time getting drunker and drunker. And finally—" Wise took a deep breath and continued—"finally, after four days of nonstop drinking and listening and breaking, he took a gun he had—an old Western six-shooter—and blew his brains out. That's the way they found him, lying on this huge pile of broken 78 records. Jesus, I got the chills when I heard it on the 6 o'clock news."

He looked at Marty. Tears had formed in the corners of the singer's eyes.

"Shit!" Marty pounded the dashboard with his fist and shook his head violently from side to side. Then he turned away from his manager and looked out the window. "He was the best," he said. "The best. All this bullshit these days about 'soul.' Wiley McKay invented the word! Some nights I would sit on the bandstand and listen to that man play his horn and I would love him because he was able to convey what he was feeling—happiness or sadness—just by playing—just notes out of a trombone. Believe me, there wasn't one night when I ever came close—"

Wynner broke off and wept unashamed. The tall, melancholy looking Texan was dead, and in shuttered ballrooms all over the country the ghosts of jitterbugs, swing fans, musicians, and promoters would welcome him to the twilight zone of a world long since past.

o

The traffic crawled ahead and Marty Wynner, lost in thought, guided his car through the rain-soaked morning toward Beverly Hills. The Game Of The Lights had started as a real bummer, so it was no surprise that he was halted at every traffic-lit intersection by an oppressive red signal.

He found a metered parking slot in front of Nate 'n Al's and pulled the Jensen into it. Much less chance of getting a door clobbered by some Beverly Hills housewife that way. He had spent hundreds of dollars fixing dents in the car, unsightly little depressions in the metal caused by inconsiderate people who thought nothing of opening their car doors into yours.

315

He was putting a dime in the meter when a flash of pain seared his eyeballs. He grabbed the parking meter for support and stood there, immobile, as the rain pelted his uncovered head. What the hell is happening to me? he wondered, frightened. Gotta get a physical soon.

In a moment he felt better. He looked around to see if anyone had noticed his seizure. Beverly Drive was nearly deserted at this early hour. Rain or not, the female denizens of this rich little enclave would shortly rise, fashionably late, and descend upon Saks, Magnin's, Gucci's, Giorgios, and the dozens of other expensive salons that dotted Beverly Hills.

When he entered Nate 'n Al's, the cashier hardly looked up, and he was glad. He didn't want to have to exchange even the smallest of small talk with anyone. He took a booth at the back, noting that the restaurant was almost empty. A sleepy-eyed waitress took his order, turning back once to stare at him in recognition.

He ate his breakfast in a fit of despondency. They were occurring too quickly and with greater frequency, these seizures of blackness he was experiencing. Thousands of dollars worth of psychiatry, and I'm getting worse, he thought grimly. Was it basically his sexual problem? Not really, although that may have been the largest contributing factor. Unquestionably, it was a combination of things. His career problems, the way the music business had changed— hell, the way the world had changed. Phones that did not work, service departments that grumbled when you wanted service and then did the work inefficiently. *Nobody gives a damn about quality any more. No wonder I'm having a rough time singing for a living.*

What galled Marty Wynner was that he knew he was at the summit of his craft. His voice had grown more resonant with age, his range had increased by a full four notes on the low end and at least two, comfortably, on top. His intonation, always good, was now superb, and what few jobs came his way these days were almost always punctuated by enthusiastic response. The trouble was, there was no future in singing for a few hundred people at a time.

He was aware of an oncoming headache. He asked the

waitress for two aspirins, and washed them down with the remnants of his coffee. He looked at his watch. Nearly ten-fifteen. His appointment with Prune-Face began at eleven. He rose, paid his bill, and went out into the rain. Marty hugged the sides of the buildings as he walked toward Dayton Way. He would drop in at Beverly Records and spend a pleasant twenty minutes or so with Jerry, the knowledgeable and courteous young man who knew Marty's musical tastes and concurred with them.

He entered the store. The sole occupant was a frizzy-headed salesgirl, in a fraying rust-brown sweater.

"Excuse me," Marty said. "Is Jerry in?"

"Do you see him?" was the tart reply.

"No, but—"

"Well, then he isn't in, is he?"

"Guess not. This is his day off?"

"Who knows? He takes off when he feels like it."

"I see. Well. Are there any new classical releases this week?"

"Third bin over."

The girl stayed at the front counter, writing figures on an order-blank pad, as Marty walked over to the "New Releases" bin and began flipping through the shrink-wrapped LPs.

He came across a recently released album by Danny Jerome, a contemporary of his who had survived the big band era, and gone on to become a middling singing star. Marty noticed the selections on the LP, puerile, schlocky bits of pop-juvenile junk. He turned the album over, saw who had produced it, and grunted his understanding.

Some months back, he had kept an appointment with Don Peterson, an excellent jazz tenor saxophonist, who had become A & R head of Premier Records. Marty had entered his office with great anticipation. At last, a knowledgeable, tasteful musician to oversee the making of quality records. Peterson greeted him in a Nehru jacket over which he wore a long gold chain and a huge sunburst medallion. Music of a sort was blaring from four speakers cranked to an ear-splitting level, the singing and playing garbled and incomprehensible. The objects on Peterson's cluttered desk were vibrating. The

317

record executive grinned at Wynner, nodding toward the speakers.

"Great, huh?" he yelled over the noise. "That's where it's at these days, baby."

Marty had turned and walked out.

Now he put back the Danny Jerome album and, after fifteen minutes, gave up trying to find something that appealed to him. As he passed the counter on the way out he said, "Would you kindly tell Jerry that Marty Wynner was in asking for him?"

The girl went right on scribbling figures. "If I remember."

Marty had already pushed the glass door open and had one foot out in the rain. He retrieved the foot, let the door swing back.

"What did you say?" he asked.

"I said if I remember, I'll tell him. If not, I won't. I'm busy, dumb ass."

Marty backed away and looked her up and down. No makeup, unkempt hair, the original who-shot-the-couch sweater. The broad was a real mess. He got the distinct impression she worked at it.

His voice pitched low and quiet, Marty said, "I'm going to step out into the rain for a moment and then come back in. I'm going to look around for Jerry, and when I don't see him I'm going to ask you to give him a simple little message— 'Marty Wynner was in and asked for you.' And if I hear one snotty word," he said, suddenly grasping her sweater in his right hand and yanking her forward over the counter, "I'm going to beat the living shit out of you."

The girl began to protest, and he tightened his grip.

"Ah-ah, not a word, bitch. I assure you, I haven't got a single qualm about pasting your insolent face all over the walls. The way my day has started, it would be a pleasure!"

He released the girl, and she straightened up, trembling. Marty smiled his sweetest smile, pushed open the door and walked out. He stood with his back to the door, did a smart right-about-face, and re-entered the store. He made a great show of looking around the shop. Then he turned to the shaken girl and said politely, "I see Jerry isn't around this

318

morning. Would you please tell him Marty Wynner stopped in to say hello?"

The girl remained silent.

Marty's voice became hard-edged. "You *will* tell him I came by, won't you?"

"Yes," she muttered. "I'll tell him."

"Thank you so much. Have a nice day."

Marty opened the door again and stepped out into the rain.

Chapter

42

"So help me, I nearly swatted that little bitch."

"Hmm. Yes."

"Jesus H. Christ! Seventy-five dollars an hour for 'Hmm. Yes.'"

Silence.

"Well, what would you have done in my place?"

"We're not here to talk about me. Let's get back on the track. About these bursts of anger and hostility."

"What is there to say? I'm having trouble controlling my temper. I don't need a psychiatrist to figure out why. My career has gone to shit. I'm not sleeping well, in spite of the pain-killers that don't kill the pain. I've been drinking more, and I haven't gotten laid in, oh, hell, I don't know, weeks. Pretty good grounds for anger and hostility, wouldn't you say?"

"I don't know. Would you say so?"

"Doc, one day you're going to give me a straight answer—"

"I'm not here to give answers, Martin. I am not 'Dear Abby.' We're here to implement within yourself the ability to solve your own problems. You're seeking simple solutions. Believe me, there are none."

"And how long is it supposed to take? How much money have I poured into this soul-searching?"

"I don't know exactly. I can go over your records—"

"Don't trouble yourself."

"Martin, I have the feeling you have been purposely trying to provoke me this morning. Am I correct?"

"I don't know. Maybe."

"Come now, don't sulk."

"Yes, daddy."

"I am not your father. Do you feel your father let you down?"

"Are you kidding? My father is the only pleasant memory I have of my childhood. He was a warm, gentle man who used to spend hours telling me stories about the old country. He's the only one who really loved me."

"As opposed to your mother who didn't? Is that what you're saying?"

"Haven't we talked enough about her?"

"Not really. You've told me a lot of facts but very little about your feelings toward her."

"Jesus, I think I've run out of things to say."

"Well then, whatever comes into your mind. How do the kids say it these days? Let it all hang out."

"That's passé, doc. The kids haven't said that for years."

"Guess I'm behind the times. Anyway, go ahead."

Silence.

"My mother. Uh—selfish, stubborn, bitchy—without morals—Let's face it, my mother was a whore! She'd screw anybody to get what she wanted."

"And naturally, you resented these men she went to bed with."

"Of course. When I thought of my father—"

"Think of yourself, Martin. You were jealous of them."

"Well—certainly. They took a great deal of her time and—"

"No, no. I mean 'jealous' in the sexual sense of the word. Didn't you think of your mother as a very desirable woman?"

"What the hell are you getting at? Look, I hated her. I've told you that before."

"Hate and love sometimes coalesce and you can't tell the

321

difference. It isn't unusual for a son to have sexual feelings about his mother."

"Are you saying I wanted to lay my mother? Christ, you're sick."

"No, don't turn away from it, Martin. Face it squarely."

"Months of this crap and I'm no better off than when I started. I ought to bust your head. You and all the rest of the parasites that bleed me for money. You're all alike!"

"Please! The whole building will hear you."

"I don't give a damn! I've had it with you, Prune-Face. Look at my hands! They're shaking. Oh, you son-of-a-bitch. You son-of-a-bitch!"

o

Dr. Emmanuel Birkenstadt, M.D., A.M.A., A.P.A., flinched as Marty Wynner ran out of his office and slammed the door.

He rose from his desk and walked into his private washroom. His hand trembled as he turned on the cold tap and let the cooling liquid run over his wrists. He dried his hands, turned off the light, and returned rather shakily to his desk, thinking about Martin Wynner.

"That," he said aloud, "is a dangerous man."

Chapter

43

Marty sat in the Jensen waiting for the parking attendant. His hands gripped the steering wheel as the rain pelted the windshield and hood. He could not stop trembling.

Indecision riddled him: to keep the rest of his unpleasant appointments or head for the beach house. A sense of futility had him by the throat.

I've lived long enough. I've seen and done it all. Why kick a dead horse any longer. He willed his hands to relax. Suicide before lunch was unthinkable.

A blond beach-boy-type in a yellow slick mac knocked on his window and handed him a ticket. Marty forced a smile.

"Take good care, will you? There's not a mark on her."

Marty glanced at his watch as he entered the Derby. Four minutes after twelve. The restaurant was packed for the lunch hour as usual. Peter, the affable Captain, smiled warmly at Marty.

"Mister Wise is here and waiting for you, Mister Wynner." He indicated the rear portion of the room. "Straight back, on your left. Table thirteen."

Thirteen! It figured.

Marty headed down the aisle, acknowledging a few friendly

323

waves. As he neared the table where Wise awaited him, he spotted Bitsy Munro in a large booth to the right of the aisle. Four varishaded young blacks flanked the pint-sized star; all were dressed outrageously. Next to Bitsy, a beautiful light-skinned Negress with superb endowments, sporting what looked like the Star of India on her right pinkie and wearing a rhinestone-studded denim pantsuit, picked daintily at a crabmeat cocktail. Bitsy himself sported a Super-Fly sombrero, laden with a band of silver conchos, an electric blue jumpsuit, and more large, gold jewelry than a three-dollar whore would have the guts to display.

Jesus, thought Marty. *Masquerade Party is back.*

He stopped at the table and said, "Hey Bitsy. What's shakin'?"

Bitsy looked up at him through half-lidded eyes, smiled lazily and said, in a deprecating tone of voice, "Sheeeet!"

"Come on, Little Bit," Marty continued, trying to salvage the moment. "You forget our old routine?"

"Who is this turkey?" said a strong-looking man at the end of the table.

Bitsy smiled again, a wider grin that showed off some very expensive bridgework. "Why, shit, baby. Don't you know a *star* when you see one? This cat's one of the biggies."

"Yeah?" answered the young black, half-rising in his seat to peer at Marty's face with narrowed eyes. "Who the fuck is he? Marlon Brando?"

"Ah, little man," Marty said to Bitsy. "You've got some real gems here. The brain trust of City National Bank, no less."

"Why, Cap'n suh," drawled Bitsy in mock-Uncle Tom. "These boys is jes' a bunch o' corner cats, can you dig it?"

"Well," sighed Marty. "As long as they make you happy."

"Dear boy," said Bitsy, switching to the English accent he often affected. "When you earn three million dollars a year, you are supremely happy."

Marty changed the subject. "Did you read about our old boss?"

"Yeah, I picked up on it."

"Too bad, huh?"

"Well, man, like, he had his day. That's tough but that's life."

"Hey, Mr. B!" The girl interrupted. "We gonna have our lunch in peace or is this jamf gonna talk our ears off?"

"And what, may I ask, does 'jamf' mean?" asked Marty, doing his best to control himself.

A thickset, flat-nosed Negro spoke up.

"Hell, whitey, where you been? Jamf! Jive-ass-muthhuh-fukkah!"

Marty addressed this last Munro man.

"How would you like to wear your asshole where your mouth is?"

Bitsy smiled as all four of his men rose.

Marty went pale, and the scene, which had not gone unnoticed by the rest of the Derby patrons, was now the center of attention.

Peter, the Captain, hurried toward the table, took Marty by the arm, and said, "Please, Mr. Wynner. Mr. Wise is waiting."

Marty, conscious of losing face, stood there for another moment, then shrugged and headed for his own table. A roar of laughter went up behind him at Bitsy's booth.

Marty Wise greeted him with a worried look.

"What was that all about?" he asked.

"Nothing. Forget it," answered Wynner, his voice tight. He sat down, aware of the many eyes upon him, and noticed that seated with Wise was Julian Resnick, Wynner's agent at the Morris office.

"What're you doing here, Julie?"

"I asked him to join us for lunch, Marty," said Wise. "I felt he could fill us in on what the work situation is."

"Yeah, Marty," added Julian. "I'd like to bring you up to date on—"

"Excuse me," said Wynner, as he pushed back his chair and walked hurriedly to the men's room.

He pushed the door open, hoping fervently no one was inside, and finding the little room empty he bent over the solitary toilet and vomited. His head spun and tears came to his eyes.

That Goddamned little nigger!

How often had his blood run hot over that abhorrent word? And now he—Marty Wynner—had thought of it in relation to Bitsy Munro! There had been real affection between them, genuine respect for each other's abilities. Marty had fought for the little man in order to preserve Bitsy's dignity.

What in the name of God was happening?

All at once, the "shooting stars" appeared again. He shook his head. Slowly they faded and, making an enormous effort to compose himself, he left the washroom and made his way back to the table.

"Hey, babe," asked Julian. "Are you okay?"

"Sure. Sure."

Martin Wise put a hand on Wynner's arm. "You really all right?"

"Yes, goddammit. Don't make a big deal out of it. What's happening, Julian?"

Resnick straightened. his tie, wriggled his neck around in his shirt collar, and cleared his throat.

"Marty," he began. "The work picture looks fairly good right now. We've got several dates lined up for you for the coming year."

"That's right, Marty," added Wise. "That's why I had Julian join us. I wanted you to hear for yourself."

Wynner brightened *This crazy business,* he thought. One minute you're in the depths and the next—

"Of course," Resnick continued. "We've got to readjust our thinking on money."

"Wait a minute, Julian. You know my price. I don't sing cut-rate."

"Come on, be realistic. Business is soft right now. Lots of clubs closing. Competition is fierce, kiddie."

"Don't call me 'kiddie.' "

"Don't get hostile. I'm only trying to give it to you straight."

"Straight, my ass, Julian. You're merely trying to take the path of least resistance."

326

"Now, wait a minute, Marty—" began Wise.

"No," cut in Julian, weary of the charade. "You're right, Marty. You might as well know. There's a lot of resistance on the part of club owners to play you. The name of the game is 'asses in the seats,' and you just don't put 'em there like you used to."

"Julian!" warned Martin Wise.

Resnick ignored the warning. "The bottom line is simply that you just don't command the money you once did. Face it, Marty. Nothing is forever."

Wynner sat passively, his hands clasped on the table before him. Staring at the saltcellar, he asked quietly, "All right, Julian. Tell me what you have in mind."

Resnick cleared his throat again. "Well, Marty, we've got a tour brewing. How does this strike you? Marty Wynner and the Johnny Waycross orchestra. One-nighters, concerts, college dates. Be a great combination."

"Give me the rest of it."

"The money? Not bad at all really. About twenty-five hundred a concert. You pay your expenses and travel fares. And, of course, your own conductor."

"Mm-hmm. What's Waycross getting?"

"Well, remember, his nut is a lot bigger. He has the band to pay and—"

"What's he getting. Personally. Per concert."

"Really, Marty, it wouldn't be ethical for me to divulge another client's—"

"What's Waycross getting, Julian?"

Julian sighed. "All right. Waycross clears about sixty-five hundred a concert. You've got to remember, the guy's hot right now. Five nights a week on the 'P.M.' show, f'chrissake. Plus records on the charts."

"As a trombone player, he couldn't shine Wiley McKay's shoes."

"Who gives a shit," said Julian. "The guy's got it made. Period. Look, if you really want it told like it is, to begin with he didn't want—"

"Julian!" Martin Wise almost shouted.

"I'm sorry but he better know where it's at. Waycross didn't want you right away. He figured there'd be a billing problem and—"

"In what way?" Wynner inquired.

"Well, you know. He would get top billing. But he figured you might object."

"Oh, really?"

"Of course, you'd get hundred-percent 'Special Guest Star' or 'Special Added Attraction.' "

Marty rose from the table and fixed Resnick with a penetrating glare.

"Now, listen to me and listen good. You can go back and inform Mr. Lastfogel that Martin Wynner is no longer a client of the William Morris Agency."

"Marty!" said the manager.

"You keep out of this."

"Like hell I will," said Wise. "You're way out of line, both of you. Sit down, Marty. Your attitude's all wrong. But so is yours, Julian. Marty Wynner shouldn't take second billing to anyone. Forget the Waycross tour. I've got a better idea."

A waiter showed up and they ordered.

Over their salads Martin Wise told Marty about a new group he had just signed, The Dawn Patrol. They were opening that evening at Whiskey A Go Go and were generating a great deal of excitement in the trade.

"They all dress nuttier than Bitsy Munro," said Wise, "but these kids can really play."

"Dandy," replied Wynner. "If you like rock groups. I don't."

"Jazz Rock," Wise corrected. "With the accent on Jazz. They're the best thing I've heard since Blood, Sweat and Tears. And you know you like them."

"So?"

"So I want you to go and see them tonight. Wait a minute, before you holler, just listen. Julian is right about competition being brutal and clubs closing. We need a new approach, Marty. Something that will show everyone you're a 'now' performer, not a holdover from another time. You're

328

the only singer in the world who can make the transition with credibility."

"You're stroking me, Wiseman."

"No," said Julian. "He's right, Marty. I see where he's going."

"So do I," said Wynner. "And I don't think I like it."

"Just go and listen," said Wise. "That's all I want you to do. If you like them—"

"I won't."

"If you like them," Wise repeated, "I've arranged to have you meet them tomorrow at Melrose Sound, that new studio near Highland. You can talk to them, trade ideas, and maybe sing a little with them. And if it works, I think I know someone who'll give us one hell of a record deal. Now, what do you say?"

Marty shrugged. "I don't know. Friday night. Whiskey A Go Go. Be jammed with kids. I probably couldn't even get a table."

Wise smiled smugly.

"I've already made reservations for you. Marty, this is important. I want you to go."

"I'll think about it."

"No, dammit," Wise persisted. "That's not good enough. I want your promise."

Wynner buttered a roll. "I'll think about it, Martin," he said.

Chapter

44

Even with raindrops glazing the paintwork, he immediately noticed the deep crease in the left door of the Jensen. He gritted his teeth and looked around for the parking attendant. The blond beach-boy-type was nowhere to be seen. Marty made a fist and pounded the roof of the car. What was the use?

He got in the car, slammed the door, and started the engine, flooring the accelerator. The Jensen shot out of the parking lot. Marty headed toward Arnold Best's law offices on South Beverly Drive, cursing to himself. Unbelievable. It had been a great morning for paranoia; the world and everyone in it seemed to be against him. A car in front of him stalled, started again, and made it through the traffic signal on the yellow. Marty was halted by the red.

I'll be goddammed!

o

Arnold Best was a fat man and proud of it. His clothes were tailored on Saville Row, and he affected a white flower in his buttonhole at all times. His cherubic features belied one of the toughest minds in the world of corporate and contract law. As he came around from behind his desk to shake hands with Marty, he smelled of a lunchtime martini and just the right amount of Brut. Best indicated a chair, walked back around to his own behind the desk, and eased his bulk into it with a sigh.

"I ate too much," he smiled. "What the hell, I always do."

Marty nodded absently.

Best looked at him. "Are you all right, Marty?"

Wynner almost laughed. "Oh, I'm fine. Do I get a blind-fold and a last cigarette?"

"Look, Marty, if you're not up to it, we could postpone our—"

"No. No postponements."

"All right," said Best. "I know how unpleasant this is for you."

Marty's attempt at a smile was a failure. "Well," he said, mock-cheerily. "When it's all over, will I have anything left at all?"

Best pulled a manila folder from his center desk drawer and opened it in front of him.

"Damned little," he said soberly.

"No chance to appeal this thing?"

"Of course, but I think you'd lose the appeal. It would only be throwing good money after bad."

"So? What's the answer?"

Arnold expelled his breath, and closed the folder.

"Pay the two dollars," he advised, looking squarely into Marty's eyes.

"Some two dollars!"

They sat in silence for a moment.

Arnold Best said, "I've gone over your holdings, such as they are. Whatever you have of value will have to be converted to cash. This Louisiana prick's lawyer has called my office already this morning. We can't ignore the court order and we can't stall too long, although the court does recognize that a period of time will be needed to divest yourself of—"

"God, Arnold," Marty cried. "What the hell have I *got* to sell? Anne-Marie got all the stocks and bonds in the divorce settlement. What's left? A little cottage at the beach, my car."

331

"Look, I'll talk with this guy's lawyer. If I can get them to agree to a long-term payoff, it should ease the pain."

"Christ in Heaven, Arnold. What am I going to do? I've gone through a great deal of money. That's all right. I was able to earn a great deal. But now! It's no secret that no one's exactly breaking down doors to hire me. How, in God's name, can I pay this judgment off?"

"I'm sorry, Marty, but you'll just have to, somehow. Look, I know things look awfully black right now but—you'll be back on top again, and this will all be relegated to the 'bad dream' department."

"Do you honestly believe that, Arnold?" Marty asked.

"I—honestly believe it's possible. You're in the nuttiest business in the world," answered Best, not quite meeting Wynner's stare.

"Oh, sure. Anthing's possible. Nixon might even get elected again."

"Don't laugh. It could happen. Marty, do you know anyone you can borrow a big chunk of cash from? Maybe if we offer it to this bum from New Orleans we can get a break on the overall figure."

"No. Unless you'd like to volunteer."

Arnold Best smiled sadly. "I hate to remind you at a time like this, Marty, but you still owe me twenty-seven hundred from the stock litigation."

Marty fingered his old knife wound, which had started to hurt again.

"Well," he said rising, "I guess that's that."

Best rose and opened the door for his client, placing a hand on his shoulder.

"Marty, I'm not going to feed you any Pollyanna crap. It's a frigging mess and you know it. Somehow, we're going to have to face it. And when I say 'we,' I mean 'we'—you and me. Okay?"

Marty managed a smile. "You know, for a hardnosed barrister, you're not all bad."

"Thanks for nothing," laughed Best.

o

He drove aimlessly around in the rain. He had nothing to do, nowhere to go, no one he wanted to talk with.

Marty looked at his watch. It was still early afternoon. Maybe he'd go to a movie. No! It would remind him of the film role he had just lost and he was depressed enough. He tried to think of some old friends he might call and decided that he had no old friends. He headed the car for the beach house. Might as well enjoy it while he could.

He removed a Wiley McKay tape from the glove compartment and fed it to the slot in the cassette player. The first selection was the old, special arrangement of "Bugle Call Rag" with Wiley playing the impossible calls on trombone and Bitsy Munro kicking the band on drums. He listened with more than a tinge of bittersweet regret. Life with the band, even his hitch in the paratroops had been simple, uncomplicated. What had happened? Merely the passage of time?

"Bugle Call Rag" gave way to a Marty Wynner vocal, "The Nearness of You," with McKay's Texas Trombone tracing lovely obbligatos in the background. He was overcome by a chilling sense of futility. What was the line from that Stevie Wonder tune, "Superstition"?

Seven years of bad luck
Good things in the past

He was certain now that the good things in his life were in the past. And it hurt.

As his own voice emerged from the speakers he tramped down hard on the gas. The speedometer leaped toward the seventy mark as he shot under the San Diego Freeway and raced for Barrington. He darted in and out of the traffic to the accompaniment of several angry horn blasts, and forced a Mustang to the curb as he careened around onto San Vicente.

He roared on toward the beach, surprised he had not yet been chased by a police car. Now the selection of the cassette changed again and "Monster Rally" blared out, featuring an

333

explosive drum solo by Bitsy. Marty hunched over the wheel and shouted: "That's right, you little shit! Play your fucking drums!"

He barreled across 26th Street in Santa Monica, ignoring the stop sign, the Jensen a frightened yellow hare amid the slower, plodding turtles. Bitsy's drums enveloped the cockpit of the car, bursting with machine-gun-like, staccato rim shots and cymbal crashes as Marty, trembling, his left eyelid twitching, wrenched the wheel to the right at 7th, into the path of a Dodge Dart. The Dart's driver, a young woman of quick reflexes, drove her car up onto the sidewalk, into a blue mailbox, as Marty raced on and hung a sharp left, downhill, toward the beach.

At the end of the street, he could see the stoplight that preceded the ocean. *Look! The light's red. Naturally. All I have to do is shoot right through the intersection and it's all over.*

He gripped the wheel tighter. Fifty yards from the corner, the light turned green.

He laughed out loud, and applied the brakes, turning onto Pacific Coast Highway, a little too rapidly but safely.

He ripped the cassette from its slot, opened the window and threw it out. He was bathed in sweat. What if the light had not turned green in time? Who would mourn him? All the people who mattered were already in their own graves—his mother, Wiley, probably his father. He was alone.

He wiped his brow and eyes with the sleeve of his trench coat and drove very slowly to the beach house.

Chapter

45

The rain had diminished slightly in intensity as Marty pulled up in front of Whiskey A Go Go. On the way into town from Malibu, he had been plagued by a tailgater. *Is somebody following me? Shape up, Wynner. First you nearly kill yourself, now you're becoming paranoid.*

The long afternoon nap had refreshed him. He had fixed himself a light meal and decided he had nothing to lose by hearing the group Wise was so high on. He'd probably hate them, but what the hell.

Upon entering the club, he was not surprised to find it jammed, mainly with young people. The place was redolent with smoke, some of it cloyingly sweet-smelling Acapulco Gold, some of it a cheaper, less fragrant product. Marty gave his name to the velvet-suited, bead-bedecked young man who served as host, and made his way through the crowded room to his table.

He had attended Whiskey A Go Go a few times; once back in the sixties with Anne-Marie, when he had been overrun by autograph seekers as the group on the stand, The Purple Penguins, had blared forth. After the divorce, he had squired Carol Lynley into the club. This time, she was the one besieged by young fans, and the group, Walpurgis, had blatted on at a decibel level that caused glasses to jump on the tables.

As Marty ordered a drink, an offstage announcer said, "Ladies and gentlemen, one of the hottest new bands in the country, please welcome The Dawn Patrol."

The lights came up as nine young men wandered onto the bandstand. They affected various sorts of uniforms peculiar to World War I aviators: riding breeches and boots, leather helmets, fur-lined goggles, and long, white silk scarves. A few of them had beards; all of them had long hair. Marty blinked and tried to keep an open mind.

They began to play. After their first number Wynner forgot the comic outfits. The group was excellent. All the players had their musical feet planted in the bedrock of jazz, and their improvisational skills as well as their ensemble work smacked of professionalism. Marty found he was enjoying himself.

He felt a presence beside him and looked up into a young woman's face. It was framed by soft dark hair, tied back in a ponytail with a green silk scarf. She was tallish, with those fine bones photographers covet, her eyes wide-set, grayish-green. Even under the green sueded trench coat she was belted into, her proportions appeared to be delicious.

So astonished by her beauty was Marty that in the moment before she spoke, he found himself wishing she would not; he was afraid her fatal flaw would be a nasal voice; a Western twang; an unlovely New York-Bronx-Brooklyn accent.

"Hello," she said, offering her hand, and Marty heaved an inward sigh of relief. Her voice was low, well-modulated, without affectation. "May I sit down?"

He sat looking at her for a moment, then rose quickly.

"Please do," he said, helping her into a chair.

"I'm Barbara," she said, extending her hand.

"I'm Marty," he answered, taking it.

She laughed. "Don't I know it. You're talking to one of your biggest admirers."

Marty felt a flush of joy. "Thank you," he replied.

They sat there for a moment as the music rose to fever pitch.

336

"How do you like this group?" she asked.

"A lot better than I thought I would."

"They're great, aren't they?"

"Well—good."

"May I take my coat off?"

"Let me help you."

She removed the trench coat to reveal an even lovelier figure than Marty had anticipated, clad in a dark green wool jersey dress. "Please forgive me for intruding, but I've been such a runaway fan of yours that I had to meet you."

"What do you do, Barbara?"

"I'm a girls' counselor at UCLA by day and a student myself at night. Liberal arts. I'm taking a postgraduate course."

"That's interesting."

"No, it isn't. I'm boring you silly."

"Not at all. Why the postgraduate? Some special goal in mind?"

"Well, yes, I have. I paint. Or try to. I want to go to Paris and live there for at least three years and see if I have any real talent as a painter."

"Why Paris? Can't you find that out here?"

"No. It has to be Paris. You see, I've always felt France is to painting what, oh, Hollywood is to movies. It just doesn't seem right not to expatriate myself."

"Hmm. I think you may be in for a disappointment. These days Parisians seem to be among the world's foremost American-haters."

"Oh, that can't be. Not after I've set my sights on living there. You're mean."

"We're having our first fight," he laughed.

She smiled. "That's right. That means we're establishing a relationship."

They lapsed into silence momentarily.

"May I have a drink, please?" she said.

"Of course. I'm sorry. What would you like?"

She told him, and he stopped a waitress and ordered it and another one for himself.

"I have a lot of your records," she said. "I think you're the best singer in the world."

"Oh, you're the one."

She laughed. "Oh, I'm sure we could round up three or four others who would agree."

"Maybe. If we had the time to look for them."

"Really!" she said, in mock exasperation. "What would the man do if I told him how attractive he is? Probably chew my head off."

"Hold it. I surrender. I am the best singer in the world and the most attractive man in the universe."

She grinned. "Well, let's not go crazy. Would you settle for the Western Hemisphere?"

He bowed his head and made a little courtly gesture with his hand. "I accept," he said, "with profound gratitude and humility."

"Good!" she said. "That's settled."

And then she said, "I started listening to your album of 'rain' songs a few months ago when I was down. I played it over and over, and don't ask me why, I began to feel you were singing the words of those terribly sad songs to me." She turned away from him, embarrassed. "Of course, I was fantasizing."

He took one of her hands in both of his and she turned back to him.

"I think," he said, "that you are just about one of the loveliest female creatures I have ever seen. I think it's wonderful to meet a girl in this day and age who can still blush."

"I wasn't blushing."

"It's nothing to be ashamed of. Listen, it's hard to talk over the music. I wonder—would you like to leave? Go somewhere else?"

She smiled her thousand-candlepower smile. "I think I'm being picked up."

"I think I am," he grinned.

They got up and left.

Chapter

46

"I'm twenty-four," she said as they drove west on Sunset. The lights and shadows glanced off her finely structured face.

"I was raised in Sandusky, Ohio. My father divorced my mother when I was two. I never saw him again. Since then, it's just been Mom and me. That is—until I came out here to go to school."

"Are you and your mother very close?"

"I miss her. Oh, I know lots of people out here, but I get terribly lonely all the same."

Marty found this hard to believe and he said so.

"I don't like dating just to date," she said.

"Where would you like to go?"

"Anywhere you say."

"Are you hungry?"

"Not really."

"Shall we stop some place for a drink?"

"Everyplace tonight will be as jammed as Whiskey was."

They drove on for a few minutes.

"I know a quiet place," Marty said. "My house at the beach."

She looked at him evenly. "I'd like that."

He suddenly realized he wanted her. For months no one

had affected him as had this dreamlike creature beside him. He felt himself growing hard between the legs.

"I'll bet it's wild and woolly around Malibu," she said. "I love this kind of night."

"I usually hate the rain. But I think I could learn to like it if we were under the same umbrella." He reached over and took her hand.

"We're going a bit too fast, aren't we?"

"I'm only doing forty."

"That's not what I meant."

They drove on in the night rain, neither of them speaking. Marty turned onto the Coast Highway.

"It's not far now," he said, breaking the silence.

"I'm in no hurry. I'm enjoying this."

As the car made its way along Pacific Coast Highway, the clean smell of the rain sifted through the air vents and . mingled with the scent of leather seats, expensive perfume, men's cologne, and natural body aroma. The overall effect was aphrodisia to Marty Wynner. After a terrible day, the strange law of compensation seemed to be evening the scales a bit.

He looked at the dashboard clock as he turned onto the beach road: 11:50. In ten minutes it would be Saturday, a newborn twenty-four hours. Barbara seemed to be lost in thought. She seemed so strangely, powerfully attractive that he decided he would gladly endure again the misfortunes of the morning and afternoon, if, at the end of the day, he could be guaranteed her presence beside him. He rolled up to the beach cottage and stopped, dousing the headlights and killing the engine. They sat there and allowed the raindrops to obliterate the night by enveloping the windows and windshield.

"I almost hate to get out," she said. "With the windows foggy and wet like this, it's as though your car was our own private little world. It's a nice feeling."

He gestured toward the cottage. "Inside is even better. Warmth, shelter, and spirits."

"Come on," she smiled, opening her door and getting out of the Jensen. Marty followed her up the stairs to the door of

340

the cottage, key in hand. It was raining hard now, and they were both soaked as they entered the house. They stood there in the dark, wet and shivering.

"We're dripping all over your floor," she whispered.

"It's terrazzo. No problem. I'll get the lights."

"No, not yet," she said, and the way she said it caused him to place his hands on her shoulders. She drew up to him immediately, her body gently molding to his, and they kissed. Her lips were cool and pliant, indescribably soft, her breath clean. With an effort he drew away from her. Neither of them spoke. He could see her eyes, wide and shining. She trembled, and he wondered if it was from the cold and the wet or their kiss.

"I'm slightly waterlogged," she said. "Why don't you build a fire and I'll find a bathrobe or something."

"One fire, coming right up," he said, as he switched on a table lamp in the living room.

She removed her shoes and started up the stairs to the bedroom. Marty's eyes followed her all the way up, noting the graceful swing of her hips and the swell of her calves as she reached the top.

He removed his wet jacket and hung it in the downstairs hall closet, went to the kitchen, and took three logs from the cupboard under the kitchen basin. He carried them into the living room and placed them on the iron cradle inside the fireplace. The flame caught with a *whoomp.*

He found some dry Levis and a turtleneck sweater, shucked his wet shoes and socks in favor of a pair of deck moccasins. In the guest bathroom at the front of the house, he ran a comb through his hair and placed a drop of Binaca on his tongue. As he moved toward the fireplace, he heard the girl coming down the stairs and he turned to look at her. She had donned his terrycloth bathrobe, and her hair was loose around her shoulders.

Never before had he seen anyone who so startlingly resembled his mother.

He was deeply shaken. How had he missed seeing it before? He trembled at the sight of her, walking slowly toward him in the firelight.

With a strong sense of guilt Marty Wynner accepted the fact: he had wanted Mary Frances carnally. He had sublimated his feelings out of shame and the knowledge that his desire was forbidden. Yet here she was in front of him, this more-than-reasonable facsimile, and all he could think of was that he wanted her badly. Time later to sort out his emotions.

He managed a casual compliment. "You look like you belong in this house."

She sat down on the floor and stared into the flames, pulling her knees up to her chin and clasping her hands around them. "I'm glad we came here."

He sat down and placed his arm around her.

"Barbara, I'm a little off balance." His throat was slightly hoarse. "You remind me of someone, I'd rather not say who."

She leaned forward and kissed him, a lingering kiss that began quietly enough and developed into something fierce. They clung to each other until, without another word, he lifted her in his arms and carried her up the steps to the bedroom.

On the bed he kissed her again. Her mouth was a magnet: once his lips made contact with hers, he found it impossible to break away. Her tongue sought his, her hands touching his face. Finally the kiss ended.

"Could we have some gentle music?" she asked.

"Of course. What would you like?"

"I think a Marty Wynner vocal would be appropriate."

"No chance! I'm not going to risk spoiling the evening. I'll find something."

She smiled and disappeared into the bathroom, closing the door behind her. He heard her turn on the taps. He went to the cassette player, and soon the opening strains of "On Hearing the First Cuckoo in Spring" permeated the room. He stripped off his shorts and stretched out on the bed. She was not long in returning.

She came out of the bathroom nude, and the sight of her both warmed and chilled Marty. The resemblance to Mary Frances was uncanny: full, high breasts, a gently tapered waist, hips flaring dramatically into soft white thighs which, in turn, made smooth transition to those superb legs. She stood there, allowing the lightspill from the hall to play upon her body almost as though she were exhibiting herself for his delectation.

A sudden thought struck him. "Just a moment," he said, rising and going over to his bureau. He opened the top drawer and took something out, returning to the bed.

"Would you mind wearing these for me?" he asked, holding out his mother's blue glass beads.

She looked at him and smiled.

"You put them on me," she whispered.

They made love.

o

Marty had never known anyone so abandoned, so giving, demure and teasing one moment, brazen the next. She was all over him, exploring every part of his body with her tongue and her hands, eliciting from him gasps of pleasure, probing erogenous zones he never knew he possessed, taking him up one peak, allowing him surcease, then carrying him up again and again.

He reciprocated with tenderness and ferocity, using his tongue, using his hands. Time became an abstract, immeasurable; their two bodies achieved a kind of fusion in limbo, a pair of beautiful machines, performing a function for which they both were created.

He rose above her, his body moving rhythmically. Her eyes were closed, her lower lip clamped tightly behind her upper teeth, the blue glass beads draped over her left breast. Mary Frances/Barbara; one and the same.. He knew he loved her and that he had never loved anyone else.

In a moment they completed in almost perfect unison. He withdrew from her and rolled over onto his side of the bed, feeling wonderful release. They lay there listening to the rain on the roof.

She breathed deeply and emitted a long sigh. "It's enjoyable with a man. I sometimes forget I like it that way, too."

Marty turned and looked at her. "What did you say?"

She smiled in the dark. "I'm bisexual, although tonight I'm

343

wondering whether I'm not more AC than DC. Anne-Marie did me a favor, even though she doesn't know it."

He sat up slowly and turned the trunk of his body toward her. "What are you talking about?"

"Now, look," she replied. "I hope you have the sense of humor she says you have."

"What the hell is going on?"

"I've been living with Anne-Marie. For four months now. We met in a bar. God, there were some great-looking girls in there that night, but she came straight to me. The next thing I knew we were back in her apartment. She's a terrific lover. But, of course, you know that."

Marty got out of bed and stood there, his back to the girl.

"Anyway, right from the start, she said she wanted you to meet me. No. *See* me, that's the way she put it."

"Go on," said Wynner, fighting to control himself.

"That's about all there is to tell. She told me where you live—both places. I went to your other house and when you weren't there, I drove out here and saw you getting into your car. So I followed you to the Whiskey. You're not angry, are you?"

Marty stood there, silent, listening.

"Anne-Marie said when you saw me you'd see how funny it was. She said you'd laugh."

"Did my charming ex-wife show you a picture of my mother?"

Barbara fingered the glass beads around her throat. "I look like her, don't I?"

He was *not* dreaming. He turned and looked at her so fiercely that she sat bolt upright and said, "My God, you *are* angry."

Marty felt as though he would vomit. Her voice now seemed to be coming from a long way off.

"I didn't think—please. You're not going to hurt me, are you?"

Her lovely face was ugly with fear. Simultaneously, the pain enveloped him, the old knife wound, his head, the shooting stars behind his eyes, all came together at once with blinding swiftness, stabbing at the very core of his being. He felt something actually snap within him, and then he was upon her, a single, fierce, animal-like growl escaping from his throat. Her eyes widened in sudden terror as he straddled her. He grabbed the blue glass beads in one hand and twisted them tightly around her neck. She opened her mouth to scream. Then with a violent jerk, Marty tore the beads away from her throat. The string broke and the beads went flying in all directions, pattering on the floor like hailstones. His body went limp.

The girl struggled free, scooped up her clothes, and ran out of the bedroom. Moments later he heard the front door slam. He looked at the few remaining beads on the broken string in his hand and laughed.

"Goodbye, Mary Frances."

Chapter

47

Wynner sat on the stool in the rehearsal studio and sang "Chicago" with The Dawn Patrol. It had never sounded better. Christ, these kids were good. The contemporary rhythm section gave the old standard brand new dimension. Marty felt great. He was singing again, and it hadn't rained for five days.

When the girl signaled him out of the studio for a phone call from his lawyer, he thought, *not bad news, not now.*

"What's the matter now, Arnold?" asked Marty.

"Relax, nothing to do with money. There's an old guy here in my office who wants to talk to you. He saw my name in the *L.A. Times* write-up and he's got this crazy story—listen, before you think I'm crazy, too, I've got to tell—"

"Arnold! I'm in the middle of a rehearsal!"

They were waving for him to get back into the studio. Marty held up a finger to signal one minute more.

"Marty, I was about to say, the old man looks like you."

Looks like me?

"I'll put him on," the lawyer said.

He heard an old man's voice. "Martin. This is me."

The accent was unmistakable.

Through the catch in his throat, Marty whispered, "Papa?"

"Yes," said the voice. "Is Papa."

"You're alive! I mean, I thought, where have you been all these years?"

"Is long story, Martin."

"Papa, listen, stay right there, don't move, don't go away, promise me you'll stay right where you are."

"Yes, Martin." Joe Wynocki sounded as if he, too, were holding back tears.

Marty hung up the phone and shouted to the girl, "I'll be back as soon as I can."

"Anything wrong, Mr. Wynner?"

But he was already taking the stairs two at a time, his heart pounding. He got into the Jensen and gunned it all the way to Arnold Best's office, the lights staying green, green, green.